REBEL YELL

REBEL YELL

A Novel

Alice Randall

BLOOMSBURY
New York   Berlin   London

Published by Bloomsbury USA, New York

All papers used by Bloomsbury USA are natural, recyclable products made
from wood grown in well-managed forests. The manufacturing processes
conform to the environmental regulations of the country of origin.

LIBRARY OF CONGRESS CATALOGING-IN-PUBLICATION DATA

Randall, Alice.
Rebel Yell : a novel / Alice Randall.—1st U.S. ed.
p.   cm.
ISBN-13: 978-1-59691-668-5 (hardcover)
ISBN-10: 1-59691-668-0 (hardcover)
1. African American politicians—Fiction.   2. Conservatives—United
States—Fiction.   3. Politicians' spouses—Fiction.   I. Title.

PS3568.A486R43 2009
813'.54—dc22
2009012492

First U.S. edition 2009

1   3   5   7   9   10   8   6   4   2

Typeset by Westchester Book Group
Printed in the United States of America by Quebecor World Fairfield

To my daughter, Caroline, with love.

All boys love liberty, 'til experience convinces them they are not so fit to govern themselves as they imagined.

Samuel Johnson

Young man, young man strong and able, get your elbows off the table. This is not a horse's stable but a first-class dining table.

Unknown

This is a work of fiction.

Part I

*T*HEY DROVE, LARGELY *in silence, from Nashville to Birmingham, in the black 1961 Thunderbird they called, on noisy days, the Flying Crow.*

Big Abel worked, alternating scribbling with blue ink on typed white pages and scribbling with blue ink across a yellow legal pad. Antoinette was at the wheel. They didn't turn on the radio.

Little Abel sat still and mute between his parents. His baby sister was back home with the grandmother. The boy had felt lucky when chosen for the trip. Now he wasn't so sure. Twice his father had slapped his leg. The second time he had told him not to wiggle, sneeze, fart, or say another word. All that because he had said he needed a bathroom. Now he thought his sister was lucky to have been left back at Grandma's, in the house full of talk and music and television, full of toilets and sweet tea and Tang.

Big Abel's tail was in a crack. Alabama scared the man and he was headed to Alabama. So he scared Little Abel. Not to be mean, or to be lazy, or to let off steam. Big Abel jabbed Abel with little frights because he wanted his son to grow immune to fear. He didn't want his son to feel, when fully grown, what he was feeling, full grown, too scared. He would teach his son to put fear behind him.

If Big Abel had to make a choice between putting Satan behind him and putting fear behind him he would banish fear and walk with Satan.

He hoped the Lord would forgive him. If the Lord didn't, Big Abel didn't mind. He wasn't afraid of the Lord; he wasn't interested in going to heaven. He was getting more eager to go to hell by the day.

It almost made him ready to die, so eager he was to see the white men, the ones who had planted the bomb and the ones who had planned the bombing, burning in hell. It was enough to make him want to pass up heaven. He stopped writing.

He imagined crackers, fat crackers and skinny crackers, tall crackers and short crackers, burning in hell, tongues parched and split. He imagined himself walking past, peeing and crying and refusing to share a drop of piss or a single tear to slake their thirst. He laughed out loud.

Antoinette glared. Carole Rosamond Robertson was dead. Four girls were blown up at church on a Sunday morning. There was nothing funny in the world. Big Abel cleared his throat and dropped his eyes back down to his legal pad. He struggled through a brief apology. Antoinette started crying again. Abel asked his wife if she wanted him to take the wheel. She said she wanted him, for this once, to be quiet.

Little Abel didn't know what to think. His mother was crying, his daddy was slapping and apologizing, and his favorite babysitter had gone to sleep forever.

Alpha was losing it. On the phone to Antoinette. She was wanting to have Carole's funeral the day before the other three girls. A separate service. At St. John's AME. Alpha's daughter was dead and she would not turn her funeral into a spectacle or a political event. She would not. She would give Carole what she was supposed to have. What she would have gotten if she had been hit by a drunk driver or caught a brain fever. She would have a service that was her very own, like her life, not something she was sharing with three other girls, one of whom she barely knew, or didn't know at all. Not something she had to share with a whole race of Negroes who were still alive.

Alpha didn't have to say any of that out loud for Antoinette to know. Antoinette came from the exact same small world Alpha came from and would have done the exact same thing, if it had been her baby girl Tess who had gotten blown up.

Antoinette was furious at the man beside her. Abel Jones Jr. His name was all in the papers. Integrating this and integrating that. She believed in it. But everyone knew where they lived. When would North Nashville become another Dynamite Hill? That's what they called one of the black neighborhoods in Birmingham. Dynamite Hill. So many bombs had gone off.

Driving to fourteen-year-old Carole's funeral thinking about the pair of strapless pumps she had been wearing when she was blown to Kingdom Come, Antoinette wished she had married a quiet man, an appeasing man, a man strong enough to play low, to play Tom, if that let the kids live.

She hated Martin Luther King. She hated George Wallace. Wallace had said they needed some funerals. Martin had gone on the radio and the teevee and more or less said that somehow privileged blacks were complicit in the death of the girls. Martin didn't know what he was talking about when he called out "Negroes on their stools complacent," or some such. She marveled at this curious thing: Martin didn't see the difference between complacent and terrified they will kill our children. And she did not mean metaphorically. She meant literally. Abel. Tess. It was bad enough Big Abel might be shot down like Medgar Evers had been shot. In front of his and Myrlie's house. Now Antoinette had to be scared Little Abel and Little Tess would be blown up like Carole.

She thought of the last time she had seen pretty Carole in Birmingham. They had run down the road for a wedding, to show off the baby, round and gloriously deep brown, Tess.

Antoinette had shimmied into a pretty silk suit, her figure came back quick, then into her husband's new Thunderbird that was just like the ones that had driven in President Kennedy's inaugural parade. That day her baby was on her lap and her husband was at the wheel. Her little boy, who had fallen in love with Carole the first time she lifted him onto her hip and her hair brushed his cheek, had been riding up front with his daddy.

Carole was a pretty child who should have lived to be a Link, and make jokes like "A Link is a fur-wearing animal." Carole's hardest teenage choice should have been whether to pledge AKA or Delta. She was a straight-A student who lived in a house with a wraparound porch who liked to cha-cha through the living room into the yard and now she was dead.

Antoinette's son was thirsty as well as needing to pee but they didn't dare give him a drop to drink, or stop to let him relieve himself properly. Any stop any day could be dangerous, but a stop a day after the bombing was impossible.

She had put cotton diapers on the boy and big rubber pants. He had screamed when she had done it but he would be fine. And she had promised herself to get the diapers off him just as soon as they got to the house.

And there would be no drop to drink. If he had a drop to drink he might soak through the diapers and the plastic pants. They had to arrive safe and presentable. The boy just needed to pee in the diapers and accept the cold wet.

She would keep the car rolling until they pulled into the driveway of Alpha's house.

Antoinette would sign up for the war if she could go fight on foreign soil. New Hampshire. Maine. Wyoming. Some place with no brown babies. Only a man would fight a bombing war so close to home. So close to home she would fly the white flag of surrender. She kept crying and driving. She had no flag to fly.

The church in Birmingham had blown up at ten twenty-two on Sunday morning. The Jones phone in Nashville was ringing before noon. Now they were three quarters the way to Birmingham.

Big Abel kept grinding his teeth and scribbling. He found flashes of comfort in his firm belief in heaven, the place where the four little girls were; and his firmer belief in hell, the place where the bombers would be.

Big Abel kept his face mean. One day the boy wouldn't be afraid of him. And that day the boy wouldn't be afraid of anything else either. He would just be mad, like his daddy, mad and safe.

To get through this day, this drive, and this night, the wake, and tomorrow, the funeral, Big Abel was letting himself get furious. He had to protect himself from seeing the church where ten sticks of dynamite had blown four girls straight to heaven.

He had wanted to protect himself by staying home. He had enough to do in Nashville. But Antoinette had insisted they hit the road. She was friends with Carole Rosamond Robertson's mother, Alpha.

Carole was in the Jack and Jill just like their Abel and their Tess. Alpha Robertson was southeastern director of the Jack and Jill of America. This had meant nothing to Big Abel but his wife had kept repeating these facts until he had assumed they were somehow of significance. Antoinette was not a woman to focus on unimportant details.

Leaning away from his wife and his son and into the cold window,

Big Abel tried to turn his mind back to the papers on his lap. He had his work cut out for him. Trying to get black students into state universities. Trying to get blacks into restaurants and stores. He didn't need to run down the road to Alabama to find something to do. There was work enough in his adopted Tennessee and his birth state North Carolina. His woman had him chasing off to a funeral in Alabama when he had fires to put out nearer to home.

Funerals were for people who wanted to see their picture in the paper or their face on television. Big Abel didn't have time for none of that. He had living children to take up for.

They had left the baby girl, Tess, in Nashville. Alabama had never been a safe place for little black girls and now it was revealed to be even less safe than previously thought. Abel didn't care what King or Bevel said, or God himself Almighty said. Abel wasn't toting his princess down into trouble. When he had agreed to "run stand by Alpha Robertson," Big Abel had insisted they leave Tess behind.

Antoinette had agreed, but not for reasons of safety. Waving her girl, Tess, in front of Alpha's face when she had just lost her daughter Carole seemed shameless.

Little Abel was in a room full of women. He was seated in a corner with a little pile of picture books. The women were swirling around trying to comfort Mrs. Robertson.

Somewhere downstairs, at an event something between a visitation and a wake, were the women who didn't know Mrs. Robertson as well and all the men.

Upstairs the women who knew Alpha Robertson well were trying to get her ready, not for the service that would be held the next day, there was no getting ready for that, but for just breathing her next breath, and

*for just stepping downstairs, for trying to look at other children, her son
and her other daughter.*

*Abel had been told to stay put in his corner, but after he had been miss-
ing his mama long enough, he forgot what he'd been told and wandered
over to where his mama was sitting in the center of the room with Carole's mama.*

Mrs. Robertson reached out and pinched his cheek.

*"You can't come to Birmingham anymore. There's nobody to take care
of you when us grown folks go out. Carole's passed. She was your favorite
and you were hers, so I guess you won't come and I won't be going out
anyway," said Mrs. Robertson.*

*"Yes, ma'am," said Abel. He didn't understand what Mrs. Robert-
son was talking about, but he knew when an older person talked real
serious and quiet, "Yes, sir" or "Yes, ma'am" are what you are supposed
to say.*

*New sobs broke free from Alpha Robertson's throat. She was in the
presence of a child as polite as her own. Perfect home training. There were
so few being raised exactly right—and now one less.*

*Mrs. Robertson's sobs frightened Little Abel. He dashed back to his
corner. His mother smiled vaguely after him, then turned her attentions
back to Carole's mama.*

*"All these men killed my baby," Mrs. Robertson said, thinking about
a girl graceful as could be. A girl who made straight A's who was going
to be a doctor's wife and move out of Alabama. Antoinette and every
woman in the room were thinking the very same thing. Finally someone
said, "Fuck Bevel," referring to the great black theologian and tactician
of the Civil Rights movement. Then someone else said, "Fuck Bevel.
If they are old enough to walk down the communion aisle they're old
enough to march. Fuck Bevel." Someone else said, "I would fuck Bevel*

and every peckerwood in the Alabama Klan if it would bring Alpha's baby back."

"I'd fuck 'em all and their daddies if it would bring any of these babies back." This last was said by Little Abel's mother.

And all the women in stockings and silk skirts, the women who would wear dark dresses and gloves and hats and pearls and girdles in the church tomorrow, so many who had walked down the aisle at their wedding intact, even some of the ones whose husbands had never seen them naked in the daylight, shook their heads in agreement. They were drunk on fear.

They were in a violent world with more children to lose. Little Abel, sitting in his corner with his picture books, was terrified by the women speaking men's words.

"I had three children," said Alpha. She was wearing the same politely pink lipstick all the other women were wearing, but only hers was all on crooked. "I had three children," she repeated, then beckoned to Abel. He didn't move. He thought the woman wanted to steal him to replace the child she had lost. The child who was sleeping forever. Carole.

Mrs. Robertson beckoned again. Antoinette silently snapped the fingers hanging at her side. The boy noticed his mother's signal. He put his book down and moved back across the room and onto Alpha's lap.

"Little man, listen here. Don't you forget these men, these black men, and these big white Birmingham mules, these men. They used you children to fight this war. Negro men were tired of what we all had to suffer and they sent our babies to die. Nothing left but the shoes. Don't you forget that, boy. I'm going to hate my husband and hate your daddy the rest of my life. And I hope you hate them too. And I'm going to hate Bull Connor and hate George Wallace and hate Martin Luther King. But I am going to hate my husband and your father and Martin the most because they know just how precious you are. Precious like my Carole, but they were willing to let her die if it came to it. They're too tired of waiting. And I hate Wallace Rayfield, that fine black architect, for designing that church and this neighborhood. If he hadn't done any of that my husband wouldn't be the bandleader in the school here and I wouldn't be a librarian and my daughter wouldn't be dead. And I hate Jesus because the Lord didn't have mercy, four little girls were in Sunday school and he let them get killed."

Alpha kissed Abel on his head. "I hate them too," Abel said.

The crow was flying home. Big Abel drove. On the return journey Antoinette lay stretched out on the backseat like a corpse. Little Abel sat up front drawing letters with his finger into the fog on the window.

Big Abel turned the radio on and tuned to a station playing rhythm and blues. He held up off the accelerator. He didn't want to get stopped. He didn't want to strangle some honky cop and get shot down in front of his son and his wife, but he would strangle some honky cop and get shot down in front of his wife and son before he would play low this day, whatever might happen to his wife and his child after he died. He drove the whole way to Nashville one mile below the speed limit.

Sometimes they were passed by a black family, smiling and waving, in a bucket of rust. One blue clunker had a JFK bumper sticker on its tail. It beeped out recognition on the horn as it passed. Apparently the occupants recognized the Thunderbird Big Abel was driving as being the same model of car as was featured in JFK's inaugural parade. Any other day that would have been solace.

This is the story gossip told.

ONE

ABEL DIED AT the Rebel Yell. He got up from the long table where he was seated with his white family, complained of shortness of breath, then headed for the toilets. His raven-haired wife, who had already made three trips (each time with a child in tow) through the door marked MAGNOLIAS across from the door marked CAVALIERS, hardly seemed to notice.

Samantha, Abel's wife, and her four almost-grown sons from a previous marriage, high school boys, two sets of twins, remained in their seats.

They were absorbed with gobbling fried chicken and swilling sweet tea. Horses were galloping through the dining room. The sound of banners and flags crackling in the dim and dusty air created a hypnotic counter-rhythm against the quintessential noise of wars from long ago, the rat-a-tat, rat-a-tat of hoof-beats. "That's the sound," Abel had said, "of horses galloping in the direction of their master's murderous gaze." The big kids, lulled into a lazy stupor at the dinner theater with horses, war songs, and Confederate battle reenactors, hadn't heard what he had said and didn't notice that he had left.

Only his three little daughters, one with immense blue eyes, one with slanty green, one with sweet gray—the children Samantha had borne Abel after his first wife, Hope, a brown-haired, brown-eyed, brown-skinned sculptress, had thrown him out of the little yellow cottage—only his creamy-skinned angels noticed. Liberated by Abel's absence, the girls rose from their seats.

Running round the table instead of eating, the girls bumped into waiters carrying heavy laden platters of canned black-eyed peas and canned corn, canned collard greens and canned sweet potatoes, keeping an eye peeled for Daddy's return, until they too forgot the man.

After a good long while, the three-year-old, sufficiently exhausted and bored to be frightened by computer-generated illusions of bombs bursting in air and rockets' red glare, returned to Mother's lap, while the six-year-old nuzzled her way back into the space between the inside of Mother's arm and her rib cage, resting her head on Mother's cool rayon-covered bosom while standing on her own small, hot feet. The nine-year-old found her way into Abel's chair.

And so it was that not so very far from their sight, just inside the gray-tiled bathroom marked CAVALIERS, but so very far from the consciousness of his white family, Abel sucked on an asthma inhaler that brought no echo hit of rushing air.

Technology was failing him. He who had, as White House special advocate at the Pentagon, sent so many young men, some boys no older than the woman's oldest teenage son, to meet their death surrounded by strangeness and strangers, armed only with the inventions of their more ambitious and more able betters, was meeting his own death amid strangeness, among strangers. Technology was failing him.

It was a good joke. If he had had breath to laugh he would

have. But he didn't, so he didn't. He sucked harder for the air that couldn't enter, sealed out by some unnamed secretion of his own body.

Breathing is an invasive procedure. Abel refused to be invaded again. Absolutely refused. Not one step back. Giddified by oxygen deprivation, the truth bounced about his brain uncensored until he spoke it aloud, *I am going to die.*

It was almost, for a moment, like he could breathe deep. He had spoken the truth that he knew to be most significant. Finally.

For once he was not banking a verbal shot off some calculated rhetorical ridge, not speaking to set in motion a series of actions and reactions that would make it all but impossible for anyone involved to discern whose intention was being manifested. He was going to die. And just like the boys he had sent to die in Iraq, he prayed his death would serve a larger purpose.

He was far from home, farther than one might think a man could travel in forty-five years.

The day Abel was born, sweet tucked deep in the dark South, Langston Hughes, out west on a speaking tour, typed a little poem in celebration. In Paris, Richard Wright received three different postcards and a letter shouting the good news, as well as, eventually, the official engraved baby announcement with its blue satin bow that would make its way to seventeen states of the Union and four foreign countries. So the street talk went.

Abel was colored-baby royalty. Related by blood or marriage to both W. E. B. DuBois and Booker T. Washington, he was also reputed to be kin to Charles Drew by marriage. Adam

Clayton Powell had been, and Thurgood Marshall was, a close personal friend of the family.

Infant Abel was as fortunate in his choice of era as he was in his choice of friends and relations. For the first time in the history of America the birth of a Negro boy was cause for almost-only happy expectations.

The bulbs of pride were in the soil, planted side by side with patience, perseverance, and our-time-is-now-ness, just waiting to peek out their heads. It was 1959. Black was just about to bust out beautiful, creating a new kingdom awaiting a new prince— and then came Abel.

"There's something about that kid," folk gathered round his hospital bassinet or peering at him through the nursery viewing glass said over and over. Born at Meharry's Hubbard Hospital, on the north side of Nashville, Abel first saw light inside the doors of one of the nation's great black institutions. At the time of his birth (the first stroke of six on a Wednesday) Meharry Medical College had graduated, if we let the gossip of North Nashville tell the story, eighty percent of all the black doctors practicing in the world, to say nothing of introducing near to a hundred percent of the most adventurous of the beautiful colored girls attending Fisk University, located directly across a two-lane road from the Meharry, to the joys of love. Hubbard Hospital was a place that thought it had seen every flavor of colored infant: the slow, the fast, the strong, the weak, the rich-as-we-get and the poor-as-we-come, wearing every hue of birthday suit from sweet cream to dark chocolate. And then came a new flavor.

Nobody had seen a baby like Abel. Born three weeks overdue, he smiled before he was forty-eight hours old. The old nurses sang "John Henry" round his crib, the young nurses sang "Hoochie Coochie Man." He slept through the night the day his mama and daddy took him home. By the time he was a month old he drank two eight-ounce bottles of milk before nodding off, and soaked through three diapers while he slept, never waking up, never getting diaper rash. Whenever he screamed he wanted something. When he got what he wanted he got back to smiling.

When he got grown he would tell that story to his children, over and over again. It was how he wanted to be remembered.

Black lawyers and doctors, funeral home owners and taxi company operators, they all scrambled to purchase one-hundred-dollar savings bonds for Abel, as Abel's daddy had scrambled to purchase bonds for their sons and nephews. Everybody wanted an invitation to his christening party.

The bonds exclaimed: This little boy owns a piece of America and I bought it for him. This baby child will grow up to be a man. He will live long enough to see this promise mature. He will go to college and need this money. He will buy a house and need this money. He is a citizen for whom I can prepare a future. It was heady stuff. It was a new exuberance. New Year's Day 1960 was sweet, sweet, sweet in North Nashville.

That Abel would one day choose to pay hundreds of dollars to eat his supper in a Confederate horse barn was bad. That he would spend money earned with the degree funded by the bonds bought for him on the occasion of his birth was worse. That Abel would have a white family to take to the mountains, to the Valhalla of country music, was near impossible.

It was as if he had forgotten what all southern Negroes know:

country music had provided the soundtrack, if not to a thousand lynchings, to the drive to a thousand lynchings, and to the getting drunk after a thousand more.

Not one of the visionary men who had crowded round Abel's cradle could have imagined Abel's final vacation. Not one would have believed the news of his peculiar death had it been foretold.

They could have imagined Abel shot down like Malcolm, Medgar, or Martin would be and like dozens of fleeing slaves had been. They could have imagined Abel shot in the ass by a jealous lover, Sam Cooke style, climbing out of his second woman's third-story window: the boy was pretty-pretty. They could not imagine this old-timey Bessie Smith death.

Too many colored people had died, too many times, on a slow drive to the hospital for men and women of color not to drive in caravans, completely avoiding snow-white counties whenever remotely possible, when they ventured out on vacation.

If hardly anyone still went to Idlewild, there was Highland Beach, and Oak Bluffs, and Sag Harbor, and Hilton Head. These were the towns of the black Riviera.

Waynesville, North Carolina. Hillbilly Land. The place was an impossibility. They did not fear Waynesville, the men who had gathered round Abel's cradle. Abel wouldn't go to Waynesville, and if he went he would not go there alone.

They knew this as certainly as they knew that when they spoke the word "alone" they meant away from the company of black people.

It might have been possible for one or two of the great personalities of the Movement to have anticipated a part of Abel's fate. Someone might have anticipated the Pentagon part of the tragedy; no one would have anticipated Waynesville.

"On your North Carolina vacation, you'll see bumper boat ponds, racing llamas, fifteen-foot frogs, and Selu the Great Corn Mother. You can dig for sapphires, pan for gold, or fish on an Indian Reservation from a stream stocked three times weekly," promised the Web page that Sammie had used to make Thanksgiving plans.

Racing llamas, fifteen-foot frogs, bumper boat ponds. Abel would have preferred to have taken his chances with the sharks at the winter beach.

Sammie had whined for the Smoky Mountains. Clog, North Carolina, between Cherokee and Waynesville, was chosen as their base. Twisted in knots by her tongue, flicking here, licking there, Abel had come to agree the kids would enjoy the Black Bear Powwow. The unused tickets were in his pocket when the funeral director returned Abel's clothes to the widow.

The old black men who would stand at his grave with their ladies in the white cemetery (men whose wives had sent baby rattles and burp cloths, and the women who had wrapped those gifts in white paper and tulle) would cry almost as much because they were being called to stand in a white cemetery as because he was dead. Then they would cry more because they would know in their bones Abel was dead, dead as his father was dead, *because* they were standing in a white cemetery. And they would know Abel had made them cry. They would know payback when they saw it.

The exquisitely bereaved: old doctors, old lawyers, an old editor, the first black this, the first black that; these men would prefer to believe Abel had died somewhere else, somewhere secret serving his country, somewhere that couldn't be told. These old men had firsthand knowledge that what the government said "ain't necessarily so."

These men would *know* that Abel had died in the Middle East or fucking the president's wife, died some way other than eating a meal at a dinner theater with Confederate battle-cry reenactments.

But it was so, just so. The fall of 2005, just after the summer 436 soldiers had fallen in Iraq, Abel ventured to North Carolina feeling completely safe. Then he started to die.

He had not feared this end. Renowned in Washington for an uncanny ability to anticipate the most likely worst-case scenario, Abel had only once trembled at the possibility of his own premature death.

In point of fact, Hope, the first wife, had not asked Abel to leave. She went crazy one morning and threatened to kill him. After that he thought it prudent to leave her. They had had a difference of opinion about corporal punishment. Abel believed in it; Hope didn't. Hope especially didn't believe in Abel doling it out. The very first time he hit the baby she told him that. The second time she told him she hadn't liked the look in his eye when he hit the baby. The third time she said if he hit the baby again she would shoot him. She would shoot him and take her chances with the courts. She had said she would wait till he was sleeping to do it. And so he had left the brown beauty. It was possible, perhaps even likely, she had been speaking in anger hyperbolically. It was likely she had intended only to get his attention and win the we-are-modern-liberal-parents argument with a bit of diary-of-a-mad-black-woman histrionics. He couldn't take the chance. He knew he would hit the baby again if he stayed. And he knew if he did she would do something.

In the last hour of his life, as a crowd of white men gathered round him, he recalled the day, years before, when he had come to know Hope was crazy. She had been wearing a flowery Laura Ashley robe. Her feet were bare. Her toenails were polished a ruddy pink. The rope of fake pearls he had given her for Christmas, telling her they were real, had been hanging round her neck. She bathed and slept in the thing. He recalled her saying she would not be aiming to kill him, but that she might if he moved.

She didn't tell him what to do. She didn't tell him to leave. She didn't tell him not to come back. She knew better than all that. She was not loony-tunes crazy. She just told him what she was going to do, given the chance, and he knew better than to go back to the little yellow cottage, to the place they had laughingly described, the day the Realtor had taken them to see it for the very first time, as the architectural equivalent of Valium.

Only minutes earlier he had anticipated the restoration of equilibrium. Her brown eyes had been soft. He had believed her to be contemplating defeat. She had whispered softly, almost strangely, "No, I'm not calling the police." He had understood her to be pondering the reality that he would have control of his child's manners, of his house, that he was the head and the neck of the household, that she was to be the belly and the breasts. And, perhaps, the hands. He liked her hands. The way she cooked. The way she ironed a shirt when he urged her to on the maid's day off. The way her hands worked with her mouth to give him pleasure. She had wanted to be the belly, the breasts, and the neck, turning the head in the direction she chose. He would let her be the belly, the breast, and the hands.

He could only imagine the joys to come. His father had taught him that a defeated woman was a pleasuring woman. Abel had believed he and his wife were on their way to that, when the softness in Hope's eyes had vanished.

He had been dressed that day very much as he was dressed at the Rebel Yell, in khakis and a Lacoste, every inch the suburban southern gentleman, except all those years earlier the sizes were smaller and way back then he wore the brighter colors. That day, standing in the front hall of the yellow cottage, his boy in his arms, he had been looking into his woman's eyes, wearing lime green, when every possibility had altered. There was before, there was after, and there was all that had disappeared.

The fear in their child's eyes had changed everything.

He had barely tapped the kid. Hope didn't know what a slap was. Ajay was only two years old but it is never too early for a smart child to start learning obedience. And he worshipped his son. Just that morning he had gotten up early, dressed for his day, dressed the boy for his, then walked with the boy, to the sound of trilling questions and faked army gun blasts, toward the kitchen, where he had sat Ajay in a little blond-wood chair at a little blond-wood table-for-four, well appointed with paper and paint and crayons. Abel would make them a hot breakfast of scrambled eggs and bacon, a little man's breakfast, but first there would be juice and Cheerios. The kid always woke up hungry. Abel had poured the cereal. Before he could pour the milk his son had demanded it.

"Milk, Daddy," Ajay had requested, smiling expectantly. Abel had smiled at the opportunity to teach his son house rules.

"Say, 'May I have some milk please, Daddy,'" Abel had said. Silence had answered him. The father had spoken again, this time more emphatically. "May I have some milk please Daddy?" Abel had repeated.

The little boy had started to cry. The strange grammar lesson had continued. *May I have some milk please Daddy?* Threats mingled with tears. Hope, who had been lying in bed listening for the bleatings of compromise and getting on with the morning, had slipped into a robe and started making her way down the front stairs.

She had stepped into the kitchen smiling broadly, if falsely, a dither of consoling words and a cloud of greeting swirling round her. She had a charm that was not lost upon either of the males in her family. They'd been immediately distracted. She had counted on this. She had lifted the boy from the tiny chair and started marching toward the steps that led to the room with the door she would lock. Abel had grabbed Hope's arm. The cheerful smell of butter warming in a skillet, waiting for eggs, had scented the air with hominess.

"Give him back to me," Abel had said, almost sweetly, as if she were crazy to think something was wrong.

"Of course, darling," Hope had said, her words dripping honey as she held her child close to her chest. With the boy's head safe, tucked beneath his mother's chin, Hope had silently mouthed, "Don't hit him."

"Of course not," Abel had snapped out loud.

Hope had handed over the baby. The child had started back to crying.

"Stop crying, or Daddy will 'pank you," Abel had immediately threatened.

Hope had focused her thought, attempting to will the child into silence while praying for the man to do right. The boy had started crying louder.

"Don't hit him," Hope had said.

Mother had barely whispered the sentence into the air when father slapped the child he was holding high on his hip, hard across the shoulder. Not perhaps so hard, but definite, and hard. Hope had snatched her son from her husband's arms.

She had known she shouldn't say what she was about to say in front of the child. And half a second later she had known she had to say it. "I will shoot you if you hit him again." Right out loud. Watching expressions he had not previously seen flicker across her face, it had occurred to Abel that his wife might just kill him. Into that moment they both had frozen.

Derangement was descending. Without moving, both the man and the boy were reaching for Hope's breasts. Without moving, both the man and the boy beckoned to Hope's womb. Man and boy made their claim on what the woman owed them. She owed them both something. Just at that moment she couldn't see what she owed the man.

Looking with the eyes in her belly, Hope saw that the boy's fear was virgin and beribboned with hope. The boy was expecting help to come. He was waiting for Mama to fix it, fix everything. The boy was hurt, but he wasn't cowed by pain.

Somewhere outside of the house, as a necessary evil of modern international antiterrorism, the man was on the road that links *I will make you wish you had never been born* to *I will hear you beg for death*. In his particular case this road passed through *I will fear nothing*, and it passed through Washington. Somehow Hope understood the truth that Abel was a dangerous man even as she heard him promise he would never harm his son.

The child was in his presence but he wasn't with him. The boy was still virgin to viciousness, still ignorant of purposeful harm, even as the palm marks welted up on his arm.

If evil is a disease, detachment provides no small portion of immunity. The child did not love the man enough to be fully vulnerable to his venomousness. He was afraid of his father but not of his body or his world. Hope knew more about this than she wanted to know. Betrayal by the mama might put a chink in the wall that fenced the boy from self-fear. If the mama looked away, or did not rescue quick enough, the wall might fail.

Hope, who had grown up in the bituminous hills of West Virginia, surrounded by sudden death and general terror—sudden death in the mines; the sudden flood at Bear Creek; Jock Yablonski, union reformer, shot sudden dead in his bed New Year's Eve 1969, his wife and daughter shot dead near him; Lawrence Jones, shot dead on a Harlan County picket line, the summer before Hope left for high school, 1973; the sudden flash of a pistol from a bra or the brandishing of a tommy gun from a car window as uncommon but not rare events that danced with the sudden burdening threat of bombs, even bombs that did not go off—had intended to live and die without her son knowing terror.

And now a strange anxiety animated her son's smile. The child's face was so oddly unlike the man's. She had picked the wrong daddy for the boy.

She had grabbed the toddler from the man who had slapped

his child for crying. Something about it had appalled Abel when, after he had warned the boy to stop bawling, or he would give the boy something to bawl about, Ajay had ascended into wailing. And neither Abel nor Hope had known just why Abel had been so bothered.

I had to hit him. The child had given him no choice. It didn't matter what the woman had said. It didn't matter what he had promised. He had forgotten it was the third time. He hadn't been counting. He didn't brook defiance. He didn't know the woman only gave two chances. He only knew he had a beautiful wife, a beautiful son, a beautiful home—and he felt ugly as homemade sin.

For a moment Abel was back in a different room in a different year waiting for a different woman to rescue him. He was at his childhood home on Fifteenth Avenue North waiting for his mother, Antoinette. And then he was returned, still in a room waiting for a woman to rescue his younger self, but the woman who arrived rescued the other boy.

"No, I'm not leaving you," Hope said. She loved him. She was as obedient as he had trained her to be.

He was pacified. He imagined himself, later that same morning, sucking on her breast, looking up at her face, and after that doing very grown-up things with and to his wife. He loved rolling in his woman's arms. If she let him do it enough times, one night, one morning, he thought he might roll out grown.

"I'm not leaving you." For a moment everything was all right. Then she said, "I'm going to buy a gun and shoot you."

The woman was crazy.

"There's nothing in me that will let me look the other way," wife said to husband just as she was falling out of love. Abel had never loved Hope more.

As he lay dying, Abel remembered falling in love with Clementine Hope Morgan Jones. He remembered knowing his son had the mother he had wished for.

The children born in his second marriage, Laura, Alice, and Nicole, called Lauro, Ali, and Nicola, had something else. They had a Sears and Roebuck white country girl, Sammie, *bless her heart sweet Sammie, pageant pretty,* who couldn't cook or keep house, but she would let him do whatever the hell it was he wanted with her big boys—from scare them straight to send them off to the war—and she looked tidy in a size-four dress. That did him some good but what good did it do the girls? He was counting on genes and money. There would be little nurture, there would be no black folk or street knowledge, but there would be money and white skins and maybe some I.Q. points. She would raise them white and they would be all right.

He lay sprawled, his inhaler on the ground, just out of reach. A stranger began to crouch over him. Abel barely noticed. Abel was too busy hoping the woman had enough sense to take his creamy angels off to Montana, or Iowa, or Wyoming, or Alaska, any place they could forget about everything about him but the fact he was White House Special Advocate at the Pentagon and that he had graduated from Harvard.

He wanted his second wife to forget his mother's Christian name, forget his grandmother's Christian name. He trusted it would be easy to forget what she had barely known. They had had so little contact with his black family. He was "the third" but he had not given any of his girls family names. Sammie hadn't wanted it. Truth be told he hadn't wanted it either. A white-sounding name was good grease for anyone wishing to slip the shackles of caste.

To be called Abel Jones was to wear a heavy-weighted chain, the key to the lock of which had long ago disappeared, perhaps down Abel the third's throat. *Freakonomics* was too thin a chisel to break that stout chain. A bigger chisel was coming and Abel would help break the chain, but right now Abel Jones was a black man's name, infamous, or famous, depending on your perspective, throughout Tennessee, throughout the South. Abel Jones Jr. had desegregated every public school system in Tennessee, except Shelby County, every city except Memphis, and half the counties of North Carolina, riding up and down winding dirt roads, bomb threats behind him, bullet shots ahead, never slowing down.

Now just outside the men's-room door marked CAVALIERS a vacationing doctor from Michigan crouched beside him and began to examine Abel's face with an air of professional competence. When Abel heard the man's flat voice calling into his cell phone for an ambulance, Abel suspected the northern tourist didn't recognize he was black. Abel was dying white. It was a triumph.

Ambulance called, the northern doctor was still jabbering, mumbling about the South. Folks were fatter here. This fellow was no exception. The fine and polished leather of the man's shoes, the heavy gold rims of his spectacles, the heavily carved shield of his class ring, and the chemically enhanced brightness of his teeth told the doctor his patient was prosperous as well as plump. Imagining a family very much like his own, a girl and a boy, ski trips and summer camps, private schools and SUVs, the Yankee doctor began CPR, cracking a rib.

Abel was thinking about his father. A Durham magazine had run an issue with a giant glossy picture of his face on the cover and a headline asking, "Is this the most hated man in North Carolina?" The black folks down on Parrish Street had thought the better question might have been "Is this the most feared man in North Carolina?" When Durham cousins recaptioned the cover as a joke they inscribed, "Is this the angriest man in the nation?" Abel Jones Jr. tore that copy of the cover in half, announcing, "The most hated man in this land is also the angriest. And he is feared, and I am he." Abel Jones Jr. said all that, then he smiled. When he smiled, the graduate of North Carolina Central, law school and college, looked just like the man on the cover of the magazine.

Abel wanted to tell this graying blond white man with blue eyes that it was not his heart that was failing; it was his body that refused to be invaded anew. He wondered how long it would take before his wife came looking for him. He wondered if the Yankee doctor had ever ventured to Idlewild. He worried that if they left this strange restaurant, this little sphere where everyone thought he was white, no one would believe the woman with the raven hair and the girls with the light eyes were his, that outside this place, separated from the family, once he was in the ambulance, alone in the hospital, everywhere else along the way, he would be recognized as a black man.

Earlier in the day Abel and this second family, seven children who kept him broke, had fidgeted, then frozen before a painted backdrop, after he had paid eighty-five dollars he didn't have, charging yet another expense to an already overtaxed credit card, to a young photographer who actively sought a sight of the souls his subjects strove so tenaciously to hide. The woman looked tired and pretty. The man looked exasperated and puffy. The children looked bored. *Sea of Whiteness*, the photographer silently titled the portrait. He named all the portraits he attempted hour after hour, Saturday through Saturday. *Sea of Whiteness*, this one was. *Sea of Whiteness*. No one would ever think, gazing at the portrait, though the photographer taking the shot had noticed before his lights washed the beige out, that Abel, flanked by his wife on one side, her children on the other, with their children folded at their feet, was anything but a normal, white man.

Abel was grateful. He was circling closer to peace when the smoke from a long-ago fire found its way to his nostrils. Abel coughed through his nose. The Michigan physician mistook the cough for a sign of life.

The ambulance attendants arrived. These men knew nothing of Italian leather, nothing of gold glasses, nothing of the black-haired woman, nothing of the green- and blue- and gray-eyed children. They only saw a Yankee doctor giving CPR to a nigger.

Close-cropped the hair might be, but it was kinky. Light the skin might be, but it was beige. And there was that face, a face neither Yancey nor Waddell could ever forget, the face of the man who had twenty-five years before, twenty years before, and maybe just fifteen years before come up to the mountains making trouble, suing this one for not serving niggers, and that one for making a separate school for niggers, and somebody else altogether for somehow mistreating their niggers. The face on the magazine cover they had long used for target practice was lying at their feet.

He hadn't aged a day. *Black magic.* He looked just like he looked when he had come up and defended the nigger that had raped the nice white lady. They didn't know the Abel they remembered was long dead, that this Abel they were lifting into the ambulance hated that man far more than they could possibly hate him. The paramedics didn't know that and wouldn't have understood it if they had been told. They simply killed the Abel they had.

Or rather, they didn't do what they could have to revive him. The Michigan doctor suspected heart attack; the country boys sent by Mountain View Hospital with the painted-all-over-green Mountain View Hospital ambulance stamped with tarheels knew allergy when they saw it: they saw it enough in this dinner theater with horses and no ventilation. Horses and food didn't belong together indoors but if people were too foolish to know that, well, then let 'em die and improve the breed. It made more work for paramedics and paramedic was good-paying work.

Except always before the fools were white. The fool at their feet was the biggest fool in the world, a nigger with no more sense than to eat his dinner in a Confederate horse barn. It was hard to believe God would make any creature, even a nigger, as dumb as that. Kind of made the men wonder if there was a God.

As they lifted his bulk onto the stretcher, Abel could feel the whiteness in the paramedic's fingertips touching the blackness of his skin. It was a familiar sensation. He knew it from basketball courts and doctors' offices; he knew it differently from featherbeds and beaches, from blankets on the grass. Sometimes with a woman it was a good thing, the frisson of white touching black. With a man it was always bad. With a man there was no difference, or there was a sad difference. Men, in Abel's experience, always want other men to be what they are, or less than they are. And if they are less than they are they want to beat them, or do more and worse.

He had come to the Rebel Yell fully prepared to see the Confederate flag waved over the dinner he paid good money to eat. He had come prepared to eat heaping helpings of white people's country cooking, humming along as the fiddle sobbed out *I wish I was in de land of cotton old times dere are not forgotten.* He had come to the mountains of North Carolina because it was what his wife's people did, when they weren't riding bulls, or playing bluegrass, or at the NASCAR races. He had crossed a final frontier.

And now, as if the paramedics were celestial minions, as if his dead father really was in charge of the world, and thus the world was wretched, for the old man had proved himself inadequate to the task of being in charge of everything—the falsely accused rapist had gone to jail and died in jail; the schools of Nashville were more segregated in 2005 than in 1965; the Klan that had burned a cross on the lawn of Abel's house during his thirteenth birthday party was still holed up in the hollers and byways of America; the Southern Poverty Law Center, when tallying The Year in Hate, 2005, would count 803 active hate groups, at least one in every state of the nation—Abel, who had crossed over into the world of whiteness, was snatched back to black, the second before his life on earth ended.

If he had been living, Abel Jones Jr., Big Abel, would have smiled seeing his son know payback when he saw it.

Abel Jones the third died in a slow ambulance ride to a country hospital. The paramedics wrote "black" so many times over the receiving papers that when the funeral home employees got the paperwork they sucked their teeth in dismay.

Something Abel inhaled in Waynesville—where people ride around on horseback, indoors, waving Confederate flags above the heads of pudgy men, women, and children and the occasional Japanese tourist—triggered the series of events that led to his tragic death en route to the hospital, or so the conventional wisdom opined loudly.

Abel knew better. *All that appears tragic is not.* He closed his eyes as the stretcher was secured in the vehicle. He did not want to see the men who had taken custody of his body. He would not let it be them who killed him by moving at all deliberate speed. *How did we forget that all deliberate speed is slowly?* He would not acknowledge the presence of the ambulance men. He knew what to withhold to confound his captors. He knew how to protect what little remained of who he had been born to be.

He had let his back be a bridge. Now he would break his back. He would slow his colleagues down. He would give the new man a better chance. ABC. A Better Chance. His wife, his first wife, Hope, would be the only person in the world who would get that joke.

As the ambulance door shut, Abel saw the face that looked so much like his own, the boy with the brown eyes and brilliance, the one whose mother would never have allowed him to bring any of them to the Rebel Yell. He saw Ajay, his firstborn, *little Abel*, his rebel who would do more than yell.

Then Abel Jones, lawyer for Abu Ghraib, crossed back over to where he had begun, the other side of terror.

TWO

THANKSGIVING FOUND THE former Mrs. Abel Jones the third standing in the middle of an appropriately cold November night, in the middle of her hypermodern kitchen, in the middle of a glass box, in the middle of Tennessee, packing old-fashioned breakfast sacks, ham biscuits with blackberry jam, pondering a half-finished sculpture in her workshop, and mulling over the proposition that black men are an endangered species.

Biscuit by biscuit she was doing her part to preserve the black men she loved—and raise the one she had borne onto a path that would (she begged God and a pantheon of ebony angels nightly, some of whom were depicted, albeit provocatively, in her current piece, a partly welded mass in the barn) lead to a fertile and sheltering maturity.

It might have all been simpler if her son had been her husband's child, but he wasn't and her household was simple enough. Abel's nature nurtured by Hope and Waycross created a fine chiseled bronze boy with neat dreads, old-school manners, and a vocabulary that ranged from a'fuck to xenophobia. He was a sweet and fearless son.

Waycross hadn't fallen in love to clean up Abel's mess but he had fallen in love and cleaned up Abel's mess.

"Ajay's what I would have been if I had been brought up by you," Abel said to Hope when he had come by to see the boy and had stood on her grass terrace a few weeks earlier, just after their six-foot-and-getting-taller sixteen-year-old boy had won some debate competition or another. Hope had had to will herself not to get taken in by Abel's unexpected flattery.

She split the last of the still-warm sweet potato biscuits in two, smeared both halves with blackberry jam, then put a big forkful of country ham in the middle, feeling fortunate.

Her present husband, Dr. D. Hale Williams Blackshear (called Waycross), and her son, Abel Jones IV (called Ajay), were, as far as Clementine Hope Jones Blackshear (née Morgan) knew, outside loading the Ford Expedition with coolers and rifles and duffel bags.

The males in Waycross's family hunted the weekend after Thanksgiving. From the first year of Hope's second marriage, her son and her husband had claimed the last days of the Michigan deer season as their almost-father, almost-son time.

Sometimes they hunted deer, sometimes they hunted grouse. This year they would hunt deer. They didn't have a bird dog ready for the field.

Idlewild was a ragtag, run-down place but Ajay and Waycross loved it. And Hope loved it for them. Mount Bayou, one of Waycross's doctor friends, who each year met them in Idlewild, liked to say, "There's something in the smell of the northwestern Michigan woods that makes your balls hang big and low and cool. Fertile." Hope teasingly referred to "y'all's black Hemingway thing," but she said it in a voice that suggested she wanted to celebrate all that was hanging low and cool.

The Blackshear family Thanksgiving Festival began with a single meal that stretched across two calendar days. It started with spiced almonds that Hope blanched, then rebrowned, in a mixture of brown sugar, pepper, and Jack Daniel's. The nuts, served with stuffed dates and cheese crackers cut into the shape of acorns, kicked off the festivities at exactly five on Wednesday.

Not having Thanksgiving on calendar Thanksgiving and doing all the cooking herself were tribute to her aunties, long dead, who, working as domestics, had often been obliged to cook for strangers and serve strangers on the fourth Thursday in November. The aunts had moved their family holiday to Wednesday and Hope, in solidarity, had kept hers there—except for the years she had been married to Abel. Drinking (cases of champagne and sparkling cider) and eating, mainly turkey (roasted, smoked, fried, and confit), continued into the early hours of Thursday morning, when a second round of sweet potato pie baked into a crust of homemade gingersnaps was served. Later on Thanksgiving Day, just before noon, Hope served a less elaborate but still big breakfast—egg casserole, twisted bacon, and blueberry crepes, all recipes the aunts had perfected working in other folks' kitchens. Only then would the hunters, laden with sack snacks, extra spiced almonds, and man-bought provisions, leave for Michigan.

"Thank you for the luscious plenty," one tipsy old lady had gasped, most earnestly, just after midnight one Thanksgiving morning after getting so high and tired she couldn't remember what she was supposed to say. She couldn't remember the word "supper" or the phrase "Thanksgiving dinner," so she said what she felt, loudly and high-pitched, with an old woman's exuberance, and everybody waiting to get their car laughed with her and started calling the meal, and the house, and occasionally even Hope, in honor of her expanding waistline, Luscious Plenty too. So many morsels of compensation attempting to eclipse so many minutes of neglect.

Now halfway through packing the breakfast sacks for the Idlewild trek, a once-a-year, middle-of-the-night task, Hope was exhausted with kitchen labor and kitchen routines. The job had never previously been disturbing or difficult, precisely because it tied her back to her aunts who had taught her to savor cooking in her own kitchen for her own family, only this morning it didn't tie her back.

She wondered if her discontent had more to do with a bad month of day-trading or more to do with being hungry for her "white meal," the last meal of the family's ritual Thanksgiving Festival. Usually by now she had already eaten it. Usually by now she was already alone. This year wasn't usually.

First, CeCe, her best friend, hadn't made it. CeCe's plane had been delayed so long departing Paris that CeCe had decided it wasn't worth traveling for two days, for two days' play.

Second, Waycross had a favorite patient in the hospital. He didn't want to leave until the woman had safely delivered her several-days-overdue-but-she-doesn't-want-to-be-induced twins. He was going to be up and stuck in Nashville half their driving night.

To save the trip, Ajay had volunteered to drive the first eight hours while Waycross slept. If they were on the road by three A.M. they would be in the field just in time to catch the last few hours of daylight Friday afternoon. The twins arrived just after midnight. Waycross got in before two. Everything was on schedule but everything was just a little too different. Yet and still, they were good to go.

Sacks finished, Hope poured both her men a big thermos near full of chicory coffee, topped it off with steamed milk, then plunked in a handful of sugar cubes. Chicory coffee, Café du Monde brand, with just enough milk to turn it the color of Ajay, was an innovation Hope had added to the Blackshear Thanksgiving hunt tradition. After twisting the tops on the thermoses, she shook one, then the other till she guessed the sugar was dissolved. Jobs done, she refilled her cup with the last of the big pot.

The cup, a long-ago wedding present from West Virginia, was between her lips when she heard a rifle shot, then the cup was in four pieces on the slate countertop.

Banjo's bed under the kitchen table was empty. She saw just barely the large vague dimple his body had left on the pillow without knowing when he had left or how she had failed to notice.

She ran toward the front of the house, in thin gray wool pants and a thinner black silk sweater, stabbed by cold she wouldn't let distract her.

Arriving at the front, she first saw Ajay standing at the truck washed in floodlight. Then she saw the silhouette of Waycross standing on the lawn, shotgun by his side. Finally she saw a huge coyote dead on the lawn. Everyone was alive.

But no one was moving. Something was still wrong. In the quarter moonlight she could just barely make out a smaller coyote, Banjo in his teeth, leaping over one brick wall—the lawn was a series of sloping terraces—headed beyond the lower wall and to the wooded wildlife preserve that abutted their property.

Waycross lifted his rifle. Another shot. The coyote was down, clipped in the hip. Banjo wriggled free, bounding on a hard diagonal, out of the line of fire and up the lawn. Waycross took aim, this time at the coyote's head, and fired again. Waycross dropped to his knees. Banjo jumped into his lap. Waycross scratched the drever's head, then felt his bones. The dog didn't yelp. There was no obvious blood. Everything was probably all right.

Waycross handed the dog to Ajay. Ajay handed the dog to Hope. She kissed the little dog's head. Her men, in their matching Barbour coats, looked more alike than usual as Banjo gave his first pleasure bark of the morning.

Waycross began to unload his weapon. "I went for the big coyote and the pip-squeak almost got Banjo. Beware the little man." With the gun empty he put his arm around his wife.

"I better go get a shovel," said Ajay, who had recently become acutely embarrassed by any physical display of affection between his mother and his stepfather. As Ajay jogged off in the direction of the garages, Waycross kissed his wife.

"I'll take him to the vet to get checked out in the morning," said Hope.

"I'm glad you didn't have to do that," said Waycross.

"Kill the coyote?" asked Hope.

"Kill the coyotes," corrected Waycross.

"I wouldn't have done it," said Hope.

"Yeah, you would," said Waycross.

"I am past ready for this house to get quiet," said Hope.

"I know that's right," said Waycross.

The sacks were in the car, the coyote corpses were in black plastic, and Hope's marathon carving session was about to begin when the phone started ringing in the glass house. A crazy patient calling. Or CeCe. Hope's cell phone started ringing. Had to be CeCe. It was not unusual for CeCe to forget the time difference. Or maybe she remembered, but also remembered when she and Hope had routinely begun conversations at two in the morning. "I would call the heifer back when she's supposed to be sleeping but she doesn't sleep," said Hope.

Her words were hardly out when Ajay's phone started ringing. He checked the number before answering.

"Dialing drunk, again, Aunt Tess," said Ajay. After flipping open his phone Ajay added, "Morning, Auntie." Whatever Tess said in response was unheard as Ajay clumsily dropped the phone to the ground and more clumsily bent over to pick the phone up. Then he vomited. Hope reached for her son. Waycross grabbed the phone.

Abel was dead. As Tess told it, her brother had collapsed during Thanksgiving dinner and been taken by ambulance to the hospital but had died along the way of an asthma attack. They had been eating dinner at a restaurant called the Rebel Yell. He had gotten up from the table saying he wasn't well. At the end of the performance, when he hadn't come back, Samantha had found out a man had collapsed in the bathroom and been taken to the hospital. He had died on the way to the hospital. The attendants had thought he was having a heart attack and they had treated him for that but he was really having an asthma attack. Abel's sister began to sob.

Waycross said, and meant, he was sorry for her loss. By habit his tone was professional. Waycross had known Tess since she was a very little girl, when he had lived next door to her family while he was going through med school. His coldness made her sob louder. He repeated the words, "I am so sorry for your loss," but this time he stripped them of the sound of his distance from the loss, the sound of his surgeonness.

Ajay's silence broke. The boy was wailing—an explosion of sound more shocking coming from Ajay's body than a flood of feces.

Hope's arms were fumbling about Ajay's torso. Mother wanted to carry her son, cradle him with her body, carry him safe inside the house, bring him as close as she could get to back into the womb, turn back time, but he wouldn't stop moving and she couldn't get a grip.

Waycross lifted the boy. They were both six feet tall but Waycross had almost a hundred pounds on his stepson. He carried the wailing boy low in his arms. Ajay tried to punch him but Waycross tilted his chin higher and continued walking toward the house.

Ajay's snot was on all of their faces as they passed through the sliding glass doors into the kitchen.

Hope wanted Waycross to give the boy an injection of something or to call someone to give the boy an injection of something. Waycross didn't think that was a good idea. It was two thirty in the morning but Hope insisted that Waycross call Opelika, Ajay's pediatrician, to see what he thought.

Opelika thought it was best to let the boy cry until he cried himself tired enough to sleep. He turned clinical on Waycross as Waycross had turned clinical on Tess. "When you lose a child everyone needs drugs. When you lose a parent most people don't," said Opelika. Then he turned soft. "Ajay's gonna be all right," he said. Waycross held the phone up to Hope's ear so Opelika could say that again and Hope could hear him say that.

When Waycross took the phone back and walked into the other room, Opelika said, "The Rebel Yell. Hard to swallow that. He was allergic to horses back in the day. Why he go to a place like that?"

Hope and Waycross took turns sitting and watching Ajay as he screamed or holding Ajay as he screamed depending on what he would allow. Minutes were long and hours were too long. Hope could sit with him for thirty or forty-five minutes, then Waycross would spell her for eight or twelve minutes. When Ajay showed no signs of tiring after three hours, and it was still not even six or light, Waycross made the boy a toddy of whiskey and honey and lemon and poured it into his mouth with a spoon like it was 1950 in Waycross, Georgia.

Waycross fed the boy what and how he had seen his doctor daddy do in a shack kneeling beside a dresser drawer that held a baby wrapped in a clean shirt, a shack that had probably fallen down by now, but that croupy baby had lived to see morning.

Waycross would do all in his power to ease the pain of this night; even a little abatement would be precious little. Hope held Ajay most of the hours but Waycross did his share of the minutes.

When it was Hope's time off she made calls. She needed to hear voices say what she had said, "It can't be" or "What do you mean Abel's dead?" until they said "Go to sleep" and "There's nothing to do now" and she knew she wouldn't be going to sleep, and then they would know it too. Each friend she called offered to come over. Each time she said, "Don't come over now. There's nothing we can do in the middle of the night."

The expectation was there would be something they could do in the morning. Hope knew that the only thing she wished would happen in the morning was she would wake up and none of this would have happened, wake up and have all of this be a very bad dream.

But it wasn't. The neighborhood dogs barked all night, the other coyotes howled, the stars disappeared behind clouds. Abel was dead and the earth was sad.

THREE

THE FUNERAL WAS odd.

The church, south of Abel's natal city, Nashville, and north of Abel's adopted town, Ardmore, Alabama, was a concrete and brick behemoth.

The dark red Expedition was just past the turnoff to the Jack Daniel's distillery when Hope and Waycross saw the stainless-steel cross. Steve Earle's *Train a Comin'* was in the CD player. Earle was slur-snarl-singing . . . *they told us that our enemy would all be dressed in blue, they forgot about the winter's cold and the cursed fever too.*

Abel's body was waiting for its November burial not so very far down the road from where the bodies of four Confederate generals, Cleburne, Granbury, Adams, and Strahl, had cooled on a porch waiting for their November burials.

Hope appreciated the coincidence Abel would have appreciated, as Waycross steered the SUV off the big road and into the driveway.

Abel's last church home reached abruptly, angrily, awkwardly skyward, signaling the rising dominance and increasing significance of a zealously middle-class in their origins, committedly middlebrow in their thinking, chosen by God, suburban southern, predominantly, but not wholly, white, led-by-their-men, Christian elite.

To Hope, on closer view, the giant doors looked like a mouth. Knowing Abel's coffin was inside, Hope imagined Abel gobbled up by hardworking, churchgoing pale people. Clearly the Xanax had not kicked in. She checked her cell phone for the time. Any minute.

Expensive tackiness and plain loud ugliness aside, Hope had to give the edifice its due: anybody who drove up or even just drove by had to be impressed with the size of the thing.

Hope imagined Abel, smiling with one eyebrow cocked, stating the obvious to him: "If the architect was directed to display the wealth, the prosperity, the blessed by God of the godly-ness of the congregation, without incorporating any of the vainglorious trappings of beauty, he, most assuredly, succeeded."

Hope laughed out loud, startling the almost un-startle-able Waycross, as she imagined Abel spitting that acid ball of words at his baffled parson.

VIP parking was designated. While Hope took offense at funeral guests being ranked beyond the classic categories "immediate family" and "other," Waycross wheeled their fancy truck through the opening between the barricades onto which hand-lettered VIP signs had been taped.

"It's not like we're bringing Ajay," said Hope.

"I'm bringing you," said Waycross.

Waycross reached toward his wife and deftly slipped his hand beneath her black suit jacket, grabbed a hunk of black-silk-shirt-covered waist, and squeezed. He was ready, if need be, to drag her out of wherever she was, by the hair of her head or the fat of her high hip.

"VIP is just another way of saying HNIC," said Hope. Waycross shook his head. Abel had said that. Waycross thought Abel was just about the last man on earth to use the phrase "Head Nigger in Charge."

"Ain't no pill for that, sugar. Ain't no pill for that," said Waycross.

It was a long walk down a hall wide enough for a parade from the front doors of Abel's church to the actual sanctuary.

There was a pulpit and a stage. There was a bandstand ready with amps and cords and instruments to back up the choir— electric keyboard, electric guitars, synthesizers, and drum sets, plural. Hope cringed.

Bad rock love songs, power ballads addressed to God, repelled Hope almost as much as over-big mega-churches. She considered it an affliction particular to living in Nashville that she even knew this subgenre of music, "Contemporary Christian."

She loved and sang loudly, when given the opportunity, the old black spirituals, "This Little Light of Mine," "Swing Low, Sweet Chariot," "Go Down, Moses." She had learned these going to church with her aunts, after her father had died, in Washington, D.C. She also treasured the old-timey white hymns "I'll Fly Away" and "The Old Rugged Cross" and "Amazing Grace," which she had sung as a girl in West Virginia. Faux-rock vanilla gospel mess she could not abide.

Hope glanced at one of the seating charts, spotted five or six color zones, and wished she hadn't peeked. Certain groups of pews, indicated by colored marker, were designated for specific categories of mourners.

Waycross and Hope took their place, as directed, in a section of pews apparently designated for black people in expensive-looking clothes, slightly to the side and halfway to the front. Hope was beginning to think, as she scooted past familiar knees, belonging to prominent members of old black Nashville, that it was good to have semi-assigned seating at a church service, that it would be nice to sit with people they knew.

And maybe Abel had chosen the church because its Sears and Roebuck aesthetics fit his new family perfectly. Maybe it was a sweet thing. And all the people in uniform were a comfort. Maybe it was a good thing his youngest stepson and his pregnant fifteen-year-old girlfriend were getting married. The Xanax had kicked in.

The service began. The immediate family, Ajay leading the way, took their place in the front row. A telegenic blond parsonman with a newscaster accent pronounced a bland yet somehow grandiose prayer, then took a seat on the stage for the opening eulogies.

The first eulogist, a white man, Abel's best friend from Duke law school days, a Houston oil lawyer's son, now a sports agent in Los Angeles, launched, in his south-coast Texas singsong, almost too exuberantly, into his theme as soon as he reached the lecturn.

"Law school lecture. 'Where is Abel?' Abel was back at the apartment watching daytime soap operas. Exam time, Law Library. 'Where's Abel?' Playing backgammon. Graduation day. 'Where's Abel?' Finally off studying. Abel was always off somewhere he was not supposed to be, doing something he wasn't supposed to do, always just a little behind, till he showed up ahead of you, right where we all wanted to be.

"The really good thing about asking, 'Where's Abel?' Just after you asked the question Abel always showed up. 'Where's Abel?' "

The Texan paused. He gave the gathered mourners a moment to comprehend, as they stared at his face and body, how young forty-five could be. Two heartbeats later, he repeated his refrain, "Where's Abel?" Gazing about, expectant, awaiting a late arrival—until he let his eyes fall on Abel's coffin. The Texan shook his head, until he shook a smile back onto his face. It was the big and goofy smile he and Abel had smiled at each other when they had been young and stoned law students. After a long dramatic pause, the Texan looked up toward the ceiling in the direction of evangelical Christian heaven.

Quiet wailing spread among some of the un-uniformed congregants, while some of the others had to bite the inside of their cheeks to keep from laughing. The uniformed were inscrutable. Abel's friend walked off the stage.

Pose struck, the choir (very blond in blue polyester robes or spiky-headed neo-punk in blue polyester robes) started singing another one of those invented praise songs, "Jesus Wonderful Savior," only this one didn't sound like a bad power ballad—it sounded like bad teenybop rock. A screen dropped down and the lyrics were projected.

Hope, leaning hard into Waycross's shoulder, missed the hymnals. She wondered if Abel had missed them too. When he was young and transgressive Abel had loved the fact that the hand holding his hymnal Sunday morning had been touching his body Saturday night. A man who thought like that should not belong to a church with a projection screen in the sanctuary. Hope shuddered, despite the Xanax, and started looking for her son in the front pews.

Ajay was seated to the left of Samantha with her three daughters, his half sisters, between them, in the front row. Samantha's four sons, the huge stepbrothers, were on Samantha's right.

Ajay's back was straight; his shoulders were not shaking. From where Hope was sitting that was all she could see and there was nothing she could do, not squeeze a hand, not pass a handkerchief. The preggers girlfriend of one of the stepsons was in the row just behind her child's daddy. She could reach forward and clutch his shoulder. Another reason not to divorce your first husband.

The second eulogist, another white man, a four-star general if his uniform could be believed, spoke of how restless Abel had always been: how he had always wanted new challenges, new faces, new views from new offices, new goals, new everything—how he was barely in a new job before he started looking for his next. Then shortly before his death this had altered. He had no longer wanted to change jobs; he had just wanted to be where he was, in the Pentagon, counsel general of the army.

Only he had still wanted to change. Hadn't it been just six weeks earlier that Hope had undergone the ex-wife interview for Abel's tryout for a position at the White House?

Abel had praised Hope for her performance during the interview. She had told the factual truth and she had told the thematic truth. To every problematic issue they had raised, *Would you say he was reliable? Did he pay the child support he had committed to? Was he good with money?*, Hope had responded, "We were very young."

He had said he hadn't been given the job and he'd said he was disappointed. Abel had told Hope he had been made to understand that the president was disappointed as well.

At the funeral they told it a different way. The general announced that Abel's achievement had caught the eye of his president and that his president had intended to announce in the very next week that Abel was poised to take on an expanded portfolio of responsibilities as White House special advocate at the Pentagon. The general didn't announce the reality: the expanded portfolio was a consolation prize. Nor was it acknowledged that before he had tried for the West Wing White House job, Abel had been trolling on Wall Street. It vaguely occurred to Hope that maybe she was the one who had been lied to. Another knot to untie later.

The third eulogist, a special assistant to the secretary of defense, apparently *above* the rank of four-star general, another white man, came up to take the stage. This gentleman declared Abel's funeral to be a marvelous example of church and state coming together.

Then he promised that church and state would soon stand braided in the public square, raising his revelation to a crescendo, "and when that tomorrow comes it will not be on little cat feet, but on large Republican hooves!"

Some, who had forgotten where they were, applauded. Some who remembered applauded, certain that Abel, soon to be on a cloud, equipped with a harpsichord and flowing robes, would have applauded too.

Hope was wondering what kind of special assistant was above the rank of four-star general, why there were so many soldiers in the room, and if elephants can properly be said to have hooves. She was exhausted by lies, omissions, and white men.

Finally a brown face. Finally a breast. Tess, Abel's sister, barely five feet tall and mahogany dark, a Stanford graduate, stood to take her turn at the podium.

As Tess walked to the podium, old black Nashville held its collective breath. Hope heard someone in her row whisper, "Lord only knows what's going to come out of that child's mouth." Then someone said, under their breath, "You got that right!" and someone else said, aloud, "Amen." Hope and Tess cleared their throats at the exact same moment.

Tess had come to stake her claim to being chief mourner. She didn't remember loving Abel; she loved Abel. Loved him enough to make her heroin-snorting jazz-musician husband sit in the back away from family. In life she had pushed the man in her brother's face and taken pleasure in watching her sibling squirm. On Abel's burying day Tess sequestered all love that was not for her brother.

She argued that their childhood had been the most important part of his life; she argued that their childhood had been the greatest challenge of his life; she argued that the hours of his childhood contained his most heroic moments. Then she told a story about a dog named Dog.

Abel and Tess had had a pet, a German shepherd called Dog. After Tess had seen a picture of two shepherds attacking a boy wearing a pretty sweater while policemen watched, Tess said, she had started to scream every time Dog had come into the room.

If their parents were gone or they just took too long to arrive and rescue Tess, her brother, who was also afraid of Dog, who had been afraid of Dog from before she was afraid of Dog, would put that fear aside and grab a thick section of newspaper. He would roll that section into a paper baton and he would hold that baton over Dog's head until Dog slunk down on the floor and his sister stopped crying. Abel had tried to teach Tess the trick. He had said it was magic. He had said that as long as you never touched the dog with the paper, and let him discover how much it didn't hurt, you could control the dog with the paper. As long as you didn't hit Dog the rolled-up paper would stay magic.

"Abel always came running, when he came to save me. Always." Tess talked about a dog named Dog, then she walked off the stage and back to her seat in the second row beside the stepson's pregnant girlfriend.

And the congregation forgot Tess. Abel seemed so far beyond his days as the king of colored kids that Tess's declarations that their childhood had been the defining time in their lives seemed foolish.

Before Tess could get settled back in her seat good, Pinigree Pinagrew started for the front of the church. Another white man, except this one had silver hair that grazed his shoulders instead of dark hair cut up above his ears, and instead of wearing a dark suit or a crisp uniform, he wore a three-piece white suit, complete with gold watch and gold chain hanging out of his vest pocket. Pinagrew was the self-proclaimed "last of the southern fabulists."

It was a challenging distance to traverse for someone who was almost falling-down drunk. Pinagrew was falling-down drunk.

He never made it to the microphones. Overlooking the fact that Hope was the ex-wife, Pinagrew spoke directly to the first Mrs. Abel Jones the third.

"I might could'a made it," Pinagrew would say later, "but you don't get to be a old cat without knowing when you're outnumbered, or a old pol without knowing how to pick your audience."

Pinagrew, a near-ancient, still-tom-catting pol, knew how to pick his audience. He stopped near where Hope sat because he had forgotten, in a senior flash, that she was no longer married to Abel. And he wanted to find John Hope Franklin and thought he might be sitting near Hope. Then Pinagrew wondered if maybe Franklin was dead and he, Pinagrew, was really wanting to see Frazier. E. Franklin Frazier. Or maybe it was the other way around, the way he'd first thought it was. All he knew for sure was he was surrounded by a lot of black people he didn't know and who didn't know him; black people and white soldiers. Pinagrew rambled for a long time. Then he got to the point.

"I wanted him to be like me. Or like Martin. Like we were when we walked together over the Edmund Pettus Bridge. I wanted him to like me. But Abel's not like me, he's like Aria Reese.

"Just like Ari, Abel was raised in a time and place of terror, a place of bombings and shootings, a place of funerals and wakes, a place of police dogs and fire hoses turned toward children, a land red with the blood of the recently slaughtered, a place where wedding bells didn't ring. My South in the sixties.

"Ari stood outside the White House, a little girl from Birmingham, a little girl who probably knew some of the girls who were in the church the day the bomb went off. That's the child Aria Reese's parents took on a trip to the nation's capital. She was not an innocent. If there was no smoke in the kinky braids of their daughter as she stood outside the whitewashed pillars of the president's home, there was smoke in her mind. Smoke in her mind. The story is told that she said to her parents, standing outside of that white plantation house where the chief executive of this great nation sleeps: one day I will work in there. How safe the green lawn must have looked just the other side of the black wrought iron gate.

"How could she know she would carry her fear with her? Or perhaps she did know. I would prefer to believe that Ari consciously chose to infect a nation with the anxieties of black children who came of age in a time of terror when the war at home rocked their churches.

"However that was, the anxieties of Abel and Ari have become the anxieties of a nation. She took her fear inside the White House, then inside the State Department. He took his fear inside the Pentagon.

"The president, smug fraternity boy he might be, had the good sense to choose worried Negroes to watchdog his world. God save us all!"

With that Pinigree Pinagrew stopped talking and started making his way back to his seat.

Pinigree Pinagrew was a fortunate man. None of the northern army men heard a word he said. When they asked the black people who had been sitting near where Pinagrew had stood, all they got out of them was he had been hard to follow.

Waycross shrugged; Hope shuddered; they both agreed with Pinagrew. Abel had been lucky about not getting the job on Wall Street, lucky about not getting the job in the West Wing of the White House. It was only within the walls of the Pentagon that Abel had felt safe. The old white Southerner had told it true.

Then they were hit with another one of those lying, pleading, crying praise songs and the truth got sugared over. "Your Grace Is Enough."

Hope watched Sammie take the folded flag from the soldier, saw her be presented with a letter from the president and a medal from the Congress. Finally the obvious struck Hope: there were *too* many soldiers in the room. The thought passed as Hope watched Tess watching Sammie. Tess looked like she was damning Sammie to hell for suggesting Thanksgiving in the mountains. And Waycross was looking at some woman Hope didn't really know. Ruby, she thought the woman's name was, but she didn't know why she knew it. She'd have to ask him about it later. Hope glanced toward Sammie and noticed that she looked like someone who might rise to the occasion.

Hope imagined Sammie eventually telling herself that things would be easier, that it was almost like when Abel was away in Washington, that things could work out, that she could run a house with seven kids and no man if she had insurance money.

Maybe now Sammie's son's girlfriend would get an abortion or put the baby up for adoption. Maybe now that Abel wasn't preaching fire and brimstone at their passion, the older twins wouldn't be thinking about getting married before they turned eighteen.

Holding the flag in her hands, the raven-headed woman in the first row of mourners was thinking about things altogether else. Sammie had come to wonder about Abel's relation to two of his closest male friends. They had made three babies but she would not swear he wasn't gay. There was an intensity of feeling he felt for some men that she knew he didn't feel for her. And she was wondering, as many people in Washington had wondered, if Abel hadn't had something going on with Ms. Reese. She didn't have to wonder anymore.

The words ended. The music stopped. The casket was lifted by a military guard accompanied by civilian pallbearers through a phalanx of white children waving posters to hail the deceased as his casket left the sanctuary.

WE LOVE YOU ABEL, read one of the posters drawn by a child forced into servitude to celebrate the passing of an American lawyer dedicated to the cause of freedom.

Drawn and colored by children who did not know Abel but who had been instructed, nay, ordered, to create kinder-care laurels for him, these bright little paintings that, so far from Beijing, so long after the Chairman, achieved what Abel would have called a Maoist Moment.

Or perhaps he would have said Leninist. Hope wasn't sure which, but she knew if Abel were alive and had attended this service on the occasion of someone else's death, he would have contrived a cutting phrase—at least inside his head—perhaps "puerile grandiosity," to describe the display.

Though the irony of the moment was utterly lost on Abel's last parson, a man who translated sacrament into spectacle, a man who knew, for certain, what the children should be doing, and how church and state should be braided. Singing "Onward, Christian Soldiers," the parson led the parade as they all left the building.

The funeral was over.

FOUR

THE LINE OF cars carrying mourners to Abel's graveside was escorted by state troopers, in sedans and on motorcycles, as it snaked its way back, from suburbia, toward the center of the city. Saying that she loved her husband too much to take the short way home, the widow had requested a path that circled Nashville, before heading across the Alabama border.

In the last of the black limousines that followed the hearse, Abel's only son and Abel's last parson had a perfect view of the cortege. Dark green government-issue SUVs with tinted black windows were followed by a motley collection of cheap and fancy cars and trucks. By the parson's silent calculation the procession was more than half a mile long.

Some drivers not only pulled to a complete stop at the green light, as directed by the uniformed officers; they exited their cars and stood, baseball caps in hand, or hands over hearts, or eyes cast down, sometimes longer than a quarter hour, waiting for the procession to pass, waiting to salute the unknown soldier, compelled by the sight of immense and martially choreographed grief.

Military protocol coupled with small-town southern burial

customs birthed dizzying display. The parson breathed deeply to take it all in. It was something he might never see again—even if he buried one of the big country stars who worshipped with him. New tears sprang to the parson's eyes. He regretted not having known how important Abel was while Abel was still alive. If he had more fully understood Abel's rank, he would have made a pilgrimage to the Pentagon to pray with his congregant. *Incertae sedis.* He didn't say this out loud. Out loud he said, "I'm sorry your father did not, in the end, choose to be buried in Arlington."

"Arlington wouldn't have punished my side of the family enough," said Ajay.

"Your side of the family?" asked the parson, who was surprised that the solemn boy had said anything at all.

"The black side," said Ajay.

"Let us pray," said the parson, efficiently ending the conversation.

The parson closed his eyes and silently prayed that Abel would be raised from his coffin and this boy with preternaturally gray hair would disappear. Aloud the parson recited the Lord's Prayer. As he kept his eyes tight shut, he didn't see Ajay's wide rolling eyes so like Abel's own.

The last family car passed the cemetery where the pillars of old black Nashville were buried. Its clovered-through grass near the center of the city where hymns of mourning were sung from memory was where many of Abel's oldest friends thought Abel should be buried. Many cars peeled off there, but the limousine carrying Ajay rolled on.

After a long drive that would have taken twice as long stopping for red lights, the procession slid through the gates of a not-so-fancy farm. A mile up a road with cows grazing on either side was the all-white cemetery, where Abel would be buried.

As he rolled toward Abel's final resting place, the parson was grateful he and Abel had ridden up to Washington on the same bus to participate in the Sacred Assembly of Promise Keepers in October of 1997.

Remembering Abel calling the rally "the white boys' Million Man March," the parson shed a sincere tear.

Cars were pulled over to both sides of the road and parked, most of them half in a ditch, half on the green that flanked the burying grounds.

Though considerably smaller than the immense group that had gathered at the church, the crowd at the graveside was still sizable. All the people in dark clothes shared one thing and one thing only, a sense of exhaustion.

The family acknowledged as immediate was seated beneath the little square open-sided tent the funeral parlor's people had erected for the occasion. Carpeted with rollout acrylic grass and furnished with six short rows of folding chairs, the little canopy sheltered the trench that had been dug for the coffin.

Even fanned out over a quarter acre, many of the bereaved felt themselves to be invisibly tethered, each to the others, by the pull of the man in the coffin. In the church, this had seemed a consolation, evidence that some conservative ideal of a rainbow coalition of well-scrubbed, expensively suited, good Christians was a living reality.

At the graveyard, connections felt over-taut and about to snap—leaving few links, if any—just as soon as Abel's coffin was covered with dirt.

Except for his co-workers from the Pentagon, all gathered felt out of place. Abel's body belonged to no coherent community; obvious and powerful factions vied for place: Abel's poor black relations and Abel's affluent black relations; Abel's poor white family and Abel's powerful white associates; and finally there was Abel's Washington group, affluent, powerful, integrated, conservative.

As the area around the cars emptied, a wide rough circle formed around the tent. Sitting beneath the canopy, in the front row, with her little girls on one side of her and her big boys on the other, was the grieving widow of record.

Sammie, in the clear light of autumn noon, looked exceptionally pretty in her pert navy suit with white piping and red wool coat. She was prissy and sexy at the very same time. And there was an air of vulnerability and kindness about her that this day gave lie to the nickname Ajay's friends, white and black, had tagged to Sammie after just a very few brief encounters: Wicked White Stepmonster. The day of Abel's funeral Sammie looked like a pretty little perfect small-town stepmom.

Hope scanned the crowd, paying particular attention to the clumps of affluent black relations, looking for James Hall, Abel's oldest friend. She couldn't stand near her son, who was seated with "the family," and just at that moment she didn't want to stand with Waycross. She wanted to stand by James, to lean on James, but she wasn't even sure he had come. She stepped closer to the tent.

On this day she would indulge the metaphysical conceit of her widowhood, so that some day soon she could embrace the truth of marriage to Waycross unencumbered.

There were so many things, too many things, in the queer construction of Abel's funeral that left Hope feeling vulgar and contorted. At the center of it all was a realization that she had misjudged something significant about the man. On the surface was the claim Abel's gaping grave made on her wife-ness.

On Abel's burying day, Waycross was for her a lover, a true love, but not the husband. She longed for the moment when no part of her would feel polyandrous or polygamist. Hope stepped away from her second husband and stepped closer to her first husband's grave.

The immediate family was telling why they had put what into the coffin with Abel—one of the boys said he had put a golf ball because he and Abel had liked to golf together; another was putting in a CD of the soundtrack of the movie *Idlewild* (they had been listening to OutKast as they drove into the mountains). When Ajay put in fifteen backgammon checkers, Hope winced.

The carved trench, above which Abel's casket was suspended on some mechanism that would lower it fluidly down, was a rebuke and liberation. She saw in the dark maw of earth the promise of a true and final divorce decree. "Till death do you part," their Episcopal priest had said at their wedding. And now Abel was dead, granting a dazing divorce.

Sammie squatted down and put her wedding ring on the casket.

Hope wondered what Abel had done with the gold band she had bought him. He had worn the token too long, for years after the divorce; then it had vanished and Sammie's ring had appeared on his finger.

Hope remembered throwing her rings, the band he had

bought and the solitaire he had inherited, across the table at him the day she had known she wouldn't stay married.

"One thing's for certain, I don't love you anymore," she had said, quoting the lyrics of a George Jones and Tammy Wynette duet. Abel had understood. He was that man who knew the lyrics to obscure country songs and the laws of many foreign lands, who loved Jane Austen and Bootsy Collins. He had not lost his equilibrium.

He had had the sophistication to be amused. "I may be the only black man in America to have his wife announce that she's leaving by quoting a country song." He hadn't thought she was going anyplace. She had promised and he knew her to be a woman of her word. He could afford to applaud the fine performance.

He had gotten her to put her rings back on that day. Then he had slapped the child a third time and she had never put them on again.

She had a settlement agreement the lawyers had worked out and a judge had approved; that notarized document bore little and no relation to reality. It was at best a crudely drawn map of the territory of relations between Abel and Hope, of the places where they would exasperate, confound, and betray each other.

Death had parted them far more profoundly than the courts had. Hope had reason to be grateful. Abel's death had delivered to her the annulment for which she had been unwilling to go to the priests. Her blood was mingled with his in a living child. She would not make that child a bastard. But now Abel was dead. Standing before his grave she felt like a widow.

Just then, when she had stopped looking for him, James Hall found her. At Hope and Abel's Washington wedding James had stood beside Abel as best man. Now Hope could stop holding herself as James wrapped Hope in a bear hug. "I used to be his best friend," James whispered. "When you were his best friend, I was his wife," Hope whispered back. James's eyes were dry.

"I don't begin to know how to mourn a lawyer whose job it was, I suspect, to parse the crazy definitions and distinctions that allow for Abu Ghraib," said James.

"What are you talking about?" asked Hope.

"Abel," said James.

Hope shook her head. She didn't want to hear it. Not in that place; not at that moment, and not ever. She remembered reading somewhere that prescription drugs had ruined Scandinavian funerals. Everyone wore sunglasses and nobody cried. Xanax wouldn't ruin southern funerals. Her mind was muted and breaking at the same time. And nobody was wearing sunglasses.

Break my mind. That was the song Abel had sung at her trying to get her to smile and laugh and let him stay. But she hadn't left a babbling fool behind—she had left the lawyer for Abu Ghraib? This did not seem possible.

If Hope had had any inkling of what Abel would become she would have stayed and fought for him to become something else, something other, some black man who wasn't even possibly the lawyer for Abu Ghraib and who wouldn't end up buried in a southern white people's cemetery.

Or, was she misunderstanding again, under-reading him again, low-rating him again?

Her train of thought derailed and landed in some harsh wilderness. She was thinking about the South without black people, of Abel's New South, the South that the Agrarians and Fugitives had dreamed, a South of hardworking, self-sufficient rural white people. This was the South Abel had loved and abandoned. This was the South that had claimed him at the last: a Scandinavian South that had nothing in common with the blue-black Deep South of Memphis or Mississippi, the state or the river.

Abel was being buried in a "white" cemetery where none of Abel's black family had ever previously stepped. On the flip side of the equation, another of his signature consistent inconstancies, Hope knew for sure that one of the things Abel would have liked about the army was that it was a "colored" place. Ditto prisons and the second Bush White House. As sure as she knew Abel liked the word "ditto," loved the movie *Ghost*, lusted for Demi Moore, and was highly embarrassed by Whoopi Goldberg, she knew he had a black and southern preference for places where black people were in abundance. She also knew he had a desire-dream of a lily-magnolia-white South, and being the one ink spot in it. So many contradictions.

Hope was running her fingers through her curls, combing these knots of thoughts through her tangles as if she had lost her good sense, when she saw, standing alone, near a broken cross, someone she had never expected to see again.

Nicholas Gordon—a spook from her past. For a minute she thought it was a trick of her exhausted mind. *Ghosts appear in graveyards.* Somehow with the bending of fatigue her thought had distorted and fractured into images of sheets in the night: Klan sheets and bedsheets and Halloween ghosts collided, creating a mirage, an apparition of a man she had almost forgotten.

She blinked and he didn't go away. Nicholas Gordon was standing in Nashville.

She closed her eyes, kissed James—whispering, "You're wrong about Abel" into his ear—and then began making her way toward the person who appeared to be Nicholas Gordon.

Hope was fully expecting to realize, as she approached, that the guest was just someone who resembled Nicholas. Or, rather, resembled her expectation of how Nicholas might look. How would she know what Nicholas looked like after sixteen years? If the man was Nicholas, she would get rid of him. Nicholas Gordon was not a person Hope ever wanted Ajay to meet.

She made her way slowly. Most eyes were focused on the parson, the grave, on Sammie, on Ajay, or on the toe of the wearer's shoes. *It is easy to move without being observed. People are so self-absorbed.* Hope remembered Abel telling her that. It was another of the many, but not enough, occasions on which Abel had been absolutely right.

She reached the broken cross.

"Nicholas?" asked the first Mrs. Abel Jones the third.

"Hullo, dear girl," said Nicholas as he reached for Hope's hand. He lifted it and held it near enough to his lips to kiss, before allowing his eyelids to flutter shut as he inhaled the scent of Hope. Her smell had changed. He wondered if she knew.

"I wasn't sure it was you," said Hope, snatching back her hand just after Nicholas, who appeared to be diving down to plant a kiss, sucked in the fat of the fleshy base of her thumb as if it were a tongue.

It was an old and courtly gesture, suggestive yet decorous, with all the risk going to him. It was hard not to be happy to see the provocative geezer.

Hope kissed Nicholas on one fine parchment cheek, then the

other. When he leaned down to help her do it, she caught the distinct whiff of hemorrhoid cream mixed with aftershave, the aging dandy smell.

Nicholas looked a lot like Keith Richards, grayer and blonder and tweedier, to be sure, but the bone structures were similar and the rebuke their ancient but reedy selves presented to her soft and spreading body was similar. Nicholas had been a dashing old toff and now he was a dashing ancient toff. She kissed her fingers and pressed the kiss to his cheek.

"It must be the end of the world. You left Manila."

"Just the end of my life."

"You said you would never leave."

"Another of the promises I didn't keep."

"I didn't know you and Abel had stayed close."

"So much you didn't know."

Hope's face registered confusion. Nicholas didn't wait for her to ask the question.

"I'm here in a professional capacity."

Hope took a step back. She had a guess about what he meant. Years earlier, he had caused her more than a bit of trouble that she hadn't rightly understood at the time. *Hindsight's twenty-twenty.*

"I'm here as the mother of a bereaved child," said Hope as she moved to place her body directly between Nicholas's and Ajay's.

"He looks more like you to me than you look like you to me. Except he's taller," said Nicholas, then he started to smile. His smile irritated Hope. It was inappropriate in the extreme. Classic Nicholas.

"I'm not amused."

"Of course not. How did you come to survive?"

"Excuse me?"

The ridges between Hope's eyebrows got deep. Nicholas smiled again. He liked it when women didn't use Botox. Botox made his job much, much harder.

It's one thing, he could see her thinking, to have sickness lurking in the back of your life when your child has two biological parents. It's another thing altogether to have sickness lurking in the background when your child is still young and one parent has already died. When your child is half-orphaned. Nicholas read wrinkles and furrows better than most people.

"You don't have lupus."

"Not now."

"You never had lupus, that's just a lie the doctors told you to get you out of Manila. Once upon a time you were a dangerous girl."

"I wasn't sick?"

"You were never sick."

"Abel . . . ?"

"Bored wives, intelligent wives, educated wives, idealistic wives: Wives are dangerous. A bored, intelligent, educated, idealistic wife with questionable friends is too dangerous," said Nicholas, reaching for Hope's hand. Hope drew her hand back.

"Questionable friends?"

"Me."

"You were KGB."

"Was."

"I figured that out."

"Eventually."

"Was I your target?"

"Was."

"I thought we were friends."

"Are, we are friends."

Hope shook her head no. The day had been too much. So many choices she had made because she had thought she was going to die. Leaving Abel. Not having babies with Waycross.

"Did Abel know?"

"Yes."

Hope wanted to snatch Abel out of the grave to put him back in it. So much exhaustion she had encountered fighting the fear of premature gloom. And all the time Abel had known it was a lie.

Nicholas remembered feeling sorry for her when they gave her what he suspected was a false diagnosis. He also remembered feeling relieved.

Manila in the eighties was a dangerous place: bad drivers; bad air in the scuba equipment; dengue fever; the occasional helicopter shot out of the air; drug pirates on the seas just beyond the bay where the rich locals sailed on a Sunday afternoon drinking calamansi soda; acquaintances who played kill or be killed, torture and release, so that others might be afraid. Manila was a place where kidnap, then ransom was a primary method of funding institutions and insurrections.

Hope had been afraid of dying when she had left Manila. Nicholas had been afraid of her dying if she stayed in Manila. He wondered if Abel had had the same fear. Maybe there had been more than what Nicholas knew inspiring Abel to shuttle the wifey off.

The funeral was getting to Nicholas just as he had gotten to her, just as once upon a time Hope had almost gotten to him. Had he approached her to turn her, or to get them to fear that he had turned her? It took him a moment to remember how it had been. Abel had been in the middle of it.

Nicholas was wondering if Abel was really dead. It wasn't a question he could ask in the middle of the alleged burial.

"Are you around this afternoon? We could have a drink," he said, affecting contrition that rapidly transformed into coquetry. "You could hit me. I deserve it and worse."

"I don't play that," said Hope.

There was true grief in Nicholas's eyes. She couldn't tell if it was because they had reached the part of the graveside service where the casket was about to be covered in dirt or if it was something else.

It occurred to Hope that Nicholas liked to be spanked. It occurred to her in a flashing moment that Abel might have spanked him. And then it occurred to her that if there had been spanking between them, Nicholas would have been the lap and Abel the bottom. How close they had all come to getting what they each had wanted.

"Where are you staying?"

"The Hermitage."

"I'll meet you in the bar at five."

Hope turned and walked back to stand with her second husband as her first husband was being lowered into the ground.

FIVE

A FTER THE FUNERAL in the church and the interment at the grave, there should have been, at the home of the deceased, at Abel's house, a repass. The meal prepared by friends for family to be presented at the end of the day of burial is a sacrosanct southern-black burial custom. Sammie didn't want it.

Of all the strange things Abel's white wife did, black Nashville judged refusing the repass to be the strangest.

She wasn't blatantly rude. Whoever wished to come, everyone attending the funeral, was invited back to Sammie's two-hundred-year-old house for a catered meal.

Folk were shocked. So shocked preparations continued: shopping, cooking, and the getting down of silver-plated serving utensils. Discreet inquiries were made: at the visitation, on the phone, and even online. On the pretense of asking what to send in lieu of flowers, or what flowers to send, mentioned somewhere in the middle of those inquiries was the dish the attendee would be bringing. On every such occasion, dutiful dark ladies were informed—by one of Sammie's sisters-in-law or brothers, or Sammie's parents—that gifts of food were not welcome.

If that had been the end of the message, the preference, most likely, would merely have gone unheeded. It is even possible some of the older ladies who had not yet developed an affection for Sammie might have begun to feel some small tenderness for Abel's starving widow. Feeling sorry for somebody, as long as it is not yourself, is not the least likely way for love to begin. But "no food" was not the end of the message.

The words "a catered meal will be provided" were tacked on. Those words stuck in the craw. Not one of the ladies who had been attached to Abel from the birth did what was supposed to be done, as it is supposed to be done.

Instead the colored ladies, from the snow-white to the blue-black, from the most sanely bohemian to the crazily conventional, took their hams and casseroles, their cakes and pies, their sweet tea and rolls and monkey bread, to Abel's grandmother's house on Batavia Circle.

There would be a repass. There would even be a widow. Hope. Black Nashville would begin to erase Sammie from its collective memory. She would be gone from Jefferson Street and gone from Batavia Circle, gone from Canterbury Close and gone from Nocturne Drive. Gone from all "our neighborhoods": from the almost ghetto in the center of the city to the segregated enclave above the ghetto, from the rich and fancy booming integrated suburbs to the fading rich and fancy all-black suburbs, gone.

Hope was hungry. And not for warmed-over-whatever in a chafing dish. She wished she were on her way to Grandma's with the other appropriate ladies—but there was no way for her not to be on her way to Abel's house, to what he had snarlingly called offay Ardmore.

Ajay was in Ardmore. Before Hope could do any other part of getting on with her afternoon and her life, she would check in on her son.

There was a doormat emblazoned with a dancing turkey wearing a cowboy hat on Sammie's doorstep, and a straw cornucopia filled with plastic fruit was hanging on the door. Standing on that doormat, staring at that cornucopia, Hope hated Abel.

She smiled wider and tighter. Waycross knocked. They waited a polite thirty seconds. When no one answered, Waycross pushed open the door to the house Abel had shared with Sammie and seven children. The distinctive odor of Thai food—basil, chili oil, and garlic—hit them immediately as they stepped across the threshold that had so recently been barred to them.

The place was god-awful. The carpet, an off shade of royal blue, was baby-, child-, and dog-stained, though it appeared, from the presence of vacuum tracks and the scent of powdered carpet cleaner, as if someone had been trying to prep the rooms for company.

Little in the antebellum farmhouse was less than two years old—and nothing was more than four years old. Everything was cheap and oddly coordinated blue and green plaid; everything was dinged or dented, much was dusty. New Barbies and baby dolls and the boxes they were torn out of and old Barbies and baby dolls in bits and pieces of pink outfits were everywhere. Waycross was embarrassed for dead Abel.

Hope was perturbed. Staring into the room, she remembered Abel making the joke "Some wives shop at Cheap and

Cheerful—my wife shops at Dismal and Depressed." Hope didn't want Ajay spending a minute more than necessary in dismal and depressed.

Abel had been amused by the near squalor of his all but white family. Amused and embarrassed. Amused and embarrassed was a favorite Abel emotional cocktail. He had developed a taste for it early in his first home and he had taken it to every home after.

Pinigree Pinagrew was talking loudly, explaining to somebody Hope didn't know that Abel had loved being linked with one of the oldest names in the South, that Abel particularly had loved spending long weekends down at the restored family plantation, Everlay. "Always came with Goo Goo Clusters in one arm and a bottle of Jack Daniel's in the other. Abel didn't hunt but he was a good drinker with hunters," laughed Pinagrew, before lifting another glass to the dead man.

Hope watched Ajay playing with the oldest of his half sisters, Lauro, holding her upside down, all the while holding up his end of two different conversations, one with Abel's old girlfriend, Margot Linden, and one with Caldwell Lyttle, the lawyer who had already called about the will. Lyttle seemed to be trying to flirt with Margot. Sammie, passing by on her way to the back porch, brushed the top of Ajay's head with her hand. The boy almost dropped his little sister before regaining his balance.

Ajay was fine. Hope could leave. She felt for her cell phone. She checked to make sure it was on. Ajay would call when he was headed to Grandma's. Pinagrew was bringing him. That was their plan. Hope would stick to it. It was appropriate for

Ajay to spend two hours at his deceased father's house after the burial. It was appropriate for the ex-wife and stepfather to make a ten-minute appearance and move on. Hope would do what was appropriate.

She found Samantha in the backyard, flanked by her brothers, standing on the concrete in her stocking feet, lighting a cigarette. Seeing them together, Hope was reminded that the three of them had been, for a hot second, a hot country act, and that they were, oddly, triplets. Somewhere she probably had had a copy of their only album. Ajay had told her they had sometimes played Branson. Hope did what had to be done, pay her respects to the mother of her son's half siblings. She stuck out her hand.

"You did a better job than me. I am very sorry for your loss. You made a lot of his dreams come true," said Hope.

Samantha didn't know what to say so she finished lighting her cigarette, shoved it in her mouth, then took Hope's hand.

Just when Hope was thinking this might be the moment their relationship changed, Samantha covered both of their touching hands with her free hand, taking custody of the moment. It was a gesture Sammie had performed a hundred times at county fairs and meet 'n' greets, a gesture that looked good across a room. Usually she accompanied the gesture with her trademark wink. This day she didn't. She was too irritated that Hope was making a good impression on her sibs.

Hope bobbed her head down, a show of respect that ended the conversation before Sammie could drop ash on her. Moments later Hope was back in the house making her way to the front door, where Waycross was already standing with Ajay.

"You're not leaving me here," said Ajay.

"We can stay," said Hope.

"No," said Ajay, walking ahead of Hope out the door.

An hour and twenty minutes later, the red Expedition was pulling up in front of Abel's grandmother's house. As he put the car in park, Waycross gave Samantha her props: "I'll be damned if Abel wouldn't have loved that, Sammie serving Thai food to New Negroes and old rednecks." Hope glared at him.

"Where did all the army men go?" she asked.

"Back to wherever they came from," said Waycross.

"They won't be at Grandma's," said Ajay.

Grandma's was on a curving street atop a hill that overlooked the old Agricultural and Industrial College that had exploded into a mainly black but definitely integrated Tennessee State University, where, before his death, Grandpa had taught studio art.

A little like Oak Bluffs on Martha's Vineyard before the celebrities came, Grandma's little corner of the world was insular and quietly triumphant, but triumphant. Neutral-hued Cadillacs, black and gray and navy and cream, were parked in front of the houses.

Grandma's street was a haven of black, well-salaried people: people with predictable incomes and insurance; people with excellent credit scores; people with birth certificates and passports; people spending their old age in homes in almost every way different from the homes in which they had spent their undocumented childhoods.

Significantly suburban, perched between the cities and the farms, Grandma's neighborhood was no Gold Coast or Sugar Hill. There was no swagger or blues about the place. It was tidy and green, a last refuge of radicals who had lived long enough and wise enough to see their ideas become, in some quarters, conservative.

Every house stood on its own two or three hilly acres. There was very little flat, not enough flat to run, or play, or remind anyone of cotton fields. There were steep sloping front lawns, houses perched on top, and steep sloping backyards. Every brick house with hill and shrub spoke of prosperity and intelligence, of modesty and modernity.

Because the houses were built into the slopes of hills, from the front you entered on one floor and from the back you entered on another. Entering Grandma's from the front you stepped into a vestibule with a staircase up and a staircase down. The down staircase led to an apartment where she put visiting family; the up staircase led to a hall that ran the length of the house. That hall was a gallery of her dead husband's lesser paintings. The masterpieces had been sold to provide Grandma's daily bread and shelter and hunks of cash to help whittle down college fees for children, grandchildren, and great-grandchildren. Off that hall you could immediately see a family room that opened into a kitchen; to the right was the large room where Grandma received her guests on formal occasions: bridge games, club meetings, weddings, and funerals.

The big room was a strikingly bright space, elegant and bohemian. Light streaming in from the windows fell on a rectangular sea of blue carpet and a large, square gold silk couch big enough to hold five grown folks, several children, and however many babies needed laps. Well-chosen, perpetually dusted gee-gaws, artifacts, and paintings, collected over seven decades of living among makers and sellers, writers and painters, beckoned the eye one way, then another, until finally the eye rested on the simple beauty of the couch and the rug and the sunlight and the charming, long and tall volumes of a Deberry McKissack–designed home.

Waycross closed the door behind them and headed straight up for the kitchen. Hope headed straight downstairs to the bar. There was a God in heaven. Mo Henry was pouring drinks.

Mo, more properly Moses Henry, Hope's favorite bartender, was a Nashville native and fixture who had left town to play football at Tuscaloosa. After a splashy career playing Alabama football, he had migrated north to study photography. He had earned an M.F.A. at NYU supported by his dentist daddy. No one could explain or got far into puzzling out why he had come back to Nashville and started serving drinks at rich folks' parties. When anybody asked him, all he would ever say was that his mama and papa had needed him to come back home; his own wife didn't like to go out much; and he wanted to make sure he got to lots of parties. It didn't make sense, but he said it often enough, and he was such a good bartender (never forgetting what people preferred to drink, never getting drunk, never gossiping about the other drinkers), that most people found it convenient to believe him.

Hope was one of the most. She didn't know why Mo made her feel safe but she knew he made her feel safe. And she knew anything she told Mo went no farther than his sweet brown Santa Claus head. He reminded her of her cousin Hat. Mo made Hope feel safer than generals. And Mo loved Abel. She quick made her way to the front of the line. Mo made strong drinks and she needed a drink. And she needed to be reminded that there were nice people who were not his blood relatives who could love Abel.

Without asking, Mo handed Hope a gin martini with three very big olives. Hope ate one, then another. Then she took her first sip of icy gin for the day.

"Good, aren't they?" said Mo.

"Used to be you couldn't get good olives in Nashville," said Hope as Mo handed her another spear of three.

"Now the Cumberland is a river in the Middle East," said Mo. Hope looked up from her drink.

"Abel said that," she said.

"Probably quoting me," taunted Mo.

"What does it mean?" asked Hope, teasing back.

Hope turned toward the sound of soft thuds: a little girl was bumping down the steps on her bottom. Mo started making a Shirley Temple. Three more plonks and the little cousin was tugging on Hope's skirt. Hope was wanted by Grandma in the kitchen that doubled as a family room.

Hope was stopped as she made her way back up the steps by a middle-aged dark man she recognized but whose name she didn't remember, an old friend of Abel's from the neighborhood. He had a message for Ajay.

"Abel was always getting popped. It didn't take no generals

or the U.S. government to make a man out of our Abel. His daddy did that. You tell Ajay."

"Thank you for coming," Hope said.

Phoebe Redmund, the messenger's mama, was sitting on the side of Grandma's chair telling her about the short film she was preparing to direct, *The Wife of His Youth*, based on the Charles Chesnutt story.

Phoebe was the grandchild Grandma said most reminded her of the aunt who had raised her—a midwife born, and full grown, in slavery times. Phoebe wore her hair in twists and dyed it a crayon-orange shade of red. She was tiny-thin, tall, copper colored, and a semi-regular on a hit television show. She supplemented her income buying and selling vintage advertisements. Phoebe looked a lot like Ajay and Hope thought Phoebe was the inspiration for Ajay's hair, but she didn't hold that against her. Hope jumped on the other arm of Grandma's chair.

Out of the corner of her eye Hope saw Waycross at the sink talking to the woman she thought was called Ruby. Hope was about to get jealous, then another woman entered the conversation by kissing Ruby full on the lips and giving her what looked to be a taste of her tongue before she said a word. Hope turned her attention to the more immediate conversation.

Grandma, round and butter colored, head to toe in black, with large clear glasses like goggles that didn't shield her angry eyes, was saying that she had met Chesnutt in 1930, the year she had married.

Somehow it made them all sad that Grandma, who had been born in 1910 and who had known someone, Charles Chesnutt, born in 1858, was still alive and someone born in 1959, Abel, wasn't.

They all three stopped talking. Grandma got up. She had to keep moving or she would cry. No one alive had seen Grandma cry.

On her way back to the chair Grandma took a picture off a wall covered with photographs, a wedding photograph of Sammie and Abel. In wedding pumps the bride was taller than her six-foot groom. With rouged red lips, powdered white skin, and jet-black hair, Sammie looked like Snow White.

"That woman ruined my family," Grandma said.

There was so much Grandma could say but wouldn't about the woman, and it all boiled down to those five words. Her grandson had had a habit of oversharing in romantic and sexual matters when he had come to talk to Grandma. It was something she had enjoyed about the boy. His stories had kept her feeling alive. She knew so much she couldn't tell. Even with her favorite Phoebe trying to pry. Dead men tell no tales, but mourning friends tell all your secrets. Grandma wasn't a mourning friend, she was mourning family. She kept her mouth shut.

Phoebe took the picture of Sammie and Abel out of Grandma's hands. She hung it back on the wall. It was near time for Phoebe to leave for the airport, to get back in time to go to work. But first, she took down a picture of a brown girl in a long white gown and a beige man in a cutaway—a picture of Hope and Abel.

She put the frame that held that image in Grandma's hands. If Phoebe and Hope hadn't looked away the two comparatively young women would have seen the old lady cry. They looked away.

Hope turned her gaze toward another photograph. A man and a woman wearing near-matching wool pants and bright yellow L.L. Bean jackets: a picture of Hope and Abel on their wedding trip to Martha's Vineyard.

Hope knew the photo. She had hung a copy of it in Ajay's room, trusting he wouldn't see what she saw.

Abel and Hope were standing right next to each other but headed in opposite directions. They didn't know this. It was a honeymoon.

Hope kissed Grandma on the head, collected Waycross, then walked down to the basement to claim Ajay—who wanted to rest a longer while at Grandma's. There was just time to drop Phoebe at the airport before Hope had to rush to meet Nicholas. Somewhere in the basement Mo was slipping a drink to Ajay.

The day was too much for all of them.

SIX

NICHOLAS GORDON STOOD in the Hermitage Hotel's Oak Bar, one of the few grand bars of the Old South that had transitioned to the modern era, trying to remember what he and Hope Jones had drunk in the time and place of the People Power Revolution.

If the barkeep hadn't had such pretty, pretty green eyes, eyes that matched the hotel's famed men's room, it would have already come back to him.

Their drink should have been gin and tonic, but Hope had never trusted his ice, and Nicholas had always liked to drink what his guest was drinking. He hazily recalled trying kir royale. She had decreed it too pink and too sweet.

He clearly recalled encounters with Hope necessitating the application of gin to brain and her vulnerability to champagne. As he processed the same facts he had processed almost twenty years earlier, a cocktail from the First World War tripped to the tip of his tongue.

He asked the barkeep for two French 75s. Three minutes later, champagne flutes in hand, he returned to the table in the bar alcove that overlooked the dining room. Curled up, with her shoes off, in one of the two tiny green leather overstuffed sofas on either side of a low table, was Hope.

She, like he, had changed out of her funeral suit. Now she was wearing a long, straight, black knit skirt, a black V-neck sweater, a triple strand of dark South Sea pearls, and cowboy boots.

She took her drink from his hand before he had a chance to offer it; he took his first sip before he even sat down. It was still that kind of day.

Settling into the couch, wearing pressed jeans, a blazer, a knockoff of a Turnbull & Asser shirt with its distinctive collar and cuffs sewn by an Ayala Center tailor, and an absurd cravat actually from Jermyn Street—wearing the very same clothes he had worn in Manila in the eighties—Nicholas felt his mind slowly adjusting to the radical change in Hope's appearance.

She was no longer the slight and precocious girl he had known. There was a new ease in her body that suggested her spirit had expanded with her waist, bosom, and hips.

He was sad for what he was often sad for since he had turned seventy, that he was so far beyond boys and women.

He didn't miss girls because he had never liked them that much in the first place. Hope had been a true exception. He didn't miss men because he still had them.

He would keep missing boys and women. They required from him passions long ago spent, some of it, if he remembered correctly, on this woman when she was a girl.

"This cocktail, this bar, Abel would have loved this."

"That's why we're here."

Hope drained her glass. Nicholas drained his. She started to rise. He waved her back down. "You don't know the recipe."

Nicholas got up and rolled back to the bar, leaving Hope perched on the sofa.

He gave the barkeep very specific instructions: "A jigger of Bombay Sapphire gin, a jigger of Cointreau, not Grand Marnier, juice from one lemon, unless it's a dry lemon, and then I want juice from two lemons, and six very thinly sliced strips of lemon peel. Mix it all in a crystal pail, a clean ice bucket will do, then pour in a full bottle of champagne. Funnel what fits back into the bottle, pour the rest into a glass for yourself."

Nicholas returned to their nook, bottle under his arm, clean glasses in his hands. They took another moment to settle. This time they made a toast before sipping.

They lifted their glasses and clinked them together, saying simultaneously, "To Abel." As Nicholas took longer than Hope to bring the champagne flute to his lips, Hope wondered whether the preposterous man had to steel himself for another encounter with the thick, flat feel of commercial glass between his lips. He took a photograph out of a man bag and placed it on the table. It was a photograph of Abel in lavender swim trunks and sunglasses on a boat. Hope was sprawled across his lap in a hot pink swimsuit. They were both smiling. The sea behind them was Kodachrome blue.

"Who's that girl?"

"That's how I remember you. The other wives stayed behind their gates, but you came to my house, you went to Divisoria Market, you jogged by the seawall with marines. He was proud of all that and of your breasts."

"We were so far from home."

"It was good for you."

"It was very good for us."

"Was it better for him than for you?"

"Some days I felt naked as those kids shitting in the street. That scared me."

"The only things I recall you being afraid of were rats and kids in the street and the sharks off Palawan."

"And mosquitoes."

"And mosquitoes."

"Abel wasn't afraid of anything."

"I think he even ate dog once."

"Do not tell me that."

They laughed together and it was a familiar thing, almost a family thing.

"But you left him."

"I left him."

"Why?"

"Ajay."

"Ajay?"

"Abel was too removed from Ajay."

"He said you left because he hit Ajay once."

"Abel lied like a rug."

"You've become so—American. You and Abel became so *American*."

"What were we then?"

"Expats."

"I haven't heard that word in a hundred thousand years."

Gin, Cointreau, and champagne were scarce commodities in Manila in the eighties unless you were a friend of Nicholas Gordon, in which case there was gracious plenty. Playing bridge and talking books as afternoon odors settled into the walls of the old town, into Intramuros, a place where nobody who was anybody, except Nicholas, lived, was something the prosperous people of Forbes Park liked to contemplate doing and talk about doing— like going down to Mabini Street and watching the exquisitely pretty virgin-whores dance—but few did.

Hope and Abel were among the few. The weary blaze of afternoon sun that fell each day on the rats of the old town often fell on Hope and Abel as the young couple scurried from the hot of their little Ford Escort—the factory air in sport compacts was no match for the tropical climate; it simply managed to lower the temperature sufficiently for the Joneses to ride across the city with their doors locked and their windows rolled up, past children who pissed in the broad daylight on streets where no dogs ran lest they wind up dinner—to the teak shutters of Nicholas's door, to the cool of his house between the river and the bay.

Abel was a college backgammon champ who played a fine hand of bridge; Hope talked books better than anyone in the city—except for Nicholas. They had an open invitation to stop in at Nicholas's any day between four and seven, except for Thursday.

Thursdays were sacrosanct. On Thursday Nicholas entertained three priests, said to be fat, old, and wrinkly, who stank of garlic and communism and couldn't be entertained with ladies, who came once a week to drink questionable (most of the bottles had turned) old wine with Nicholas and play mah-jongg.

When Abel and Hope found themselves exhausted with the opulence of the pink and vicious city, whenever they could pull themselves away from the pool or the Polo Club, away from tennis and work and calamansi soda, away from the merry-go-round-dull din of expat existence in Manila, they made their way to the hazy dark of Nicholas's house, where little was abundant and everything was exquisite.

Nicholas said he lived in the old town because he liked to be near the water. Some people thought he lived where he lived because he was running out of money. Other people thought it was because he didn't want to run out of money. Hope thought it was because he wanted to be able to see both his guests and his enemies arriving from across a great distance.

Nicholas's house, built in the eighteenth century, was a sculptured wood translation of a Gothic manse, erected by a Catholic priest who had arrived in the Philippines just in time to discover, at least in the version of the story Nicholas told to beguile Hope, that he loved women more than he loved God, a day before he discovered, so far from Spain, that he could have them both.

The priest could tell the very first time he kissed his pagan Indian woman that God didn't care, or that if God cared, God was pleased. The sun, the day after the priest made love to the woman, seemed an unusually bright red-gold, the sky a purple-blue. Everywhere about him the flowers were colors and shades the priest had never seen. He believed God was winking at him, goading him onward into love. When the woman gave birth to twins, a boy and a girl, seven months later, the priest saw it as a sign of God's continued favor. He didn't know a pregnancy lasted forty weeks. Until Manila this man had paid no attention to the bodies or calendars of women.

As baby followed baby, the priest came to know and count the days he was invited and the days he was prohibited by his woman. He came to see the short season of the first pregnancy as a miracle that had returned the woman's body to him sooner than would usually be possible, a miracle provoked by the ardor of his wishes.

Because the woman let him make love to her every day the week before the babies were delivered, none of the mistresses he took in the months between the time she began to swell and the time she allowed him again ever took hold. Between the privilege of lolling in the pleasure of her immensity and the joy of a little baby created by his desire laid into his arms to cry into his ear, between this and the pleasure of suckling at the woman's breast as if he were the baby, while knowing he was the man who had brought the baby to life, the young priest grew older and happier and wiser, without growing into the knowledge that the father of his twins was his gardener, a man who lived, if not precisely under his roof, in his shed.

The bishop threatened but never visited; after a decade he sent an emissary. For this occasion the priest built a house for his woman and their children that was separate from the house the church had built for him.

To keep his lady happy he required that the house he built for her be twice as large as the house the church had built for him. To keep his flock happy, he had required that the house they built for him be quite small. He did not wish to drain too much from the collection plates passed through the aisles of the poor.

When the impending visit from Spain precipitated the building of the new house, the priest saw the importance of acquiring some sugar lands far to the south in Leyte. In this way he was able to rob poor people he never had to meet, poor people who didn't love Jesus, and give generously to the poor people who prayed, on bloody knees, to Jesus in his church, and who worked in and about his house.

Nicholas told Hope the passionate priest story early in their relationship. Hope was charmed but incredulous. She asked a skeptical question.

"How would you know any of that?"

"Oh, but she kept a diary," Nicholas said.

"She could write?" Hope asked.

"The besotted priest taught her," Nicholas replied.

"And you have her . . . ?"

"Papers . . . Young wives should never keep diaries or journals. They have a way of showing up at the most inopportune times."

"I'm glad she wrote it all down. The story makes your house more beautiful."

"I don't think the descendants would share your opinion, nor the church. They can excommunicate you after death, take away lands as well as laurels. The bastard descendants of gardeners do not enjoy the privileges of the bastard descendants of priests. Young wives must be so careful of what they put on paper."

"I don't commit anything but drivel to paper. I have a more than excellent memory. I inherited it from my Melungeon great-grandfather, a famous moonshiner, who kept nary a note of recipe, still location, or accounts received or expended. Often arrested, never convicted. I take after him," Hope said rather proudly.

"Don't be horrible, Hope," Abel warned; he had been silent

up to that point. He hated it when she talked about her poor white relations instead of her rich white daddy.

"I quite like her attitude," Nicholas said.

"You appreciate the primitive instincts," Abel rejoined.

"I have a particular fondness for the primitive passion for secrecy and magic. I won't have an affair with a woman, can't even propose an affair with a woman, if I think she's the kind who keeps a diary, she'd be far too . . . unmagical."

"Hope, buy one tomorrow, and promise to make daily entries," Abel said.

They all laughed. They drunk more French 75s until the other guests, bridge players, had arrived. When the dealing began, Nicholas called for his maid, Tola. The shoeless and beautiful girl led non-bridge-playing Hope back to one of the guest bedrooms, where her feet would be washed, then massaged before her toes were most delicately polished.

As Hope left the room, following behind Tola, Nicholas called after her, "Don't put tonight in that diary he buys you. When they look back on our time, don't make it easy for history to say we were a decadent lot."

The banter had been so light and erotically charged, so seemingly translucent, and pleasurable, that Hope hadn't thought much about it when Abel asked her later that night to destroy the diary she had been keeping.

"It's not like you're in the CIA," Hope said.

"I don't want strangers telling our secrets two hundred years from now," Abel said.

"That was rather appalling, unless Nick made the whole thing up," Hope said.

"Why would he do that?" Abel asked.

"To flirt with me," Hope replied.

"I should encourage you to keep a diary so I can spy on the both of you," Abel said.

They digressed to kisses. When Abel awoke the next morning, Hope was burning the little journal she had been keeping of marriage.

The day the picture of Abel in lavender and Hope in pink was taken by a waiter who sometimes doubled as an extra boatman, Hope and Abel had set out from their hotel, the Bohol Beach Club—forty thatched rooms set out over a two-mile crescent of chalk white sand—in a small open boat with a single outrigger motor, for a reef off Pamilican Island.

By noon Hope and Abel were snorkeling and swimming above what the boatman, whose father was a fisherman, had told them was the deepest crevice in the ocean floor. If it was just the deepest tear any of them would ever know it was plenty deep enough. Swimming there was paddling through an aquarium. The fish—barracuda, lapu-lapu, parrot fish, angelfish, and so many species none of them could name in English, only knew as brightly-colored-luminescent-beautiful-fish—were plentiful. Hope and Abel held hands as they swam, her hair trailing in the water shadowing the sea grass.

Eventually, with the help of life buoys, Hope and Abel made love in the water, off one side of the boat, while the boatman caught an octopus off the other. Later when the boatman showed the young couple his catch, Abel told him he could take the octopus home for his family's dinner. Later still, the boatman climbed a palm tree on a small islet and brought back coconuts. He hacked off the coconut tops with a machete. They all drank coconut water rich in coconut fat for their lunch. She remembered wondering not if there were sharks in the water, but why it was the sharks didn't attack, and how it became likely or unlikely that would ever change. It was an exquisite day.

They were back in the water snorkeling again. As Abel pointed out a barracuda to Hope, she was thinking, *Nothing can hurt us here.* Her feeling was contagious. She could feel him catch it when he touched her fingertips. Behind her dive mask, defogged with her own spit, she wept tiny tears into the big sea. She was stepping back from a ledge.

Eventually, Nicholas and Abel had partnered to win the Polo Club bridge championship. After that Nicholas had invited Hope to join the small book club that was more intimate and more bohemian than the elitist English Speaking Union, which many of the other well-educated wives had joined. Nicholas hadn't wanted Hope to get jealous, bored, or disaffected. He had had other plans for her. And then Hope had been medevaced from Manila to Nashville pregnant and allegedly ill.

At the time she had burned her journal, Hope had thought Nicholas had had nothing to do with it. Now, staring at him from across the table at the Oak Bar, tapping on a photograph of a best day in her life, she wasn't so sure.

"You were dazzled and dazzling."

"We liked it that you let us think we were."

Nicholas placed a picture of Abel in a suit, standing in front of a flag—what looked to be his official White House or Pentagon portrait—next to the picture of Hope and Abel on the boat.

"How did he get from that to this?"

"Was Abel in the CIA?"

"Yes."

"Abel was in the CIA?"

"Or something very like it. You were at the funeral. Did it look like a civilian occasion to you?"

"No."

"Why do you care?"

"Why?"

"How is the CIA any worse than White House special advocate at the Pentagon?"

"I didn't put it all together: September eleventh. Waterboarding, Guantánamo, Abu Ghraib. Abel."

"What did you think White House special advocate at the Pentagon did?" asked Nicholas.

"I think I thought he dealt with personnel matters. He told me he handled personnel matters. The army has a lot of employees, and provisioning . . . Abel seemed so incompetent," said Hope.

She sounded offhand and convincing. It was apparent to Nicholas that Hope had been lying to herself about Abel's employment. What remained to be seen was how far, in the face of Abel's death, she would progress toward abandoning denial. For the moment she was looking down and flushing.

"You underestimated him."

"And?"

"You hear the *and*. You were always so good at hearing the *and*. And I was in love with him. I will not divulge whether or not he was in love with me or whether or not we were lovers but I will claim I was in love with him," said Nicholas. He turned the champagne bottle over into the ice bucket.

"I thought you were in love with me," said Hope.

"There was that too," said Nicholas.

"We were very young," said Hope.

Hope let her face go soft. Nicholas had provoked her to remember an earlier self she had forgotten. She leaned in and kissed Nicholas on the lips. A woman's kiss. For Nicholas it was something like tasting the will of the world to keep spinning; so different than what he tasted on the tongue of every man he still knew, the will to keep fighting to the end.

Nicholas was starting to wonder if it might not be interesting to give women a second chance.

"I think I might like to stay and see a bit of Nashville. And you," he said.

"Go home, Nicholas. I've got a family to tend to."

"You sound so black and southern."

"I am black and southern."

"I'm deciding between seeing what Abel would want me to see and seeing what I want to see," said Nicholas.

"What do you want to see?"

"Where Abel grew up."

"What would Abel want you to see?"

"Whatever is shiniest about the place."

"That used to be me. May I have the photograph?"

"Will you play tour guide?"

"No."

"You may still have the photograph." Nicholas picked up the snapshot of Hope and Abel on a boat in the sun and handed it to the woman who used to be the girl in that picture. Hope put it in her purse. Nicholas put the formal portrait of Abel back into his breast pocket.

"Was that story about the priest and his concubine true?"

Hope asked, but that was not what she was thinking about, not as she spoke, not as he gave his answer.

"Of course. We wouldn't have persuaded you to burn your writings and to stop writing with a lie. It's a true story, just not the story of my house," said Nicholas.

Hope was thinking about perversions. And politics. It was hard to think about Abel and Manila without thinking about politics and perversions. Rebuff. Break my mind. How was all of this connected?

Just as once upon a time someone had figured out that bright young women who had been sexually exploited by powerful, well-educated men, particularly fathers, would have both the temperament and the opportunities to make very successful assassins, someone had figured out that black southerners had a very complex relationship to law.

People who have been tortured by the state make ideal just-inside-the-law torturers, just as people who have been tortured by people they love make excellent executioners.

Children who have been hurt by strange and extreme acts grow into adults who want to believe that certain strange and extreme acts are not strange and extreme. An abused black southerner presented all kinds of interesting political possibilities.

Who had exploited the possibilities? Hope didn't know, but she suspected Nicholas might. Tomorrow she would try to find some time to squeeze him in maybe in the late afternoon if Ajay wanted to see friends and Waycross went out to his office. Hope wished she could meet Nicholas for breakfast. Once upon a time champagne in the early morning light with Nicholas had been a very good thing.

Nicholas was thinking about the same very good thing. And he was thinking about marrying a woman. Maybe even having a child. An old man with a pocket full of money and a will to write can get a young and pretty wife in any nation of the world. Comes a time we all stop thinking about joy and love and start thinking about progeny.

The rules of life, unlike the rules of war, cannot be rewritten.

SEVEN

Driving from the hotel home, Hope was surprised to discover that some of her love of Monday night had seeped into the bitterness of the strange day. She was finally feeling less stunned and less stoned. She was starting to be able to imagine waking up Tuesday sober and ready to help Ajay start sorting out life after Abel.

It had been a long weekend. After Waycross had dosed him down with whiskey before dawn on Friday morning, Ajay had eventually cried himself to sleep at about eight o'clock. He had awoken at noon.

Ajay had joined Hope and Waycross at the big dining table, picking at, but not eating, the remnants of Thanksgiving breakfast: cold grits casserole, cold peppered brown-sugar bacon. None of them had known what to say, so they had babbled banalities until Hope had reached across the table for Ajay's hand and toward the head for Waycross's. Reflexively, Waycross had taken Ajay's. Together they'd gone silent.

To someone glancing into the room at that moment it might have appeared that they were about to pray except for the fact that their heads weren't bowed and all their eyes were wide open. Hope was saying, and Waycross was seconding, with no words spoken, "Our circle will not be broken." Then it had been. Hope had started clearing off the dishes and Waycross had started reading the paper.

"I have so many questions I want to ask him," Ajay had said. The circle had reformed, quickly.

"Your daddy loved you so much," Hope had said, walking back to Ajay's chair and placing the hand not full of plate on his shoulder. He had shrugged it off.

"That's not one of my questions," Ajay had said.

The tall boy had slid from the table and shuffled, in bare feet, up the floating rosewood stairs to his bedroom. Not knowing what else to do, Hope had followed Ajay. Waycross had followed Hope.

They had sat in the boy's room in forlorn silence, Ajay and Hope on a sofa, Waycross in a chair just beside the sofa. Eventually Ajay had broken the silence.

"Do you two have to be in here?" he had asked.

"Yes," Hope had said.

"Is it possible Dad's not really dead?" Ajay had asked.

"No," Hope had said.

Ajay had risen and put a movie into the DVD player. *Citizen Kane*, Abel's favorite. When the card reading "In Xanadu last week was held 1941's biggest, strangest funeral" had filled the screen, Hope had excused herself, mumbling something about a contact lens. Ajay had settled deeper into the couch, moving closer to Waycross's chair.

"Promise me somethin'?" Ajay had asked.

"Anything," Waycross had said.

"We go to Idlewild," Ajay had said.

"Now?" Waycross had asked.

"Soon as Daddy's buried," Ajay had said.

Waycross had not been blindsided by this request. The quiet particular to Idlewild had frequently scared the kid and sometimes like to driven the boy crazy, but Ajay loved the quiet and noise of the place. It was a particularly male quiet and a particularly male noise. Waycross had promised.

They had come a long way from that Thursday and that Friday of wails and promises to get to Monday night. She turned on the car radio, tuned to a country station, and did her best not to think.

Thirty minutes later, still high from Nicholas's cocktail and longing for a bath, she walked through her front door and was surprised to find hunting duffels in the front hall. She wouldn't have been if Waycross had told her about his conversation with Ajay, but he hadn't.

Banjo trotted out to greet her. When she lifted the dog he gave a quick yelp. She would take him to the vet tomorrow. She should have taken him three days earlier, should have but hadn't. Silently chiding herself for failing to be a good dog mother, she kissed Banjo, then put him back down.

The dog followed beside her back to the kitchen, toward the sound of Waycross's voice. She had a staircase to climb and several rooms to walk through before she got to her men. She made her slow way, vaguely beginning to wonder when Ajay should go back to school.

They were leaving for Michigan. She wanted to argue. Waycross shook his head.

"We're going to Idlewild," said Ajay.

"I'll go with you," said Hope.

"No. Just Waycross," said Ajay.

"Why?" asked Hope.

"Because," said Ajay.

"I promised him," said Waycross.

"When?" asked Hope.

"Now," said Waycross.

In their bedroom, just before Waycross joined Ajay, already in the Expedition, Hope extracted a promise. In the strange event anything happened to her, in the event she dropped dead anytime soon, Waycross would tell Ajay his mother had run off with her hairdresser.

She sealed the deal with a kiss. It would be better, they both agreed, for Ajay to think he had a nut for a mother than to know that he had another dead parent.

EIGHT

WAYCROSS LET AJAY drive. It had been what was planned and just then getting back to some part of the plan was an urgent need of his stepson's. Almost as urgent as getting Ajay away from the world of too many women and too many soldiers.

Driving upset could be as dangerous as driving drunk—which, despite having had one drink five hours earlier, Ajay assured Waycross he was not—or driving upset could be a great way to regain a sense of control of one's journey through the universe. Waycross was hoping to provoke this latter response.

And Waycross, who was tired of thinking, wanted to get comfortable in his seat, close his eyes, and ride a few miles.

Having established on earlier trips that each hated the other's music with a passion that did not allow for compromise, they rode in silence. Inside his head Waycross was hearing—note for note—Miles Davis playing "Some Day My Prince Will Come" and trying not to think about "what if's," particularly "What if I dropped dead and Hope found out about me and Ruby like she found out about Abel and some bullshit with the military?" Inside his head Ajay was cussing Abel out, cussing him and accusing him of all manner of sin—large and small—from being responsible for Ajay's ugly ears and allergy to nuts to being responsible for the use of waterboarding as a tool of interrogation.

Alternating cussing and imagining his father standing in the middle of the road with cussing and imagining driving Abel down, Ajay made a hundred and some miles while drinking sixty-four ounces of Coke without a squirm or a pee break. When he finally tired of cussing Abel, he lit into Sammie.

"That bitch is a fucking whore. A horny non-fucking whore. A rose-tattooed non-fucking whore."

The third time Ajay said "whore" Waycross decided it would be inappropriate to continue ignoring the fuck-storm of profanity. He opened his eyes and craned his neck in the direction of his stepson. "Have you seen the tattoo?" Waycross asked.

"Sorry," said Ajay. He hadn't realized he was talking aloud.

"Ass, breast, or ankle?" asked Waycross, wanting to assure his stepson that there was nothing the boy could say that would shock a man who had started off life as a small-town doctor's only son and then spent the last thirty years practicing gynecological surgery.

"Seen it all, done most of it twice," Waycross was fond of saying. He didn't say it just then. With Hope and Ruby so recently on his mind, and awkwardly close together, that phrase wasn't something he wanted to pull out and mouth to Hope's boy just at the moment.

And "ass, breast, ankle" was a better invitation to the boy to speak. There was less boast in it.

Something more than the death of his father was troubling the kid. Waycross wanted to put a finger on it and hadn't yet found it, but he found a joke to cheer himself up. *"Ass, breast, ankle?" is a probing question, particularly the ass part.* Waycross chuckled in his head when he thought that. He kept his face solemn for the kid's sake and didn't speak the joke aloud. Waycross loved Ajay.

"Face," said Ajay.

"How'd I miss that?" asked Waycross.

He couldn't tell if Ajay was lying or taunting or starting to go crazy. All he knew for sure at the moment was that he needed a rest room. He'd been counting on the kid needing to go first. He wasn't counting on it any longer. Surprise and age had made Waycross's need urgent.

"Pull in at the next rest stop, we can get some coffee," directed Waycross.

"A'right," said Ajay.

"What was it, some of that makeup eye shadow tattoo mess?" asked Waycross.

"Naw," said Ajay.

They were fast coming up on a sign for an exit with a McDonald's and a Wendy's. Ajay started moving across to the far right lane.

"I slapped Sammie," said Ajay.

"You slapped Sammie?" Waycross repeated.

"I slapped Sammie and Daddy died," said Ajay.

The OnStar indicated they were somewhere outside Fort Wayne, Indiana, as Ajay pulled into the McDonald's parking lot. Driving erratically across empty parking spaces, hesitating between the painted lines, oddly unable to pick a parking place, Ajay started talking about how he had read somewhere that Wendy's was better than McDonald's. Waycross kept his face blank but began to wonder if a crack-up hadn't started. Ajay, like his mother, was an excellent driver and Ajay thought Wendy's was for girls and geeks. Something was very wrong with Ajay. He kept talking and driving and not parking.

Just as Waycross was deciding a U-turn back to Nashville might be prudent, Ajay swerved into a wide turn and then pulled the Expedition, rather precisely, between two parked cars in the row closest to the arches. Waycross breathed easier.

As a teaching physician Waycross spent a lot of time worrying about the almost grown. He had a long time previously come to the conclusion that the almost grown were uniquely delicate. Possessing little wisdom and fast losing possession of their innocence, the almost grown were overdependent on insight they rarely had and visceral knowledge they found confusing. The young person beside him was no sturdier than most.

All Ajay knew was he had something he needed to tell Waycross before they got to Idlewild, before they got to what both his fathers had called the black Eden, before they got to the ghost town, before he polluted the place in some fundamental way that could not be undone, before he finished puzzling over the proposition just crossing his mind that maybe curiosity was the opposite of fear.

They got out of the car, both slamming doors. Ajay's khaki pants and blue button-down shirt, similar to the one he had worn to the funeral (he understood this journey to be a "class dress" occasion), were already more than a little wrinkled. Waycross (in an old-school jogging suit he had owned since the seventies but since the nineties had only worn twice a year, on the drive to and from Michigan—except the year it had been given to the Goodwill and he had had to go and buy back what he had already owned) looked sharp. Purple jogging suits do not wrinkle.

Waycross put his arm around his Ajay. The boy was as tall as the man, six feet, and he would be taller soon, might actually be a hair taller already, but neither of them was quite ready to see it. "Tall and a string bean," Waycross had been heard to brag. Because he could think of nothing else to say that was both true and innocuous, he said it now, "Tall and a string bean."

The boy hesitated at the heavy glass door. Waycross opened the door and waited for his stepson to pass through.

"I can't go in," said Ajay. Waycross gave the boy his fierce do-as-I-told-you-to-do glare that had gotten so many residents through their first difficult cesarean section, then quickly let the glare morph into something less belligerent.

It wasn't fear animating the boy's face; it was plain determination and sharp sorrow. If Waycross pushed, something might break. Something might even break without his pushing.

"After I pee and buy me a coffee we can go wherever the fuck you want," said Waycross. He threw Ajay the keys. Ajay caught them in his hand high above his head. The kid was down but he wasn't out.

They laughed as they found themselves wedged into seats that seemed designed for shorter people: women and children. Ajay ate a bacon cheeseburger and Waycross ordered two Frostys and a burger. He wanted to drink some scotch for lunch but that wasn't happening. He'd make do sucking on two straws jammed into a shake.

"And why exactly are we avoiding McDonald's?" asked Waycross.

"We were in that fucking 'roll tide, roll' kitchen, Daddy's plane was late, or he had missed the one he was supposed to be on, some redundant shit," began Ajay.

"And this has something to do with McDonald's?" asked Waycross.

"Yeah," said Ajay, "somethin'."

Ajay and Sammie had been in the messy Crimson-Tide-red kitchen. The little girls, Ajay's half sisters, had been out of sight but their light high voices, shouting commands to one another as they had played a game of freeze tag, had carried over the wide board fence that separated the yard from the field. The room had smelled like the McNuggets and fries they hadn't finished. Abel's plane had been delayed but no one had called to tell Ajay, so he had shown up, knocking, at the back door.

He had caught Sammie scavenging. Her big children had been at a movie and Sammie had been making lunch out of her little daughters' leftovers. She had said she was saving to buy something. She hadn't said what, but she had said "saving" in a way that had made Ajay ashamed of his Bills Khakis pants, ashamed of his leather wallet, ashamed of his expensive school, ashamed of all the things her kids, both the ones she had had with the car wash owner and the ones she had had with Abel, would never have.

She had offered Ajay the unbitten end of a baked-fried apple pie. He had been surprised that she had offered him a half-eaten piece of food, surprised when he had accepted it, surprised when he had bitten into it to find it still warm.

With his second bite into the apple-filled dough some of the filling had squirted out, then had landed back on his chin.

Sammie had laughed at Ajay; she had wiped the sticky stuff away with her fingers and then she had licked them.

"Do I look old enough to be your mother?" Sammie had asked.

"No," Ajay had said.

"My oldest twins are older than you," Sammie had said.

"You're a lot younger than my mother," Ajay had said.

"Is that a compliment, Abel Jones the fourth?" Sammie had asked.

"I guess," Ajay had said.

"How old are you?" Sammie had asked.

"Sixteen," Ajay had said.

"I was seventeen when I had my first babies," Sammie had said.

The boy hadn't said anything. But he hadn't stepped back. She had stepped closer.

"What do you like to do, Abel Jones the fourth, except get good grades and wear fancy clothes?"

He still hadn't said anything. Samantha had worked harder to get his attention. She had touched his belt buckle, gold and initialed, when she had said the word "babies." She had drawn happy face smiles in the air, as if she were directing a little orchestra, as she had pronounced, singsong like, taunting, "get good grades."

When she had got to "wear fancy clothes" she had ever so softly, lightly enough so it had been impossible for him to know if she had done it by accident or on purpose, grazed the fabric of his trousers with her hand.

She hadn't seen his hand rise. She'd been too busy trying to work her way into setting him up with one of her young cousins;

she hadn't even thought of how he might misconstrue or construe the introduction of her eventual invitation.

He had slapped her. Hard. An inking. She had been wondering how she was going to explain the palm print to Abel when Ajay had thrown a box of fries at her head. Two or three stragglers had fallen into her cleavage before the red box had hit the ground. Ajay had bolted out the door.

Waycross was laughing. It was a tonic for Ajay. He started laughing too.

"You did not do one thing wrong, boy," reassured Waycross.

"I felt kinda stupid throwing the fry box," admitted Ajay.

"Insignificant," declared Waycross.

"Insignificant," Ajay said, starting to mean it.

"You did not do one wrong thing, and you helped that crazy bitch not do *another* thing wrong. You a better man than me, boy," said Waycross.

"Truth," said Waycross.

"Word," said Ajay.

"Word," said Waycross.

"I know about Ruby," said Ajay.

"Ruby," repeated Waycross.

"She called the house. Told me she wanted me to tell my mama about her. Said you made her have an abortion in 1964 and she couldn't have babies after that. Said you wouldn't marry her because she was a hairdresser," said Ajay.

"Did you tell your mama?" asked Waycross.

"No," answered Ajay.

"Thank you," said Waycross.

"Is any of it true?" asked Ajay.

"Some," said Waycross.

"She sounded crazy," said Ajay.

"She's not crazy," said Waycross.

"Are you in love with her?" asked Ajay.

"Everybody loves Ruby," said Waycross. It hurt him to smile. But he smiled anyway. Ruby brought a smile to his lips. "It's not so much love. I knew her from when we were kids in Georgia, back in Waycross. She's the only person left in this world who calls me Dan."

"It's like that old blues song, I've only loved four womens in my life, my mother, my sister, my girlfriend, and my wife?"

"Something exactly like that, except, Ruby's gay," said Waycross.

"Ruby's gay?" asked Ajay.

"Yes," said Waycross.

"Have you slept with her?" asked Ajay.

"On long past occasion," said Waycross.

"Why did she call our house?" asked Ajay.

"That would have been her gal friend," said Waycross.

They finished the rest of their meal in a silence punctuated by the snorting sound of Waycross sucking too hard on his Frosty. He was sorry he had lied to Ajay but it was a necessary sorry. After they cleared the remnants of the meal to the trash bins and the tray stacks, Ajay refilled his Coke and Waycross bought a coffee to go.

They were back on the road. Waycross took the wheel. He needed to achieve a semblance of control for himself.

Ajay turned on the satellite radio and quickly found a jazz station.

"I'm starting to like Miles," said Ajay.

"And Thelonius?"

"Not Thelonius. Gil Evans."

"Born Ernest Gilmore Green."

"He changed it to his stepfather's name."

"Or he changed it to make it sound less Jewish."

"I prefer my explanation."

"Me too."

Ajay wasn't as sad as he'd thought he would be. He wasn't even as sad as he'd thought he should be. *It was, what it be.* And the man sitting beside him, the man who had told him something near the whole truth and nothing but the truth, even when it hadn't looked pretty on him, the man who had spilled his own secrets to distract Ajay from sorrow, wasn't the only daddy Ajay had but he was his best daddy. Hope Jones hadn't raised no fool. Ajay knew he was lucky to have a daddy driving him to Idlewild to mourn his daddy.

Waycross was flattered that his stepson wanted to bury some of his sorrow in the same lake where Waycross had buried his daddy's ashes.

It was half sideways but Hope had given Waycross a son, and Waycross was going to do what he could to help Ajay mourn Abel.

Ajay and Waycross were listening to Kenny Burrell play "This Time the Dream's on Me" as they passed the sign that read, WELCOME TO MICHIGAN, GREAT LAKES, GREAT TIMES.

Part II

O N Saturday, March 6, 1965, Abel and his daddy were headed to Selma. Big Abel pointed the Flying Crow south for what turned out to be its last trip to Alabama as the Jones family vehicle.

Big Abel's school-teaching frat brother, Randall Pettus, a part-time deacon who worshipped at Brown AME Chapel, had invited them down for a local march.

Abel, going on six, a young veteran of the Movement, was his father's traveling companion of choice.

When they drove past the turnoff to Birmingham, Big Abel started talking about "the funeral." Abel claimed he didn't remember the little girls' funeral. Instead of stopping talking, his father told him all about it again. About the little shoes. About Addie, Denise, and Cynthia as well as Carole. He said Denise had been only five years older than Little Abel was now. Little Abel was wondering why they were headed to a church if children got blown up in churches. He knew better than to pose this question aloud.

They arrived in Selma in time for Saturday night supper. Abel liked the other boy, Wade. Wade was yellow and wide with brown plastic glasses. Saturday night the daddies wore blue jeans and plaid shirts and the little boys did too. The daddies drank scotch and grilled hamburgers while the little boys watched teevee.

The next day the fathers wore suits and ties and overcoats and the little boys wore their Sunday suits with their warm school jackets over them. With the boys in the middle holding hands and their daddies on the outside, they formed a phalanx of four. They marched from the church about six hundred strong down to the bridge.

Wade and Abel traded jokes along the way and they sang one of the songs they had been taught to sing, "Ain't gonna let nobody turn me round, turn me round, turn me round, I'm gonna keep on walking, keep on talking, Lord, keep on praying, Lord."

They were so noisy, and the crowd was so noisy, they didn't notice, and their fathers didn't notice, how silent the town had become. They made six blocks and then it was horrible.

People, men and women, were falling, in lines, to their knees to pray. Other people, all men, were hitting the kneeling men and women in the head with thick sticks.

Later Abel learned these sticks were called billy clubs or batons. Some of the people didn't drop to their feet to pray or sing, they screamed and ran.

The police looked like toy army men all dressed the same way, in light-colored pants and dark shirts and helmets, with some kind of strap across their chests and guns on their hips.

Young Abel saw this, then he saw nothing. He and Wade dropped hands. He felt his father lifting him in his arms. Abel's eyes were burning. Big Abel fell to the ground. Abel wasn't holding his father's hand anymore. Abel was running away from the river.

He found his way back to the church with the help of a woman in a neat dress and hat and pumps and stockings. He was sucking on a peppermint stick in the church basement when Big Abel found him.

Later that night they watched themselves on the teevee news. King was coming. Big Abel wanted to stay and march with King. Antoinette called and told Big Abel to get his ass in the car and get her son home to Nashville or come home whenever he came to an empty house. He got himself and his boy into the car.

Abel rode all the way back to Nashville thinking about what he had seen in Selma. The people were sad, and they were angry, but some of them were something else. He didn't know the words for it but he recognized defiant and angry and sure when he saw it.

Walking across the bridge and hanging back at the church, hearing the folks with the different way of talking talk, the people the others called Yankees, black Yankees and white Yankees, Abel realized, for the very first time, there were people who lived in safe places. He wanted to live in one too.

He had seen the reporters and seen the photographers. He had met somebody who'd said he was a panther. Some of these people had talked to him. Some of them had even taken his picture. One of them had told him about a place called South Africa. He didn't know what the man was talking about but he knew he wanted to be like one of the white people from somewhere else who couldn't believe that places like Selma existed even when they were standing right in them.

A few days later, the march was attempted again and a few steps were taken but the bridge was not crossed. A few more days after that Martin Luther King went down with a lot of famous people. Wade's daddy called to tell them all about it. Abel's daddy called Abel to the phone and told Wade's daddy to holler for him. It was the first time Abel had ever talked long-distance. Big Abel wanted his boy to remember the victorious day.

All Abel remembered later was Bloody Sunday and the telephone call from Wade's daddy and the reporters who hadn't believed the place where he lived existed.

Saturday, April 9, 1967. Abel ran right through the door of Craighead's Barber Shop and smack into the knees of a man in a dark suit.

The man grabbed Abel by the sleeve of his new blue and white seersucker Easter suit. Abel was about to be in trouble.

Bumping into grown folks because you're rushing to get a Coke from the machine was not the kind of thing his daddy tolerated.

If the man was old enough Abel might get switched. He didn't look up to see the man's face. He didn't want to know how old the man was. Abel wanted to get his soda before his daddy announced he had lost his privilege.

"Slow down, son, before you knock somebody over," said the man.

Abel's fortunes changed. He slowed his move toward the Coke machine and happily fingered the coins in his pocket. His daddy hated anybody calling his child "son" worse than he hated his son bumping into grown folks.

Abel didn't look back. He didn't want to see what was about to happen to the man.

Big Abel could tear a person up with his tongue. Sometimes after his daddy quit cussing and fussing a man would look so crumpled Abel believed the man might have preferred getting whipped with a switch. He knew what was about to be said because he had heard it so many times before.

"You calling that boy 'son' is like you calling my wife a whore. You don't want to do that. Apologize."

Depending on what the man said back the conversation could get ugly quick. This stranger was in trouble.

And then he wasn't. Big Abel was saying something and he was stammering as he said it. He said, "If y-y-you want him he's y-y-yours." And then he was welcoming the man to town and apologizing for his boy. Big Abel didn't apologize—for himself or for his children. Abel's world wobbled.

The boy turned around to see who the man was that was making his daddy act strange.

Dr. Martin Luther King. Abel recognized the face immediately. Dr. King's picture was hung up in his classroom. Dr. King's face was on six different magazines on the cocktail table in his family's living room. Dr. King's likeness was plastered to telephone poles and the sides of buildings and the fronts of buildings all over North Nashville. And Dr. King was standing in Craighead's Barber Shop at seven on a Saturday morning looking like he had just gotten scalped by Craighead himself.

Abel blinked to see if Jesus, John Henry, and Muhammad Ali weren't sitting up in Craighead's three barber chairs with white towels wrapped around their necks.

He shook Dr. King's outstretched hand reluctantly. He could not help but be a little afraid of any man who could make Big Abel stammer.

Dr. King crouched down to look Abel in the eye.

"You got your suit on and you getting your hair cut. You coming to hear me speak?"

"Yes, sir."

"How old are you?"

"Eight. The nuns read us 'Letter from Birmingham Jail' at school this week because you were coming."

"Did you understand any of it?"

"Injustice anywhere hurts justice everywhere?"

Dr. King patted the boy on the head and looked up at Big Abel. Dr. King was impressed. He stood and shook the father's hand.

"T-t-tell him something else you remember, son."

"My feets is weary but my soul is at rest!"

The room erupted in laughter. Even old Craighead, who never laughed and hardly ever talked, laughed. Big Abel lifted his son onto his hip. King kissed the boy on the head, then Big Abel kissed Abel on the cheek. Then Big Abel stood his son on his own two feet and looked at him like he had never seen him before. King reached out to shake the boy's hand again. This time Abel shook it like a little man.

Dr. King reached into the breast pocket of his jacket and he pulled out a candy bar. He kissed the boy on the head again, then handed Abel the treat. Apologizing for having to be on his way, he was due on the Vanderbilt campus across town, King was halfway out the door.

Abel was climbing into one of the three barber chairs. Big Abel was sitting in another. King turned back to speak.

"You don't know what that means now, but one day you will. And I predict when that day comes it will be as true for you as it was for that lady. If it's not, don't you eat my candy bar."

As soon as Dr. King closed the door, Abel unwrapped the candy bar and gobbled it down quick.

The preacher, the poet, the pol, and the rabble-rouser, Martin Luther King, Allen Ginsberg, Stokely Carmichael, and Strom Thurmond, were coming to town. April 9, 1967, the weekend of the Vanderbilt University IMPACT Symposium, was promising to be more exciting than Christmas—and then it was more exciting than Christmas.

Big Abel's son, Abel, had been kissed by Dr. King after Abel had quoted, correctly and without prompting, from "Letter from Birmingham Jail."

For the first time in his grown life Big Abel wanted to go to heaven. He wanted to thank Jesus. Come Monday morning Big Abel was sending the nuns at St. Vincent de Paul, the little black Catholic school, a bright bouquet for preparing his son so well. That story was all over town and for a few hours Abel loved hearing it.

When he walked out of Craighead's Barber Shop with his fresh-cut head and Dr. King's chocolate on his breath, he was the prince of a proud place.

There is a stone wall around the Fisk campus that guards the students and raises the lawn that connects Jubilee Hall, the chapel, the old library, the Van Vechten collection, and all the original campus above the street. In April 1967, as Abel and his father drove, in a new navy Cadillac that had replaced the Flying Crow, from Craighead's alongside the wall toward Vanderbilt, Abel thought the stone wall beside him enclosed the most beautiful place in the world.

Then they stepped onto the grounds of the Vanderbilt campus to hear Dr. King speak. Abel didn't hear many of Dr. King's words that day. He was stricken by the realization that the Vanderbilt campus, which he had never seen but had always heard derided in his home and his neighborhood, was, in fact, prettier than Fisk's campus. The trees were taller and more plentiful. More flowers were planted. He couldn't say the buildings were more beautiful, but they were bigger and there were more of them. He was profoundly startled. Then the speech was over.

They tried to shake King's hand again but there were too many trying to shake it for the first time. Big Abel and Abel dashed back to North Nashville and Fisk; Antoinette was cooking and Stokely Carmichael was giving a talk. Stokely promised to be something bigger and badder than King. Lunch was great. Halfway through Stokely's talk Big Abel walked out, dragging his son with him.

He said he could do more to help the race down at his law office, and Abel could do more doing his homework, than either of them could do "listening to that mess." In the morning Big Abel had thought Strom Thurmond was the rabble-rouser; now he thought Carmichael was a rabble-rouser too.

Abel was intrigued that a black man and a white man could provoke his father to the exact same kind of rage. He had never seen that before this strange day.

Later that Saturday night, Big Abel and Antoinette were off to the home of friends for a Circle-lets party. It was rumored King might stop by. Pretty Sonia babysat for Abel and Tess.

Soon after Abel's parents left, a war began. This war wasn't carried on the national television or much noticed even in the rest of Nashville, but two blocks from where Abel lived a battle occurred. Students fought with rocks and sticks and stones and police fought back with bullets. All night long Abel could hear gunshots as he lay in his bed in the dark. By the second evening one black boy, a Tennessee State University student, had been shot in the neck and the chancellor of Vanderbilt University was defending academic freedom. Molotov cocktails were thrown that night through the windows of homes. Abel thought it was the night he and his family were going to die and the black people were going to kill them just like black people had killed Malcolm.

The next morning Abel's daddy, who had been bailing students arrested for nonviolent protest out of jail, using his own money—Little Abel's patrimony—to do it, laid the blame for the mayhem at the mouth of Stokely Carmichael. Nobody was talking about Strom Thurmond anymore. Everybody was talking about Stokely's speech. And not in a good way. Abel was a most bewildered boy.

NINE

HOPE WOKE UP Wednesday morning in the bed she shared with Waycross sick that her week was buried in sorrow and Abel was buried in a white people's cemetery. Bigger things than that were wrong but none of them was as absolute and for-sure wrong. For better or for worse Abel should have been buried in Arlington. It was the worst kind of spite that Sammie had buried Abel in Alabama.

Hope pulled the phone, a blah white touch-tone with a hyper-sophisticated caller-ID system, into her bed before even getting up to go to the bathroom. She called Ajay, who wasn't answering. She called back and texted the obvious: "I love you, precious."

She wanted her son to be fine again. Abel's death had stripped away a layer between the boy and mortality. Anything that made the child feel precarious made Hope feel precarious. She thanked God that Grandma was still alive providing an illusion of buffer, but Grandma was closer to a hundred than ninety. How long could that last?

Before she had time to answer the question the phone rang. Caldwell Lyttle was on the line. Republican, Christian, and southern in all the expected and easy-to-deplore ways, he was calling to talk about the will. He was calling so early because he was headed to the airport.

With mourning settling so prickly into and onto her morning, she found it comforting to hear the voice of someone who understood Christian-soldier Abel and perhaps could help her understand him.

Lyttle continued to speak, working hard to maintain the appearance of being an aw-shucks modest man (pride is a significant sin in the New South) while conveying the impression that he was a very big deal and it was a very good thing, a right true and Christian thing, that he was extending the shelter of his authority to a *raggedy* part of Abel's history.

"By 'raggedy part' he had better only mean me," Hope thought as soon as Lyttle had let that particular bit of idiocy slip his lips. *Only I am raggedy.*

Hope wanted to slap Lyttle, but the phrase had originated with Abel. "My raggedy-ass divorce" was a common phrase of his. She could hear him talking in his fake Negro-speak that so amused him when he was drunk.

Lyttle mimicking Abel talking black, Lyttle saying, "It's time I tend to the raggedy parts of Abel's life," was, like the old folks say, uglier than homemade sin.

Lyttle didn't like Hope. She was not what she once had been—nor what she should be by his lights. Lyttle only knew Hope as she was now: expanded untidily into middle age, and aged to a complexity unsuited to him. At best he thought of her as Abel's unfinished business; business he, Lyttle, would be honorable enough to finish. She felt his distaste, but as long as he didn't project it onto Ajay it was of no concern to her. She liked her raggedy parts.

It was barely seven but Lyttle started reading bits and pieces of Abel's will to Hope to illustrate the need for him to get together with Ajay. He was talking about a "bonus round" and about Ajay inheriting the house on Fifteenth Street and all its contents, but Ajay had to live in the house a month a year, and he had to be on a pre-med track. Hope woke up. Lyttle noticed. She started paying attention. He really noticed. The conversation got difficult.

She had been making prompt and proper responses; now she began idling, withholding words. Abel had some crazy friends. He didn't have many dumb ones. Lyttle was smart enough to get off the phone.

Hope got up from the bed and walked toward her blue and white and gray bathroom. She brushed her teeth with an electric toothbrush, washed her face with a simple cotton cloth.

Her mind wouldn't get quiet or it was too quiet. She had to find a lawyer. Maybe two lawyers: one to sue the Confederate horse barn restaurant and one to represent Ajay's interest as the will got settled.

Hope, who knew what it was to be a black child who had never had a bill paid for by a black father, would not separate her son from that increasingly rare privilege or the always rare privilege of being a black child who inherits from his black father's estate. She would find a way for Ajay to inherit from Abel without complying with any strange bits.

The will as quoted to her seemed more a truckload of strange carrots and stranger sticks than a tool for the transference of wealth.

Hope pushed a button and was ringing back the number Lyttle had rung her from, hoping he hadn't turned his phone off. He hadn't.

"There are a lot of prohibitions in Abel's will that you mentioned, lots of instructions, but you only mentioned what you called one simple bonus round."

"The two hundred thousand for going to medical school."

"Yes. Why?"

"Abel wanted to be a doctor when he grew up."

"No, he didn't."

"You didn't know Abel very well."

"A fact becoming increasingly apparent."

"Does that mean you'll set up a meeting between me and Ajay?"

"It means you should expect a call from my lawyer."

"If you're represented by counsel we shouldn't be talking."

"Right."

Hope slammed down the phone. Had Abel wanted to be a doctor? Why hadn't she known that? She called Waycross. He answered. He always took her calls.

"Did you know Abel wanted to be a doctor?"

"Yep, for sure."

"When did that change?"

"He was thirteen."

"Thirteen?"

"Yep."

"You remember that specifically?"

"I remember he was thirteen."

"Why?"

"Why, what?"

"Did he stop wanting to be a doctor?"

"Hopie, I'm freezing my ass off in a deer blind."

"Tell me."

"Abel started thinkin' people like me didn't have much power. And he didn't have the right name."

"Right name?"

"Daniel first, Hale middle."

"What?"

"Bougie black medical world circa nineteen fifty. *Good-bye.*" She appreciated the fact that her second husband had taken the time to say the word.

TEN

Driving downtown, Hope was thinking about how it came to be that her first husband had named her second husband. A thousand miles away, Waycross was thinking about the very same thing in a slightly different way.

Once upon a time there was a man forgotten by time, but not by CPT: Daniel Hale Williams. Colored people in colored people's time remembered the boy who began his working life poking a needle through animal skins (in the employ of a shoemaker, sewing hides) and who then became a barber quick with a blade (cutting hair, shaving beards) before his transformation into a surgeon, all preludes to his final metamorphosis into the world's first heart surgeon.

"Firsts" often involve tricky distinctions. Almost always the validity of the designation is dependent on a quantity of unknown information as well as on the quality of the known information. Claims of being the first this or that, and especially claims of being the first black this or that, are often disputed—and this one was—outside of the Negro world. Within the

Negro world, Daniel Hale Williams was granted his laurel without dispute.

The white world was different. Some argued that Williams hadn't operated on the heart, he had operated on the sac surrounding the heart. Some argued that a person in St. Louis had performed a similar operation a year earlier but hadn't reported it widely. Eventually there would be those who argued that Williams wasn't really black, that he had had too many white ancestors to be counted as a Negro, negro, black, African-American, colored, or nigger.

The Fantastic Four, Waycross and his three med school roommates, believed what they had been told: Daniel Hale Williams was the world's first heart surgeon and he was a black man. They were entranced by those twinned facts and simultaneously scarred and made fraternal by the understanding that their names were his tombstone.

Their shared history as sons of fathers who wished they had been born Daniel Hale Williams's sons was also a profound connection. Sometimes it was as if they had been spawned, and this was discussed aloud one drunken night at Howard University, by one man off four different fathers, with no mother in it anywhere. The Fantastic Four reveled in a mystical sense of special camaraderie, drunk or sober.

That they shared an idea—Abel's eventual favorite writer, Machado de Assis, would have called it a fixed idea—about Williams's surgery, as well as sharing names, served to make the bond among the physicians in training that much stronger. Their fixed idea was that they had been present at, and witness to, as the sons of their doctor daddies, the emergence of a black man as disciplined actor informed by theoretical knowledge.

That Dr. Dan, such an elevated black man, would have put himself in the service of a street criminal, would have determined to save a fallen warrior's life, and that he would have been audacious enough to invite witnesses to watch the rescue, they understood to be an assertion of the significance of every black life, including the poor and the foolish, including the violent. Dr. Dan's audacity added immeasurable sweetness to the deal.

And so eventually Waycross and Mount Bayou and Opelika and Yazoo City were called by the towns from which they hailed and not by the name of the great pioneer. Daniel Hale Williams was too damn popular. Abel said that when he was still a boy, just before he named them Waycross, Mount Bayou, Opelika, and Yazoo City. Just after that he begged Waycross to continue with the story of Dr. Dan and how he had changed the mythology of the Talented Tenth. That day in the little house next door to Big Abel's, Waycross had said, "Into the history of the Swordsman arrived the Surgeon." He had begun to tell Abel about an alternative warrior identity, an alternative construct of male competencies in a new and modern era.

How far beyond the dull tool of John Henry's hammer was Williams's sharp scalpel? The scalpel that required brains and balls to approach the very heart of a man did approach, on the evening of July 9, 1893, the heart of a specific man, James Cornish, and there were invited witnesses, black and white, male and female. Williams would later speak of the nurses repeatedly, and they did something, *gossip*, to further the news. All of this came together to make Williams, for black men of science, what Pushkin was for black men of letters: a reason to hold your head up high.

The hammer, John Henry's hammer, only touched materials. John Henry bested a machine. With hands dripping blood, Daniel Hale Williams bested God and other men. Williams aimed to snatch a man back from the jaws of death, renouncing heaven's or hell's claim on the body, telling heaven or hell, or just death, to wait.

That was the story Waycross had told Abel, and that was the story he told Ajay on the road to Idlewild. He didn't tell Ajay that Dr. Dan had cheated on his wife, Alice, with a French woman and had applauded Alice's stoic silence with a midnight-blue Woods electric coupe. He didn't tell Ajay that somehow this gave Waycross justification for his affair. He didn't boast and say, "My daddy alone actually studied directly with Dan at Provident." Didn't say, this gave me more than justification, it gave me immunity. Didn't say, the hospital Williams founded, Provident, closed in 1987 only to rise phoenixlike in 1993. Didn't say, I've been a hard dog to keep under the porch but that's going to change and some of it's because someday soon you going to be big enough to knock me down if I do your mama wrong.

Hope wasn't ruminating on any of those salacious bits; she was wondering who the first black American spy was—and pondering the probability that his, or her, name would have tripped quickly to the tip of Abel's tongue.

ELEVEN

Nicholas, wearing an amazing black western tailored jacket, jeans, and cowboy boots, was standing just inside the glass front doors of the Hermitage Hotel when Hope pulled up in her red MINI Cooper. He did a little spin before he got into the car. Rhinestones and sequins sparkled, outlining black-on-black appliquéd palm fronds.

"Do I look like Gram Parsons?"

"You look like Johnny Cash channeling Gram Parsons."

"Thank you."

"You're not exactly dressed for Silver Sands."

"Where?"

"Soul food."

Silver Sands started serving breakfast at five A.M. to cater to working men and women who had to be on their jobs by six or seven. The restaurant was housed in a building with orange and white checkerboard walls just off Jefferson Street, the main commercial thoroughfare of North Nashville, home to the old black bank, Citizens Bank, and to many churches, several fast-food franchises, and the one and only Mary's barbecue. It was also the road that connected Fisk and Tennessee State University. Silver Sands looked more like a place to drink and shoot pool than a place to eat, but that appearance was deceptive. The eating was good.

Hope pulled right up to the place. The noses of the other cars were almost touching the building and their butts were hanging out on the street. The MINI Cooper fit easily on the blacktop.

Inside the restaurant there was odd paneling and no table service. Diners stood in the shortest cafeteria line in the world and picked their dishes from a steam table that offered a clear view of the food and let them point to what they wanted. Hope loved the fried bologna topped with grilled onions and the grits swimming in butter and the country ham. Folks came from miles for the tender liver.

At seven thirty in the morning the restaurant was halfway through breakfast and bustling. Hope and Nicholas were comfortably ignored. People stopped in to pick up to-go orders, and people arrived to walk through the line, then sit and eat. There was a sign that reminded customers to put the money in the servers' hands because drafts created by opening the sliding doors would blow money into the food on the steam table. The place was full of people, most of them men, who didn't have anybody to cook for them.

Nicholas and Hope were seated at a wooden table. Each of them had a plain white china plate in front of them filled with grits and pork and stewed apples. She had the country ham; he had the fried bologna. They both had coffee.

"Is this a place Abel ate?"

"Places like this scared Abel."

"Places like this don't scare you?"

"The first one I went to scared me, the first few times. Then I fell in love."

"Where was that?"

"Ben's Chili Bowl. Washington. The seventies."

"I play good shrink."

"You play shrink?"

"Do you want to talk about him?"

"Yes. I don't have to worry about making you jealous or sad."

"Jealous would be Waycross, sad would be Ajay?"

"Exactly."

"Are we near the barber shop where Abel met King?"

"Craighead's? Very near."

"You're taking me on a battlefield tour?"

"Battlefield?"

"Abel's Civil War."

"I forgot that phrase."

"You coined it."

"What did he tell you about his Civil War?"

"He talked a lot about the student riots."

"Black student riots."

"Abel thought he was going to be killed."

"He hated his father for not moving out of this neighborhood after that," said Hope.

"And now, you say, he's left Ajay the house."

"It seems he had already had the house put in Ajay's name, but his inheriting other things is dependent on his living, at least part-time, in the house," said Hope.

"That's wild."

"That's Abel."

" 'Dave Evans played Cupid.' That's how Abel liked to start the story when he told the story of how you met and fell in love. Who was Dave Evans?" asked Nicholas.

"Dave Evans was, and is, a Harvard admissions officer. Dave began life as the son of sharecroppers, then rose to play a pivotal role in defining the shape of forty Harvard classes. He admitted Cornel West. What did Abel say about Evans?" asked Hope.

"That Evans had said three sentences on behalf of him: there were a few low grades to overlook, or perhaps more than a few, but there were perfect SAT scores. And maybe five sentences on behalf of you. They had so many excellent St. Paul's candidates that year, but two Dickeys and being from the same state as Skip Gates held sway, and envelopes that might have been thin were fat," said Nicholas.

"You've heard his version; do you want to hear mine?"

"If I'm allowed to embellish and amend."

"You are."

Hope and Abel had fallen in love while undergraduates at Harvard, but the tumble, at least for Abel, had occurred not in a Yard dorm or classroom, or in a River House, or up at Radcliffe Quad; it had happened in a Beacon Hill dining room, on Pinckney Street.

Abel had been secretly proud of this fact. Falling in love with a 'Cliffie on the Yard or in a River House was too *Love Story* for him.

Their first kiss occurred a year and a half after first sight. When they were both far from home (and close to the place where they would come to think they had begun, the Flying

Horses, a carousel on Martha's Vineyard), he did not resist her and she did not resist him.

The Sunday lunch had been hosted by a Mr. S——, who was a descendant of a more famous Mr. S—— who had been the subject of a book, albeit one commissioned by S——'s family, written by Henry James.

Hope and Abel had been interlopers, both dragged in tow by a roommate who had a father who had gone to Harvard with this S——. CeCe, born in Hong Kong (when her father had been a war correspondent in Vietnam) but of Japanese ancestry, had been there because her parents had crossed paths with this S——'s wife, first in Paris and later in London (her father circulated from bureau-chief post to bureau-chief post), and the wife had promised to entertain their daughter in Cambridge. Windsor Armstrong, whom Hope had met in Washington, had been there with her sister, whose name Hope could never remember. And the man who would help found the Lampadia Foundation, which would rescue elephants in Africa and children in Brazil and republish Machado de Assis, who had been at Harvard with S——, he, Bob Glynn, had been there as well. He was the one who had brought along the Armstrongs.

The rest of the group had been shiny, smug, and bright in the way one might expect of the sons and daughters of Harvard men who had graduated between the dropping of the atom bomb and the sparking of the Sexual Revolution. The progeny of a new modernity, having endured their parents' wild vacillations, bold experimentations, burgeoning wealth, and various therapies, had been almost jaded, over-entitled, oddly earnest, and definitely hungry.

They had swarmed the sideboard laden with savories prepared by S———'s Danish wife, a tiny woman with a blond
and silver bob who had been married to a famous photographer. With several of the young guests claiming to be aspiring
photographers, and all Harvard students of this ilk being bud-
ding philosophers, the conversation had quickly turned to Su-
san Sontag and her new book, *On Photography*.

Before too long, the wise wife had deftly redirected the conversation toward sculpture, her present husband's most famous ancestor having been a sculptor. Somewhere in the middle of that
discussion, Hope had stated that she had always been puzzled by
the black soldier depicted in the Confederate Memorial at Arlington National Cemetery.

Someone else had quickly explained it away by saying that
he must have been just some man sent to the war with his master, and Hope had said he looked like something else to her, a
Hatfield. Everybody had just stared for a moment, until she had
explained, "Hatfield, like Hatfields and McCoys. I'm from West
Virginia, y'all." When she had said that, everyone had laughed.

And Abel had fallen in love. He had been fifteen years old
the first time he had gone to Arlington National Cemetery, and
he had noticed that same black man. He had gone in a school
group, on his private high school's official Washington trip, to
see Kennedy's grave. After they had got through that, before
they could head for the gates, someone in the class had announced he had Confederate ancestors buried in the Confederate section. Then someone else had said he had one too. Before
they knew it the entire group had been heading toward the
Confederate Memorial. Abel too. Abel had refused to be so
typical a black and proud "Negro" as to say no. He had refused

to make his displeasure known. He wouldn't be scared off any acre or inch of the place. He would stick in the middle of the group. He would blend in, until he could safely vanish.

Walking around the base of the Confederate monument, Abel had first noticed the mammy, holding up the child to be kissed. The mammy had made Abel wince. Then he had seen the soldier—seen the soldier and known in that moment that he was to be a soldier.

After that it had taken him years to find Bob Shropshire, his favorite black Confederate; years to find his sharpshooter, his most effective black Confederate; years more to find his proof that the South would have won if they had only armed their blacks. But the wish for the knowledge had been born that day.

Later that week his class had visited the Pentagon, and Abel had made up his mind then and there that one day he would work inside the five-sided fortress.

And when Hope said, at the house on Beacon Hill, that she had seen his black Confederate, that she knew for sure, with certainty, when challenged, backed up by no facts, that his Confederate was a soldier and not a servant, Abel had known that one day he would marry Hope.

S——— himself had been enchanted. By Hope, and by Abel. By the fact that they all three of them knew the Confederate Memorial. He had known it because he'd known the sculptor, Moses Ezekiel. S——— had added that "piece to the puzzle," as he would later tell the tale at the wedding.

That day at lunch S——— had been thinking Abel and Hope might get to their second marriage the first time. To wave them on, S——— had told them tales of his ancestor's studio in Rome, of parties at his famous house. Parties attended by Moses Ezekiel, Edmonia Lewis, and, most fabulously, Moses's black daughter, Alice. *That was the kicker.*

None of them had forgotten that particular beef Wellington, that potage parisienne, that chocolate mousse, that Sunday lunch in September of 1977.

"For Christmas I gave Abel an out-of-print copy of *Dr. Dan.* I wonder if it's still in his old house," said Hope.

"The biography of Alice's husband? Abel gave it to me, when he married Sammie," said Nicholas.

"Why?" asked Hope.

"He said he was afraid Sammie might destroy anything you had given him," said Nicholas.

"That's why I was always terrified of her spending any time with Ajay," said Hope.

"Did he name the second of the girls Alice for Dr. Dan's wife?" asked Nicholas.

"Probably," said Hope.

"Nicola is named for me," said Nicholas.

"I didn't know that," said Hope.

"How long before Abel knew your father was white?" asked Nicholas.

"A good little while," said Hope.

"Why?" asked Nicholas.

"I was just so newly black. I didn't want anything to mess it up," said Hope, looking up.

"What do you mean 'newly black'?"

"My mother died when I was very young. She was black. My father was white. He raised me isolated in coal country.

When he died I was taken in by my black great-aunts who lived in D.C.," said Hope.

"When did you tell Abel about the rich part?"

"After the aunts died."

"So money was part of why he picked you?"

"And it was the sin he couldn't forgive."

"Rumor has it you've made a tidy profit eco-investing."

"I do all right."

"The sin he couldn't forgive wasn't yours; it was his."

"Wealth?"

"Jealousy."

It had been a good little while before Abel had known that Hope's father had been white, months into their courtship, after they had become lovers.

She had told him one afternoon when he'd found her in the African-American reading room in Lamont Library crying over Nella Larsen's *Passing*.

"I don't want to be some 'tragic mulatto.'"

"I am a tragic mulatto. You are a . . . my . . . Rebel Yeller."

She had fallen in love with him precisely, as precisely as he had coined the phrase, at the moment he had coined the phrase. Rebel Yeller.

Soon after that, they had gone down to Washington for the weekend to see the great-aunts who had raised Hope. He had imagined that her mother had been a well-loved but debauched maid who somehow had obtained a degree of respectability and some funds. He had imagined that Hope had attended St. Paul's as part of some ABC program. He had felt sorry for her. He had taken her to Arlington and shown her, again, the Confederate Memorial and reminded her of all they knew about Moses Ezekiel and Alice. Abel had feared Hope didn't believe her white father had loved her.

He hadn't been able to imagine anyone not loving Hope. And somehow the fact that he had snatched her from a white man, from her white father, from all the white boys who had had her—at St. Paul's and at Harvard—before she had fallen in love with him, was unspeakably sweet consolation for losses he would not name.

Walking together around the Confederate monument, they had first voiced their wish to spend the summer after their junior year together in Rome.

Two years later, when the wish had come true, he had spent his days preparing to write a thesis on the rise of fascism; she had spent hers rereading Hawthorne's *Marble Faun* and retracing the steps of Edmonia Lewis, the black sculptress. And Hope had begun to whittle little pieces.

Neither Hope nor Abel had got much work done. Instead they had drunk wine, eaten gelato, and walked around the city telling each other the stories they had told no one else.

He had told her about the Fantastic Four, the four young residents who had lived next door to him when he was a teenager—one from Waycross, Georgia; one from Opelika, Alabama; one from Mount Bayou, Mississippi; and one from Yazoo City, Mississippi—all named Daniel Hale. She had told him some about West Virginia—that she had been raised in Harper's Ferry—and then Washington. She had told him that her father had been some white guy who had disappeared. That she had always been black, had not started sorta being black away in boarding school and then arrived at Harvard just black; that she had never been exiled from the world of Storer College, from the bubble that is the world of historically black colleges, the buildings, the people who attend them, the people who teach in them, and the people who run them.

And so, ever after, when anyone had said Harper's Ferry, West Virginia, Abel hadn't thought of a crazy white man, John Brown, or of Heyward Shepherd, the first black casualty of the Civil War. He had thought about what he knew of Hope's family, of her grandparents Charles and Emmaline, who had taught at Storer, and whom Hope had hardly known but was able to construct quite vividly for Abel; the great-aunts who had raised her in Washington after her parents had died, whom Hope loved dearly with a love she feared Abel wouldn't share. She had kept their joys to herself.

He had borrowed a guitar and she had taught him three chords, and they had sat down and written a blues song called "Redboned Woman in a Bluestone House" and a protest song called "Buffalo Creek," about the mining disaster. He had played lead on his guitar and she had kept the rhythm on her banjo. That was the best work either of them had done that summer, except perhaps for her little whittles.

When they had put their guitar, their banjo, and their wine bottles down, when they were not walking and looking through the city holding hands, they were urgent and awkward in their search for sex. She kept reaching for his blackness and he kept reaching for her whiteness when he should have been reaching for her breast and she should have been reaching for his penis.

As Hope and Abel had wandered round S——'s rooms, imagining what Alice, the slave woman's daughter, had seen or done, and how she had been viewed and treated, they had understood themselves to be among the few or the only who cared that Edmonia Lewis's *Cleopatra* was finer than S———'s. Though Edmonia's sculpture would be lost and forgotten in barrooms and storage rooms, Hope and Abel would love it best, and Hope and Abel were among the few who tried to reconstruct just what might have happened to precipitate young Alice's return to America from Rome after eighteen months. Even as Hope withheld and left unspoken the story of the dark lady she loved deepest—her own mother, Canary—Hope and Abel would remember the other dark ladies of Rome. And Hope and Abel would imagine what Alice had made of her father being a white Confederate soldier—a Confederate soldier who had cared enough about his African daughter to send her to Rome and send her to Howard, or at least that's how the story went when Abel told it to Hope. Later, after telling her that story, he would serenade her to sleep, singing "My Creole Belle."

By the end of the summer they were not living in Rome; they were living in Hope and Abel Land. And they didn't need their hands to give each other best gifts. He had found her breast and she had found his penis and they had found love.

Senior year they had both been busy writing, catching up on the work they hadn't done in Rome. Diploma in hand, he had headed for law school, down to North Carolina and Duke. She, not knowing what she wanted to do, had gone to work for a senator from West Virginia. He'd been surprised she had the connections to grab that plum. They'd broken up.

High blood pressure had taken the aunts, who had not liked swallowing pills. Stroke had taken one; heart attack had taken the other just days later. Hope had buried them both the same day. She had called Abel and asked him to come to be with her. He hadn't. The old lovers were no longer friends.

Eventually, Abel had gone to Washington for a New Year's party. Fortunately, or unfortunately, Hope had been invited to the same party. They had avoided each other all the night but couldn't avoid talking when they found themselves alone in the same cold gravel parking lot waiting for the rest of the small group that had hiked the towpath on New Year's Day. Nor could she avoid him in the way-backseat of a Volvo station wagon, squashed into his lap, on the crushed drive to the downtown hot tubs, Making Waves. In the chlorine-scented darkness their fingers had brushed and he had looked so like her that she had believed she could be swept into a southern family and belong; he had believed he could be swept into all her big-world wildness and get free. They had made a date for the next night.

He was still broke from Christmas, from trying to trick the only people who knew for sure he was poorer than a church mouse, his mama and his daddy, Antoinette and Big Abel, into believing that small sparkling presents—a money clip and a gold locket— meant prosperity, not lack of sense and a willingness to sell your blood.

Wanting to treat Hope to a memorable meal, he went round to the fancy grocery store his friends from Washington talked about, Neam's, and purchased a fancy loaf of bread, wishing he could afford a jar of caviar—wishing that he had saved the best gift for the one who was most dear to him. Abel never did that. He saved his best gifts for whoever needed the most persuading.

Loaf under his arm, he walked down to Cannons Fish Market

and bought a few dollars' worth of fresh mussels. His hands were no longer empty.

In a borrowed kitchen, he scrubbed the black shells clean with his toothbrush, then boiled them until they popped open. He threw the steamed mussels into a baggie and wrapped the baggie in tinfoil. Throwing the foil packet into a paper bag with the bread and a fifth of Jack Daniel's, Abel was proud of his feast.

He waited in a borrowed car in a dark that had arrived so early it could rightly have been accused of having stolen the remains of the day, waited in front of the house she rented with friends who were also working on the Hill, waited until she tapped lightly on the car door.

He rolled down the window and she kissed his cheek, then twirled that prep-school-girl look-at-me twirl in funny vintage white go-go boots and black tights and a tweed coat. When she turned her face back to his, and he looked into her dark eyes and she looked into his, she saw that he saw she was more beautiful than any other creature on earth; he saw that she saw they were almost exactly alike.

She tugged at the scarf round his neck, she pulled his face toward hers, and then she kissed him.

By the time she ran round to her car door, he could hardly breathe. He wished he had brought his asthma inhaler. But he didn't tell her that. He told her where they were going. She told him to stop the car. She ran back into her house. When she came out again she was wearing a black mink coat. She looked like the most magnificent bear.

Some snow was on the ground when they walked into Rock Creek Cemetery. In the shadow of the monument (called by locals *Grief*, called by its creator, Saint-Gaudens, *The Mystery of the Hereafter and The Peace of God That Passeth Understanding*) that Henry Adams had placed on the grave of his photographer-socialite wife, who had committed suicide by drinking photographic developing chemicals, Abel asked Hope to marry him just after he came in her mouth and she swallowed.

She should have run. In years to come, she would wonder why she hadn't. When she recalled the scene to the front of her mind to reimagine it, he was left alone, her mother's black mink coat on the ground and her footprints, tiny size-six boots, marking the dark path of her escape.

But that wasn't what she had done. It had been so strange him walking her into that cemetery, so muddled his wanting to show her that monument, so real all the statues they had seen, that she had just had to reach for his scarf again, pull his face to hers again, take him by the hand, take off her coat, lay it like a blanket on the ground, take his hand and put it on her breast, then rock him like her back had no bone.

She had liked the view she had had of the stars when she'd been lying on her back looking up with him on top of her. On top of her he had liked the smell of the earth.

They had thought they could cheat death. She had been so hungry for everything he had wanted to escape and so she had invited it all in—all his junk and all his beauty. He had never before felt and would never again feel so welcome. Not even the afternoon in Baguio, in the shower after tennis, in the hills of the Philippines, when they had made Ajay.

TWELVE

H E GRADUATED LAW school in May of 1984. "We were
engaged in July. One September later we were married,"
said Hope.

"He once told me freedom had a specific flavor," said
Nicholas.

"What did he say it tasted like?" asked Hope.

"Mrs. Abel Jones," said Nicholas.

"Was he talking about me or Sammie?" asked Hope.

"Don't be a bitch. Where was the wedding?" asked Nicholas.

"St. John's Lafayette Square," said Hope.

"Church of Presidents," said Nicholas.

"Where but," said Hope.

Abel and Hope had been married at St. John's Church,
Lafayette Square, an eighteenth-century gold-domed Episcopal
church just across from the White House. Thurgood Marshall,
a close friend of Abel's family, had attended the service and
later had sent a Waterford pitcher to decorate the new home.

She had told Abel that she was rich and they had had the

harder conversation about wills and trusts, which meant he wasn't rich but their children would be. He hadn't seemed to mind.

Some of Hope's friends from St. Paul's had come, and a very few of her father's friends from Exeter. There'd been a divided phalanx of Harvard folk—his Finals Club people and her Institute of Politics and *Crimson* buddies. And her cousin Hat from up on the mountain had come to walk her down the aisle. Gordon Lyle, one of her father's Exeter buddies and an old China hand who had begun his career in Hong Kong when Vietnam had been the problem of the day, had dashed over from the White House on a bicycle.

Lyle's wife had sent a little blue and white teapot decorated with Chinese characters, as if she'd known the young couple would soon be headed for Asia, but there wasn't a way for them to know that already, or at least there wasn't a way of which Hope had been aware on that day.

Their gift had been an interesting departure from the mounting collection of large and dramatic silver-plated trays, which would have constituted decorative bric-a-brac for most young couples but which Hope would put to hard and regular use in Abel's new world.

The senior senator from West Virginia, Hope's about-to-be-former boss, had broken from the pack and sent a porcelain cake plate that had looked too fragile for the life Abel and Hope had been headed into. Like Hope, the plate would make it across the world and back, little worse for visible wear, but there would be a crack.

The near-ancient black Baptist minister who had married Abel's parents and the young black Episcopal priest whom

Hope and Abel knew from Harvard and who had prepared Abel and Hope for marriage had flanked the unflappable Reverend Harper, who had given no indication, as he had gone about the Lord's work, that the 1815 edifice was not daily inhabited by a tribe of southern black poets, politicos, and preachers.

With a former ambassador, a White House aide, a Supreme Court justice, and a senator studding the crowd of professors, preachers, doctors, and lawyers, more than one of the brilliant and brown of the dearly beloved filling the pews (forming, for this day, a predominantly black but integrated congregation) had been shouting inside their head the words to an old cigarette commercial, "You've come a long way, baby."

One dowager dragon had whispered, behind her perfectly manicured espresso-colored hand, into the beige ear of the young matron beside her, all the while keeping her amber eyes turned toward the crew of clerics waiting at the altar. She had stated plainly, if quietly, "It's not Abel and Hope getting married, it's our South to their America."

When the first chords of Vivaldi's "Trumpet Voluntary" had sounded, everybody had stood to welcome the bride. Cousin Hat, sober and trembling in a new blue suit, and perceived by many to be a light-skinned black man, had given Hope away.

After the service, which had begun as the last bell of noon had rung and had ended before the strike of one, the guests had been herded onto rented yellow school buses that would carry them to the reception. Everyone had got the joke.

Thrown together on the black vinyl seats, everybody had talked with everybody, the people from Washington hearing how it was in the hinterlands; the people from the hinterlands hearing what was about to come down from Washington; everyone agreeing they had done their share of good work—that the young couple was proof. It had been a good day.

And things had only got better at the Cosmos Club. The menu had included shrimp étouffée, jambalaya, *pain perdu*, and French champagne and American cake. The cake, made with organic flour and eggs and real butter, had glowed the palest yellow that isn't white. It had been perfect. The groom's cake had been a perfect full-scale replica of a backgammon board.

As jeroboams of champagne had been drained, negritude had given way to creolization. Guests had danced and guzzled and snuck off to have their picture taken with the sign that proclaimed, MEMBERS AND THEIR MALE GUESTS ONLY. In this crowd that sign was an issue.

When people recalled anything bad about the wedding they would recall the sign; then that, too, was forgotten when the Cosmos Club inducted its first woman. Mainly everyone recalled Abel replying "Absolutely," not "I will," when asked, "Do you take this woman?"

To be dancing in the ballroom of the Cosmos Club on that Saturday afternoon in 1985 as Big Abel danced with his new daughter-in-law or as Abel danced with his new bride was to be convinced that Lyndon Johnson was the greatest president who had ever lived—that his dream of a Great Society had become a reality.

The time for Abel and Hope to cut the cake had come almost too soon. Bride and groom had each taken a demure bite from a single slice on a glass plate. The recipe was from an earlier era, an era so far back that few present remembered—a time before hand mixers and measuring cups, from back when some women knew and loved their way around their kitchens and their homes, from back before the black South had been defeated. It was the kind of cake black women bake for their families on special occasions and never, no matter how well they might be paid, for the families of white women. It was an old recipe of the aunts.

A few of the older ladies had wrapped their slice of cake up in their napkin, remembering being young women who had slept with a sliver of equally dense wedding cake beneath their pillow, hoping to see in dreams the face of the one they would one day love, men they had now put in their grave.

Slipping a bit of Able and Hope's cake onto their tongue or a slice into their purse, or a bit into their pocket, had been a moment to forgive the old dead Texan, the thirty-sixth president, who had begun his career with stuffed ballot boxes.

Abel and Hope had walked (she in her going-away outfit, a green and black corduroy dress with a black hat complete with veil; he in a gray silk suit and patterned orange Hermès tie) toward the limousine that would whisk them off, getting pelted with birdseed. As they had folded themselves into the stretch Cadillac that would take them to the airport, they had looked good enough to stand atop any bright tiered cake.

They had taken a ridiculously expensive first-class flight to Boston on a plane so small it had barely had a first-class section. The stewardess had poured them cheap champagne and announced the wedding over the loudspeaker. This, for Abel, had made the journey worth the price of the ticket.

Mr. and Mrs. Abel Jones the third had spent the first night of their honeymoon at the Ritz, in the presidential suite, a large and then-shabby room with wonderful windows that had looked out onto their rosy future and the Boston Common.

After love and breakfast they had lit out, as they'd put it, to see the territory. Which of them was Huck and which of them was Jim they didn't bother to declare. Their raft was a rented green Porsche convertible.

With the first picture Hope had ever seen of herself in the pages of the *New York Times* on her lap, Abel and his bride had headed for Martha's Vineyard and for marriage.

Abel had known that Hope had no real idea why they were honeymooning in New England. It wasn't cheap, it wasn't easy, and possibly it wasn't romantic. Except it was romantic that she had let him completely plan the honeymoon, much as he had let her completely plan the wedding.

He had intended to celebrate the conservative conventions; she had intended to celebrate his black beauty and brilliance.

They didn't know this. It was a honeymoon.

THIRTEEN

THE PIG FEET weren't out yet, at Silver Sands, but Hope could smell them cooking. The people who didn't have early jobs to get to but needed breakfast before breakfast stopped being served were starting to drift in. All but one of the tables were full; there was about to be a line. It was time to leave if Hope and Nicholas weren't buying more food.

They had a place to go. Hope still had a key to Abel's old house. A large red painted-brick structure, it stood a stone's throw from a gate of Fisk. Two stories tall, and it had five pillars, not out in the front, but off to the side. In the front it had a kind of bay window that jutted out in three sharp angles.

Hope was pointing to the bay window as Nicholas fiddled with the key in the lock.

"Abel was terrified of this bay window when he was a boy. He thought this was where the bomb would come in," said Hope.

"Like they bombed Z. Alexander Looby's house?" asked Nicholas.

"He told you about that?" asked Hope.

"More than once," said Nicholas.

Now Hope was pointing to the much smaller house next door, a Victorian with a basketball court out back.

"That's where Waycross lived when he was at medical school."

Finally, the key turned and the door was opened. Inside the house, time had been slowed in about 1970 and had come to a halt in about 1980. Explaining that the home décor owed much to the pages of *Southern Living* in the seventies, Hope led Nicholas through the rooms as if she were taking him on a historic-house tour. Then she explained that *Southern Living* was a lifestyle magazine out of Birmingham, Alabama.

Gesturing with an upturned palm, Nicholas suggested Hope take a seat on the parlor sofa, and she did. He sat beside her. "Is there any whiskey?" he asked, and she was up again making her way to the bar in the kitchen.

Hope found a half-full bottle of Gentleman Jack and two jelly glasses. Then she joined Nicholas on the sofa. From the breast pocket of his jacket, he took out a stack of photographs and laid them down on the table as if he were playing eccentric solitaire, three rows of three.

The pictures—photographs—were disturbing and familiar. Naked men, dogs, leashes, piles of bodies, simulated sex acts, a uniformed smiling soldier, hoods, framed in a neat white border.

"Abu Ghraib?"

"Abu Ghraib."

"What do they have to do with me?"

"My question exactly."

"Nothing."

"Nothing?"

"Nothing."

Hope hoped she was telling the truth. Seeing Nicholas pull the pictures out of his inside jacket pocket, seeing the images as photographs touched by fingertips, not beaming from a computer screen or glossy in a magazine or flat in a newspaper, brought the poses closer, alarmingly close. Seeing them on Abel's cocktail table was painful. Seeing them after having listened so recently to Tess and Pinagrew talk about Abel and dogs it was especially painful.

Right after the pictures from Abu Ghraib had been published, Hope had had to schedule extra sessions with her shrink. They hadn't got very far and then she had lost interest. Her interest was returning.

"I can't know this, Nicholas," said Hope.

"Why?" asked Nicholas.

"Ajay," said Hope.

Nicholas didn't have an answer for this. He had thought of the question but he hadn't thought of an answer.

Nicholas took out his pack of cigarettes, Gauloises. As he tapped one out and started to light it, Hope pointed to the front door. She stacked up the pictures and handed them back to him. He slid them back into his breast pocket and headed for the front door. He had pushed her too hard and too quickly. He had forgotten how strong she was and how cold she could be. As if she could read his mind she said, "You've forgotten what a mama is."

Hope found her way up the stairs and into Abel's room. All four walls were lined floor to ceiling with books. There was an extra-long single bed. At the foot of the bed was a desk. Beside the desk was a nightstand. There was a closet with a mirror on the door. She lay down on Abel's bed. The pillows smelled like him.

She was surprised. She wondered how often Abel had come to the house. As she settled herself into Abel's pillows, she felt herself growing intimate with the dead. She closed her eyes to intensify the feeling, then she opened her eyes to see what he had seen from his pillow. Hanging from a pushpin stuck in one of the bookcase shelves was a little plane, the plane she had made him—she didn't remember exactly when—a replica of the one flown by Lauro de Bosis.

She was sitting cross-legged on Abel's bed with that plane on her lap when Nicholas, carrying the Gentleman Jack and the jelly glasses under his arms, walked in without knocking. He put the glasses and the bottle on the desk.

"I think Abel named his first daughter, Laura, for Lauro."

"I used to call Abel Icarus."

"Neoconservatism gave him wings?"

"Something like that."

"And the second President Bush was the sun he flew too close to?"

"Or, his conscience came back."

Abel had named his first daughter, Laura, for Lauro de Bosis, a charming unfortunate who (on October 3, 1931, after flying above and papering with antifascist pamphlets the Spanish Steps and much of central Rome) had vanished: into midair, or into the sea, or crashed to earth and obliteration; or, mayhap, had glided to a quiet shore and simply chosen to abandon lover, mother, sibs, and friends.

History records, if you exclude the reports in the fascist papers, that except for his poetry, Lauro was never heard from again.

"He told me he was taking you to Rome to patch things up."
"We stayed at the wrong hotel."

Lauro's act, the overly dramatic, silly gesture of an embarrassed son betrayed by an enchanting mother—she had written a groveling letter to Mussolini—had appealed to Abel mightily.

The part Abel had seemed to like best was not the thing that had happened, but the thing that had unhappened: The significance of Lauro's parents, Adolpho and Lillian, had been diminished. They had been rather famous and acknowledged to be glamorous, but over time they had come to be known, when they were remembered at all, as mere relations of the bold antifascist and ardent lover Lauro.

By a failed feat of sufficient imagination and bravado, the father had been eclipsed, and the son was to be remembered.

For Abel, who had shivered long in the chill shadow of paternal imminence, this flavor of gone-from-the-face-of-the-earth had been indescribably delicious. He had wanted to gorge on it. Or so it had seemed to Hope, when Abel had told her the story sitting in the café with a view of the Spanish Steps where he had attempted to woo her to remain in the life they had chosen, when they had returned to Rome one last time to talk about divorce or fall in love again.

On that trip, out of the blue, Abel had quoted to Hope fragments of a poem by Jacopo Sannazzaro that was supposed to have something to do with Lauro, and with Abel and Hope:

Happy the man who meets with such a fate
And by his death obtains so great a prize!

The days after death are filled with dreams. The night after Abel
died, Hope dreamed that the pilots Lauro had rented his wings
from had lied when they'd stated to the police investigators that
they hadn't been informed of his intentions when he had rented
the plane. She dreamed that the pilots had known what Lauro
had been planning to do and they had filled his tanks with extra
fuel, and that Lauro had made it to North Africa.

On the day after the presumed death of Lauro de Bosis, a copy
of a letter Lauro had written, titled, then mailed before rushing
skyward toward the center of Rome and oblivion appeared
in a Rome paper. He had called it "The Story of My Death."
Lauro had effectively seized the last word.

Abel had believed in the possibility that Lauro was alive.
Hope hadn't. According to Hope, if Lauro had been alive he
would have returned to his woman, Ruth Draper. Ruth had
died manless. To Hope, Abel's arguing that Lauro was alive had
just been a way of playing *torture wife*, not a true conviction. To
her mind, Abel's belief that Lauro could be alive but not return
to Ruth Draper was vicious love-blindness.

If Lauro were alive, Hope had thought and said, he would
have returned to the woman he could suckle and fuck, to the
second of his two *caramadres*, Ruth Draper. And Hope had feared
anew Abel's ignorance of heart-chivalry.

Lauro had been not a little in love with his mother. In Ruth
Draper, an actress seventeen years his senior, he had found an
outlet for that ripe passion.

And Ruth had wanted him—boy and man. His passion for her—she would describe him as the most ardent lover she had ever known—had split her life, as his hips had split her legs (she had been forty-one when they'd met), right down the middle. He had plunged firmly into her pierced but unbroken center. Then he had vanished.

Icarus. Jesus. It was occurring to Hope to associate her first husband's evolving infatuation with Christianity with his affinity for sons who abscond with their father's power. God may have created the world, but Abel's world was fixated on Jesus. His red words in the Bible. A funky bracelet on a child's wrist: WWJD? What would Jesus do? Something radical. Something perhaps even God wouldn't understand.

Underlying the fervently Jesus-centered faith of the Promise Keepers was a fear of God the father.

Promise Keepers resolved this fear, and perhaps a few oedipal anxieties, by asserting that the father's time was plain over. Hope told Nicholas about men by the stadium-ful flocking to hear charismatic preachers deliver, under the rubric of "Biblical Manhood," variations on the theme.

Prompted to remember that Abel had been standing in the crowd when evangelical Christian men—five hundred thousand strong—had rallied round the Washington Monument by a photograph of the event sitting prominently on his desk, Hope and Nicholas shook their heads.

"Their question isn't 'Is God dead?' " said Nicholas.

"Their question is 'Why won't God die and give us a turn?' " said Hope.

"I wish Abel had been kind enough to leave us a 'Story of My Death,'" said Nicholas.

"I wish he hadn't tried to get Ajay to wear one of those WWJD bracelets," said Hope.

Eventually, Abel's Christianity had been less about the triumph of sons over fathers and more about the movement to the authority of a society of men, the Apostles, above the rule of one man, Jesus, than it had been about forgiveness and tomorrow. It had been more about the abandoned baby in the manger with no human father at all than about the man hanging on the cross, certain he would soon be with his father. It had been about flying too close to the sun with wings that did not melt, and thereby gaining the sky.

"Il mourut poursuivant une haute advanture." Nicholas was reading out loud the words Hope had painted onto the wing of the plane she had whittled for Abel.

Nicholas knew the poem the line on the wing came from: *Icare*, written by Philippe Desportes in the sixteenth century. He remembered the bit more of it Abel had long ago recited to him:

> Icare est cheut icy, le jeune audacieux,
> Qui pour voler au ciel eut assez de courage:
> Icy tomba son corps degarny de plumage,
> Laissant tous braves coeurs de sa cheute envieux.

Bad as her French was, Hope understood enough to translate all of that to the question, How wide is Abel's tomb?

Even as death reframed all the events of Abel's life, Hope had a growing sense that death did not completely contain him. Surprising ripples were felt. The peculiar wildness and originality of his death underlined her forgotten awareness of the peculiar wildness and originality of the man.

"Why did you show me the pictures?"

"I wanted to know if you recognized anything."

"Like what?"

"I feared I recognized a signature."

"Feared."

"I didn't want my darling to have done that."

"I don't want Ajay's daddy to have done that."

Nicholas took the plane from Hope's hand. He sat in the old desk chair. He poured them both a drink.

"Then you were a 'dependent spouse.'"

"A shocking title for me."

"Married to an intelligence officer."

"A fact I didn't know at the time. Did he ever talk to you about when we lived in Old Town?"

"He told me about Philoctete, and the day he told you about Manila, and about onion tarts."

"Lord, have mercy, *today*."

"But mainly he talked about your Christmas in Rome."

FOURTEEN

ON SEPTEMBER 15, 1985, they were in the State Department's A-100 class. Hope lasted three days tagging along as a dependent spouse before realizing that her presence was tolerated but not required. She stopped going to class, but she still drove in with Abel to the office so that she could have the car.

By the end of the first week they had been chosen to house-sit for an ambassador who lived in the Old Town section of Alexandria, Virginia. She attempted to fill her days with her new and still novel domestic duties and with light-of-day Stoli martinis when she didn't have too far to drive.

It was a busy and expensive first fall. They had agreed to spend only one hundred dollars on birthday presents. They would splurge on a long weekend in Europe for Christmas but they would try to live much of their life on his salary. On Hope's birthday Abel had given her a box full of hair ribbons. On his birthday, Hope gave Abel a *National Geographic Atlas of the World*. They savored their frugality.

★   ★   ★

They landed in Florence and it was more of a honeymoon than their two weeks in Massachusetts had been. They stayed in the Hotel Tornabuoni Beacci, a place where, they decided, the Brownings had stayed—and they agreed with each other that both Elizabeth Barrett and Robert Browning had been black.

Hope gave Abel the little copy of *Sonnets from the Portuguese* that her mother had given her father, and that her father had given Hope.

She showed Abel where her father had underlined the words that her mother had woven into her wedding ceremony, "I love thee freely, as men strive for Right" and "A place to stand and love in for a day." Abel asked Hope why they hadn't used the same words in their wedding. Hope confessed she had thought they might be bad luck. She was thinking about her mother's death in Rome but she still wasn't speaking of it. Abel said he preferred the words she had chosen anyway. Then he took out the fancy fountain pen she had given him as an engagement present and underlined twice the words they had spoken, "I love thee to the depth and breadth and height my soul can reach."

They had a cocktail near a tree Hope had planted in a hotel roof garden as a baby girl and she told him the story her father had told her, about her mother decorating a tiny live tree in their room with earrings, heavy and shiny with precious and semiprecious stones; and she told him about another year with CeCe when they had decorated a larger tree with Lifesavers and foil-covered chocolate candy.

Abel loved the stories about Christmas in Italy so much that she didn't tell him Christmas in Italy was how her mother had died.

She wasn't sure if she didn't tell Abel because she was afraid he would no longer be able to boast, "My wife's family *Christmased* in Florence," or because she feared that even after he knew, he might be able to boast with undisturbed pride, "We always cook Italian food for Christmas; it reminds Hope of Christmasing in Florence as a child."

She hated those stories the way he hated the double strand of fake black South Sea pearls that she thought were real. He loved the stories like she loved that necklace.

They ran down to Rome, took ecstasy, romped for a day and a half, and thought they would be in love forever.

She had stared at one, then another inch of him; she had been deliciously amazed. She lay naked in a claw-foot tub of cool water, thinking slowly, turning over harder and harder remembered visions, as all fractured into color and shape, and as tinier and tinier bits formed into larger and larger and more beautiful and more colorful patterns. Any pain she had ever experienced was now fractured and vanquished and returned to her as glowing jewels of now and know—joy past pain. Her mind was like a kaleidoscope. She lay back in a chipped tub, arms draped over the side toward the dull floor, a window open to the street, and she was thanking heaven for 1985 and friends, and ecstasy and mommies, even if they died, and daddies even if they killed people, and for husbands and vaginas, and for the very spit on her tongue. That December in Rome she accepted all of it—thanks to a pharmacological wedding gift from the best of Abel's Duke law school friends.

FIFTEEN

W HEN SHE PULLED up to the agreed-upon corner not at the agreed-upon time, in their tiny tan Ford Escort, that mid-December in 1985, Abel was standing, slightly slumped, stomping his fleece-lined duck boots into the concrete sidewalk. Snowflakes fell on his tweed-covered shoulders and on his bare head.

"Now comes the big lie," said Nicholas.
    "And so many little ones with it," said Hope.

Watching her young and new husband from across the intersection, waiting for the red light to turn green, Hope had imagined for the very first time a son, a boy with sherry-colored eyes and dark hair and full sweet lips.

Abel was a beautiful man. She remembered seeing it, his beauty, clearly in the gray light of the streetlamp that December evening. The rush she felt was akin to coming upon a lost and valued item in an unexpected place at an unexpected time, long after hope for recovery had past. An inch over six feet, well muscled, with dark-amber-colored eyes, an aquiline nose, and exquisitely sculpted Greek lips, Abel was crowned not with a wreath of laurel, but with close-cropped curly dark hair that had sprouted preternaturally, at twenty-six, four or five silver hairs.

Whenever Hope noticed his silver kinks she shivered. The silver hairs on his head reminded her of the three silver hairs that had appeared south of her belly button. They each of them had their worries.

She was not late accidentally. Puttering around Alexandria, fluttering and dithering about the Federal-style town house where she spent her days ironing napkins and shirts and making dinner and feeding the pets and making the bed and worrying about what she would cook her new husband for breakfast, then dinner, then wondering where she would walk on her own for her lunch—between all that and going to the grocery store, Hope searched for the life she had misplaced, the self she had lost without warning or fanfare.

Or perhaps there had been fanfare. The trumpet voluntary. With her opportunities limited to "rush toward Abel" and "be dragged behind him" it was hard to make a choice, any choice, including "What time shall I leave to pick my husband up from work?"

And she wanted to make him wait for her, wanted to control the timing of some small event in their lives, to feel something of her old power, to remind him that she was the ladder and when the ladder got knocked out the man standing on it fell.

She was a trophy wife of a very particular persuasion. He loved having a stay-at-home wife, a woman with a Harvard degree, ironing his undershorts and his shirts; he loved having something his white and northern peers would never have because white

Ivy-educated girls were past (having seen their mothers entombed and having witnessed their mothers' revolutions), way past, dreams of isolated homes as castles.

She had propped him up high, she would prop him up higher, she would be his high horse, his stepping stone, his ladder—but as he understood it, then, she wanted him to adore her for it. He couldn't. He wanted to find all of that inevitable.

She had chosen the wrong day to make him wait. She could see it through the windshield and across the cold air, in his posture a slump-shouldered but high-chinned resignation. He looked too changed.

The light turned green. As she began to accelerate through the intersection she was glad that she had dressed as he would have wanted to see her dressed, in gray wool pants, a red turtleneck, and a cream-colored fisherman's sweater. She thought of telling a lie, of saying that she had been stuck in traffic, or that she had taken a wrong turn trying to take a shortcut. She didn't. Those days they told the truth whenever they could.

She pulled up to the curb beside Abel. His face was red, she supposed from the bite of the wind. Usually he came to the driver side and waited for her to run round to the passenger door and let herself in before he settled into the driver's seat. That night he just opened the passenger door and slid in beside her quietly, unexpectedly, like husbands sometimes slip into sleeping wives.

They hadn't gone half a block when he realized his door wasn't completely shut. He cussed the weather as he slammed the door hard, leaning his head toward the cold window instead of leaning in for a kiss.

Everything was wrong. There was a baby softness in his face

she had never seen before; his smile looked premature. His chiseled lips, engorged, perhaps from crying, appeared like plump bumpers between the world and his throat. It occurred to her to wonder if he had just swallowed, or choked, or retched. What she could see for sure was this: sometime between the time she had dropped him off in the morning outside the Crystal City outpost of the State Department where he daily took instruction, in she didn't know quite what, and the time she had pulled up to the corner of Roxindale Avenue and Kefauver Place, he had lost a skin. She was sorrier than sorry that she was late.

The young bride wasn't ready, was no longer ready, to injure her groom. She was spooked.

And she didn't know it. She didn't know that she was driving into a scene constructed to elicit her sympathy and mute her hypervigilance. His defeat had been coached. She was walking into a sweet-as-arsenic lie.

He said they were going to the Philippines. He said he hadn't been given any of the posts he had requested, that he wasn't getting to learn Chinese or Arabic, that they were headed almost immediately for Manila. His flat voice begged for pity.

She had none to give. No pity for herself; no pity for him. She had something: a towering hopefulness that things would work out. She had a faith, which she tried to disguise and feminize in a ditzy mantra of "When life sends you lemons, squeeze them in your sweet tea and thank God you were born southern." She believed herself to be a find-a-way, make-a-way, or die-trying woman.

She had that and it tethered her to him. He loved the gray slacks. He loved the red turtleneck. He loved the fisherman's sweater. She was classic and exotic. She was so far from the blues, and so far from irony, she was unlike any black, brown, yellow, or white girl he had known. He liked that best.

She's my Alka-Seltzer: plop, plop, fizz, fizz, o-o-o what a relief she is. That's what he had been thinking as he'd walked down the left aisle of St. John's Lafayette Square toward the one white priest sandwiched between two black ones. Just before the chords of Vivaldi's "Trumpet Voluntary" had filled the sanctuary he had thought: *I have dropped effervescent intellect into the half-empty glass of my life and soon my cup will runneth over.* As he had stood at the altar with James Hall, waiting for Hope to come down the aisle in her grandmother Emmaline's gown, those had been the words in his head.

And there was the thing that Abel liked best about her, the thing he was counting on: dust, or shit, or mud, she could change all that to black gold. She could change an asshole into a penis. Erotic alchemy. She would transform him into someone wonderful, someone commensurate with her capacity for making dreams go real.

"Nothing on your list?"

"They called me in and asked if I would take Manila."

He said it as if he were saying, they called me in and asked me if I couldn't please sit in the back of the bus, told me that all the buses were going to the same place at the same time and it was too much trouble for everybody, for anybody to make trouble. If he would suck it up and sit in the back of the bus everyone would get where they were going. Eventually. He spoke in a way, hanging his head down low, contrived to provoke Hope into thinking all of that.

"Manila."

"Manila."

She didn't really know where the Philippines were more specifically than somewhere on the other edge of the earth, somewhere in Asia, somewhere not Europe or Africa or America, and not China or Japan. All she knew about the Philippines the day they were assigned was that it was a place maids came from and where soldiers served. She imagined it like some giant West Texas army base.

No Chinese lessons, no Arabic, no Guangzhou, no Ankara, no Istanbul, no place anyone would want to come and visit, or anyone would want to live. Manila. It was like being assigned to McDonald's. She'd rather face the open toilets and the strange food in South China. It was a second blow.

The first had been the list itself. No London, no Paris, no Rome. It was what the State Department called a hard-language list, full of postings that required Chinese, Arabic, Hindi, and maybe Russian—a job list top to bottom of hardship posts with hardship pay. Manila was one of these. For Abel and Hope it was the bottom of a bad list. Manila had not made their short list.

She had imagined being sent off to London, or Rome, when she had imagined herself a diplomat's wife: a chic young woman, in some chic old place, husband and wife, broke and brilliant somewhere with a culture she could immerse herself in and learn; a culture that would entice her to go native and abandon her old and contradictory cultures of origin, perhaps even discover that her own cultures were inferior, or better still, reconciled. She sought a city where they, Abel and Hope, together, could represent what it was to be American, even if he had never felt fully American in America.

Identity arbitrage. She almost told him he should quit. Almost reminded him he didn't need the job. She didn't say this, though, mainly because she didn't want to make it harder for him to do what he wanted to do: accept his first honors, and his first duties. She loved him that much.

He had been chosen to represent his country. He would be the face of America for foreigners. He liked that. He liked it a lot. There was a simple irony in the thing that enticed him at the beginning and consoled him to the end. And the Department had chosen him blindly, based on the Foreign Service Test. He liked that too. He wanted to believe that meritocracy and level playing fields were the American way. That was the mantra he had chanted to himself every morning for a year when he had read, from first page to last, the first section of the *New York Times* in preparation for the entrance exam.

One way of looking at it was that Abel and Hope had found themselves side by side, but one was moving in one direction, toward the large world, and one was moving in the other, toward the South. For a moment they were side by side in the same place and the future outstretched before them was alluring and obtainable.

All she could think about as she attempted to steer the car back to Alexandria through the rain and traffic was the little blue and white china teapot the Lyles had given them with Chinese characters written all over it and how she had secretly doubted Abel's ability to learn Chinese. She feared that doubt had cursed them. It wasn't that he was not smart; it was that he was undisciplined and easily bored, or so she believed. She had wished for a posting where he could succeed. *Be careful what you wish for.*

And now they were leaving in February, almost immediately, too soon.

She had expected a year or more of hard-language study, a year and a half probably because he wouldn't pass his language tests the first time, a year and a half of getting to know this man she had married and of saying good-bye to the city where she had started her life as a more expected kind of black person. She had wanted to see the city while hanging on his arm, hiding behind his back, peering over his shoulder, but now that was something she thought she would do later—but she never did it at all.

They would return to live in Washington, return for their halcyon time in the federal city, but that would be after. After two armed marines, sent to fetch them and shuttle them home safely, had found them walking arm in arm, oblivious, in Manila outside the CCP Main Building, still talking about *Tokyo Story*, the Ozu classic film they had both managed to previously miss. After they had feigned, each to the other, their shock at having missed the film previously, they didn't have to fake being pleased that their chosen life had demanded that they see it now. After the marines had shuttled them from the movie theater back to Sea Front on the night the People Power Revolution had begun. After they had broken curfew to leave the compound and dance at the Playboy Club till dawn, into the first morning of the Revolution. After Abel had been called to the palace to help pack the Marcoses up and move them out. After he had been one of the ones standing by as the Marcoses had boarded the helicopter, checking, he had teased, to make sure they hadn't tried to pack up any of General Yamashita's gold. After she had wandered around for ten days with her wedding silver in her purse, in case of quick evacuation; after the Marcoses had left and she and Abel had started weekending in Baguio, once spending a house party weekend at the ambassador's residence with the sultan of Brunei. After she had missed so many occasions to see what he was really about. After all of that, they would be back in Washington, she would have a baby, and he would be learning French, a language (and an easy language) at last, and they would be going down to Martinique.

The next time she returned to Washington to live with Abel she didn't look, or feel, or think, back toward Alexandria or even LeDroit Park; she just started a new life in a different enclave, in Georgetown. She succeeded in putting out of her mind all she had seen in the Philippines. As a young Georgetown matron she would take her baby for walks in Dumbarton Oaks and go to the same early-morning aerobics classes as Sandra Day O'Connor at a dance studio called Somebodies. But that baby had yet to be conceived. She had to not flip out the night they were assigned to Manila for Ajay to get born.

She had to close her eyes to follow him. And stop her ears. She closed her eyes and stopped her ears. She wanted to follow him. And he looked so good to her. And he played so well with her.

Hope believed everybody black enjoying all the new opportunities of being young, gifted, and black owed a debt to the youngest black southerners whose childhoods had been slaughtered by the march to freedom. She accepted the responsibility of providing compensation.

She was twenty-six years old and she thought she knew how to give them both back their innocence. She would have his baby.

The night they got their first tour assignment, before everything that came after, they drove the rest of the way to Alexandria, toward their first neighborhood and their first home, in silence.

The Gabbons would have to find someone else to take care of Philoctete, the huge rottweiler; someone else to use the silver and the china, to change the cat boxes, and walk the dog, and play house in their exquisite home; someone else to make the onion tart Mrs. Gabbon had taught Hope, the onion tart she had served in posts around the world, the onion tart that Hope would cook in Manila and in Martinique, though she didn't know that yet.

The house was beautiful. The kitchen and dining room were on the floor below street level; the kitchen was tiny and tidy, with green-blue planking quite Federal, and the dining room was lovely, with a stone floor and inset shelves and beautiful brass chandeliers.

Philoctete, called Philo, had been trained by the South African police. He weighed more than Hope did those days and all the weight was muscle, 135 pounds. They said his bite could kill a man. They said he was so heavily muscled and so well trained that he could kill a man after he had been shot. He only took commands from one person. It was decided it would be Hope because she was home all day. Or so she was told.

She would miss Philoctete; he made her feel safe. When she cried, he put his huge head on her bed pillow. He put his wet nose in her curls when she cried and she felt safe as houses. West Virginia safe.

"You my Rebel Yella." Abel had said that more than once. And he had said, "You are my rebel yeller." Both phrases had changed things more than once. She was waiting to hear any of those words that night in the car.

A previous night, halfway through A-100, Hope and Abel had got to fighting about money. He had said something mean and idiotic about the need for them to save money by her ironing his shirts, and something meaner and more idiotic about her cooking the food—culminating in his esoteric calculation that the total worth of what she brought to the marriage was less than fourteen thousand dollars a year. He had clearly been en-acting a scene from an earlier marriage, his parents', but she hadn't known that then. She had just known, then, that he was crazy and mean. She had come back at him with an equally contrived and idiotic comment of her own. Then she had laid her head down on the pillow and cried.

When Philoctete, teeth bared, had started herding Abel from the bedroom, he had called out plaintively, "It don't have to be this way. You my rebel yella."

When she had called back, in a whisper, "Absolutely," the dog had stopped showing his teeth. Getting the inch, going for the mile, Abel had recalled a funny story from the wedding. When Hope had started laughing again, Philoctete had let Abel back into the bedroom.

Then Hope had let Abel into her body, and just before they had made the turn toward home, just before he and she had come, she'd whispered into his ear a question that she hoped she already knew the answer to: "Am I your rebel yeller?" He had answered her without words. Sometimes each found the other to be a fine and silent witness.

The next day, they had returned to the Confederate Memorial. This time they had noticed the grave where Moses Ezekiel had been buried in 1921. Together they had wondered if his daughter, Alice, had attended the service. Out of the blue Abel had said, "The Institute will be heard from today." Neither of them had been able to remember who had said it. But they had both known that whoever had said it hadn't meant what Abel had meant: that the Institute would be used to attest the significance of black women. And then they had both, at the very same time, remembered it had been Stonewall Jackson.

"You my Rebel Yella." He didn't say that in the car the night foreign posts were assigned. That night he wasn't her safety, Philoctete was.

Philoctete didn't protect Abel the way he protected Hope. He protected Hope from Abel. Or so the dear girl thought.

She didn't believe she needed any protection the day he said foreign posts had been assigned. That day they wondered aloud if they should stop in the city for dinner as an offsetting treat, but they both agreed they had to get back to the dog, before he shat in the house.

In their borrowed dining room with the stone floor and the eighteenth-century Tidewater Virginia table with its eight perfect chairs, with beeswax candles burning, and with old silver heavy in their hands, over the meal she had prepared in the early afternoon (chicken breasts stuffed with sausage nestled up to roasted apples and green beans), a snowy napkin in each of their laps, a napkin that Hope had ironed with her own hands, a squared-off goblet in each of their right hands, Hope looked into the face of her husband as he spoke, trying to make sense of Manila.

What she thought she saw on Abel's face was hope dashed. What she thought she saw was a man who hadn't been given a proper chance. She thought wrong. They had chosen him for the Agency; they had chosen him for a secret and important life. They had anointed him with the right to tell necessary lies to his wife, and to whomever else he chose.

As he spoke to her that night, spoke and watched the candlelight flicker in her eyes, his mind kept flashing back to watching her waiting on the other side of the intersection, watching her wait for the red light to turn green. A taste of sweet sage on his tongue perfectly suiting the chicken and the apples reminded him: She is too bright to cheat. She is more than they think she is, she is more than I thought she was. I must step farther away from her if she is not to know.

The woman or the world would be his eventual choice, but this night he could have them both. He inhaled deeply the overheated air that irritated his lungs, puffing deep on the pleasure of knowing something even the establishment did not know.

He knew, he could see down the pieces yet to be played, that she wouldn't go with them for long, wouldn't go with him for long. He knew, because he had made love to her, tentatively, curiously, felt her abundance, and love, washed in her sweat and scent, that she believed love eclipsed any and every darkness. He knew, because he knew she was fundamentally romantic and fundamentally powerful, that she would never be long intrigued by war games or warriors.

She wasn't Mrs. Right. She was Mrs. Right now. He would use her to assure his place in the ascendancy. She was his ticket to ride. As a tandem couple he and she were without peer or rival. No government could or would ever make her a regular agent. She was too much of a cowboy for that. But she would be an effective contractor, a true asset, for him and for his people. He knew all of that; he just didn't know when or how it would happen.

He seated himself across from her at the Gabbons' table; he was establishing a distance. If he could keep his distance, he might keep her love. She might stay long enough to roll him a good way up the road, before she rolled on without him. *Hopie be my Bobby McGee.* He said it right out loud. It was an invitation and a description. It was his prayer. He wrote it in a Hallmark card. She kissed at the card. She loved him. He knew this when she said yes to Manila. Just like he'd known, when he hadn't sat the second day of the bar exam, and had taken away all of their choices but one, that he didn't really love her at all.

Abel wanted to walk through the world with Hope because he thought she was a creature with an all-access pass to the planet. He wanted her to walk ahead of him opening doors, then he wanted to trip her up and have her fall in step two feet behind him.

He wanted to be something more than a black southern politician, something more than the one who took the pleadings of an injured class to the powerful men in the nation's capital on bended knee, with eloquence. He wanted to be an international man. An unhyphenated man. He wanted to be something more and the nation had chosen him for something more. Chosen her too. Only she didn't yet know it.

He didn't think she would forgive the bugged house. Or, forgive the simple way they had taken advantage of her willingness to be of use. The Gabbons had had to go on an inspection tour. The ambassador and his wife had needed them. The Gabbons had told a lie very near the truth when they had set up the interview for house-sitting. They had said that they always chose someone from the A-100 class to look after their house when the ambassador went on a long inspection tour. They hadn't said that they always chose the spy who would be in deep cover, that Mrs. Gabbon gave that man's wife skills to be used in entertaining that would further the purposes of the government—some as simple as a recipe for an onion tart, a tart so pungent with olive and anchovy that it could hide a variety of off flavors, a tart without delicate eggs that might betray the presence of foreign ingredients by curdling.

The importance of obeying rules precisely; they had used the dog to teach her that. Another thing she wouldn't forgive if she knew.

To give him an order she had to say his name, then the order, then his name, or he wouldn't obey. On Thanksgiving morning she had been walking the dog and it had been arranged without her knowing that she would cross paths with a little Maltese Philo had been trained to attack. Philo had lunged at the little dust mop, but he had dropped back on his haunches when Hope had thought to order, "Philoctete, sit, Philoctete." She was a natural. She used the ordinary and familiar tools at hand to do the unusual and unfamiliar job. So much she learned without knowing that she was learning.

When Hope had turned up late on the day foreign posts had been assigned, it had occurred to Abel that she might bolt before the adventure began. The possibility that he would enter his self-imposed exile from his family and home and from Hope all at the same time had chilled him colder than the wind and snow. He'd been wondering how high he could rise without her when he'd caught sight of her waiting for a red light to turn green.

It would be a while before he discovered he could rise very high, very high indeed, as long as she played along a little. She misread his sadness and fear and said she would come with him. Said it would be all right. Said it was only eighteen months. She would pack up all her silver trays and he would stamp visas in Manila.

How bad could it be? She could continue to sculpt. There would be amazing Philippine woods. They would be far, far away from everything, together. She loved him. She didn't want him to hurt. It was Asia. She remembered that people spoke Tagalog there and that some people spoke Chinese. It would be all right.

Eighteen months. They would smoke cigarettes, and drink, and make love, and when he came back he would have something more than a wrinkled white linen summer suit. They would make a baby. They would see the world. She was his girl.

He didn't know why he wanted to lie to her, but he did want to, and he needed to, and so he lied and enjoyed it. It was one of the first things he truly loved about being inside the fortress of the strong: the complete privacy of the thing. No one knew him. He was an authority unto himself. No one understood him; but for once it was not a bruising thing. He would wear the mask on every occasion. His government required it. He was happy to be of service, to the nation, to his woman, to himself.

He was beginning again. This woman didn't know his significance or insignificance. This woman would not punish him. He treasured all his masks, but each of the masks that served him best had been formed on his face just after some part of him had died.

His birthday-I-am-a-man mask was on him now. He had put it on to tell her about Manila. And he had worn it to receive the invitation of the Agency. Just after the government's proposal the man doing the asking had put his arm around Abel's shoulders, looked him in the eye, and explained, "It's a little bit like getting engaged: we don't ask until we know the answer."

Abel had proposed to Hope very differently. The night they had made love in the cemetery on the snow, he'd been absolutely unsure what her answer would be. He'd thought she might say no. She had still been a bit angry with him for not having gone to the aunts' funeral. She could be angry and love at the very same time. This was a revelation to him. He didn't know it was a basic maturity. He knew she was smarter than his daddy and unafraid of his daddy—a man who had made strong grown men cry. She loved him and didn't love his daddy. Hope was perfect for Abel.

"I was not raised in your house," she had said to Big Abel during their Roman summer, when, after she had gone down to Nashville to meet his parents, Big Abel had stormed at her for some trumped-up infraction but really for having lived with his son in sin. "I'm not afraid of you." The way she loved him more than his father it was almost as safe and sweet as the feeling of the policeman picking him up in his arms. He would try to give her that feeling. He would be the policeman and one day he would pick her up in his arms and she would feel safe. Until then, while they lived at the Gabbons', he did not begrudge her Philoctete. When Hope took Abel in her arms he felt safe.

"What did he do in Manila?" asked Hope.

"He packed the Marcoses out. He was there when they got on the helicopter. He was the last one to look into their bags before they took off. And he tried to find out how and when and if Cardinal Sin had communicated with the communists. But he failed at that," said Nicholas, sounding sorry and proud.

"If I had known more about him, and he had known more about me, things would have been better," said Hope.

"Different, not necessarily better."

"What policemen do you mean?"

"Did I say policemen?"

"That made him feel safe."

"All policemen."

Nicholas went out for a cigarette and a stop in the hall toilet. Hope, after availing herself of Abel's en suite bathroom, went searching for a bottle of water.

SIXTEEN

B Y F E B R U A R Y T H E Y would be off to the South China
Sea in time for the People Power Revolution. On to all
their new secrets. And to making Ajay.

"And meeting me," said Nicholas
   "And meeting you," said Hope.

But first they had to finish their training. They were the king
and queen of the silent shout-outs. They were taught that skill
before their first post in a chock-full class on coping with violence abroad. They had been taught to always have a place
where they could meet in case they became separated—a place
preferably nearby and a place far away. A place they never talked
about. A place you have never been, preferably a place they could
signal without naming. When it had been their turn to per-
form the assigned practice exercise in front of the group—
communicate an evacuation location to your spouse during a
conversation about impressionist painting in such a way that the
others involved in the conversation can't guess what it is—Abel
had cheated and chosen Idlewild. She had guessed right off, and

no one in the class, though all were armed with the most detailed biographical profiles and world atlases and all possible AAA TripTiks, had guessed where Hope and Abel were headed. A first, small career and marriage triumph.

To celebrate their success he gave her a book by Bernard Lewis called *The Assassins.* She found the sect almost as intriguing as he did. They'd been followers of Hassan-i-Sabbah, a branch of Shia Muslims who had lived in Iran, Iraq, Syria, and Lebanon long before those places were called by those names. The sect had disappeared in 1272 when their last stronghold had been invaded and seized by the Moguls. They had referred to themselves as *al-da'wa al-jadida.* Hope noted that Lewis's book had come out in 1967. In the time of the Summer of Love, in a time of pot, and hash, and LSD, she wondered if some had been chastened by the existence of a cult rumored by Marco Polo to have ingested hash before they killed.

When Hope started talking about the Summer of Love, Abel said, "Where I come from, the summer of sixty-seven was the summer of the war nobody noticed."

"Abel's Civil War."

"That's what you call the riot on Jefferson Street?"

"That's what I call all of it."

"All of it?"

"The bombings, the murders, the funerals, the neck shooting, what you saw."

He kissed her. He liked the way his new wife always reframed everything to make him heroic. She loved him more than she loved the truth. He kissed her, then changed the subject. He turned from his private anxiety to a more common public anxiety.

He told her about the strict rules the Assassins were said to have worked under. Told her that they had preferred to kill in a public place, close up, often wearing a disguise. Told her that they had preferred to use a blade, they had preferred to put themselves in danger with their action. And later they would allow themselves to be killed by their leader. Sometimes instead of killing they would leave a knife at the home of an enemy as a silent way of saying, we could have gotten to you; change course, or you are dead. All of that disturbed, but what disturbed Hope most, and what disturbed Abel most, was the alleged method of initiation into the club. Initiates were tricked into thinking they were about to die, then they were drugged, and when they awoke from their "death" they found themselves in a beautiful garden with wine and were told that they were in heaven. Everything they heard in the garden they believed.

"When did they first approach him?"
    "Probably during Harvard, but not at Harvard."

Abel and Hope left for their first post barely six months after the wedding, in February 1986. In his pocket and in her purse was a diplomatic passport. Abel had proof that he was an important person married to an important person.

"What was it about Abel and planes?"
    "Trains, buses, and boats all had a history of being segregated."
    "Planes weren't part of his family trauma story?"
    "Exactly."
    "Why did they call their car the Flying Crow?"

"That was the nickname of a train that carried people south from Chicago. It started out integrated and got segregated when it crossed into a Jim Crow state. The aunties said you could hear big grown men, black soldiers going down to those southern camps, crying in the night when the train crossed into Dixie," said Hope.

"Abel's family knew about that too?"

"Everybody black knew that."

"And the Joneses called their car the Flying Crow because . . ."

"A black man rich enough to own a traveling car didn't need to subject himself to a train. It's a joke."

"You get him."

"I got him."

"Then you left and no one did."

"He didn't choose a someone who could have."

"Sammie. I didn't see that coming . . ."

"When his parents got shot and killed . . ."

"Outside a restaurant in New Orleans?"

"A black man shot them."

"Big Abel wouldn't give up his wallet."

"If we had been together Abel might have gotten over it."

"Probably not."

"Unfortunate Negroes in America are more unfortunate than unfortunate white people in America."

"I've heard Abel say that so many times."

"Now you've heard me."

They flew from San Francisco to Tokyo on a 747 with a staircase that led to a lounge. She drank Baileys Irish Cream in the bar. He drank champagne and orange juice in the big leatherette seats.

Hope had never known, and never was to know, a person who took as much pleasure in commercial aviation as Abel did. To speed on one's way with a toilet and a kitchen, with pretty women to serve you, in always integrated splendor; to be able to sit in the big seats in the front just because you could pay; to be, takeoffs and landings aside, completely safe, or at least as safe as anyone—these were among his favorite things.

They changed planes in Tokyo and landed in Manila. She woke up the first day with a mosquito bite on her eyelid. Her eye was almost swollen shut. It was as if the planet didn't want her to be happy or easy.

SEVENTEEN

THEY LIVED IN a compound, owned by the U.S. government, called Sea Front that neither of them quite liked. He found it a bit plebeian and felt slighted that they hadn't been given a townhouse, which he understood after a week in Manila to be the compound's best living quarters; she found the compound confined and militaristic. The fact that a single married marine lived next door irked them both. That first night they didn't know any of this yet. They just moved into the temporarily furnished apartment on the compound determined to bloom where they were planted and opened the trunk.

She was proud of her trunk. She had black plastic dishes, Hellerware, and some wonderful espresso cups that a friend's daughter had collected flying on Pan Am in the sixties, and the Lyles' fat funny little teapot, and packets of tea, and her silver, and even a small tablecloth and napkins, and two hand-embroidered pillowcases, and tins of soup and smoked oysters.

That very first night she was able to make dinner for her husband. They sat out on a screened porch and drank soup and ate smoked oysters and she said, it's all going to be OK. For after dinner she had a tiny silk nightgown and *The Thirty-Nine Steps*. They both went to sleep happy. She woke up with the swollen eye and a paranoia that had invaded her with the mosquito juice.

Abel was gone when she awoke. She had slept longer and deeper than she had expected. Quickly attributing her drowsiness to jet lag, she examined her eye. Swollen till it had a single eyelid fold, the eye looked Asian. It was as if she had gone to sleep and half-changed ethnicities. The eye itched; she scratched it. The eye stopped looking Asian and started looking angry and red. Hope found a pair of sunglasses and put them on her face. It was far ruder to eat in public showing that angry eye than to wear sunglasses inside a building.

"Do you think he drugged me?" asked Hope.

"Possibly, but probably not," said Nicholas.

"Do you think he brought in the mosquito?" asked Hope.

"I think he was a spy and now you're a paranoid ex-wife," said Nicholas.

Then there was nothing to do but walk over to the club and order and eat her lunch alone. She took with her the materials provided in the apartment, the papers that had been folded into a welcome basket and that told her all about the club and the women's club and the shopping.

The club looked like any half-fancy country club built in the sixties, all poured concrete and glass. She was told she could sign her name rather than pay for anything; she was told that this was the one place in Manila where she could drink her drinks iced. When she asked the waiter if there were any local items on the menu, he smiled and said calamansi soda and fried lumpia, and so she had a kind of lemonade and cigarette-slim eggrolls for her first lunch in the Philippines.

It was before cell phones and voice messages, but when she got back the phone was ringing and some local hire, in the administration area, was calling to invite her to the office to pick out things for their new home. The U.S. government in its infinite wisdom had decided it was more efficient to buy them new furniture than to ship their possessions across the world.

All at once they would have everything new and superficially perfect. Someone said it was a little like having rich parents.

From a big book with drawings of furniture and fabric swatches, Hope chose a pink and green Chinese-looking tropical fabric palette and black lacquer furniture. With a living room, dining room, bedroom, guest room, and office to furnish, Hope was finished in an hour. Once the furniture had been chosen, the admin officer was ready to help set up maid interviews. Somewhere distant, but on the compound, was a little warren of rooms where their maid would sleep, after they chose her.

Hope wondered how it could be that she had traveled across the world to awaken in a place where people thought it fine to pay a maid two hundred dollars a month and have her work every day of the week. Going along she hired Ting Ting: the whole thing was too much like West Virginia.

That fall, after the revolution, after falling into friendship with Nicholas, after all that was her Manila, just before she knew she was pregnant, Hope baked Abel a flan for his birthday in Manila. She put sparklers into the pudding.

That night after they made love he kissed her between her legs for an hour. It was the first time after their wedding that he had saluted her sex with his mouth in that most intimate fashion. After that they kissed, mouth to mouth, and she tasted herself on his tongue. When she wiped a tear that ran from his eye off his cheek he said nobody had ever bothered to notice he hadn't eaten a bite of a slice of birthday cake since he'd turned thirteen years old. "Until you. Until now." Abel loved Hope that night.

"What happened on your thirteenth birthday?"

"Somebody burned a cross on our lawn."

"Oh, God."

"No God. I knew."

"And you stopped eating birthday cake?"

"I couldn't swallow it after that."

Nicholas didn't know that story. He understood Abel's atheism to foreshadow and balance Abel's overzealous evangelical Christian promise keeping. He found it touching. In exchange he told Hope a story he hoped she would find touching. Abel hadn't destroyed her naked pregnancy-belly photographs as he had promised at the time of the divorce. He had had them photoshopped so that it appeared she was wearing a discreet white Victorian gown and he had kept them in a black portfolio along with pregnancy pictures of Sammie. Hope wasn't sure whether that was touching or alarming. She decided to let it be touching.

EIGHTEEN

AJAY WAS BORN in Nashville. Three weeks later the little family flew to New York, where Abel was assigned to the United Nations.

They lived in a duplex in Chelsea across two gardens from the famed Chelsea Hotel. Abel was working long hours at the UN, leaving early and coming home late.

After her husband went to work Hope fed the baby, then took the baby on a walk through the garden of the Episcopal Theological Seminary, then fed the baby and put the baby to sleep. While Ting Ting tidied the house and kept watch over sleeping Ajay, Hope would take herself out to breakfast, usually a place called the Chelsea Café, where she saw, or imagined she saw, Kinky Friedman every morning eating breakfast. Not infrequently friends would come to see the baby on their lunch hours. More often friends would come for a viewing and stay for dinner. Ajay, the first baby in their group of friends, coupled to Hope's home cooking, was quite the attraction.

Except to his father, who left for work before the baby was awake and came home after he was asleep. And when the baby woke up howling in the middle of the night—he slept in a

Moses cradle by the side of their bed—Abel didn't stir. Hope was never alone that fall in New York, and she was seldom with Abel.

It was an overblown time in the life of the world. Banker boys preposterously calling themselves "Big Kahunas" and "Masters of the Universe" attempted to seduce all, indiscriminately, into entering the masculine fairy tale of money mattering fundamentally.

Hope had entered into an ancient feminine fairy tale. Her baby was a wilderness and she got lost in it. For her it was a raw and simple time. Her nipples hurt and her cesarean wound itched, but she was enchanted by her journey into the much-charted but still entirely mysterious territory of a baby boy who wakes every four hours hollering for mommy and milk.

Abel missed his own birthday dinner because he was working late. When he finally got home the guests were already gone, and she tried to make a party for two, inviting him to enter her body for the first time since the baby's birth.

Wanting to spare Abel the sight of stretch marks and pounds that would be shed soon enough, wanting a period of sole possession after having shared her body for forty weeks with the baby, she had not been quick to return to the role of lover.

The birthday was a catalyst. She attempted a seduction. They tumbled timidly.

The coupling only lasted a few minutes but the immensity of the event eclipsed her sense of the immensity of her body and his sense of the immensity of her abandonment. They were doing what had got them the baby and what had got him a birthday. It was a powerful doing and being and knowing. He tried to sip on her breast. She playfully pushed him away and playfully bit his shoulder; she was pulling him back to her, trying to create a gesture that was loverly not motherly, when the baby cried in another room and her milk let down. The sex that had been delicious a moment earlier became for them impossible. When she returned to the bed he was asleep.

On Monday, October 18, 1987, the day appointed for the second attempt at an Abel birthday party, later to be called Black Monday, the financial markets loudly expelled a goodly amount of whatever it was that had been keeping them overinflated.

Hope didn't notice. She was busy grocery shopping and cooking a second birthday dinner. Come seven, all the regular guests showed back up for Abel's second bite of the birthday apple—and this time the guest of honor made it.

Stocks and money were the talk of the evening. In his cups, Abel got almost snarky about being "just a government worker, a not-invested nobody," then he turned bitter, making jokes that weren't funny about the baby losing all his money and Hope losing all of hers. When the entire table, except Abel, agreed the only thing to do was leave everything where it was, Hope was relieved. First because Abel shut up and second because leaving everything where it was was all she had the energy to do.

After Manila, after the United Nations, after what she thought was some language training in Washington, D.C.—but Nicholas thought probably had been language and *other* training in Washington, D.C.—Abel arrived in Martinique before his wife and son.

He moved into a rambling bachelor pad overlooking the bay.

The apartment that had so thrilled the previous political officer (it was close to the nightlife of Fort-de-France, to the dance clubs where the zouk pulsed until the short hours of the night turned into the long hours of morning) disappointed Abel. He hated the low-walled balcony; he hated the dodgy neighborhood. Nothing about the rooms seemed appropriate to what or how Abel understood his position to be.

He wanted a house in the *beke* community. He wanted to live among the old money of the place, or so he said, loudly and widely. What Hope understood was that he wanted to live among the white descendants of the aristocratic French planters.

By the time Hope arrived, Abel had a reputation as a braggart, a boozer, a cheat (this third she never knew), and a pretty, pretty boy who knew just how pretty he was.

Even so, Abel was invited everywhere and not just because he was the chief political officer of the Caribbean. He was invited because he was chief political officer of the Caribbean, because he was serious about nothing but having a good time, and because everybody wanted to be a guest at Hope's house.

Hope was a surprise. They had taken bets about Abel's wife. Half the town thought she would be white, perhaps some trippy, tiny California girl, from a rich family, who smoked pot and had had an adolescent crush on Bobby Seale. That kind of white American girl, the kind whose parents had taken her to vacation in Martinique in the seventies and eighties, was the kind of American girl Fort-de-France knew. Others thought he would have married a black woman very much like himself, with very light skin, perhaps with green or blue eyes, a lawyer or a doctor, someone precise and professional, someone to keep him in check.

Black or white, she would be pretty and as stupid as a bright woman could be, an ornament to hang on his arm and look up adoringly in his face. Pretty but thick.

Perhaps she was thick, but only if you were thinking about thighs. By the time she arrived in Martinique, Hope had taken much of her baby weight off. But upon her arrival there was consensus among the chic *beke* ladies and the chic-chic brown ladies that her curves needed editing.

After a few parties the ladies changed their minds. Too much of Hope turned out to be a good thing. Abundant hair, abundant smiles, abundant laughter, abundant breasts, abundant hips, abundant knowledge, abundant thoughts equaled a compelling diversion. The town stood corrected, and amused Martiniquais enjoyed a surprise. The doors of the city opened wider to Abel.

You are my key. He said this to her a month after she had arrived on the island. He was whispering into her ear. Then he was drawing his tongue across the side of her face, leaving an invisible trail of his saliva from her ear to her mouth that opened wide for him.

When she poked her tongue into his mouth he knew what she wanted, but first he sucked hard on her tongue, like a hungry baby. She didn't like that but he didn't notice. She did what she could to make him feel big and clean and significant. She surprised him with flicks and nips till he abandoned every concern but how long he could last before he came and the pleasure ended. *She worships me. You are my key*, she said to him, spreading her legs.

The black sand of Martinique makes promises it does not keep. It promises that it will never let you go. It promises that it will always call you back. *Pays revenants.* It promises that you will always be beautiful. It promises that the world does recognize the prize of darkness as equal to, if not greater than, the prize of lightness. And because it makes those promises, and because she did not know that they would be broken, or how soon they would be broken, for a few hours Hope lay upon the volcanic sand and dreamed her last dreams of the bedazzled.

She imagined staying on the island. She imagined speaking a French that her servants could untangle, that her best friend, CeCe, would not mock. She imagined meeting Gauguin's daughter, or great-granddaughter, who would be brown and round and brilliant and would take Hope into some old Creole house, some abandoned place, and there on the walls would be paintings of a brown round woman who was wholly beautiful in her lover's eyes—and wholly unconcerned with his judgment.

She read *Wide Sargasso Sea* and determined that she wanted to write a screenplay of the book, only to discover, in expensive long-distance phone calls that she insisted on paying for out of her own money, that an Australian director had already optioned the rights.

Trying to inspire his wife back to sculpture, after she'd been distracted (by a revolution, an illness, and a baby) away from the work he perceived to be most compatible with his own, Abel told Hope about William Edmondson.

Edmondson, the black Nashville sculptor who had been given a one-man show at the Museum of Modern Art in New York City in 1937, intrigued Hope immediately.

Hope began to move past imagining herself to be an artist, to being an artist. In addition to her own *objets* she started sculpting funeral pieces for people who could not afford a monument, and giving them away.

To celebrate their anniversary they took a sailboat, the *Seastar*, across the Caribbean. She danced in Basil's Bar in Mustique, and climbed over the desert cactus landscape of Little Palm Island. The waters that had compelled Lafcadio Hearn compelled Hope and Abel too.

She liked the Caribbean better than the South China Sea, better than the Sulu Sea. She had swum joyfully in those Asian Crayola-box blues with the neon fish in the southern islands of the Philippines; but she preferred this *bleu* of Gauguin and Hearn and Césaire, probably because she had not sinned in it. They were no longer brazen enough or simple enough to make love in the water two feet beyond the boatmen.

But more than the colors of the waters it was the colors of the people that compelled her, bronze and black and cream, every shade of chocolate, flavored her evolving sense that the Martiniquais had found some way to be at once wholly African, wholly French, and wholly Creole.

Some days she encountered this as a rebuke not to her experience but to her American people. Where DuBois had spoken of double-consciousness, what she encountered in Martinique, over and over, was something quite opposite: people inhabiting multiple identities at different times.

She had a new ambition: to inhabit, at once, multipleness. She read Aimé Césaire and Frantz Fanon and thought about her own history in a whole and new way, but this was not the most important thing she had to think about.

Abel was not falling in love with the baby, Ajay. Hope sensed, then feared, then refused to know, that he had concocted a reason for them to travel down on separate planes because he didn't seem to be able to stand to fly with his child.

He said that the baby's crying embarrassed him. He offered Hope a hundred foot massages, without question, if she would, without question, fly with the child alone.

"Has it occurred to you that Abel wanted Ajay on a different plane because a different plane was safer?"

"Did it occur to you that Abel wanted Ajay on a different plane because he hated riding in cars with his daddy?"

"Maybe we're talking Ron Brown in Croatia *and* Big Abel and Abel riding to Birmingham."

"We didn't have a chance."

When Abel came home from his office in Fort-de-France he would sit out on their terrace that wrapped around the apartment and gulp a gin and tonic as Hope nursed a Coke with lime. She always offered him a tiny bowl of something to nibble on, warmed nuts or tiny squares of pastry flavored with cheese. They would talk for a half hour, about things in the newspaper, about her day, never his, and then, finally, he would allow the baby to be brought out by Ting Ting, who would appear in a starched white or pink cotton dress with full skirt and lace-trimmed button top. The baby would be on Ting Ting's narrow hip, howling as he reached for his daddy, slapping softly at the nanny he loved dearly, angry that she had kept him from Abel.

Every time Hope witnessed this little drama she grew infuriated. The way Ting Ting held her body, the way she opened her green eyes so wide, she asked a question without saying a word: Why can't you make your husband more interested in the child? All this was accusation. If Hope lifted the baby from Ting Ting's arms in the middle of the tragic performance, the child completely ignored her, not even bothering to be mad. It was as if the baby knew she had no power, knew that her power had vanished as suddenly and completely as the city of Saint-Pierre.

Somewhere, someone, every week, mentioned to Hope the natural disaster that claimed thirty thousand lives, the imagination of the island, and eventually Hope's imagination. She was that tired and that sad.

When finally admitted into his father's awareness of his presence, Ajay would be exhausted from crying, from having wanted to see his daddy since the moment Abel's key had been heard in the door and his tread had been heard in the front hall, from having had to wait to be acknowledged by his daddy for minutes after entering the balcony.

Hope hated to watch their strange reunion: the child so angry, the man so annoyed that the baby hadn't been born a little girl patient and sweet. Hope had to watch all of that before she got to see that the child was too lovable not to love. A few moments with the weight of his son in his arms and Abel was standing at the terrace balustrade singing to the boy and pointing at the sights of Fort-de-France. Ajay hugged his daddy and tussled with his daddy, soft-punching his arm, as they, in their own way, fell back in love, much to everyone's surprise, every evening.

Twenty minutes later Abel would have had enough. He would start yelling for the nanny to come get his kid and for his wife to come get him.

He liked to have sex before they went out to dinner. She liked it too if they were very quiet. It was the thing she didn't like about the apartment; it had precious few doors. It was open to the air in a way that made public too many intimacies.

Eventually the Creole sun seemed to sap her strength. She didn't seem able to get settled in good or well. There continued to be the matter of language. She spoke French with a West Virginia accent the island folk found perplexing verging on hilarious. Everyone understood exactly what she was saying but she sounded so strange few paid attention.

And there was the matter of mice. It was as if the rats of Manila had created an allergy to rodents that even the small kitchen mice of Martinique could provoke. Mice and mosquitoes were every hour challenging her authority in the kitchen. Abel said he had seen bigger mice and rats on Fifteenth Street.

And gas. Gas for the stove had to be delivered in tanks. And food, with everything being shipped in from France, was ridiculously expensive. All of this could have been ameliorated by the hiring of a local woman to shop and cook and clean, a woman familiar with the ways of the island, but instead she had brought Ting Ting with her from the Philippines, hoping to offer herself a significant continuity. And it was something Abel had wanted.

None of this would have mattered if it hadn't been for what she perceived to be his unwillingness to fall in love with the baby and her subsequent belief that things would have been very different if she had borne Abel a daughter. He wouldn't have wanted to hit a daughter.

She attempted to distract herself from this truth by worrying more about black souls and skins and white masks and about how Frantz Fanon had tried to treat the victims of torture abuse with psychoanalysis and had almost gone crazy doing it. Hope was holding hard to some ideas Abel refused to understand, about Fanon's idea that the mammy who managed to actually love the white child she took care of was a true humanist and revolutionary. She told him it was as important to understand the mammy in the Confederate Memorial as it was to understand the soldier. He didn't hear her. Abel thought Fanon's and Hope's idea was a lie. He didn't know anything about missing home.

He kept talking about Louis-Auguste Cyparis, the black prisoner in the jail who had been one of the only ones, or the only one, saved when the entire city of Saint-Pierre had been destroyed by a volcanic eruption in 1902.

The aristocratic white family, the new American diplomats, the New Englanders, and all the other inhabitants had been killed. He talked on and on about that. Hope accused him of being a nouveau Puritan obsessed with Divine Providence.

He said he was obsessed with fortunate Negroes. She allowed that there were few enough of those that he probably could indulge in the obsession. She liked this idea of Abel's. They laughed together and he told more of the story of Cyparis, who after surviving the eruption had become a circus performer, appearing as "The Man Who Survived Doomsday" with Barnum and Bailey.

The story made Hope sad. She didn't want to be married to the man who wanted to survive doomsday. Still, they stumbled into each other, as married people will—if one is not determined to avoid the other. Often, but not often enough.

In Fort-de-France it came to seem the only thing Abel felt comfortable sharing with Hope was the location of the next party. One bizarre afternoon the party was on the deck of a Royal Navy battleship. In a black and white linen dress she reviewed the troops or some such. Later she ate tiny éclairs with two or three young officers seemingly assigned to keep her company. She hated it. He could feel her recoil from the militaristic and somehow he took it as a reproach. She didn't know why.

The silences expanded. She didn't know if it was his work he wasn't talking about, or a woman he wasn't talking about, or some strange feelings about the baby he wasn't talking about, or he was having an affair with Ting Ting he wasn't talking about, but he wasn't talking about something. "Angel from Montgomery" became her favorite John Prine song. "How in the hell can a man go to work in the morning and come home in the evening and have nothing to say?"

He had nothing to say, but the town had much to say about him, about his growing reputation for putting his feet up on his desk and reading the paper all day when he wasn't at parties or receptions or lunch. She was furious at his apparent incompetency. She didn't know he was doing his job exactly as his handlers wanted it to be done.

"You were paranoid about the wrong thing."
    "He was lying, but not about typical things."
    "Absolutely."
    "And I was paranoid about some of the right things."
    "Such as?"
    "Abel hitting the baby."
    "Occasional baby swatting is a major sin?"
    "Abel occasionally swatting a child was like an alcoholic occasionally having a white wine spritzer. And he knew it. Big Abel used to beat the hell out of Abel. He had no business laying a finger on any child."

She tried to orchestrate it such that they ate one meal together as family each week despite their heavy social calendar. On those nights they would sit in the kitchen. One evening during dinner, when Ajay was about fourteen months old, the boy discovered it was amusing to throw his plastic sippy cup on the floor. Abel picked it up once with a smile and told him not to do it again. Ajay threw the cup to the ground again. Abel picked it up, put it on the tray, waited for the boy to smile, then slapped the boy's hand. Ajay began to howl. Hope picked the cup up from the floor and put it back on his tray.
    "Don't hit my child again."
    "You're spoiling him."
    "You can't spoil a baby."
    Ajay threw the cup down on the floor again. Abel picked it up and put it on the table.

Two nights later the baby threw his cup and Abel slapped him again, this time on the shoulder. Hope didn't say anything about it until they were alone that night.

"Hit him again, I will divorce you."

She came back to the States for the wedding of a boarding school friend. Baby Ajay got a high fever on the plane, some variant of measles, roseola, probably from swimming in the pool at the fancy hotel a week earlier. She missed the wedding. They never went back down to Martinique.

NINETEEN

WHEN HE "LEFT the State Department" she thought it was for her. It seemed a sweet proof of love. The marriage was reborn. She didn't know quitting the State Department was a deeper move into cover, not a deeper move into marriage.

They settled into the little yellow cottage. His relations were happy to have the foreign-smelling couple back to reestablish the political significance and ascendancy of their family.

Abel ran for the state senate and was defeated. Then he slapped the baby a third and too-hard time and that was it. Hope was ready to get rid of Abel and ready to get rid of Ting Ting. She was ready to step alone into the world with her son.

My Creole belle. She was lying atop Egyptian cotton sheets in the Hotel Splendide Rome near the Spanish Steps; it was the trip they had taken to try to patch things up. She remembered lying on scratchy sheets in some *pensione* the name of which she had long ago forgotten, remembered lying in a room closer to the Trevi Fountain, where she'd been given a key for the squeaky-clean shower down the hall. She had washed herself all over with a handheld sprayer contraption and had come back pruny and content, so content, having just discovered watery self-pleasuring. In that room Abel had traced the outline of her breast to her hip, slipping his fingers into what he called "the figgy stickiness of your fecundity." In the presence of the promises to be kept, children that would be made and sheltered, steeped in Africa old as Eve, and in the world as young as tomorrow, he had said, "You are my Rebel Yella." In this better room he didn't say it. She was very far away from that room and that shower, that man, that girl, and then. They were tragic mulattoes for the very first time.

Hope wondered whether, if she and Abel had stayed at the old *pensione* on their make-up-or-divorce trip, they might have stayed married.

"You left out the part about the story you wrote."

"What story?"

"'Belisario.' Abel's birthday present."

"I had forgotten about that."

"I had too, except I saw it in the bookcase in the toilet."

"Which I need."

"I think I'll just go out and get a smoke, then."

He grabbed his cigarettes and lighter and left the room; Hope headed for the hall bath. Her little manuscript, hand-sewn pages of old perforated computer paper, was easy enough to find on the shelf full of Trollope and Balzac.

From his studio in one of the towers Belisario had ordered constructed to defend Rome from swarming hordes from the north, Moses Ezekiel could see both the

Villa Borghese and the Via Veneto. The Roman government had been kind and had moved him from the stable that had been his studio into a fortified perch in the Roman Wall. And then the king had given him an honorary Italian knighthood to match the one bestowed by the second William to be emperor of Germany.

He was planted. Without effort he had obtained a high place for himself in Roman society. "The old world," he said to himself many a night while falling asleep over some inky-dark and dusty wine, "has a sweeter appreciation for this southern Jew and soldier than my upstart Republic ever did."

He had imagined he would never venture back, never again cross the ocean. Even the planned unveiling of what he believed to be his masterpiece, in the presence of President Warren G. Harding, was not enough to tempt him to quit the Eternal City; he had written the letter to decline the invitation and would have posted it had he not taken a nap and dreamed of a certain young woman in Washington.

He wanted to see his masterpiece through her eyes.

In preparation for his return to America he had ordered calling cards that read, SIR MOSES EZEKIEL. It was an affectation, but not precisely a lie.

Everything else would be a lie.

The worst the cards could be truly accused of was poor translation. And most people, Moses assured himself, walking to calm his nerves through the Vatican gardens, underestimated the significance of that sin.

Moses, a man who had, in what he perceived to be an

act of superb translation, transformed himself from a Confederate soldier into a Roman sculptor, from a southern Jew into a European Buddhist who held the most charming Christmas parties for Rome's expatriates, was not most people. Moses did not low-rate translation.

He was, however, otherwise careless. One chill afternoon, with rain coming down and influenza blowing in, when coughs and tales of disasters of the body had strained the nerves of his visitors, he had made the mistake of showing sketches of the monument. D'Annunzio, Michetti, and Adolfo de Bosis had been there, drinking his wine and talking about Madame Helbig. Finally someone had hoisted the rusted barb calling her "the most immense figure in Rome with the single exception of Michelangelo's Moses."

He liked the woman. She was married to the director of the German Archaeological Institute. A student of Liszt's, the Russian princess formerly known as Nadja Shakhovskoy entertained on Janiculum Hill—and in her own wonderfully large way had been indirectly instrumental in Moses's rise. They shared two loves: sculpting and Pushkin. He had trotted out the sketches to save her. Or perhaps he had done it to impress Edmonia Lewis. However that was, Moses found himself mocked. It was an unfamiliar and infuriating sensation.

His Roman friends had little feeling for the defeated army. Rome is a city of the victorious warrior, a city to which warriors returned with the tokens of their victories. Someone asked him how he could get so involved with lost causes. Someone else said that Roman slavery had been completely different from slavery in America because the Roman had acknowledged the humanity of his slave and the American didn't.

He discovered that he felt himself free to quit Rome—precisely because he felt able to discern that Rome would wait. He wasn't so sure about Alice.

The year and a half the girl and her mother had spent with him had been a dream that had come true, revealing the disproportions of dreams. Neither woman could be made to fit into the home and life he had made in Rome without hacking something off—and neither woman would stay still enough to let him hack at her. If they had stayed still he wouldn't have had the stomach to hack at them. They were not marble.

Moses had started dreaming of Rome when he was still in Virginia, when he and Isabella, Alice's mother, his father's slave, had first become lovers. She had asked him, "Ain't there some place you can take me where we can always be together?" She had offered one answer to the simple question: Montreal. He had proposed a different answer: Rome. Then he'd gone off to war and hadn't taken her anywhere. And she had picked up words of French anywhere she could. She had kept raising his child, first in Virginia, then, after Emancipation was declared, in Washington. The girl was a student at Howard University when he sent for them both to go live in Rome with him.

He had taken her to the S———s', to the fabulous Palazzo Barberini, where S——— and his wife entertained in a tiny palace of forty-five rooms. *Tableaux vivants*. He had a nightmare about one of the evenings. He dreamed he had slapped his daughter in one of those tapestry-hung rooms with so many sofas shoved up against the wall and then in another. She had run through one room and then another and he had run after her, slapping her face and her shoulders. She wore the red print of his palm on her cream-colored shoulders like a brand.

She had sat as Cleopatra. Draped and undraped. Her left breast exposed. Bracelets on her left and right wrist. Someone had found the exact necklace the model had worn. It had been a strange performance. First she had sat quite still, the sleeve of the gown up on her shoulder. Cleopatra every inch: from the curl of her fingers to the lift of her toed sandals. And then she had let the draping on her shoulder fall. S——— had begun the applause. There had been nothing prurient in it; most were simply remembering the work of 1869. And then she had changed positions. Removed her headdress. Turned her back to her audience and put on a new necklace and ear-rings, rearranged her hair, taken off her sandals, crossed her legs, placed her elbow on her knee, then leaned heav-ily into her hand. Her feet had looked big. Her gaze had turned off to the side. She had become the Libyan Sibyl, all but the soft fold of flesh and two exquisite breasts—and then had allowed all of her draping to fall to her waist. The room had filled with louder applause.

The mother was almost proud. Her daughter was ex-quisite and untouchable. So much more beautiful than marble. She had lived too long in the South to be shocked by a black woman's nakedness, even a white-black woman.

There was every kind of shiver and shudder: from desire and awe to fear and aversion. But she wondered at the responses of the others. This tableau was not a display, but an encounter. It was evident that someone, perhaps Charlotte Cushman, had been teaching Alice to convey. She was not flatly posed. The young woman leapt without moving—from the confines of the gilded frame into brown eyes and blue eyes and gray eyes, into hazel eyes and black eyes, flickering as they blinked. Only the father appeared to stare without blinking.

Isabella saw that Moses Ezekiel's motivations were too intricate. Most simply he wanted to impress and outdo his host. He had succeeded. He also wanted to seek a Roman husband for the girl. If he could marry her off to a Roman or a permanent exile, she would be that much more likely to stay with him in Italy. All that was simple.

But perhaps he wanted to see her. Not her body displayed for his pleasure, but her body celebrated inviolate. His fear during the war had been that the South would win and he would die and slavery would be continued and his darling would stand in some showing room, a commodity to be inspected. He wanted to see that she was untouched. He didn't understand his wish to be a violation. He did not understand his wish as Isabella did. He wanted to replace the images from his night terrors with an image from daydreams, a tableau of his daughter, almost white and cold as marble, but alive and forever most significantly draped. He wished he could assure and ensure that no one but her mother and her future husband would ever see whatever there might be between her legs. If she couldn't have a baby it wouldn't surprise him. He imagined she might be missing an essential part. He imagined her not merely inviolate; he imagined her inviolable. He wished her sex away without blinking at the violence of the hope.

Her mother was noticing something else. Or trying to take notice of something she couldn't quite catch sight of but could sense. One of the women was falling in love with Alice. Who was looking at her daughter through too-shiny eyes? Eyes full of tears. Her mother was wondering what had put them there. And how it was that her daughter was intact; she had had word from a Roman doctor, an authority on such things, and yet something about the girl was different. When asked, Alice would only say, "I've seen Rome and Rome has seen me." Alice was not the same country girl she had been in Washington.

She confessed to her mother what she would never tell her father. She had been kissed by Charlotte Cushman. She would have preferred to have kissed Emma Stebbins. And of course she was exceptionally curious about Edmonia Lewis, the black lady sculptress, who had appeared in Hawthorne's *Marble Faun*. The kiss was of curious origin—provoked by Alice's own awareness of two Cleopatras, S———'s version and Lewis's. Only Charlotte and Alice and Emma had paid attention.

Moses Ezekiel had miscalculated. Shortly after the *tableau vivant* incident, his woman packed up his daughter and returned to southwest Washington.

If he wanted to see the girl, he would have to go after her.

When Hope came out of the bathroom the pages were in her Dial-soap-washed and Jergen's-lotioned hands. She smelled like Abel.

"He loved that story," said Nicholas.

"I don't think so," said Hope. "I remember being so very disappointed that he didn't. I remember all he said after he finished reading it was 'Are you a lesbo?' All I could think to say to that was 'Are you an idiot?' so I didn't say anything."

"If you had said, 'Yes, I'm a lesbo,' he would have said, 'I'm queer sometimes too, aren't we perfect for each other?'" said Nicholas.

"Then I'm very sorry I didn't tell that lie."

"I'm sorry too."

"Was Abel gay?"

"No, he only sometimes feared he was."

"What an odd thing to say."

"And sad thing to feel."

"Lunch?"

"After a stroll through the Country Music Hall of Fame. Abel would want me to see Elvis's solid-gold Cadillac. And no more soul food unless it's at Prince's Hot Chicken," said Nicholas.

He leaned over the bed and picked up a medicine bottle three-quarters full of what appeared to be black sand.

"Is this what I think it is?"

"Do you think it's volcanic sand?"

"Yes."

"Yes."

"And this critter," Hope said, pulling a small white limestone carved rabbit or squirrel off of a shelf, "is the Edmondson I gave him for his birthday the last year we were together."

"What's this?"

"A starfish from Bohol."

"Here's another copy of the *Dr. Dan* book."

"I'll take that for Ajay."

Hope added this last to the pile she had been creating all morning, a pile that included the books next to Abel's bed, *Epitaph of a Small Winner*, *Eugénie Grandet*, *Man's Fate*, and *Where the Wild Things Are*, as well as a Ringling Brothers ticket and a picture of a fountain in Central Park. All this she slid into her large canvas bag.

Nicholas put on his black jacket, Hope put on her shoes, they rinsed out the jelly glasses, and they locked the front door. The house was empty again.

TWENTY

STANDING IN FRONT of Elvis Presley's "solid-gold Cadillac," a cream-colored pearlized 1960 Fleetwood, Nicholas Gordon did not appear impressed, not with the gold-plated refrigerator that froze ice in two minutes, not with the gold-plated shoe buffer, not even with the gold records embedded in the roof of the automobile.

"It was a very good thing we did for you Yanks, the British Invasion. Without Mick and John and Ray . . ." said Nicholas.

"Ray?" queried Hope.

"Davies," said Nicholas.

"Davis, the Kinks," said Hope.

"Davies . . . without the Beatles, the Stones, the Kinks, and Van Morrison, America would have been doomed to hearing the blues raped rather than reinvented," said Nicholas. Hope shook her head.

"I am not a big fan of either the Beatles or the Kinks," said Hope.

"But you appreciate the Stones," said Nicholas.

"Love the Stones. Manuel designed 'the lips,'" said Hope.

"God designed those lips," said Nicholas.

"But Manuel, the man who made your jacket and Parsons's, Manuel turned the lips into a pillow as a make-up gift for Mick after they fell out when Mick was hitting on whoever it was Manuel was with at the time," said Hope.

" 'No shit,' as the young people say," said Nicholas.

" 'Word,' as my young folk say," said Hope.

"How did you know Manuel made my jacket?" asked Nicholas.

"No one but Manuel could make that jacket, or those boots," said Hope.

"You recognized a signature," said Nicholas.

"This time," said Hope.

"Take me to the nearest martini. Did I see a Palm?" asked Nicholas.

"You saw a Palm," said Hope.

Walking through the tourists, they made their way from the half-light of the Country Music Hall of Fame galleries to the bright light of the Nashville sidewalk.

Turning to take one last look back at the building as Hope pointed out the notes for "Amazing Grace" decorating the rotunda, Nicholas laughed out loud—with, not at, the building. Finally Nicholas was impressed. He was amused by the visual evocation of a stack of records, a piano keyboard (the windows were the black keys), and a late-fifties car fin. Nicholas had fond memories of the backseat of a certain 1957 Chevy and a certain piano player.

They were seated beneath the faces of Trisha Yearwood and Jennifer Aniston. Having downed a steak, two martinis, and a full plate of Half & Half—a mess of fried onion rings and matchstick potatoes—Nicholas was asking for pudding and waving toward a tray of large but not luscious desserts. Hope ordered a cappuccino. Nicholas ordered a very tall slice of chocolate cake embedded with what appeared to be malted milk balls. After the cake arrived he took one bite, then pushed it away.

"You didn't ask me how I got the jacket," said Nicholas.

"I assumed it was a gift from Abel," said Hope.

"On the occasion of my seventieth birthday," said Nicholas.

"How did he seem?" asked Hope.

"Guarded," said Nicholas.

"Guarded?" repeated Hope.

"He couldn't say anything about his work to me, being who I am, or who I was, but I suspect he was tired of parsing 'perpetual detainment.' And he was strangely worried about some marine named Seamus," said Nicholas.

"Seamus?" asked Hope.

"Like the poet," said Nicholas.

"Killed by friendly fire?" asked Hope.

"Just heading out to Iraq, if I remember correctly. From somewhere in Illinois, I think. Abel said he had met someone who had asked him about this Seamus. Whatever Abel found out about Seamus changed how Abel was seeing things," said Nicholas.

"Seamus? What did he say about Sammie?" asked Hope.

"That she was a mistake. That she was God's punishment for what he and I had done," said Nicholas.

"Whoa," said Hope.

"And 'the picture was prettier,'" said Nicholas.

"What did he mean by that?" asked Hope.

★ ★ ★

Abel's habit of over-sharing in romantic and sexual matters had extended past Grandma to Nicholas. He had indulged the habit when he had gone out to Manila for Nicholas's seventieth birthday celebration. Nicholas had always enjoyed Abel's indiscretions even more than Grandma had. His stories had kept Nicholas feeling sexually competitive. Nicholas knew much that he couldn't tell.

When Sammie's pink and white skin turned red, as it often did—she was a woman given to blushing with embarrassment and flushing in anger—it complemented her blue-black hair most particularly.

She bought simple tailored clothes that made her look like Jackie Kennedy dressed from Wal-Mart, a credit to her taste and a boon to Abel's bank account. Sammie knew how a thing was supposed to look—she had developed her eye for clothing by regularly reading news magazines and perusing the society pages of the newspaper—she just didn't know how they were supposed to feel.

One of the first things Abel had noticed about Sammie was that she always looked good in pictures, and it was something he had told his grandmother the day he had taken her a picture of Sammie and said they were going to get married. *The picture was prettier.*

I want some of that, he thought, but did not say, the first time he saw the woman who would be his second wife. He waited to speak the thought aloud inside his head until he was leaving his office, until he was walking out the tall plate-glass doors that separated the glass-sheathed tower that housed his office, on the always perfectly sixty-eight-degree twenty-third floor, from the wildly fluctuating temperatures of the sidewalk. He was moving toward his perfectly wet and cool five o'clock scotch after a hard day's work in municipal finance.

I want some of that. He spoke the words to himself, but softly. He was in the habit of taking himself into his own confidence. Back then he had had to speak a thought aloud, or commit it to a piece of paper, or type it on a screen, to allow himself to know a thing, especially a thing about himself.

He raised his hand to cover his mouth as he spoke. His ring finger (encircled by a gold band engraved with the Harvard Class of 1981 insignia) caressed his chin.

He did not say he was slightly anxious. Anxiety was an emotion he wished to forget. He would not state this idea to himself. He would not commit it to paper or screen. Soon he would not know it.

"She is pretty enough," he said, "pretty enough for a white prince, pretty enough for me."

Sammie, a runner-up to Miss Alabama and the winner of the Miss Peanut Festival, worked for the same bank as Abel did, but in the District of Columbia office, planning and setting up parties where the lobbyists lobbied, instead of in the Nashville office where Abel worked.

He never did tell Samantha that the reason he had developed such a strong and sudden interest in banking regulations was that he had seen her picture in the bank newsletter. And he never told her *the picture was prettier.*

Abel had ducked out of his office early for his perfect scotch. Needing something to read while he waited for his buddies to arrive, he had grabbed the in-house rag he never read.

When Caldwell Lyttle, then a newly minted lawyer serving a

tour of duty as vice president of municipal finance, sat down beside him, Abel made way for his buddy by laying his reading material on the bartop. As Lyttle settled onto a stool and ordered his drink (Heineken in a bottle), Abel tapped a photograph on the glossy page, while commenting that the woman was pretty. Lyttle laughed. Then he set his glass bottle down on Abel's newsletter.

"Nobody's gonna go near that! She's got four or five kids, all boys, a dead husband, and liberal, unemployed, hippie bluegrass musician parents," said Lyttle.

Abel wasn't so sure. Of course, if a girl had liberal parents, it helped if they were rich, preferably wickedly rich of the trustafarian persuasion.

Abel grimaced. He was thinking about Margot "Gogo" Linden. Gogo was smart, and funky, and fun, and white. She was too pale to be pretty—her hair was white blond, her eyes were light watery gray, and she wore too much makeup trying to give herself some color—but she had a dancer's body and bearing and she knew her own powerful mind. Her momma was a judge and a former Junior League president. Her father was a physician. Abel had very much wanted to marry Gogo Linden, but she couldn't or wouldn't abide his politics.

"She can't abide my politics," he had typed onto the screen of his computer monitor the day they had broke up. He didn't say, she is afraid of my sorrow, and my anger, and of the way I drink the way her daddy drank. He didn't say it. He didn't write it. He didn't type it. For a few days he felt the pull of temptation. He had a love for truth. He had professional knowledge that knowing the lay of the land, of the emotional territory surrounding a moment or a self, could be useful.

He had a more profound knowledge that embracing certain dark ideas, no matter how truthful, could slaughter the future. To know that Gogo Linden held within her pale self the potential to loathe him was a dagger, even if it was sheathed in the knowledge that her potential for loathing was born of a loathing for her brilliant daddy.

He bit his tongue. He kept his hands down by his sides. When his fingers were curled over his keyboard he bid them work only on the documents at hand.

Soon all he knew about Margot Linden was that her politics were too liberal for him and her chest was too flat. Soon he was silent about that knowledge, allowing it to be replaced with *My old girlfriend, Gogo, was an amazing gal, she's a producer on* The Dennis Miller Show, *she's their token liberal.*

He spoke of Margot so often his friends often felt invited to ask him questions about her. Lyttle was no exception. He was asking when Abel would be next going out west. Abel smiled. Abel liked it when his white friends pushed him back toward white girls.

When Abel left the bar, with one of the secretaries from Caldwell's division, *a bubbly girl*, he took the stained bank newsletter with him. He dropped it atop the burled-walnut and bird's-eye maple Art Deco chest of drawers that stood sentry across from the bed as he walked into his room. The bubbly girl was following him.

Abel pulled the secretary's shirt over her head. He liked the look of her breasts in her front-closing bra. He smiled. He was proud of his ability with clasps. He had it undone with one hand.

He was a breast man. He liked the moment everything but

the breasts was covered. The moment before he touched them, the moment before he made the nipples hard and made the tight slit wet. He liked it a lot, more than he liked the feeling of the stiffening in his pants. Before was always for him all about the female. During was all about him. Just as he sank into her slit, he wondered vaguely if his buddy was giving his secretary a bit of the same at the very same time.

After he came, after he threw her front-closing, purple, thirty-four double-D bra out of the bed, wishing it would be as socially acceptable for him to throw this new pale, blond thing beside him out of the bed, it struck him hard that he was bored with new beginnings, blonds, and breasts.

Sometime before midnight the girl left. She had a kid to go home to. He liked white girls with kids. Usually their families— their mummy or their mama, their poppa or their daddy, their ex-husband, their somebody—kept them from getting serious about him.

He woke up, as was his habit, around two when the bars closed and publicly loud people poured onto the street. He went into the bathroom, then into his kitchen, comforted by the familiar sounds of the night. He poured himself his usual, a glass of milk with a slug of brandy. Listening to the shouting back and forth of happy promises as they morphed into worried queries—*let's get together soon . . . stay in touch . . . see you tomorrow . . . where did we park the car . . . that's my cab . . . I've got to get home*—intensified his intimate connection to the city. Every night he got up to stand on the fringes of the party as the other guests were leaving. Usually it made him happy. This night was different.

Long after his glass was drained he moved toward his bed.

On the way he grabbed the newsletter from the top of his bureau. He glanced at it for a moment, put it next to his Westclox travel alarm with round face and glow-in-the-dark hands, then stretched out beneath his Italian linen sheets and clicked off the light. It was almost four o'clock.

Sitting up in his bed, after the alarm had gone off, Abel drank his coffee from a porcelain cup decorated with chevrons, while watching the barges float on the slow-moving Cumberland River. In the morning quiet, he began his day's work. When he was finished reading the *New York Times*, article by article, he glanced through the headlines of the *Tennessean*. When he was finished with the *Tennessean*, he grabbed the bank newsletter. He liked the look of the pretty face encircled by the beer halo.

Samantha Weekly, the caption announced: a pretty face atop a boyish body in a pert pink suit. With ebony hair, magnolia skin, and red lips, she looked like Snow White in the picture book he'd seen a thousand years earlier. And she had the longest legs he had ever seen.

Abel phoned up a reason to visit the bank's Washington office. *The picture was prettier,* he thought but did not say the first time he met the woman who would be his second wife. He asked Sammie out on a date after that first meeting. Walking to join her for drinks at the Old Ebbit Grille, he whispered to himself *the picture was prettier.* A month later he fucked her for the first time in the middle of a two-day team-building seminar held in a Pennsylvania Avenue hotel during a coffee break. Her hair let down reached almost to her knees. Then she got pregnant and they set a wedding date.

Samantha suggested that they marry in the garden of her

grandmother's farmhouse, out in Limestone County, Alabama, Abel suggested they marry in the parlor of his grandmother's house in Davidson County, Tennessee. It was decided.

Except Grandma would have no part of the thing. This threw Abel for a loop. He had always been a preferred, perhaps the preferred, grandchild. His mother had been the eldest of seven girls, the first to marry, the first to provide a legitimate offspring. It seemed ridiculous for his grandmother, whose skin was so pale, the color of honey mixed into the richest cream, to refuse him this small honor because his bride's skin was the color of eggshells.

"It is not her color I don't like," Grandma said.

"What?" Abel asked abruptly, hoping to scare her out of answering.

"It's her station," Grandma, who was too old to be scared, replied.

At the time, Abel thought he understood. He had always suspected his grandmother was some kind of snob. He thought he could use that. If Grandma was speaking out of high-yellow supremacy, she should understand, if she did not share, his pleasure in choosing a spouse he could place himself above. She herself had chosen a husband she had placed herself above, until the world had placed the famous painter above her.

"What?" asked Abel again, this time more gently. He was curious about anything the old woman might have observed that he hadn't.

"In my time always-poor white people were far more dangerous than rich white people, or even used-to-be-rich white people," said Grandma.

Abel smiled. In Abel's experience, Grandma's experience

was rarely relevant. He was willingly informed by her observations and her analysis of the present. But when she started talking about her history—about her great-aunt, the root doctor in some town in Georgia where she'd fed white sawmill workers turpentine when they'd got syphilis; or about her mother, the young maid, who'd been raped by her employer's son the first week on the job; or about how the young man's family had felt so sorry they'd eventually sent Grandma away to school in New York—Abel's eyes glazed over.

Over-told stories of vanished civilizations did not interest him. Grandma's quibble with Sammie, couched as it was in history, was brushed aside as an insufficient obstacle.

Abel married Samantha at a wedding chapel down on Music Row. There was no budging Grandma. And no budging Abel. The wedding took place at noon.

Her parents out of their stage clothes in their Sunday best were presentable: dear, intelligent, curious. They had raised their only daughter vaguely in the southern suburbs when the land had still been the out-acres of played-out and broken-down, poor southern towns, then fancy suburbs, surrounded by cousins. The brothers and their wives and her cousins, were, thought Abel, decidedly NOCD.

Samantha and her female cousins had grown up bored and drunk and flirting with any man who looked like he would carry them away from bored and drunk and suburban.

One of the brothers lived in a big house in Decatur out on Wheeler Lake. After the band broke up he had gone to the University of Alabama, majored in mechanical engineering, and gotten a job in Huntsville. The third of the triplets lived in Ardmore, within walking distance of Samantha. He was an electrician.

All summer long the electrician's wife kept three inflatable kiddie pools inflated, two on the back lawn and one on the porch. The one on the porch contained ice, beers, and wine coolers. One of the two pools on the lawn usually contained splashing children. The other usually contained Abel's electrician brother-in-law-to-be, watching the splashing children while downing adult beverages.

The attendants were Samantha's sisters-in-law and Abel's son. Her four boys, in jeans and red checkered shirts, sang "I've Got a Never Ending Love for You" as the crowd gathered. Grandma hated to see Ajay, the youngest in the group, squashed under and surrounded by trash. Raised as she had been inside the walls of a decaying plantation house, a petted and pitied high-yellow house servant hired to brush an old white woman's hair, Grandma had been carefully trained, by ladies propped up high by invisible distinctions, to distinguish between different shades of white.

There was too much white southern lady blood and too much persecuted slave blood in Grandma for the lady not to wonder whether these new people were trash, or hippies, or hippie trash.

When she was young, Grandma could tell trash, dressed up or costume covered, just as easily as she had been able to recognize the lightest-light-skinned Negro. Since about 1970 it had become hard to tell who was who, black or white.

She knew in her heart God didn't love her so much that he'd have to chastise her so hard as to make these new relations hippie trash. Hippie trash was the worst of all.

There was one simple but real consolation. Grandma was

glad the new wife's sons weren't near as handsome as Ajay. That was the good part.

Grandma was also glad the boys were short and scrawny. She hoped they were short enough. She would not bother to learn their names. Their shirttails were out and their shoes were dirty and their hair was unkempt. The grandson was making a mistake. Abel believed he would make of this woman a servant. Grandma was not so sure.

Already Sammie had succeeded in insisting that both she and Abel transfer to jobs in Huntsville (she from Washington, he from Nashville) and start married life together in Alabama, explaining she wanted her boys to go to the University of Alabama and she wanted them to go cheap. Saying she wanted her children to know and to love the state where she was born and raised, Samantha, in one fell swoop, got Abel away from Washington women and Nashville black folk.

When the bride entered, carrying a carefully trimmed bouquet of crimson grocery-store roses, Samantha's parents beamed.

Her two sisters-in-law held hands, crying softly, each absolutely overwhelmed by how much their husband's sister was willing to sacrifice to provide for her four children. She was a good mama.

Silently, her brothers cursed Sammie's first husband, the college football quarterback, for dying. Then, again silently, they cursed their sister for bringing the family to this strange wedding with strange black people. They'd liked it better when they hadn't known there were any rich blacks except in sports and on teevee. The only black person they wanted to know personally was Curtis Lowe.

Leaning against the back wall of the wedding chapel, the electrician brother was chastising himself for not having killed Sammie's first husband or her second husband before they were the first or second husband.

Then he remembered there hadn't been a moment he had known she was going to marry either man before he'd known she'd been knocked up with the man's baby.

Sammie got engaged the old-fashioned way. The electrician shook his head. He checked his watch. The longest two minutes in the history of his world had just passed. He wasn't killing his unborn niece or nephew's daddy. No matter what. *Hell, come this summer I'm gonna be sitting in a blow-up baby pool drinking beer with a colored dude.* The only good thing about it, the electrician could figure, was that the colored dude pretty much just looked like a white guy, except maybe a Jewish white guy, with a tan.

The bride and groom exchanged vows. Samantha's parents sang a cleaned-up version of "Willin'." Her boys shuffled and kicked and whispered, ignoring the hand their mother put on their shoulders.

Grandma had to sit down. She was carried back to plaster-wall Georgia, to sudden knowledge, to an understanding that when this many white people get together in a house, the black folk are working for them. Grandma wanted to faint.

Sammie's sons continued to fidget and whisper, oblivious to the scowls directed at them. This didn't worry or irritate Abel. There was no one in attendance it embarrassed him to have see the boys' misbehavior. Only immediate family was present. He would teach the boys better and soon enough.

★   ★   ★

"Did you come to the wedding?"

"Phoebe came. I've started to collect old American advertisements. Phoebe Redmund, Abel's cousin, is my primary dealer. Phoebe fills me in."

"Has anyone ever told you you have boundary issues?"

"Where shall we go next?"

"You tell me."

"The Islamic Center."

TWENTY-ONE

T HE MOSQUE LOOKED stranded. Nearby houses and
hedges were just beginning to be decorated with white
lights. On three different lawns inflated snowmen stood sentry.
On another an inflated giant snow globe glowed. Christmas trees,
fake and real, foil and green, were in almost every window. Atop
each indoor tree was a star placed to celebrate the bright light that
guided wise men to a baby.

What Hope considered to be the first big mosque in
Nashville stood on Twelfth Avenue. On Fridays the mosque
hosted a market: black olives, pita bread, falafel. But mainly it offered conversation and a rapidly growing community. This was a
Tuesday. The neighborhood anchored by Corner Music and by
Katy K's Ranch Dressing, a vintage clothing shop, looked like
what it was: a boho-honky-tonk-cool subset of gritty American.

As she searched for an always-hard-to-find parking space in
the quirky South Nashville neighborhood, Hope tortured
Nicholas by crooning along with Merle Haggard, who was declaring, "If we make it through December everything's gonna
be all right I know," an earnest promise that sounded false.

By the time she was squaring up to wedge her MINI Cooper

between two gigantic Suburbans into a nonexistent space, Chrissie Hynde was harmonizing with the Blind Boys of Alabama, "in the bleak midwinter, a long, long time ago." Abel would have liked that one. He'd loved the Pretenders. Nicholas joined in when Hope and Chrissie added their voices to Clarence Fountain's, Jimmy Carter's, and George Scott's when they got to the words "Hear me."

Hope didn't care to or dare go into the mosque. To enter so close to Abel's death, hyper-Christian promise keeper that he had become, seemed both disrespectful and dangerous. Nicholas went in alone, leaving Hope to wander the seasonally expectant streets.

After Nicholas disappeared inside the yellow brick building, Hope invited the ghost of Abel to wander with her. The ghost did not appear. She was sorry. Abel knew, and would tell anyone who would listen, that there was no greater joy than being a black child at Christmas. When he had told Hope that, he had expected her to chime in harmoniously; he had been certain that she would know what he meant. But she had held silent. She had *kinda-sorta* known what he meant, but because she had read a lot, not because she had had any personal experience of what it was to be what Abel had drunkenly and repeatedly called "the good hope of a bad people."

Or had he said best hope of a plagued people? She was beginning to forget the details—but she remembered this: when Abel talked like that she tasted some of what she imagined her mother's life to have been before her marriage.

Both her mother and her first husband had been campus kids who had grown up in the immediate vicinity of black colleges. A sense of what Hope's mother's life had been during her girlhood, before her marriage to Mad Morgan, was one of the things Abel had brought to Hope. A better thing was a sense of what it was to be a black child at Christmas. Abel had given Hope that when he had given her Ajay.

She would remember this as the year she and her son were twinned by the isolating sorrow and rage of precipitous father loss. It would be her second unmitigatedly sad Christmas, unless they mitigated the sadness with anger.

"Onward, Christian Soldiers." That was the song played at Abel's funeral that had made sense. And it was the song that had made Hope saddest. Walking through the neighborhood surrounding the Islamic Center and mosque, Hope couldn't avoid knowing how some of the neighbors would have offended her ex-husband. He would have loathed the dusky faces and dusky eyes, but most he would have hated the sounds and sights of the Muslim call to prayer.

As she walked around the periphery of Christmas and the Confederacy and the Nashville Islamic Center, all of it wrapped up together and placed in stark relief for Hope how *peculiarly* religious Abel had become.

When Hope had first known Abel in college he had claimed to be a Buddhist and officially been a Baptist; he had barely tolerated being married in a church. Before their wedding, at Hope's prodding, he had taken a course to be welcomed into the Episcopal Church. At the end he hadn't wanted to change denominations. He hadn't believed enough to warrant a change. He had remained a Baptist, baptized, who claimed Buddhism as an inspiration. But somehow he had died claiming to be, and claimed by, an evangelical Christianity.

★　★　★

She had gotten up from her bed in the earliest, shortest hours of Tuesday morning to do an Internet search for an article she had vaguely remembered. She loved Google. The article that twenty years earlier had taken Abel days to find and hours to copy, feeding coins into a slot at the Library of Congress, she had retrieved and printed in a matter of minutes.

She pulled out the little notebook she kept in her purse where she had made her notes and read, "From the Fall of 1862 until the last days of the civil war, religious revivalism swept through Confederate forces with an intensity that led one southerner to declare the armies had been 'nearly converted into churches.' "

According to Drew Faust, southerners were long and peculiarly experienced in defining their political cause as godly and discussing war in terms of God.

A fact Faust had unearthed that had intrigued Abel and had bored Hope was that "nearly two hundred million pages of tracts were distributed to soldiers during the war." Abel had been impatient when he had explained to Hope that the tracts Faust referred to had been printed sermons. "They were something like Lauro's," Abel had said.

In Abel-speak, what did it mean to fly away? To die? To escape? To escape by dying? How did he tie the Italian experience to his Dixie memory? Hope wished she had taken the little plane from Abel's bedroom.

She was starting to think of her ex-husband as a modern-day black Confederate. And she was wondering if she shouldn't stop. Hope had been born with a good memory. Brief, intensive, state-paid training had made it great. Nevertheless, there was something Faust had written near the end of the article

Hope had read that she wanted to remember but already couldn't.

She willed her mind slack and it came back to her. Deserting soldiers had been punished with "thirty-nine lashes and a brand on the cheek." That was the fact that had intrigued Hope and Abel at the time they had first read Faust's article. Abel had been visibly disturbed by the fury and frustration provoked when white deserters, as reported by Faust, had been punished exactly in the manner of runaway slaves.

Abel had experienced a complex fury and frustration of his own when confronted with "thirty-nine lashes and a brand on the cheek." It stole something from the slaves. It branded their boldness cowardice, even as it stole something from the white men's identities. *The Thirty-Nine Steps.* They had read aloud to each other Buchan's 1915 "shocker" during their early days in Manila. *Thirty-nine lashes and a brand on the cheek.* Had Abel translated that indignity into new sets of gestures, gestures he could misuse at Guantánamo and Abu Ghraib?

The only tools she could quickly grab to use against that possible reality were ignorance, lies, and the special kind of lie that is storytelling. And they were barely enough after having seen those photographs on Abel's table.

She and Abel had met a couple in the Philippines, a black tandem couple, the Winters, a beautiful couple, who had allowed Hope to attempt to sculpt them in exchange for the pieces. The Winters had wanted to be immortalized in a spy movie. Hope had distracted them while they sat for her by making up an elaborate Hansel and Gretel spy story, about a man who left a trail that could be followed only by the woman who loved him.

The hero in her story had been a rogue Foreign Service officer who avenged people who had been tortured by torturing their tormentors. She had developed her character by crossing the Winters with an urban legend she had first encountered in Manila, the legend of Fearless Laurel.

This was the kind of tale that was told over the heel of a bottle in the middle of the night. The kind of tale that was spoken in whispers by drunks to drunks.

Fearless Laurel. The first part of the story was always the evolution of his name. Over time, in cells throughout the world, Fearless Laurel had been shortened to FL. After that, eventually, he had started to be called Florida, first in a small house in a South American city, but the nickname had stuck and had traveled. The three little syllables had made it around the world. Florida. Those three beats made it possible for men and women who were being tortured to alter the balance of power—if not the hour of their death. They could call out, "Florida!" It was a promise that someone, Florida, FL, Fearless Laurel, would come to torment the tormentor.

Florida. After those three syllables were whispered, shouted, spat, or even mumbled, the fear was never just on one side.

Stories swirled in the quarter-world of spies, spymasters, operatives, contractors, and international crazies, the world of diamond merchants, oil merchants, and arms merchants, and of do-gooding NGO runners: of flayings and faggings, of peelings and proddings, of brandings and beatings almost beyond telling.

Fearless Laurel afflicted people not for pleasure or gain but for vengeance, deterrence, and solace. He offered each and every anonymous victim in each and every anonymous cell, room, or basement the joy of knowing that each and every anonymous tormentor had reason to wonder if what he or she was doing, what he or she was about to do, would be done back to him or her and worse. Florida. Three little syllables that kept minds from breaking even as bones crick-cracked.

When Hope first heard the story she dismissed it completely as an urban legend. Then one night in a zouk in Martinique it was told to her again by a man who swore he knew someone Fearless Laurel had nearly killed. His own brother, and his brother had it coming. The young man in the zouk was ready to worship Fearless Laurel. Then he drank some more rum agricole and couldn't say anything at all.

"Do you think Fearless really exists?" Hope had asked.

"I hope he does," Abel had replied.

Hope wondered if before he had died Abel had feared that Fearless was coming for him. She sadly suspected Abel had exhausted himself creating variations on "thirty-nine lashes and a brand on the cheek."

There was a line she wanted to remember that wasn't coming back. To bring it back, Hope tried to imagine Abel reading the Faust article to her. Then she imagined herself quoting the missing line. The words returned: "Evangelical religion provided psychological reassurance to southern soldiers struggling with the daily threat of personal annihilation in its Christian promise of salvation and eternal life; conversion offered a special sort of consolation to the embattled Confederate." Hope decided she would rather have Florida. She was that Hatfield. And Abel had preferred Christ. He was that southern.

★　★　★

Cold, and tired of walking, Hope returned to the car and turned on the heat. She was just beginning to thaw when Nicholas began pounding on the passenger window. Like a magician pronouncing, "Ta-da," Nicholas announced, "Look who I found."

Nicholas stood back to reveal the jolliest man Hope knew, Mo Henry. Mo came around to Hope's side of the car as Nicholas moved toward the passenger side. When she rolled down the window he leaned in to kiss her.

"What are you doing here?" asked Hope.

"Coming to see you," replied Mo.

"Getting in?" asked Hope.

"Running round to Sinbad's. We can grab a coffee and something sweet."

"Perfection," said Nicholas, getting into Hope's car. As Mo moved toward his car, Hope took her car out of park but did not take her foot off the brake.

"You ran into Mo Henry at the mosque?" asked Hope.

"We met at the funeral. I asked him to meet me here and introduce me to the imam," said Nicholas.

"How do you really know Mo?" asked Hope.

"You don't want to know," said Nicholas.

"Yes, I do," said Hope.

She took her foot off the brake. She never stayed tired or furious long. Nicholas put his hand on her knee, stroking across the bone as he had done years earlier, only then her knee had been naked. Through the nylon of the stockings and the wool of the pants she felt the call of old times. The old man made her feel like a younger woman. "Don't you feel my leg, don't you feel my leg, 'cause if you feel my leg, you'll want to feel my thigh, if you feel my thigh, you're gonna get a surprise, don't you feel my leg," sang Hope.

"Blue Lu Barker," said Nicholas.

"You know everything," said Hope.

"Yes, I do," said Nicholas.

It is hard not to like a man who knows that Blue Lu Barker sung "Don't You Make Me High" a half-century before Van Morrison, who remembered, or even knew about, Danny Barker, the jazz banjoist, even as she realized that he was romancing her, now as then, for purposes that had little to do with lust and even less to do with love, but had everything to do with staying amused during violent times in desperate places.

She launched into a peculiarly twangy "Things Have Gone to Pieces." Singing loud about a faucet dripping in the kitchen and a picture falling down from a wall, getting fired and a lightbulb's going out—singing a stone country song Nicholas couldn't possibly like, she pushed him away with a smile. She didn't want Nicholas getting a big head or bigger ideas.

TWENTY-TWO

HOPE DRANK WHAT she fondly called sweetened black silt but was otherwise known as Sinbad's Turkish coffee, hoping Ajay and Waycross, somewhere in the far North, were finding their way to having the time they needed.

Sinbad's is in a little strip of restaurants and shops across from Belmont University, a Baptist college famous for its music business program. Situated at the corner of "Baptists don't believe in drinking" and "Beer is a food group," the neighborhood had a charm born of geographic irony.

Sandwiched between the round and brown Mo and the skinny and silver Nicholas, it was impossible not to realize Mo and Nicholas had each appealed to an opposite pole of Abel's identity. Mo had appealed to Abel's old-timey black servant self; Nicholas had inhabited and inspired all Abel's dreams of double-zero-seven cosmopolitan spydom.

Mo was both what Abel had longed to leave behind and the best of Abel—a sense of tradition and the capacity to be loyal. Nicholas was what Abel had longed to attain—unbridled power—and Abel's shallowest love of shimmer, international tailoring of the most complex sort.

Abel had failed in both directions and he had triumphed in both directions. It occurred to Hope that she too was reaching for some part of Abel she didn't know, that she had hoped to know better, but now never would, unless she gleaned something essential from the memories of these men. They were the poles Abel had connected just before vanishing.

Nicholas tucked into his second diamond of baklava. Mo was eating hummus and drinking a Coke while he waited for a falafel sandwich. Hope's attention drifted to the street and across it to Abel's favorite Nashville restaurant.

The International Market, directly across from where Hope was sitting, now vaguely swabbing a dab of Mo's hummus onto a torn triangle of pita, had sustained a generation of aspiring singers, fading stars, students, and other near-homeless people; but Hope had never gone there. Abel had frequented the place, making it too likely a venue for a chance encounter with a difficult ex-husband. He had said it reminded him of Manila. He had said he appreciated the tastiness of Styrofoam takeaway containers filled up with noodles and broccoli and rice (cooked Thai, Chinese, and Vietnamese style) from the International Market steam table.

Hope wondered if the waiter now bringing her second cup of coffee and Mo's falafel—one of four waiters wearing black pants and white shirts and looking distinctly Middle Eastern as they moved about the room—was from the Kurdish part of Iraq.

Knowing that most of the seven thousand Kurds in Nashville came from Iraq, she thought it would be a very good guess. As she started to let herself get pulled back to half listening to the jerky conversation, part hide-and-seek, part tug-of-war, going on between Nicholas and Mo, it seemed to Hope that both men were doing exactly what she was doing: reaching for some part of Abel they didn't know, that they had hoped to know better, but now never would, unless they discovered the missing part at this table.

Mo was teasing Nicholas about not heading over to Little Kurdistan. Nicholas gibed back with faux acknowledgment that he might just be a little conspicuous. They agreed that one of Abel's great advantages in the life he had chosen had been his chameleon face. He could have been anything. White, black, Jewish, Arab. Hispanic. People had mistaken him constantly for everything but Asian, and wearing a barong Tagalog he had been, on more than one occasion, mistaken for Filipino.

With Nashville having been designated an official Iraqi voting location (just like Chicago, Detroit, and Los Angeles), Abel's little band of mourners agreed a significant change was taking place in the geopolitics of the American South. It was not an exaggeration to say that Nashville was a focus of attention in the Kurdish world. As Iraq prepared for the first open elections in fifty years, Iraqis everywhere were talking about how the Samir who had discovered Saddam Hussein hiding in a spider hole and punched him in the face had come to Nashville to register to vote. The gossip was smoke that patterned the walls of Sinbad's.

Hope, Nicholas, and Mo each silently wished Abel had lived to see this day, the day somebody he loved recognized his—and Nashville's—significance to the international scene. He had been in his last year of high school when the first of four big waves of Kurdish immigrants had hit Nashville in 1976 and the first fifty

Kurds had been settled; he'd been back in Nashville, working as a banker and paying more attention than anybody had known, when, after Saddam had targeted Kurds working for nonprofits for extinction, the final of the four waves had hit in 1997.

Hope wondered if some of those folks had been spies in Iraq. Abel would have known. Abel had lived long enough and weird enough to coin the phrase Hope and Nicholas and Mo had all in their time quoted: "The Cumberland is a river in the Middle East."

"What if Abel saved more lives than he stole?"

"How much would that justify?"

"There are people in this restaurant Abel saved from dying?"

"Which people?"

"You know I can't tell you that."

Mo was gesturing to Hope to take the last bite of hummus. She appreciated his good manners. And she appreciated a fact Abel would have appreciated: his little town had become an international power and he was a part of making it so. She suspected the Cumberland was not merely a river in the Middle East, but that the Cumberland was an important river in the Middle East.

"Why did Abel leave Huntsville?"

No one answered her. The conversation veered back to the personal. Hope was surprised to hear Mo and Nicholas ragging on each other by throwing pithy Abel put-downs. She was surprised that Abel had told Nicholas and Mo so much about each other. She would have thought Abel would have feared Mo would find Nicholas too fey and Nicholas would find Mo too servile. She would have thought wrong.

Nicholas was feeling comfortable enough to venture aloud a theory he expected Hope would find silly. He wanted to gauge Mo's reaction. Nicholas raised the possibility that Abel wasn't dead, that Abel was in some kind of international witness protection program, or self-generated exile. Mo was sure Abel was dead.

"I saw the body," said Mo.

"And you are absolutely sure it was him?" asked Nicholas.

"Changed, but yeah. I've known Abel since he was a gleam in his daddy's eye," said Mo.

"Were you surprised he went to the Rebel Yell?" asked Nicholas.

"Very," said Mo.

"Do you think it was some kind of signal?" asked Hope.

"I think it was suicide," said Mo.

"Suicide," repeated Nicholas.

"I think he wanted to die. He couldn't stand living with Sammie anymore. He knew his choices were hard on Ajay. Maybe too hard on Ajay," said Mo.

"Change the subject," said Hope.

"Abel said you knew more about Hope than anybody, because you knew her family from back in West Virginia," said Nicholas.

"I dated one of the aunts," said Mo.

"Did I know that?" asked Hope.

"No," said Mo.

"Did you know my mother?" asked Hope.

"Everybody brown who passed through the state of West Virginia back in the day knew, or knew of, Canary, and that's a story for a bar and a bourbon," said Mo.

"Unh-unh. You owe me after dropping the 'death by self-inflicted horse barn' bomb," said Hope.

"I'll tell you, but it's time to change venues."

"The wake cycles back," said Nicholas.

Hope was checking her watch as Mo started sing-talking "make it a Hurricane before I go insane, it's five o'clock somewhere." Nicholas laughed and started singing along. Hope joined in too. In the last year, "Five o'clock Somewhere" had become a favorite song of Abel's. They, the only three people in the world who knew this odd fact, were a cadre.

As she drove from Belmont Boulevard toward downtown, Nicholas told Hope that Mo was some kind of homeland security officer or operative. Hope almost believed Nicholas.

TWENTY-THREE

THEY WERE ENVELOPED by the Oak Bar's green couches, Hope and Nicholas sharing one and Mo across from them, bourbon in hand, on the other. Nicholas was in possession of a martini; Hope, a glass of red wine. They were settling in for the duration.

Spinning the history to become a suitable grown-up cocktail-time story of a pilgrim's tale, Mo began, "I dated this gal, up in Washington, distantly kin to you and Canary, met her on the Oak Bluffs tennis courts, but that's a different story. That gal took me to a party where I hooked up with one of the aunts, Grace."

"Aunt Sweet."

"Yeah, Aunt Sweet."

Canary Morgan came back to the mountain with a belly full of baby and no new name. The town was dazed. Their predictions had been precisely right and completely wrong. When any Negro from anywhere near around Harper's Ferry, West Virginia, remembered 1951 that's how they remembered it.

When the belle of the town had rejected the local colored

college, Storer, in favor of the flat cornfields of Oberlin, Ohio, colored Harper's Ferry had vaticinated, almost in one voice, "That chile be knocked up by some white boy and home before two semesters get good and gone."

Colored Harper's Ferry was tight braided to the college. Canary's parents, Charles and Emmaline Morgan, excepted, nobody at the college understood why anyone needed to leave the prettiest spot on earth to get an education.

According to the wisdom conventional on the campus as 1951 turned into 1952, to enroll a pretty Negro girl in a white college or university was to invite trouble.

"If she is to go away, she should go to Howard," said Emmaline's best friend, the chair of Howard's Women's Department. The unspoken implication being that if Canary was to go away she should go to the best and closest place—as long as it was a Negro place.

The decision to send Canary to a white school in Ohio had been community business. And community sorrow. All the dark folk of Harper's Ferry, including Canary's parents, had started missing the girl just as soon as she had started receiving thick envelopes with postmarks from the glamorous world— from towns called Cambridge and Bryn Mawr and Wellesley— addressed to the girl's certificate name, Mary Hope.

Mary Hope had been born with two pale eyes, milky skin, and bald. The day of her birth the midwife had laughed at her infant pinkness, reassuring Emmaline, her young mother, that the brown would come in within the week. Then it hadn't. Her skin had stayed light and one blue eye had turned brown.

She could tell things. That was hard on her daddy, who was

a man of science, and easy on everyone else. By the time she turned nine the entire town was convinced that her one brown eye was just God's way of signing his best work.

There wasn't a pair of ears that could still hear that didn't listen out for the sound of her song; the town counted on her to tell them today what would happen tomorrow, at least the important things.

When she got quiet, trouble was on the way. That's how she came to be called Canary. She knew when the weather would get bad; she knew when the sickness would be coming; she could tell when the white folks' mood was going to change.

Mainly she sang sweet and hot from morning till night—her own songs and pop songs, "Honeysuckle Rose" and "You Are My Sunshine," that migrated to the mountains with the bands who came to entertain and fleece the miners black and white— except when she was talking or laughing. And sometimes she stopped. Just like a canary in a coal mine, she was.

The happily noisy child grew to be a beautiful noisier woman; there wasn't much trouble that came to the town. The old folks said she was a second sun in the sky except on hot days; on hot days she was a cool breeze.

A few who imagined the possibility of a larger world meeting Negro Harper's Ferry by meeting Canary contemplated with pleasure the idea of her going to school at one of the Seven Sisters. These folk welcomed the big envelopes with applications for admission from Radcliffe and Wellesley and Bryn Mawr. Girls' schools. Academic convents, well and long organized to keep boys at bay.

The town had a special appreciation of Mount Holyoke, both for its geographic isolation in mountainous western Massachusetts and for its place in colored history as the first of the Seven Sisters to enroll an American girl of color.

That all ended when she started talking about Oberlin. When an envelope from an institution that enrolled white boys appeared in the Harper's Ferry post office, all support for any white school vanished.

Since just before the Second World War, coal land had been hemorrhaging colored men. The town needed Canary to lure a black boy back to it or to hug one tight from leaving. If colored Harper's Ferry were to survive it would be as a son-in-laws town. Canary's beauty and Canary's charm were a significant community resource.

Canary just knew she was getting bored having a whole town love her in general and no one love her in particular. She wasn't willing to wait for someone who *might* come to town, particularly when she heard daily gossip that the colored college *might* be closing soon.

She could defend her ambitions but she knew she'd only make matters worse and folk would call it backtalking.

And everybody she wanted to argue with knew the same facts she did: Oberlin was the first college in the country to accept Negro students, the one that was accepting *us* before the Civil War; Oberlin had been enrolling Negro students in 1837 and Storer hadn't even been founded until 1867; and last but not least to her or them, Oberlin had been stop ninety-nine on the Underground Railroad. Canary and the town knew the same facts—but she had seen something that had caused her to weight the facts differently.

Or rather, she had seen somebody. In Martinsburg shopping with her mother one Saturday afternoon she had caught a glimpse of male prettiness laughing, an unworried power, Mad Morgan in an Oberlin letterman jacket, leaning against a Jaguar XK-120. It had been enough to make her start chasing after the future—not waiting on the future to come to her.

And so she had gone away to the white school. Cold days were colder and hot days too hot at Storer.

When she rode back into town in a car too wide and too long for the narrow curving streets, in a yellow Rolls-Royce with a white boy at the wheel, no one noticed the ring on her left hand; all they were looking at was her belly—it appeared flat— and the white boy. All they could hear was the sound of her voice saying she had dropped out of school.

When they could see again people were flabbergasted to learn that Mary Hope, called Canary, had legally wed Mad, officially Madog, Morgan, coal baron and descendant of coal barons.

The town started talking again. She had married a rich white boy. There was a big diamond on her hand and no shot-gun in the picture.

It was a moment to take in. Marriage between a Negro woman and a Caucasian wasn't legal in West Virginia. Ohio. They had gotten married in Ohio. If it was probably true she had gotten knocked up before the tiny church wedding she wanted to tell them all about, it hardly seemed to matter.

On one fact everyone was in agreement: the strangest things in the world happen when you send a colored daughter out of town to a white school.

Mad Morgan fell in love with Canary Morgan the very first time he sat beside her in class and heard her talk.

She sounded and smelled so much like home that he didn't even notice she was black. It wasn't until he had her in his bed, until her clothes and his clothes were lying on top of each other down on the floor, until he was kissing her chocolate nipples and kissing her pillow lips and getting his fingers stuck in her long curls, that he thought to ask if he was her first man. Too embarrassed to answer yes, she just kissed him again and answered his question with a question of her own: "Am I your first colored girl?"

She was. He hadn't thought he liked colored girls. He liked her. Though her nose was broad and flat, her pillow lips were narrow, like her behind. Her hair was wild with long tight, tiny curls. Her skin was the yellow color of cream. One of her eyes was the color of the sky. The other eye was the exact color of earth. All that light skin framed by all that gold but niggerish hair. All those Latin and Greek thoughts, spoken in that hillbilly accent. All this had distracted him from knowing that she was colored.

By the time she asked her simple question, his simple desires were too urgent for verbal investigations to continue. He had to feel the inside of her. He had to feel his own surface surrounded by her. Looking into her blue eye and into her brown eye, he knew she had something to give that couldn't be purchased or stolen, something that could only be boldly gifted; and she was ready to gift it. With his nose in the curls of her hair that smelled just like mountain roses and wild thyme, the boy was drunk on love and poontang.

She was on her way to New York. To meet strangers. To be a painter. To have lovers and art openings. Their first night together she wanted him as her first, not her only, not her forever.

She closed her eyes and opened her legs and did what she had to do to begin her great adventure. He was, she thought the night she surrendered her virginity, the best way possible of slamming closed forever the door that led back to the mountains.

She would never return soiled where once she had ruled as virgin queen. Disgrace, even private disgrace, would propel her toward the land of strangers, toward the wider world.

After the initial gasp, and the bit of blood, after the first time, when the kisses held longer and the touches slowed, when he got over his fear that he would hurt her and she got over her fear that she was submitting to him, the coupling became a crowning.

He wanted her for every day and night to come and he began to convince her that she wanted it too. Two weeks after their first time, a package arrived from his bank. When they married in the little Episcopal church on the Oberlin campus, his dead mother's immense heart-shaped yellow diamond was on her hand. She would carry her canvases back up with them to the mountain.

They named their boy baby Madog after his daddy. From the day the boy came into the world hollering and red, he was affectionately called Mad Dog. Though no one said a word, everything about the baby, from his unfortunate nickname to his very complexion and demeanor, served to remind the aristocrats of Bramwell—where the baby had been born because the millionaire's village was where the best doctors were—that Mad Morgan's father had plucked his wife, Mad's mother, out of a coal camp.

As soon as mother and blue-eyed, redheaded white child were decreed fit for the everyday isolation of country life and for travel, they moved into a series of interconnecting glass boxes the elder Mad's father had commissioned and abandoned overlooking the Pocahontas coalfields.

Reading books and painting and watching the baby grow into a fine boy, dancing sometimes before breakfast, sometimes after dinner, to old jazz band records, for Canary the first years passed as good and prosperous time does: too fast.

When the baby born in 1959 looked more than a little brown, no one said a word except that it had always been known that Mad Morgan's mama had been a Melungeon as well as a Hatfield, and that Canary was for sure a Melungeon. Melungeons, as anyone who cared was well aware, were a mysterious people and in no way to be understood as Negro. The family was completely fine and completely white. Or so said the rich folk who wanted to attend the Morgans' winter ball and otherwise be entertained by the Morgans.

When the baby girl was big enough, and their big boy was eager enough, in 1960, Mad flew his family to New York in his own small plane. From New York they set sail for England on the SS *United States*. From England they flew commercial to Italy. In Italy he hired a chauffeur and car to move them about the countryside. As they were traveling from Rome to Florence, somewhere near Monte Oliveto, there was an accident.

Mad Dog died by the side of a dirt road with the scent of olives or almonds, something foreign, in the air. Canary was holding him. A week after her son died, Canary followed him. Remembering something his darling had said standing at Elizabeth Barrett Browning's grave, Morgan buried his wife and son in Rome's American cemetery. Only the baby girl, Clementine Hope, returned with Morgan to his mountains from Italy.

When Canary died the elite of West Virginia were shocked but were hopeful that Morgan would wipe the slate clean and just start over. With his wife and son dead, the descendants, relatives, and hangers-on of the coal barons expected that Morgan would soon entrust Clementine Hope—the baby gossip now claimed wasn't his child at all—to the care of nurses while he looked to find himself an appropriate wife and have a real baby. Some folk said Canary had cheated. Some folk said Canary hadn't been able to have a second child and Morgan had bought her a baby. Nobody, gossip said, in their right mind would leave all Mad Morgan had, and the more he would have when his daddy died, to a beige question mark. As far as Morgan was concerned, babies did not get more real than Clementine Hope.

Beside his daughter's crib he prayed for forgiveness. If God was angry at him for something, Mad for sure knew it was for stealing Canary from the Negroes.

"So that's how you got raised white," said Nicholas.

"*Whitish*," said Hope.

"Black enough," said Mo.

"Let me tell the rest," said Hope.

Mad Morgan taught his daughter to drive as soon as her feet could reach the pedals, the year she turned eleven. He taught her how to navigate the narrow and curving country roads and he taught her never to entrust the driving to anyone but herself, or him, or her cousin Hat. After that when he was too drunk to drive, he let her.

As the years passed she drove more and more often. He pressed her hard to drive fast through the hills. When he had a belly full of corn-likker he got paranoid and believed not what he had told her—that some of his people had set up a still on the place and the revenuers believed he had something to do with it—but that the devil was chasing them.

Mad stopped going to New York, or New Orleans, or anywhere out of West Virginia. Fearing God would punish him again if he didn't, a few times a year he would send Clementine Hope over to Washington to visit her aunts.

Clementine grew to be an odd and elegant girl. She had her mother's same wide Negro nose, pillow lips, and high forehead, but she'd been dipped into a milky-gold caramel color. If she hadn't had the strange accent she'd picked up from constantly changing tutors and nannies, anyone anywhere would have immediately recognized her as black. With the strange accent people thought she was some peculiar white island child marooned in the mountains.

Sometimes when just the two of them were having dinner, when there was no tutor or cook or housekeeper or guest staying over, she would wear his old boyhood tuxedo, the tuxedo her father's father had worn before her father. Old, black, hand-tailored silk looked good on all three of them, her father would attest on every such occasion.

One particular feast day, Clementine made herself and her papa dress-shirt studs out of wildflowers and stream rocks and said she was going to be a jeweler. He said she was going to be a coal baron's granddaughter. She said she hated coal; that it killed people. He looked at her hard. He raised his hand. He wanted her to dart away, or grab his hand, retract the idiocy, somehow break the chain of eventualities, but she didn't. She didn't have any idea in the world what was coming. He slapped her. She started to cry. Eventually she started blubbering. She wasn't thinking about coal.

"Grandpa doesn't want me."

"Doesn't want *me*?"

"He doesn't think I'm his."

"Little pitchers have big ears."

"Am I?"

"Are you what?"

"Yours."

"What do the aunts say about it?"

"They say they hope you drink yourself to death and I can come live with them. They say you've got a wedding certificate and a birth certificate that say they can't raise me."

"I got all of that."

"They say you make them mad Ohio made it legal for a black woman to marry a white man 'cause it's only getting legal in West Virginia now and if Mama had stayed at home and gone to school like she should she'd be alive today—but I wouldn't be and they guess God knows what he's doing."

"Clementine!"

"Answer my question, Papa."

"You're mine and you may have some little half sisters and half brothers up in any of the finest families of West Virginia, but you're the only child I'm claiming."

"What about my brother in Rome?"

"You know about him?"

"For a long time."

"Him too."

Eventually she left for boarding school, St. Paul's. Angry that she was being banished, she refused to even consider attending his alma mater, Exeter, just down the road.

In her third year at St. Paul's her father decided they would spend the Thanksgiving holiday with his father, who was growing old. When her father left with all the youngish men for a morning hunt, her grandfather went to her room and said she would give him something to be grateful for, or he would shoot her favorite horse that very morning, that very hour. Looking into his eyes, she knew he would do it. While he worked his way into her, she couldn't decide if she was being raped. She had already had a lover; she could already imagine telling her boy about this yuckiness and how sweetly he would console her. The chief violence of the thing was the words her grandfather said about her mother as he did it. He didn't believe Clementine Hope was his grandchild.

She told her father as he dropped her at the airport to send her back to school for the two weeks of term before the Christmas break began. A few days later she received a package containing two books, a first edition of *Their Eyes Were Watching God* and a paperback of *Tender Is the Night*. Inside the Hurston he had written, "I was your mother's Tea Cake." Inside the Fitzgerald he had written, "Remember it was Nicole who turned out all right at the end."

Clementine and Mad had a happy enough Christmas, keeping very much to themselves, with the exception of hosting the twenty-four-hour blowout between Christmas and New Year's that had become legend. And they watched *How Green Was My Valley* together.

A week after she returned to school in January her grandfather was making one of his extremely rare visits to his son's home near Bluefield when a fire at the old house killed both men.

Clementine immediately returned to West Virginia for the funeral. With her aunts standing beside her she buried her father next to her mother's parents in Harper's Ferry.

The grandfather was cremated. His ashes, at Clementine's request, were entrusted to some of his former miners for an appropriate burial.

When she finally returned to school, in the large pile of mail, mostly condolence notes, she found a postcard postmarked Bramwell. Scribbled across the reverse side of a picture of a cowboy hat was a heart.

After that, Clementine Hope started spending her time off from boarding school at the aunts' house in Washington according to the dictates of her father's will.

"If Grandpa weren't dead, I'd be fixin' to go kill him," said Mo.

"My poor girl," said Nicholas.

"Abel was not my first strange accident," said Hope.

Rising from his seat, Mo wished Nicholas a safe and soon flight home. He shook Nicholas's hand and kissed Clementine Hope. Mo had a party to work.

Hope followed Mo out. She wanted to thank Mo again for a taste of Canary. It had been a consolation.

TWENTY-FOUR

HOPE WAS ON her way home. Even at rush hour, she appreciated the long drive from downtown on the river to her house on the edge of the woods with the big pot of red flowers that brightened her front step every season of the year. This winter it was the reddest purple kale she could find. She had half fallen back in love with Abel. Understanding him as having been a young soldier in the Civil Rights movement and getting convinced that he had loved the baby had done it.

She pulled out her cell phone and punched in the numbers of the Idlewild house. Waycross answered. Ajay was sleeping. He had shot a buck. Waycross had feared that it might be, coming so quickly after Abel's death, an unfortunate triumph, that the boy would too sadly miss being able to show his father the photograph of the properly downed, killed, and tagged deer.

But it had been a triumph. For the first time ever, Ajay had field-dressed his own kill. He had worked slowly with knife and string and hands as Waycross had watched him tie off the rectum and carefully remove the bladder. "He pulled the innards out and didn't spoil the meat," Waycross boasted. Then he went on to describe how they had hung the animal upside down to let the meat begin to chill, how Ajay had insisted, when they'd left the field, that they drive to a processor who would contribute Ajay's deer to the Michigan Sportsmen Against Hunger Project. How after they had dropped off the meat Ajay had announced he was done with hunting.

"I think he might just be a doctor, like me," said Waycross.

"You mean the next time he's in blood up to his elbows he's going to be saving somebody's life?" asked Hope.

"Or trying to," said Waycross, who was grateful his wife knew what field dressing was and he didn't have to tell her.

"You should tell him the story of Dr. Dan."

"I've already told him the first half, and he's getting old enough for the second half," said Waycross.

"And that would be?"

"How Dan ended up abandoned by black people and white people and alone in Idlewild after all the good he'd achieved."

"Ajay's not old enough to hear that," said Hope.

Waycross said nothing. He didn't lie to the woman and he knew different. There was no sweet way to say, "Today I saw your son take off his blaze-orange field jacket and hang it over our heads on a tree limb so we wouldn't get shot and he wouldn't get his sleeves bloody. I saw him slice from the breast bone to the anus, saw him cut around the penis and balls and get up to his elbows in gore thinking about feeding somebody hungry. We dragged a deer so heavy it could give a man as old as me a heart attack if I had dragged it alone." He didn't say any of that. He expected she remembered enough about deer hunting to understand how grown her boy was getting.

"I've got to get some dinner going," said Waycross.

"I'm going to miss venison," said Hope.

"We ate our share," said Waycross.

As Hope had turned up the drive leading to her house, the coyotes had been yapping. She could hear them yapping again. There wasn't much time but she would have a shower and a bath before heading out for dinner in a dress that would be as close to a robe as she could find in her closet.

Hope was in her high soaking tub. Mo's stories, Canary's story, had made Hope remember lost and young. In the hot water filled with her favorite Dr. Singha's Mustard Bath, she remembered more.

TWENTY-FIVE

WHEN SPRING TERM and what St. Paul's called fifth form—and most of America called junior year—was over, Hope took a cab, which she refused to share, from Milleville (the two thousand pristine acres just outside of Concord, New Hampshire, on which the campus of St. Paul's School posed in a kind of mock bucolic true splendor) to Boston's Logan Airport.

She owned land in West Virginia but it was not her residence. Her residence, according to her father's will, her aunts' preference, and her own wish, was now at 428 U Street in Washington, D.C.

She had felt queasy on the plane to Washington. Naked in warm bath water, Hope remembered wondering if she were pregnant then thinking that she couldn't be. She always took her birth control pills exactly at the same hour each day. It was her new address that had her sick to her stomach.

As much as she had always loved visiting with the aunts, as safe as she felt in their cramped, chaotic house, as sated as she got on all their good food, and as exciting as she found their neighborhood animated by noisy and sometimes nosy strangers, she wasn't sure, with arrival imminent, exactly how she felt about their house being her house, about LeDroit or Shaw—she wasn't even sure of what to call it (the aunts said LeDroit; the Washington friends from St. Paul's said Shaw)—being her neighborhood. Safe, sated, and excited was no part of it.

She told herself it would help her fit in at St. Paul's. Most of the black students she knew who attended boarding schools were bright kids who lived in the inner city. And now she was one too. Sort of.

When the beverage cart came down the aisle she palmed one of the vodka minis from the side of the cart without waiting to be served. The stewardess raised her eyebrows but didn't say a word. First-class passengers are always right.

Moving to U Street could not be a good thing.

Drinking straight from the tiny bottle, she started thinking about Cornel Brown. The meanest thing anyone had ever said to her at St. Paul's had been said midway through winter term of her first year, her third-form year, by Cornel Brown, a boy she wouldn't kiss. At the time, the aftermath of the Mish Holiday dance, she had yet to kiss any boy, but Cornel Brown hadn't known this.

Her next significant encounter with Cornel occurred one of the first warm days of the year. There was a big group of kids smoking pot down by Library Pond. Cornel was the one black boy, and Clementine Hope was the one black girl. While they were untangling the fate of the universe, a white fifth-former from South Carolina, who was interested in Cornel Brown but feared Cornel Brown was interested in Hope, had asked Hope if she went to St. Paul's as part of an ABC program. Hope had said, "No," simply, but way too loud.

Her passionate negation had been inspired by her strong attraction to the six-foot-four-inch Nubian warrior prince. She wanted Cornel Brown to like her, and she had formed the impression—growing up with a father who always responded to anyone who said they wanted to match him up with someone with the question "Does she have big breasts and big bucks?"—that it would be a good thing for her if Cornel Brown thought she was rich. About the breasts she wasn't worried.

Or had only just recently begun to worry, which probably had increased her anxiety about the money.

She knew she had big breasts, which would have been perfect, according to the girls in her dorm, if her nipples had been pink or apricot instead of brown. That day, as a skinny-dip was being contemplated, and as the girls were teasing the boys by teasing one another about the parts of their bodies they wanted and didn't want people to see, she was worrying about nipples. She was wondering how many of the other girls present—none was from her dorm or team so she didn't know—had pink-tipped breasts. She didn't want to be the only dark-chested one. A girl from New York with olive skin and a severe dyed-black bob, with black bangs grown long enough to hide her eyebrows and chopped straight across, declared, "Orange and pink nipples are like eyelashes without mascara: not enough contrast."

Before anyone could disagree, the girl, Tatiana, flashed the group, lifting the waist of her neon-blue spring sweater above her head and treating all present to a peek at large chocolate teats on tiny vanilla mounds and downy armpits.

"Anything more than a mouthful's a waste," Tatiana squealed loud enough to be heard through the veil of the sweater. She too had noticed the charms of Cornel Brown.

Some very bad boy asked, "Wouldn't that mean you should have only one breast?" A girl jealous of the attention Tatiana was receiving purred, "I guess you haven't seen *Jules and Jim.*"

The display of tiny breasts, perfect mouthfuls, made the amply endowed Clementine Hope feel eclipsed. In a breath she was out of her clothes, into Library Pond, and back to being a center of attention. In another breath the others were in the water with her.

The girl from South Carolina, in retaliation for Hope having what the boys were now calling "chocolate yummies," said something, again, about ABC programs. Again Clementine Hope said, "No." But this time there was some irritation in her voice. Cornel Brown dove deep and reappeared between Hope and the South Carolina girl.

"Why you want to lie and say that?" Cornel asked. When neither girl replied, as neither was paying a speck of attention to what he said because both were fully distracted by how good he looked, Cornel plowed on. "Y'all's both," he was mimicking Clementine Hope's accent, "on the original ABC program, the RWD program."

"What's that?" asked Clementine Hope.

"RWD," repeated Cornel Brown.

"RWD?" repeated Clementine Hope.

"Rich white daddy," said Cornel Brown.

Someone laughed. Cornel kept talking. "All y'all's got rich white daddies. Don't keep signifying about *my* better chance. All y'all's on the original A Better Chance Program." Now everyone was laughing.

It was a little like applause for Cornel and somehow for Clementine Hope too. She could hear in the merriment that the white kids had finally decided she was just like them after all, which was a very good thing. It was a very bad thing that the boy she found so intriguing, a black boy, was thinking she was just like them, the white folks, too.

After the winter dance, she had turned away hoping he would snatch a kiss. He didn't. Cornel Brown thought Clementine Hope was shying away from his brownness. He cut her with his eyes. Then he cut her with words. He had said he thought kissing her might be a violation of his promise to his mama that he wouldn't kiss a white girl. What had made it so bad was he had said that before he even knew her daddy was white.

She had told him, walking away, that her father was, for a fact, white. He hadn't said four words in a row to her between the day she'd bitten him and the day they found themselves swimming naked together in Library Pond.

The vodka mini was empty in her hands. She could do this. If all those A Better Chance kids could live in hard places and go to St. Paul's and Exeter and Groton, she could too. They were no better than she was. She could do it. Those kids were great. She could be one. This would work. Her papa was dead. It had to work.

Or maybe not. As the plane from Logan prepared for its final descent into Washington National, Clementine Hope peered out the window and wondered if she wasn't moving into a whole neighborhood of Cornel Browns.

Again, she wanted to heave. She looked imploringly at the young businessman beside her and pointed to the suit pocket where he had stuffed three vodka minis. He handed her one.

When he said, "I went to Groton," she was happy she was traveling in her St. Paul's sweats.

Aunt Sweet was waiting for her at the gate. She said Aunt Hot was waiting at the curb outside of baggage claim. When Hope got seated between the always-late-for-everything-but-work aunts in the front seat of their 1969 Duster, everything was all right.

Eventually the Duster turned onto U Street. The neighborhood that had once been a celebrated Negro enclave was now dilapidated and dangerous—a ghetto with gorgeous architecture. One row house was in picture-perfect condition with a pot of red flowers blooming on every step. Hope was home.

The aunts decided that to ease Clementine's transition to Washington, they would spend the first week together as if it were a vacation, as they had always done on her visits, sightseeing: driving out to Arlington National Cemetery, looking at the jewels at the Smithsonian, where the aunts told her that the Hope diamond had been named for her, walking over the Mall, visiting the Capitol, taking pictures in front of the huge sculptures at the Hirshhorn Sculpture Garden, eating dim sum in Chinatown—having a big time.

It was a good time and a good week and would have been a great time and a great week, if it had been just a week. Seeing each other through the eyes of "family who reside in the same house" as opposed to "family visiting" changed things.

Both aunts worked as domestics. One aunt worked for a black family and one aunt worked for a white family. Their world was more divided between those people who made messes and those people who cleaned up after them than it was between black and white.

At St. Paul's everyone—teachers, students, prefects, the rector—had always praised Clementine Hope for how hard working she was. If her papers weren't usually in on time, they were always long and dense, and boldly argued. Nobody at St. Paul's cared that her clothes were scattered across the floor or that she sometimes forgot to pick up her plate or glass in the dining room.

Nobody picked up after anyone else at the aunts'. The aunts did not understand skirts splayed on the floor just where they fell from your waist to your feet, or jeans thrown across a chaise lounge with, likely as not, bloodstains in the crotch, or wet towels on a tile floor, not folded neatly to dry on an aluminum bar. Hope began, for the very first time in her life, to worry about her deportment.

And with very good reason. Over the course of the single week Hope and the aunts had roamed around Washington, the aunts had become increasingly fearful, eventually reaching a point of anxiety between panicked and deathly afraid, that their grandniece, before they could "get her straight," would reveal to the world she had "No Home Training."

"No home training" was an indictment severe and broad: a critique of mother and child and relations. "No home training" was a pronouncement to be avoided by whatever means necessary.

Real life started on a Saturday when the aunts, exhausted by a week of "looking at the mess on that chile's head and not saying a word," did what any two sane black women with a phobia of hair salons and a nappy-headed niece would do: they hustled down to the corner store and bought a box of Ultra Sheen relaxer.

They did this while the girl was still sleeping. When she got up they fed her grits and bacon instead of French toast and strawberries and introduced her to the other joys of a regular Saturday. Go downtown and look through the stores. Go to the grocery. Clean the house. Have lunch late in the afternoon at Ben's Chili Bowl. Get Sunday's supper started. Re-clean the kitchen. Get out the magazines, black skillet, Wesson oil, the pop-corn, and the salt. Find some phone books to plop into the kitchen chair. Grab the clean-stained towels.

Promising to get her "fixed up right," the aunts got Clemen-tine set up on a stack of telephone books in a kitchen chair tilted toward the sink. She thought they were washing her hair or putting on some kind of conditioner. Something started to burn. They kept working. She started into screaming questions the aunts ignored.

"You hollerin' loud enough to wake the dead, chile."

"Then let them get up!"

"Hush!"

"My head's on fire!"

"Hush."

"Did you do this to Canary?"

"She got wicked white folk ways!"

"What?"

"Calling yo' mama Canary."

"It's her name."

"It ain't her fault, Hot."

"Sweet, you say a thousand times we should go snatch Canary's daughter back."

"Yeah, I did."

"This white stuff stinks."

"You get used to it."

"What happens if you leave it on too long?"

"We don't."

"I think my hair's falling out."

It wasn't. Clementine Hope let out a wail anyway. The aunts smiled. Complaining about the stink and fearing your hair was all going to fall out was a normal sixteen- or seventeen-year-old-girl thing to do mid-relaxer. They had heard their friends complaining about their daughters and granddaughters complaining about the very same things. This was the first very good sign. In the aunts' minds they were turning into a near-to-normal family. They would laugh about all of that eventually, but that would be later.

That afternoon Hope kept whining, and they kept putting the white paste on her hair and combing it straight. And she kept on keeping on whining and they kept on keeping on cracking jokes about her being "tender-headed." Hope just kept whining and their hands kept moving.

They rinsed her head in the kitchen sink. They gently poured warm water over her and when that was done they went at her with a blow-dryer, and when that was done they went at her with a hot comb and a curling iron and some blue hair grease. When they were finished they announced she looked just like a *Jet* magazine beauty.

They stood her before the big mirror, each of the aunts taking a hand as they walked her from the kitchen up the front steps, toward the mirror that stood on three clawed feet in Aunt Sweet's bedroom. It was Clementine Hope's first time in the room.

In the drunk that was the first summer after her father died, everything in the mirror was fragmented and reconnected wrong. Someone pretty was looking out at her. Someone she didn't know.

"You look just like Lena Horne."

"Who's Lena Horne?"

"What this chile doesn't know, Hot . . ."

"We teach her."

"I used to look like Canary."

She spent her first summer as an orphan cooking and getting fat. She grew from swimming in a size four to squeezing into an eight. She was sad and silent and the best the aunts knew to do for that was feed her. They taught her to cook, they said, because their catering business was finally getting going good that year and they could use the extra free hands, but really it was because they wanted her to be, just a little, like them.

It was the summer of the Bicentennial and the summer Barbara Jordan addressed the Democratic National Convention.

Because both of the aunts had arthritis in their hands, soon it was Hope putting the color on their heads and Hope letting her curls grow back. She thanked them in their language. "You love me enough to let me grow that mess back on my head?" she said, and the aunts nodded back "yes." They were settling into their summer.

The bank started bugging the aunts about moving. Sitting in their cosy U Street living room, as clean and polished as any in the city, the aunts listened as the trustee at the Riggs National responsible for Hope's trust asked the aunts how they could possibly imagine Hope making friends in their neighborhood or bringing friends from out of the neighborhood to visit. He declared the neighborhood unsuitable. He warned the aunts that they would find somewhere appropriate to live before Hope left for St. Paul's in September or find themselves in court.

The aunts were more than a little surprised. Like an old man who looks at his wife of half a century and sees the girl he fell in love with, the aunts looked down the U Street corridor and saw an enclave of black achievement.

When they had first come to town, LeDroit Park had been *the* place for blacks to live in Washington. And now the bank declared Shaw, as the trustee called it, an unfit neighborhood. The aunts, particularly Aunt Hot, wanted to poison the bankerman. Aunt Sweet said, later, that the bank would just send somebody else in this bankerman's place and it might be a worse somebody.

Aunt Sweet spoke the names Mary Terrell and Benetta Bulloch Washington and Alain Locke and Georgia Douglas Johnson, intending to impress. The bankerman sitting in their best front-room chair digging his elbows into a hand-crocheted doily had no idea in the world who those people were. He didn't know why they were important, or where they lived, or had lived. Hope only knew a little more than the banker, but she could hear clearly that the aunts thought the neighborhood had a lot to boast and that the bankerman thought it had nothing.

And she knew something far worse. Walking down the street with the aunts, sitting in the pews at church with the aunts, and watering flowers on the stoop with the aunts, she had come to see that some of the fancy people who remained in the neighborhood thought that the aunts, being maids who had never gone to college, were almost as emblematic of LeDroit decay as the dope fiends and the welfare queens, if not the dope dealers.

"I don't want to live here," said Hope.

The bankerman started to speak. Aunt Hot silenced him with a raised hand.

"Hush!"

"I want to live with you, but I don't want to live here."

"Hush!"

"No one lives here who's not a thousand years old who can live somewhere else. I'm not a thousand years old."

Aunt Sweet stood. She walked over to her sister and took her hand. She had lost the child's grandmother and never had her mother. She wasn't losing Clementine Hope. Sweet squeezed Hot's shoulder.

"Who's gonna pay for this new house?" asked Hot.

"The bank," said Hope and the bankerman at the very same time. It was a lie that approximated the truth.

They found a real estate agent and started making rounds. When they weren't looking at houses they were cooking pies for restaurants and reunions.

Eventually they found a pretty house on a tree-lined street with beige and brown and black families, lots of doctors and lawyers, and some people working for the antipoverty programs. Unfortunately, some of the wives toting casseroles to their porch recognized Aunt Sweet from her housekeeping job and a few even recognized Hot from hers. It was a frosty late July. The aunts sought the help of a dear friend of their dead sister Emmaline, a woman called Red. Red had gone with Clementine Hope's grandmother to Dunbar and to Howard and then, having married well and been widowed twice, had advanced considerably in the world. They invited Red to Sunday supper.

Just after the soup they asked her to make some appropriate introductions to the new neighbors on behalf of Clementine Hope. The old friend said the neighbors would be tough—and that the neighbors were not enough. The child also needed the Jack and Jill. As the aunts were not, and never would be, in the Links, it would be hard. She offered the aunts the loan of her house on the Vineyard. She advised the aunts to take it for all of August and give a big party. She would charge them a very fair rent. A Vineyard stint would do the trick. She asked them if they still knew the old mayor's wife. Before Hope's new patroness was gone the aunts had Benetta Washington, their old neighbor, on the phone. Benetta said she would get Senator Ed Brooke to attend whatever it was they gave, whenever they gave it. August was settled.

Clementine Hope drove the aunts north. The old ladies spread out in the backseat of the little blue Volvo station wagon that Hope had insisted they purchase, and the Duster was left behind.

Hope had the front seat and the radio to herself. After the four hours it took to get to New York, they stopped and ate at Sylvia's in Harlem. Four hours after that they were in Boston, where they ate at Bob the Chef's on Commonwealth Avenue. Two hours after that they hit the ferry port at Woods Hole.

★   ★   ★

For Clementine Hope the simple pleasures of the Vineyard, like the simple pleasures of life, were few. Clementine had spent way too much time living wild in West Virginia to readily pass for conventional anything. And her worlds kept colliding. She ran into friends from St. Paul's at an ice cream shop. They wanted to join her on Inkwell Beach, the gathering spot for black kids. She reluctantly issued an invitation. The presence of the white friends from St. Paul's did nothing to enhance Hope's social cachet with the black kids until one of the Milleville friends whisperingly declared her Oak Bluffs friends to be "horrible snobs." When Hope said, sounding just like the aunts, very loudly, "That's the pot calling the kettle black," everybody, black and white, laughed.

The aunts did a better impersonation of typical brown Vineyard people than Hope did. They wore pale cotton clothes, pearls, and espadrilles. They boasted about their child's SAT scores and worried aloud about the relative merits of Howard and Harvard. They fit in because they were all about family and genealogy and because they were tired and obviously grateful for a cool place in the sun. And they were pretty in a coral and bronze kitchen-beautician Revlon makeup kind of way. If they had not come of age on some historically black college campus or another, or on a Seven Sister, Ivy, or Little Ivy campus, or even on the dreaded campus of Oberlin, they had come of age working for doctors' wives in a city where the families of physicians were aristocrats. They knew how to do, from years of helping those other people's families do. And they did what they knew because they thought it would help their grandniece Clementine Hope.

On the ferry to the island they even started calling her, and insisted that she call herself, just Hope. Clementine and Clementine Hope sounded too country.

Hope's living on the island wasn't easy until at Larsons, the lobster place, she ran into a white boy from school, a D.C. boy she had expected to be in touch with earlier in the summer—except he had headed directly from school to Chilmark. Or so he had said. Later he confessed he hadn't wanted to see Hope on U Street.

After that most afternoons she pointed the blue Volvo up island and spent a few hours with her classmate in a guesthouse converted from a barn. Some mornings she would rise and pick him up before anyone in her house was awake and they would drive out to the very tip of the island and eat breakfast on a deck hanging off a cliff overlooking the ocean, hoping for a James Taylor sighting.

Sometimes while eating breakfast at the cliffs they ran into friends from New York. All the New York kids wanted to talk about was it being the Summer of Sam. Hope hadn't heard much about that because even rich kids didn't call long-distance often in the seventies and black Washington wasn't worried about the white girl–killer. Over blueberry pancakes on the cliffs, someone told her this was one summer she was really lucky being black. Thinking about playing kitchen beautician and long gossipy family stories, Hope agreed.

Their party, a barbecue, was held on the Wednesday before Labor Day. Everything conspired to have it be well attended. The aroma of the aunts' cooking allured. Senator Ed Brooke, America's only black senator, was on his way over, Benetta Washington, wife of D.C.'s first black mayor, having called him four times earlier in the day to gossip and to remind him of the engagement. It was fun to have a new party given by new people. And the house they had rented was fabulous, right in the thick of Cottager life, newly decorated with tasteful furniture funded by the exorbitant rent the aunts were paying.

The aunts had a good time. Hope had something else. One of the families brought a daughter who attended Exeter. The girl, having been in Germany for the summer, had only just arrived on the island the night before the party. Her name was Victoria—after the queen, she said—and she looked like Dorothy Dandridge, or so the aunts said. Victoria wanted to know if Hope was in the Jack and Jill. Victoria made jokes about having to help serve at Link functions and didn't understand when Hope didn't understand the jokes. She said, "The whole thing," referring to the aunts' party, "might as well be a united meeting of the Boule and the Links and the Girlfriends and the Circle-lets with a Carousel or two thrown in."

Hope had only half a hold on what this lithe brown girl—who, to add insult to injury, was wearing the exact same Lilly skirt she was except two sizes smaller—was talking about. The little clique surrounding her, all wearing perfect Lilly Pulitzer tennis skirts and twinsets and carrying Coach bags, seemed to share a secret handshake to go with their tiny diamond tennis bracelets and their fancy dialect that was even more exclusive than St. Paul's slang. And far more beautiful. She loved the funny words and phrases—bougie, copacetic, fathom, hincty—that she added to the jargon she already knew: heifer, trifling, home training, no half-doer. She loved the drawn-out syllables, the sentences that swirled on and on and back on each other, traveling up and down a musical scale, peppered with frequent allusions from and to the King James Bible. Just as she had heard Italian and had known she wanted to speak it—not the first time she'd heard it but the first time she'd heard it spoken in a certain Fellini film—she first heard Bougie Black spoken by Victoria in Oak Bluffs and she wished she could speak it fluently, speak it as Victoria spoke it, just as she wished she could wear Lilly like Victoria wore it.

It amazed her that all the exact same Lilly pieces that she had known in St. Paul's could be worn so differently in Oak Bluffs. She had been trying to pull her worlds together all summer. And just as all the various constituencies seemed to be reconciled in the person of Vineyard Victoria, they began to fly apart.

The boy from the carousel arrived at the party. She heard someone say his name was Abel Jones the third. She heard someone else say he was going with Victoria.

Hope took a wrong step. Someone meaning no harm asked her what the aunts did. When she told them they had a catering company, one of the girls sneered. So Hope told them the rest of the truth: that her aunts were retired maids. The bossy-glossy brown girls closed ranks against her—the arriviste with a mess on her head who didn't wear her Lilly right—against Clementine Hope Morgan. When Victoria made a face like she had just smelled something awful, Hope hauled off and slapped her.

"No home training."

"How do we even know these people?"

"We don't."

Most of the crowd was too drunk to care, but those who

weren't, particularly those with daughters or sons near the wild child's age, turned on their heels and left. Eventually, Ed Brooke left too, wondering what in the world Benetta had gotten him into.

And so the summer she spent ostensibly learning to make pie but in reality trying to learn to be black—and part of that was simply learning to be afraid of the same things the aunts were afraid of: a fear of missing underpants, a fear of being hit by a car and having it discovered you are wearing a bra and panties that don't match, a fear of unshod feet that left women suffering in stockings in the summertime, a fear of being accused of having no home training or of providing irregular home training—ended in a kind of colossal failure.

Hope had no home training and she didn't care if the world knew it. And she would be accepted as a black girl or die trying to be—probably wearing no underpants at all.

She hadn't known why she was doing it when she was doing it, but before the hot wore off her hand Hope knew her second-best reason for having slapped Victoria was that the girl was in full and flamboyant possession of things Hope wanted for herself, most particularly Abel Jones the third, the boy she had seen on the carousel.

As the ferry pulled out of Vineyard Haven, taking Hope and the aunts back to the mainland, Hope was thinking about what diet she should go on. By the time they reached Woods Hole she had started imagining her life after St. Paul's, her life at Radcliffe, very, very differently than she had imagined it before. She would let her hair grow long and she would straighten it.

While the aunts ate Sylvia's sweet potato pie, Hope drank hot black coffee. They all agreed they didn't need to do that, go to the Vineyard, again, or at least not anytime soon.

The water had turned cold. It was time for Hope to get out of the bath.

TWENTY-SIX

NICHOLAS WAS WAITING for Hope in the lobby of the Hermitage, sitting beneath the ornate stained-glass ceiling, martini glass in hand. Having changed out of his country-and-western attire, he now was wearing black cashmere sweatpants and sweatshirt, black velvet loafers, and a bottle-green smoking jacket with deeper green toggles.

As Hope approached, wearing a black cashmere wrap dress, her workhorse Chanel black ballerina flats, and Wolford tights, she could see that Nicholas's jacket looked old enough to have been worn by Nicholas's grandfather in a withdrawing room when Victoria still sat on the throne.

"Great minds think alike," said Nicholas.

"Fools seldom differ," countered Hope.

This time instead of kissing him on both cheeks and one cheek twice, she kissed him on the lips and then on a cheek. The aging-dandy smell was gone, replaced by something less familiar.

"Jicky?" asked Hope.

"You remember," said Nicholas.

"I remember," said Hope.

"I like your new scent," said Nicholas.

"I'm not wearing any," said Hope.

"The scent of the skin of your neck," said Nicholas.

As they made their way down the steps to the dining room, she was surprised to feel how much weight he was leaning on her. She couldn't tell if it was gin or age.

"New or new and improved?" asked Hope.

"And improved," said Nicholas.

Hope rewarded him with a kiss, linked her arm into his to give him more support, then started moving, more slowly, down the stairs.

They flirted through dinner, aimlessly, speaking of meals they had eaten and people they knew; how skinny she had been, how round (and radiant, Nicholas added) she had gotten almost as soon as she'd become pregnant; how he had finally gotten to go to Moscow; and how she had finally gotten to go to St. Petersburg. They discovered that they still had the same favorite food movie, *Tampopo*, and that both had added *Babette's Feast* and *Big Night* to make a list.

When the coffee was served Nicholas told the waiter to leave the silver-plated urn on the table, fill the water glasses, then leave them alone until he waved a napkin.

"So tell me the rest of the story," said Nicholas.

"There's no more to tell," said Hope.

"The aunts," said Nicholas.

"The aunts are mine," said Hope.

"I have a story to tell you. There was an unforgettable birthday party," said Nicholas.

"You mean when the Klan burned a cross on his lawn on his thirteenth birthday?" asked Hope.

"The Klan was the least of it," said Nicholas.

Abel felt gypped. It was his thirteenth birthday and it was a Saturday. He preferred it when his birthday fell on a school day. Then he got a party at school and a party on the weekend, cookies as well as a cake. Monday, Tuesday, Wednesday, Thursday, and Friday were the days to have a birthday.

Opelika, Mount Bayou, Yazoo City, and Waycross knew all of this. Ever since the four medical students had arrived, in a caravan of polished cars loaded down with copious stuff, and had moved into a rented house around the corner from Meharry Medical College and down the street from the home of the Abel Joneses, the kid had carried his complaints up the street to their blacktop.

On this morning he had brought his complaints into their kitchen. The smell of fried bologna and hot sauce mingled with the smell of coffee. Plates shared place with textbooks on the crowded chrome and Formica ice-green dinette table. Abel slumped in a corner drinking hot, milky coffee from a turquoise Melmac cup into which he had poured four spoons of sugar before a large brown hand had slapped his smaller beige hand away. Abel had just laughed, then started gulping down the coffee.

"You just make sure you come to my party," pleaded Abel.

"Why you think we up here before day hittin' the books?" asked Opelika.

" 'Cause you goin' out with nurses tonight?" teased Abel.

" 'Fore long we be taking you with us, little man," said Mount Bayou.

"Thirteen is more'n half grown," said Waycross, before grunting like he was remembering something and then cutting his eye back to his chemistry textbook.

Abel put his dirty cup in the sink.

"Your mama live here, boy?" asked Yazoo City.

"No, sir," the boy replied. Everybody laughed. Yazoo City sounded just like an old man when he scolded.

"Just bring my presents," said Abel, before stopping to wash and dry the cup and slip it into the plastic dish rack.

"What makes you think we got you anything?" said Waycross, not bothering to look up from his textbook.

"I know y'all," said Abel.

Abel snatched another piece of fried bologna, got his hand slapped again, by Opelika, and was out their back screen door.

Four dark men dressed in light-green scrubs, shooting hoops in back of a little Victorian cottage that had survived long enough to find itself standing in the vicinity of Meharry Medical College's twelve-story Hubbard Hospital, is an amiable scene.

Opelika, Mount Bayou, Yazoo City, and Waycross were show-boating for any ladies who might happen to see them from the other side of the chain-link fence that divided their backyard and the alley from the Meharry parking lot when they caught a whiff of something sweet: smoke.

They'd been waiting for the stars to come out before dashing down the street for a piece of Abel's thirteenth-birthday cake—when they inhaled the scent of smoke and thought of daddies and uncles and granddaddies. They thought of burning leaves, whole pigs roasting in sawed-open tin drums, and store-bought chicken parts grilling on poured-concrete patios; they thought of the South of their childhoods in the early fifties: gentle lives lived sharply circumscribed with prim surfaces.

Recollecting their mothers running off to sorority conventions, their fathers with stethoscopes in their ears or black leather bags in their hands or paper masks across their faces, their families sitting in the first pew at church, and the gifts of preserved peaches and patchwork quilts and collard greens that had shown up on swept-clean back steps, they found themselves, for a moment, missing clapboard home-houses, far away from North Nashville and 1972.

But only for a moment. The pride of Mount Bayou, Mississippi; the pride of Opelika, Alabama; the pride of Yazoo City, Mississippi; and the pride of Waycross, Georgia, would have four young social-workers-in-training eager to be Mrs. Doctor Somebody waiting for them in front of Jubilee Hall at precisely seven o'clock.

The Fantastic Four, as they were also privately called by many a Fisk coed, did not plan to linger long at the kid's party. They had places to be. They liked Nashville, Fisk, and Meharry med school; and Nashville, Meharry med school, and, perhaps most important, Fisk seemed to like them. One of Nashville's prominent black citizens, Abel Jones himself, had invited them to attend a family party. This was a stark contrast to their recent experiences at Howard University.

These scions of big black southern doctors had not found much welcome in Washington, D.C. The Fantastic Four had been perplexed fresh boys when they'd arrived at Howard in 1968.

The matrons of black Washington society dreaded the "country-colored" undergrads, knew them "for certain" to be dangerous. The young men had felt the chill. Washington had seemed for these boys to be almost a northern city; still they had swaggered even as the brown dowager-dragons had clucked. With their daddy-bought, all-cash-paid-for-Cadillac cars, these drenched-in-the-South Howard-ites could turn a government worker's daughter's head. Before you could say "Jack's cat" a daughter could be folding baby diapers and reading novels behind the Cotton Curtain, dressing in silk to eat dinner with the very same Negro night after night—when he wasn't called out to stitch up some nigger mess or white-folk folly, or to doctor one of God's more taxing mysteries.

As soon as they got their Howard degrees the Fantastic Four had refugeed south to Meharry, four singular decisions that had braided them into a brotherhood. When they had rented a house together it had seemed more than a suitable decision; it had seemed an inevitability. The four, each of whom had once known no one who was not black, and known no black person richer than himself, now knew each other.

Mount Bayou made another basket. Waycross said that he hoped the new basketball they had bought Abel would make up for his birthday falling on a Saturday. Opelika opined that for sure the Nike Cortezes purchased to supplement Abel's everyday Chuck Taylors "could make a grown man feel lucky." They laughed anticipating Abel's joy. Mount Bayou made another basket.

Yazoo City got the rebound; Opelika fouled him. "Cain't let Mississippi take over," Waycross said, making the winning shot, a layup; then everybody agreed it was time to get down to the kid's party.

They dodged back into the rented house, grabbed the gifts

(carefully wrapped in the colorful "funny pages" of the previous Sunday's newspaper), then gulped down ice water from jelly glasses before they began making their way up the street.

The smell of smoke was too sweet to ignore, and they began to sense, without knowing for sure, that Abel needed them.

Abel was in the kitchen drinking Coke from a bottle with his school friends, four black boys and a white one. The white boy, Ben, was Abel's best friend and the only kid from his class. The brown boys were his friends too, but they were more like cousins than friends, and they were all younger, or at least in a different grade. James Hall was almost Abel's age but James's mother had let him stay home a year longer instead of rushing him off to kindergarten.

James Hall was sure of himself. Abel liked to think it was because James was the oldest in his class. Abel liked being the oldest in the group. In his neighborhood gang he was usually the oldest. At school he was usually the youngest.

Today Abel would be the first in the neighborhood gang to become a teenager. It felt significant, as if he was leaving his cradle friends behind and joining something bigger, the company of men, the world his white classmate Ben had been ushered into at the temple off Harding Road. Already this year Abel had been to two bar mitzvahs. The previous year he had gone to six.

It was going to be a good day, better than Abel had expected. His grandparents had given him a trip to Los Angeles as his present. His father had given him the silver saxophone that Big Abel had used to play his way through college. And Abel knew the Fantastic Four had something for him, something big, something sharp, something he could show off with in front of the others and be proud of, something they would say he could "showboat"—if short, thick black boys with wire-rim glasses could *showboat*.

He could almost imagine one of the kids from Buchanan Street sneering derisively, "Tugboat," except they wouldn't know the word. That made him smile. My arsenal is larger, he thought. Then the thought was amended. Abel had a vivid imagination. "Fat fuck," the boys from Buchanan Street would say and snatch away whatever he had been given. "Fat fuck," they had said when they'd taken his bike.

When they punched him about the head, gently, not so hard as to make a mark or to really hurt him, they called him "white boy." "You think you a white boy," they said over and over again, but it was a lie. *They* thought he was a white boy, or at least as close to a white boy as they were ever going to see riding through the neighborhood, and so they showered him with soft punches, touching his nose and his mouth at their will. *Les enfants terroristes.* It was almost nice.

Gnawing on the hot chicken drumsticks that his mother only fixed on holidays—chicken so crisp on the surface but so moist and soft inside, chicken just peppery enough in the crust that the Coke made your mouth explode, putting tears in his eyes (tears he never admitted were there, or let run down his face; Abel was excellent at fast blinking)—was not just a good thing. For Abel it was an almost perfect thing.

Abel had silently acknowledged that chicken hot with fire and hot with spice and cold Co-Cola was his favorite meal. Then he had announced the thought to the group. It was his practice to check out what he said by stating it silently inside his head before saying anything aloud. Many thoughts he spoke inside his head he did not speak aloud. His favorite dessert was vanilla ice cream eaten with a barbecue potato chip as a spoon. He didn't tell this. It was an uncool preference. When he invented that snack it surprised him that nobody else tried to dip into his bowl. He always got his fill of hot chips and ice cream. *Odd tastes have their advantage.*

This day would be different. Watching the mouths of his friends as they chomped down on his mother's fried drumsticks and chicken breasts, watching their hands as they grabbed for more, watching the napkins come back from their faces not greasy (Antoinette's cooking was never greasy) but red with the traces of pepper and paprika, Abel's stomach began to growl in protest. The likelihood he would get his fill that day was rapidly diminishing. The meat on the platter was vanishing faster than Abel could bite, chew, or swallow.

They were talking about Bobby Fischer and the Munich murders and Abel even said something about Ferdinand Marcos declaring martial law in the Philippines, but he didn't say much about it because no one else knew anything about the Philippines; so he just used the comment as an occasion to remind everybody that Thurgood Marshall was a close family friend by reminding them that he knew the Supreme Court justice's wife was a Filipina. After that the conversation turned back to what all the neighborhood gang conversations turned back to that year, except when Abel was working to turn them in another direction, *The Godfather.* They all wanted to be Sonny, but Sonny who didn't get killed; they were all afraid of being Fredo.

The old men were in the backyard barbecuing ribs and

shrimp, whatever Antoinette had marinated in her orange sink, drinking scotch and talking politics, lying about each other and telling on themselves—when they weren't telling dirty jokes. Abel could hear their voices and their laughter rolling low and loud, like October thunder.

The women were in the living room whispering and calling out, remembering and warning, their boozy high-pitched voices knocking together like chimes in the rising storm that carried the men's words. Sitting on the floor with her legs spread out and a glass of something gold over ice between them, Abel's mother, Antoinette, was looking at Sonia, the only young woman in the room.

Sonia was beautiful. Tall and as dark as a light-skinned black girl could be, Sonia, the daughter of Antoinette's best friend, also named Sonia, who had died a year or two earlier, had long tapering legs, large breasts, and a high, round, small derriere that made Antoinette wish she could wrap the girl up in tissue and put her on a shelf and give her to Abel as a birthday present three or four years down the road.

She would have to surprise him with someone else. Sonia was courting an architect. If the architect didn't marry her, somebody soon would swoop her up. *You can't hide a ripe mango.* Or maybe you can. The University of Tennessee was a desert of whiteness in which Antoinette could imagine Sonia's beauty being ignored, that rare place where the scent of Sonia's attraction could hang in the air unnoticed. Antoinette wasn't sure Sonia would be dating the old architect if she weren't attending UT Chattanooga. *He sees me,* Sonia said to the older women, as if that explained everything. To the old women it explained nothing. Everyone they knew saw the girl.

Antoinette winced. Big Abel had not done right by her god-daughter. There was nothing Antoinette could do about it, or at least nothing she knew to do. It would all work out, or it wouldn't. Antoinette lifted her glass and drained it dry of every-thing but the ice. She slid a few cubes of ice into her mouth and began crunching on them. Someone was prattling on to Sonia about the University of Tennessee, about how lucky she was to be going to one of its campuses. Antoinette held her empty glass up above her head, letting the tinkling of the cubes announce her wishes. Somebody got up and filled her glass high with more of the blended scotch Antoinette preferred.

UT Chattanooga was a good thing. It had the allure of the unobtainable. It was a new thing. Big Abel had encouraged it in a moment of true Big Abel—ness; the community was still applauding, still not comprehending, even with Sonia in their midst threatening to rot on the vine.

Sonia, beautiful Sonia, was the punch line of a joke only Big Abel and Antoinette heard. Abel had encouraged Sonia's daddy, his law partner, to send her to UT Chattanooga because he wanted to torture Chattanooga with her existence. A fresh black beauty just off the farm, whose daddy was a lawyer and whose uncle was a judge and who was wholly unavailable to white men. Big Abel wanted the white boys, he wanted the white men, to see this, to know this. It was something for his mother and something for himself. Abel Jones didn't let himself think, or didn't bother to think, what it was Sonia would see in Chat-tanooga. He didn't care. He wanted Chattanooga to see Sonia, and want Sonia, and not have Sonia.

He had struck a sharp deal to keep her safe. Big Abel had not thrown Sonia into the lion's den. She was a woman. She was a girl. He would protect her body. He did not know if it was because he wanted a female body, or because he *wanted* a female body. He would not ask himself that question. Big Abel Jones master of blooming in the soil in which he was planted, never let a thing he couldn't have remain significant. This was his advantage over other men. And he made it a great advantage by exploiting it. *An advantage is not an advantage unless it is exploited.*

Abel had carefully structured the events surrounding Sonia's matriculation. He had gotten the fathers of the city of Chattanooga to agree that they would see to it the girl was not molested in any way; in exchange Abel would push for no further integration of the university—at least not during Sonia's tenure.

Her situation was so different from that of the other female students of color that the other girls had begun to ostracize the privileged one. Very quickly Sonia had started dating her old man, an architect whose wife had left him.

Antoinette wondered, sitting so close beside young Sonia that she could, and did, push locks of the washed and pressed glossy black hair behind the girl's ear, so everyone could see her pretty face, how it could be, with all her beauty, that Sonia would throw her life away on a middle-aged man, a man who had given her an emerald-cut diamond ring but who clearly, at least to middle-aged brown female eyes, had no intention in the world of marrying his young lover.

Antoinette coughed and took another swig of her drink. She knew exactly why it was *she* had thrown *her* life away. She had done what she had done for a good reason; she had done what she had done for the same kind of good reason most of the women gathered round her had sacrificed their lives.

There were so many good reasons and they all had something to do, Antoinette was thinking, with finding a way to get into the room with the circle of women, getting to hear the thunder from the men in the distance, getting to hear the grunts of the sons close by your elbow, welcoming the silence of your own daughter and the other young girls, even as their scent rose in the room until it made the air hard to breathe and you sent them away on a fool's errand.

You throw your life away to get a house of your own. You barter your adventures for shelter, when the shelter comes with the sustenance of home.

A home of one's own was worth the price of whatever you did in the room with the bed, or whatever it was you didn't do there. Or, so the little swirls in the scotch glass told Antoinette. How much time did anyone spend in bed not dreaming, anyway?

Antoinette suspected Sonia wanted more from marriage than what Antoinette had; the late lamented Big Sonia had had something more with Sonia's father. As much as Antoinette had loved her friend, she had been jealous of her, but not so jealous that she had not also been mutely adoring.

Big Sonia had been the sweetest little drunk-girl-mama-wife anyone had ever seen fall into a bottle and drown. Maybe, Antoinette was thinking, gazing at Sonia, if the mother had figured out more about the living room and the kitchen, Big Sonia wouldn't be dead and her husband wouldn't be left looking backward with a smile, and her daughter wouldn't be kissing old men.

Antoinette wanted to tell Sonia to find her daddy the way he'd been when her mother had first found him, not the way she, the daughter, saw him now. Antoinette winced thinking of Sonia's father, Vernon, looking into the eyes of his old friend the architect, just after one of the other ladies tried to coax from Sonia some understanding of the dimensions of the architect's . . . *richesse*. Antoinette knew what Vernon, who never heard the raunchy side of any double entendre, would say: *This old man, my old friend, will treat her like the piece of crystal I would treat my woman as if she came back to me from the grave.*

This was not true, but it did not matter to young Sonia, who was trying hard not to burst out and tell all the women in the room that she didn't care if her old architect married her or not, it had done something for her to have him touch her body.

What the architect had made her feel, other women had felt, but Sonia did not know this. Beige ladies did not talk to their brown daughters about such. Looking into the eyes of the women ringing round her, Sonia saw that the secret that was with her now was not now with them. Adding that knowledge to what her girlfriends told her about the fumbling of their young suitors—who want it again and again, but never for more than three minutes at a time; who bit your nipples so hard that however wet you were getting the little garden just dried up— all the gossip she heard over and over again, and all the gossip girls at the university whispered almost just out of her earshot, made her want her old man for as long as she had him, even if she knew this wanting had nothing to do with love. It wasn't that he had made her a woman; it was that he had made her love being a woman.

It was Sonia's silent birthday wish for Abel that when he grew to be a man he would be a lover like the architect—not like his daddy.

There was something nasty about Big Abel. Sonia didn't know exactly what it was and never wanted to know better than she knew. But when she sat close to Antoinette, Sonia could feel that truth coming out of Antoinette's pores smelling exactly like moonshine, like homemade liquor that left you dead not drunk, like something she had encountered in Chattanooga.

As if he were still a baby and she were checking on him sleeping while his parents were across town carousing at some big event in a hotel with her parents, Sonia got up, walked through the breezeway, and entered the kitchen so she could see her boy. She was tired of explaining, and tired of withholding, and she loved little Abel.

Only he wasn't so little now; he was almost as tall as she was.

Sonia found Abel sitting with his friends at the long bar dividing the cooking area from a dining area, in the kitchen Big Abel boasted was the size of a large small New York apartment.

This room was filled with young people from Fisk and Meharry and a few from Tennessee State University making friends in the rising dim and din of early fall. School had been in session for a month and a little bit, just long enough for the new to wear off and the courting in earnest to begin. The dark was creeping up earlier and earlier. Al Green was on the stereo when the Jackson Five wasn't. Sonia was slipping into a chair near the fireplace just as Michael Jackson was making promises he was far too young to keep, *I'll be there to comfort you*. The phone started ringing. A TSU student answered it, then announced, to no one in particular, that the neighbor across the street was saying, "Go look outside your front door."

Sonia got up to go look. She was as close as it came to a responsible adult host in the room and it was an excuse to keep moving. Abel detained her. He called Sonia over, ostensibly to give him advice on playing his hand of rummy, but really to let Ben see, again, just how pretty she was. The phone was ringing again. Another neighbor was on the line.

The next thing anybody knew, someone was banging on the front door and screaming, and then someone else was screaming and then everybody was up and rushing to the front of the house.

Abel and his friends stayed rooted. Commotion was a frequent visitor in the Jones household. Abel knew from experience that it was usually best to stay out of grown folks' way when they got real busy. The kid started dealing a second hand. He started feeling grown. He was for certain feeling superior and able. A white boy had come to his party and so had the neighborhood gang. His worlds were coming together. And Ben was the top of the class. Abel felt accepted in some "we are superior" way that amused him deeply—until the shouting started in earnest.

Looking from the kitchen through the breezeway into the front room, he could see his mother rise from the floor. It was like seeing Niagara stretch and yawn. Antoinette didn't rise from her chosen spot on the floor once a party began until after the last guest was gone except in cases of dire emergency. Antoinette started yelling for folk to stop acting a fool; her favorite all-purpose admonishment was consolingly familiar. Abel couldn't see exactly what was going on, but he knew somebody was pressing on the doorbell because it rang and rang. A stout woman was barring the door from the inside, as if shielding Antoinette and everybody else from something they shouldn't see. And somebody kept pressing on the doorbell. Out back, his

294

father was drinking with the men, watching the meat on the grill, oblivious to the commotion.

It was an opportunity. Abel put his cards down. Soon the very young man and his boys were dashing out the back door, dashing up the side of the house, leaving the old men—whom no one had informed about the phone calls, who couldn't hear the doorbell, who ignored the shouts of the women—watching after their wake, unconcerned and unobserving, except of each other, as the kids made their way to the front of the house.

There he saw it: seven feet tall and maybe three feet wide, a blazing cross. The flames looked alive, licking and taunting the air, even as they bit and danced.

Abel peed his pants.

On the other side of the blaze he could see his big friends from down the street completely stopped, frozen, at the moment they knew what they were seeing. A neighbor woman coming out to her porch screamed loud enough to be heard for blocks. Soon, Abel could hear his daddy's voice behind him, cussing. Beside Abel on one side was Ben; on the other was James. Whacked upside his knuckle head by the absurdity and fright of the cross, Ben started laughing.

Abel wanted to pee his pants again. Instead he ran, almost through the flames, abandoning Ben—as he wanted to abandon shame, and the hour, and the day, and his birth—to stand beside the biggest of his big friends, beside Opelika, who held a package shaped just like a basketball wrapped in newspaper.

And so it was looking from across the flames that Abel saw his father slap Ben, then saw James rubbing at his own eyes as the smoke began to sting. From a distance Abel saw his father blinkingly observe the darkness down the side of Abel's leg.

He saw Opelika drop the basketball wrapped in the funny pages, saw the basketball bounce and roll into the gutter, saw Mount Bayou drop the box he was carrying, from close up.

The heat from the rising flames seemed to melt the freeze that had suspended the Fantastic Four. Opelika pulled off his jacket and started beating the blaze with it. His housemates followed suit in a misguided attempt to extinguish the flames that only managed to fan the fire.

Big Abel was struggling with the spigot on the outdoor water hose as one of the jackets exploded into flames. After what seemed like too long, the water started running, a half trickle out the nozzle, then spews, strange arcs, and splashes down the green length of the hose. It had been slashed. *Get me some fucking tape . . . no, get the hose from next door . . . no, don't fucking call the police.*

James and the boys from the neighborhood, all but Abel, unscrewed the hose from the house two doors down and dragged it right over to Big Abel. They knew from hot days playing hide-and-seek and war over and through the lawns and flower beds of their summer kingdom, slaking their thirst at any convenient tap or faucet, that the house next door had neither gardener nor hose.

Ben felt ashamed, ashamed of getting slapped, ashamed of being white, ashamed of standing out in the street in this neighborhood that was getting stranger by the moment. More than this he felt, without knowing what it was exactly he was feeling, the shame of all the dark, the pale-dark, and the hard-dark people around him; a shame intensified by the presence of a white witness to their humiliation.

Whoever had set the fire had had the good sense to rush off

before it was discovered, before the police could be called, before their license plates could be written down. The perpetrators' cowardice was the victims' good fortune. It was a bad enough thing to see the cross. To have a white boy see you see it, to have a white boy laugh as you saw it, was a thing almost unbearable. Everybody on the lawn hated Abel for having invited the white boy to the party. Ben felt the shame and Abel felt the hate. A police car arrived and two white policemen got out.

"Shit."

"Shit. Radio the fire department."

The white policemen looked so calm and unperturbed, so uninvolved yet powerful, that they appeared to Abel to be stronger than all of the men running around angry and agitated. Mistaking their disinterest for courage, he ran to stand in the sheltering space he imagined between their two bodies. The larger of the two men lifted him into his arms and cradled him like a baby.

Ben walked around the cross, toward Abel, thinking the heat he felt on his cheek came from the fire or from his embarrassment. When he touched his face he felt the raised welts, the imprint of Big Abel's palm. Ben wanted to vomit.

Everything was scary and strange: the whooping and crying of the women, the silent eyes of the men, Abel soiling himself. The policeman lifting Abel in his arms like he was a baby. Ben was ready to leave. He didn't wait for his father. He just started walking. Ben, who considered Abel to be the first person he'd ever loved of his own free will and volition, had exhausted all of that love in a single evening. All he wanted was to be again who he had been that morning.

Abel wanted the same thing. Only he hated himself for wanting it. Ben and Abel had seen pictures of bodies hanging from trees and fiery crosses and people in white sheets with pointed hats. They knew what the Klan was from social studies class at school. In school it had seemed to both of them to be distant, horrible but distant, true but impossible, no scarier than a vampire in a horror movie. It wasn't a fear they triumphed over; it was a fear they didn't have. Abel wondered what it was he could do so that he could not know tomorrow what he knew today.

Can I not know tomorrow what I know now? What young Abel knew now was that his daddy wasn't powerful. *Big Abel can't protect me. Can I not know tomorrow what I know now?* It seemed an impossible necessity. All his thoughts, all his understanding, all his abilities, starting with a toddler's ability to hold his own water, were fleeing.

Big Abel waved to his son to go to him. Abel couldn't let go of the policeman's hand. He was too afraid. Big Abel shut his eyes.

The stout woman who had barred the door, who had tried to prevent the other women from witnessing what she had witnessed, was now standing on the porch hollering to Big Abel.

"There's some rednecks on the phone and they wanna know how you like your boy's birthday present."

"Tell them to fuck themselves," said Big Abel.

"Yep," said the woman.

It seemed to Abel that his father was asking a woman to do what he couldn't do. The crowd saw it another way; they applauded.

Despite the best efforts of the Fantastic Four, the fire blazed until the white firemen arrived and put it out.

After the fire trucks and the policemen had driven away, Big Abel announced, "Time for cake and ice cream."

Abel didn't want any.

"He can save that for a better year," said his mother.

"We're singing and you're eating," his father responded.

"I don't want to sing 'Happy Birthday' or eat cake," said Abel, who had not had a chance to stop and change his clothes.

"We're singing and you're eating," Big Abel repeated. He didn't like repeating himself.

"Why?" asked Abel.

"Terror disrupts rituals," said Big Abel.

The party reconvened. Abel changed clothes. As soon as the cake was eaten, Big Abel approached Abel. His son's eyes were as full of fear as his discarded pants were full of piss.

"Go get a strap and wait for me in your room." Abel's eyes went hard. A whipping was a familiar thing. He was stronger than a whipping. Maybe everything would be all right. When he walked upstairs toward his bedroom away from the noise of the party, he walked angry, not scared. *Copacetic.*

Waycross approached Big Abel.

"Sir, about Little Man . . ."

"A Negro boy afraid of white folks is worse than dead." Waycross dropped his head. *A man raises his child as he sees fit.*

Sitting on his bed waiting for his father, Abel was thinking, the only thing worse than a Saturday birthday was a Sunday birthday. It was getting so Abel didn't like church. He didn't like the preacher, didn't like the way they, the family, were all so visible, didn't like the way his father always had them arriving late, didn't like taking communion after singing that creepy song,

There is a fountain filled with blood drawn from Emmanuel's veins, didn't like getting on his knees, didn't know for sure that Jesus was the son of God, wasn't sure there was a God to have a son, didn't want to be someplace where one person, the preacher, was free to stand up and tell what and why and how he was right about everything, while everyone else was free to keep their mouth shut and smile. Considering how bad having a birthday on a Sunday was made Abel just a little grateful.

Mainly he was jealous. He was turning thirteen. He half wished he were having a bar mitzvah. He liked bar mitzvahs. Even from the pews, even as a twelve-year-old waiting to turn thirteen himself, he'd been able to see something change when he'd watched his newly turned thirteen-year-old friends read aloud from the Torah for the very first time before the whole congregation. He could feel, though he could not name, the sense of entitlement bestowed, the sense of arriving, the sense of recognition conveyed to the bar mitzvah boy as his community began to try to understand him to be a man. Abel wanted all of that for himself.

He lusted for recognition like he lusted for the big-bosomed white-skinned centerfold ladies. He wanted it all the more acutely for knowing this too was something his daddy didn't have, that his granddaddy hadn't had.

Sitting on his bed, swinging his legs restlessly, waiting to be released, for punishment to be over, for the whipping to be done, he wondered what portion of the Torah had been read by the Swiss-German Jew who was kin to him, his father's great-grandfather.

Don't think about that. Think about something else. Think about what was supposed to be.

Abel was supposed to have had a birthday party. A grown-up fill-the-house-with-people birthday party, the kind he hadn't had since he had begun real school. Since he'd begun school he had had single-sex parties at some public place: a bowling alley, a skating rink, a movie theater, someplace neutral, someplace familiar and comfortable to the white kids in his class. The only problem was that his mother had never been comfortable and his father had never come. If he had known how bad it could get he would have left his parties as they had been.

Except he wanted his mother to be comfortable and he wanted his father to be present, and he wanted something different for turning thirteen. He had learned his lesson about wanting.

Big Abel always kept his law office open on Saturday, always worked on Saturday, usually coming home around four. *I should have left it the way it was.* Every year on Abel's birthday and his sister's birthday, Big Abel would take his wife out to dinner. "She's the one who did all the work," Big Abel would say, patting his wife's arm. "And you've already had your party." *I should have left it alone.*

It was one of the few things that Abel and his sister agreed on: birthday nights were very lonely and quiet. This year he had wanted it to be different. He hadn't wanted to eat early with Tess while their mother was out getting her hair fixed or in the back of the house getting dressed for dinner. He hadn't wanted his parents to leave after hearing his and Tess's prayers and kissing them each on both cheeks, after telling them they were to be in bed asleep by eight thirty.

Ever since they were old enough to stay at home alone, since they were eight and ten, at eight thirty on birthday nights they would be in their respective bedrooms with the lights out. But neither could quite fall asleep that early. Abel would be in his book-lined bedroom just above his parents' and Tess would be in her white bedroom beside his. The parents would come home whispering loudly. Then the sounds of moans and cries would start rising from their bedroom.

This year was different. This year they were all together. This year everything had gone wrong. *I am wrong.* Abel held the belt as he waited, stroking some of the length of it. *I am wrong.* He repeated the same sentence over and over again when he couldn't make himself think about something less frightening.

Abel knew himself to be an odd little boy. He was hoping to be a simple man.

Because everyone who knew him knew he was black, and because everyone in North Nashville knew Abel, the boy with kinky golden curls flying past on a bike, everyone in North Nashville except Abel knew that Abel was black. He remembered the day he'd been told. It had been in this very room, in his bedroom. He didn't want to remember.

When he went downtown it was a different story. He rarely went downtown—except with his grandmother. Antoinette and Big Abel, remembering downtown from its most recently segregated days, preferred to wait and shop for clothes only when they traveled to Chicago or New York. Sometimes Grandma took Abel downtown. Grandma was an adventurous woman with a love of fashion and a taste for changing times. If she could go in the stores and get proper help from a saleswoman, she would go in the stores, driving the little car her husband had bought her on her sixty-fifth birthday and then had taught her to drive a year before he died of a sudden heart attack, almost as if he had known death was coming. And Grandma took her little grandson with her. Sometimes people thought she was his mammy. And sometimes he liked it. *I should be punished for that.*

Whenever Abel was going to get a whipping, he tried to think of a reason he deserved one. Usually it wasn't the reason he was getting one. His father didn't whip him often but he whipped him awfully—and almost always for reasons Abel didn't understand. Waiting was the worst part. He was almost happy when Big Abel finally entered the room.

"Take off those soiled clothes."

Big Abel looked away as his son disrobed. The boy didn't say he had already changed. It was beside the point.

"Are you a baby?"

"No, sir."

"I should save those clothes and make you wear them tomorrow and the next day, shouldn't I?"

"No, sir."

"No, sir?"

"No, sir."

For a moment Big Abel looked as if he saw something in this naked man-boy he couldn't be cruel to, no matter to what purpose. Then he saw something else.

"You afraid of crackers, boy?"

"Yes, sir."

"Didn't I tell you not to be afraid of anybody or anything but me and God?"

"Yes, sir."

"But you afraid of them."

"Yes, sir."

"I'm going to do you a favor, boy."

"Yes, sir."

"When you walk out of this room, you're not going to be afraid of anything but me."

Big Abel closed the door. When the sun rose the next morning there were two men living under Abel's roof and they hated each other. *Happy Birthday.*

Big Abel left for church before any of his family awoke. He left a note saying he was going to early service, then down to his law office. When Antoinette, who had stumbled into her room drunk and exhausted long after her husband had finished doling out discipline in the next room, saw spotting on the sheets as she made the bed, she made a note to schedule an appointment with the gynecologist. Then she stripped the sheets, bleached the mattress with a sponge, and put the linens in the washer with more bleach. After that she got her girl and her boy into the car, then into church for the eleven o'clock service.

In the afternoon the Fantastic Four called down to the house for Abel to go up to their house and get his presents. Gardeners were arriving in a flatbed truck, loaded down with sod to redo the front lawn, as Abel marched up the street. The Fantastic Four fed Abel McDonald's hamburgers and French fries and told him stories of the whippings they had gotten as boys and the whippings their daddies had gotten. And in case that was insufficient balm in this particular Gilead, they told him the story of the beatings they had taken to cross the burning sands into their fraternity.

After a time, Abel let their stories make him smile. The stories did make things better. Not good, but better. His big friends had not protected him. Abel hated them for that. He hated the Fantastic Four for not having protected him from his daddy. And he hated his daddy. He hated the people he trusted so much that he had no hate left over to hate the Klan.

My worst day is behind me. He would find his safe place. He would find the strong men. He would make all the weak people and all the vicious people and all the weak and vicious people pay. Abel made that promise to himself as he fell asleep. It was a promise he would keep. He cuddled to the truth like it was a stuffed bear: *terror is bigger than love, and shelter sweeter than excitement.* Touching himself in the safety of his anger, he soiled the sheets the woman, the mother, would have to wash. *He knew a truth and would exploit it.* Abel was a man.

Hope drained the last of her glass. Nicholas drained the last of his.

"You and Abel played a better game of 'Show me yours, and I'll show you mine.' "

"Different, not better."

"Who can tell us how much Abel had to do with Abu Ghraib?"

"Your friend from Birmingham."

"Aria."

"I've taken the liberty of booking us both on a flight to Washington."

"That's not the liberty I'd anticipated."

"Allow me to accommodate you more cordially."

"If I cheat on my husband it will be with a ghost."

"A waste."

"You don't know the power of my imagination."

He took Hope's hand and kissed it again. She kissed him full on the lips without opening her mouth. Then she was gone.

By the time she was halfway home Hope had almost decided not to accompany Nicholas any farther on his journey. She had no strong wish to be with Nicholas on the plane to Reagan Airport. His Abel was too different from her Abel. But she needed to know what Aria knew, and Aria's Abel might be more different still. Hope needed Nicholas.

When she arrived at her house she showered and slipped into her bed. Touching herself, she thought of the girl she had been and the boy Abel had been that summer in Italy. Then she turned off the light and tried to settle into the sleep of the grown.

Instead, she started thinking about the Bible. Abel's Bible. She was thinking about the numbers he had always used for his computer password back when she had still known his password: 4133132. But it had really been 4,13,31,32. The four was for the fourth book of the Bible, Numbers. The 13 was for the chapter; 31 and 32 were the verses.

She turned the light back on. She sat propped up on the bed in the pillows. She pulled the King James Bible she kept in the nightstand out of the drawer. She turned to Numbers:

These are the names of the men which Moses sent to spy out the land . . . And Moses sent them to spy out the land of Canaan, and said unto them, Get you up this way southward and go up into the mountain: and see the land, what it is, and the people that dwelleth therein, whether they be strong or weak, few or many; And what the land is that they dwell in, whether it be good or bad, and what cities they be that they dwell in, whether in tents, or in strongholds, And what the land is, whether it be fat or lean, whether there be wood therein, or not. And be ye of good courage, and bring of the fruit of the land. Now the time was the time of the first ripe grapes . . .

But your little ones which ye said should be a prey, them will I bring in, and they shall know the land which ye have despised. But as for you, your carcasses, they shall fall in this wilderness.

Thinking that God himself punished less-than-intrepid spies, and that she owed Abel much, Hope was headed to Washington.

Part III

*T*HE NEWS TRAVELED *faster than any other news ever. Dr. King had been shot dead. The date was April 4, 1968. Abel's house quickly became a gathering place. Friends and even some people they didn't know arrived at the house on Fifteenth Street without invitation until there were fifty or sixty grown people in the house, crying and getting drunk.*

It was a fifth and final blow. Medgar Evers, June 12, 1963, shot walking into his ranch house, leaving two boys and a girl. The four little girls bombed in church on September 15, 1963. November 22, 1963, John F. Kennedy killed in Dallas. February 21, 1965, Malcolm X. Now the daddy of Yolanda, Little Martin, Bernice, and Dexter was dead.

In Big Abel's house it was the end of an era that in Nashville had begun with the bombing at the home of Z. Alexander Looby in April 1960. Abel didn't remember a time when politically active black men weren't dying.

He was over black men. King's death did it. He heard all the sadness. He heard other things too. That King was up in that hotel with a white woman. In his little boy's mind and in his grown man's mind, Abel always blamed Coretta for the death. It would take Hope to almost undo that. No one could undo his sadness that he hadn't saved the wrapper off the candy bar Dr. King had given him.

That very night eight-year-old Abel started saying no when people asked if he wanted to run for his father's seat on the city council when he grew up.

He was over black people. Ever since he could remember he had heard the phrase that all he had to do was be black and die. And now the only two things he for sure didn't want to do were be black and die.

TWENTY-SEVEN

O N T H E S A M E flight to Washington that Abel had taken every third week, commuting to his office at the Pentagon from his house in Ardmore, Hope was thinking about Aria Reese. She was wondering if Abel had thought about Aria on the flight too. Nicholas's eyes were closed. His thumb and ring finger were bent to touch, forming a circle. His breath was slow and deep. Nicholas believed pilots and planes benefited from his serene concentration.

Aria was the only woman Hope had ever kissed as she had kissed Abel and Waycross and, a long time past, Nicholas.

Hope's and Aria's enchantment had lasted only a long weekend. They'd been, each for the other, an atypical diversion. The friendship was long-standing.

The women had first met when Hope was at Harvard and Ari, the future national security advisor, was at Wellesley. They had both been invited to an AKA sorority event. Discovering a bouquet of shared preferences and experiences ranging from the uncommon (each had created a diorama of the Hanging Gardens of Babylon) to the common (claiming Zora Neale Hurston as their favorite writer), the women had quickly become friends. That Easter, Hope had gone home with Ari to Birmingham.

They saw the Wedgwood at the museum. They saw the church that had been bombed. Aria said one of the girls, Denise McNair, had been a friend of hers and Angela Davis's. She said Angela had called home from the Sorbonne when she'd heard the news. Just after that Aria showed Hope the statue of Vulcan standing on the hill. And then they kissed. In Hope's mind that day the beacon in Vulcan's hand was red. Looking back she doubted it had been shining at all.

After the divorce, Hope and Ari had rarely crossed paths but the friendship between Ari and Abel had intensified. Then in 2002 Hope and Ari had found themselves staying at the same hotel in Los Angeles. They'd both been attending the NAACP Image Awards. They had sat up in the bar drinking vodka shots as Aria had recounted her dreams and Hope had interpreted them.

It was a game they had played. West Virginia hoo-doo.

There had been three dreams. All these years later Hope couldn't remember anything about the first and she could only remember her interpretation of the second: "No fun being an undercover brother." The third she remembered with awe and amusement. It had disclosed that Aria was having an affair with the president and that she called the president's most private part Mr. Wonderful. To Hope this had seemed a small victory for dark women everywhere. Usually, Ari had very patriotic and very erotic dreams. Every once in a while Aria had the same nightmare. Aria had kept rubbing her flat stomach as she'd told this last dream. Then it had been over and she had taken another sip of what she called "moloko" that was just plain vodka without the milk.

"That means you know that the white woman whose hus-band you've been sleeping with is going to kill you dead if she gets a chance to come away looking clean," Hope had said.

"What she doesn't know won't hurt me."

"Ajay could use an aunt."

"I recuse myself."

"Because?" Hope had asked.

"I know Abel almost as well as I know the president."

"Invitation withdrawn."

In the sober morning, Hope and Aria had smiled in each other's direction and kept moving as they had crossed the hotel lobby.

Hope gave the taxi driver a twenty and asked him to wait when they pulled up to the entrance of Arlington National Ceme-tery. She said there would be another twenty if he was there when they got back. It was the unlikely thing to do and there is safety in doing the unlikely thing. Doing the safe and unlikely thing was a way of paying homage to Abel. Arlington some-how commanded a new respect for Abel. If you don't act pre-dictably, people can't plan for you. And if people can't plan for you, it's harder to get waylaid.

That was another thing they had taught her in the seminar on coping with violence abroad: Don't stick to routine. Don't go home the same way each day. Don't make it easy for anyone to target you. Hope remembered Abel saying he wished somebody had taught that lesson to Martin Luther King.

At the time she had thought it an offensively bitter, sarcastic remark. Now she understood Abel to have been staggeringly sincere.

Dr. King and Reverend Abernathy had used the same room at the Lorraine Hotel so often that folk in Memphis called it the King-Abernathy suite. Don't stick to routine. Don't go home the same way each day. Don't make it easy for anyone to target you. The knowledge kept rare—that was the knowledge Abel wanted for himself and his.

By being black and playing by the insider's rules of self-protection, Hope did Abel what Ajay would have called "a significant solid."

Inside Arlington, Hope and Nicholas scanned the crowd, wondering who was busy with the same kind of business Abel had once been busy with.

She started on the path that led directly toward the Confederate Memorial. Nicholas pulled her back and put them on the path that led toward J. F. K.'s grave.

Arlington was crowded, now as before, with citizens and foreigners. Standing again at Kennedy's graveside, Hope was surprised to see a long and literal crack in the monument. She wondered when it would be fixed; then she stopped wondering. The crack was irrelevant.

Standing in front of the eternal flame that she had always found magical, or mythic, and perhaps even fairy-tale-ish, that she had always found to be evidence that not so long ago the nation had been young and innocent, Hope began to mourn for Abel, who had known from childhood's hour, from before the first time he stood at this grave, that the nation was not innocent.

Wrapped warm in the Burberry trench coat Abel had loved to see her in, with Nicholas beside her, in front of Kennedy's words etched in stone—*Ask not what your country can do for you; ask what you can do for your country*—Hope cried for Abel for real.

A group of Albanian nuns scuttled away, frightened by the arrival of a group of silent tight-lipped skinny German girls with black-painted nails, belly rings, nose rings, and tattoos.

One of the pierced German girls began to read aloud, "Now the trumpet summons us again. Not as a call to bear arms though embattled we are But a call to bear the burden of a long twilight struggle. A struggle against the common enemies of man: Tyranny. Poverty. Disease. And War itself." The inscription didn't end there but the girl stopped reading. The young women stood in silence. Finally one girl had it all figured out. "It is ridiculous," she announced.

The German girls moved on, laughing and chattering in a German peppered with French, leaving Hope and Nicholas alone at the grave.

Hope picked up reading aloud near where the pierced young one had dropped off. "Let every nation know whether it wishes us well or ill that we shall pay any price bear any burden meet any hardship support any friend oppose any foe to assure the survival and the success of liberty . . . In the hour of maximum danger I do not shrink from this responsibility I welcome it . . . The energy the faith the devotion which we bring to this endeavor will light our country and all who serve it and the glow from that fire can truly light the world."

On the rise above Kennedy's grave was the Custis-Lee mansion. Hope and Abel had both intimately understood that the national cemetery had been placed to defile a family home, the Custis–Lee home, with bodies—with the bodies of victims and conquerors, slaves and soldiers. She wanted to explain this to Nicholas, but he was going on and on about blind people and elephants.

Sitting on a bench in a cemetery of warriors, he was concluding there were three kinds of villages in the world and every one of them was populated by blind people and elephants.

In one village everyone had hold of a different part of the same elephant. The people there were always arguing as each kept trying to convince the others they knew what an elephant was.

In a second village everybody had an elephant of their own and someone arranged things such that when a whistle blew once everyone caught hold of the tip of the trunk; when it blew twice everybody grabbed hold of a rough, fat toe; and when the whistle blew three times everybody grabbed hold of the tail. Each hour of the day everybody was changing their mind about what an elephant was but they were always all in full agreement.

And there was a third village where there was only one elephant but everybody took the time to touch him all over. In this place the villagers shared an understanding that an elephant was many different things and all at once but you could only deal with the part you were touching.

"Most people live in the first village. People like Aria and Abel live in the second village," said Nicholas.

"And they are the whistle blowers," said Hope.

"And you want to set your tent up in the third," said Nicholas.

"But that one doesn't exist," said Hope.

"Abel told me he met someone he thought might help that village come to be," said Nicholas.

"I can't imagine anyone getting to that third tent," said Hope.

"Abel thought it was going to happen," said Nicholas.

She wanted to return to the small southern town that had been Nashville before seven thousand Kurds had settled near the banks of the Cumberland. Before Samir who had found Saddam hiding in a spider hole had driven in a green BMW to Nashville to register to vote in the Iraqi elections. Before new thefts had begun at Oak Ridge. Before the Cumberland had become a river in the Middle East. Before the world got smaller and smaller and the contradictions got increasingly savage.

She wanted to return to a Nashville that no longer existed. And when she got there she wanted to enjoy a kind of safety that no longer existed. It was a sorrow to know that it had leavened something in Abel's spirits to move from "I am not safe" and "We are not safe" to "No one is safe."

"Do you think she will turn up?" asked Nicholas.

"She might show up faster if you disappear," said Hope.

Nicholas flipped the collar of his coat up toward his ears, then put his arm around Hope's waist for warmth, pulling her closer. She pushed him off and away.

Perhaps at the end Abel hadn't wanted to be buried in Arlington because he hadn't wanted to participate in any more desecration.

She wondered if he had arrived at that point. If it had come to that she hoped it was not because he had defiled so much that he could defile no more. Or perhaps it had been a simple act of humility, that at the last Abel hadn't believed himself worthy.

Or, maybe it was the man he had met—he had said it was on a plane—his first unhyphenated black man. Abel had declared himself, to Nicholas, ready to die after the chance meeting. He hadn't remembered, or at least wouldn't tell Nicholas, the man's name except he had said it had been a stranger and blacker name than his own and he had talked to the gentleman for an hour and a half and found not a single syllable or hint of race-based double-consciousness.

Maybe it was that. And maybe Abel had simply figured out that when you're ready to die, it doesn't matter where you are buried.

She found her way back to the place where all the losing had begun, the Confederate Memorial. There was the black soldier and there was the mammy. There was the white man who had carved the memorial and the black daughter he had educated. And there was the black man that daughter had loved who had pioneered open-heart surgery that would allow so many soldiers to survive battles. And there were the babies Alice hadn't been able to bear, and the white Frenchwoman who had consoled Alice's husband. It was all an unbroken circle like the statue itself, interlocking betrayals, rescues, and mysteries.

"Hello, Hope." The words came from behind. Hope turned to see an elegant woman in a brown wool pantsuit and a camel-hair topcoat: Aria Reese.

Her old friend was wearing exquisite faux riding boots that added two inches to her height, making her six feet tall. Nicholas was nowhere in sight. For a moment Hope felt wide and small.

"Hey, Ari."

"Let's take a walk, girl."

They linked arms. For a moment all either woman felt was safe.

Arm and arm and slowly, Aria led Hope to the plain white tombstone in section thirty-six with the number 1431 carved into the back. On either side and in front and in back of the stone, other stones ribboned the grassy flat. On the front of 1431 the word MISSISSIPPI, all in capitals, was most prominent, then the given name: Medgar Willey Evers.

"We came to the fortieth anniversary," Aria said quietly.

"We who?"

"Me and Abel."

"I forget how much Evers meant to Abel."

"Didn't forget, didn't know."

"Tell me."

"I can't. You've got to be from deep down south to know. You can't read and learn what it is to be a child in war. You just learn what it is to be lucky reading about the unlucky."

"I remember Abel kept a framed picture of Myrlie and her son in the pews at the funeral, on his desk."

"The *Life* cover."

"The boy's crying and Myrlie's wearing a double strand of pearls and white gloves . . ."

"And a hat, don't forget the hat . . ."

"And a tailored black cap-sleeve dress."

"Medgar got shot down in front of the pretty house where he lived with his pretty wife and his pretty children and the governor of Mississippi walked arm in arm with his accused murderer during the trial. Abel wanted to get inside the government because he knew it was dirty as much as because he knew it was strong."

"And."

"And after Ajay was born if he had to choose between his ideals and his safety, he chose his safety. Not Abel's safety, Ajay's safety."

"When I had the baby I doomed him?"

"You radicalized him."

"I don't believe that."

"It's truth. And the rest of the truth is, whatever it is Abel did or didn't do, knew or didn't know, you are the one person who has reason to love him despite it all, no matter what all is."

"Because?"

"Ajay."

"Ajay?"

"Ajay."

"Is that all you have to say to me?"

"It's all I can say."

"Why didn't you come to the funeral?"

"As I had been sleeping with the widow's husband, I thought it would be in very bad taste."

"Nicholas thinks there's some possibility he's not dead."

"He's dead. If he wasn't I would know. And I would tell you. However many rules or laws it broke. Even if I never told Stokely Carmichael the CIA was really following him and he wasn't going crazy. And you can fucking tell Nicholas. Abel's dead. Go home."

"First, I've got to finish burying the man," said Hope.

When Hope got back to the cab Nicholas was sitting in the back-seat blowing smoke out the window. She told the cab driver to head to Dulles Airport.

TWENTY-EIGHT

NICHOLAS AND HOPE were in a bar at Dulles Airport. He was waiting to board a flight to Tokyo. She was waiting for the flight to Rome. Waycross and Ajay were still in Michigan. She had tried to call and tell them she was about to board a plane, but they weren't answering their phones. It was her first fortunate moment in many days.

Nicholas had a last photo to show her. A photo from his seventieth birthday party: Abel and Nicholas walking on a beach. Abel looked serene. Nicholas was talking animatedly, a moving hand blurred in the frame. Hope asked if she could keep it. Nicholas politely refused.

"I will be on a plane to Detroit later tonight and in Tokyo seventeen hours later. Four hours after that I will be back in Manila and two hours after that I will be back home in my barong Tagalog walking by the South China Sea waiting for three girls who love each other to start massaging the plane crunch out of these old muscles. And three hours after that a very pretty man will allow me to explore the inside of his toothless velvet mouth."

"Toothless?"

"Toothless."

"Did you have his teeth taken out?"

"Of course not. He was a beautiful boy. I never afflict beautiful people. Manila is not what it once was."

"The Wild West . . . a place to warehouse agents."

"Far superior to being a place to torture people legally."

"I don't know anything more about that than what I read in the *Times*."

"I saw Abel."

"You saw Abel?"

"While we were flying."

Another person telling her another dream. Usually she envied Canary her birds. Another not usually.

Nicholas Gordon rolled the cuffs of his blue-gray linen pants that exactly matched the color of his eyes, propped his white Gucci loafers up on two coconuts on the deck, then began to wade to shore.

Halfway to the island he looked back at the open boat outfitted with a sputtering outboard motor that had brought him to this edge of paradise. The boat was headed for the next atoll, an uninhabited as opposed to sparsely inhabited destination. He had instructed the boatman, a lazy boy, to have a look-see around the spit, find and feed himself lunch, probably a coconut, and return in two hours.

If there are ten thousand islands in the Philippines there are too many tiny spits and sandbars to count. And too many pirates down round Mindanao for tourists to come looking for pretty beaches. If anything happened—a heart attack, a pirate attack, a bout of radical disobedience—it might take Nicholas days to get off this little empire of palm trees, if he got off.

Wading through the soft warm water with museum-quality seashells scratching his toes, Nicholas inhaled his own scent, the scent of expensive cologne and old-man sweat, thinking that some ends of the earth are far more beautiful than others.

Out of the jungle came what appeared to be a woman, wearing a kind of sarong and a large hat woven of palm fronds. The person was wearing a cross like a timeless necklace and Chanel sunglasses that signaled a recent connection to the larger world.

Nicholas and the sarong wearer greeted each other affectionately. Bumping arms, they walked the path from the beach to the house, a quarter mile. At the house they didn't go inside; they walked around and sat in the courtyard. There was a book on the table, *The Thirty-Nine Steps.* The island was so small that this courtyard overlooked the sea.

"Abel's dead?"

"Abel's dead."

"Everyone's certain?"

"Everyone's certain."

"Excellent."

"Where are you actually staying?"

"If I told you that . . . I would have to kill you." It was a bad joke but they both laughed.

"There is that. Are you a woman, too, wherever it is?"

"No."

"A pity. You're quite pretty."

"I came back to you."

"What will you live on?"

"General Yamashita's gold."

Nicholas laughed. The laughter didn't stop Nicholas from worrying that the woman Abel would hit him up for funds.

"Really?" Nicholas was incredulous. He wasn't of the camp that believed that the gold Japan had stolen from Manchuria and China in the 1930s had ended up in booby-trapped underground mazes in the Philippines under the direction of General Yamashita. Nicholas would pay if need be. Pay and be amused by his front-row seat to the destruction of colonialization. Even Fanon could not have imagined the "new woman" sitting before Nicholas. The moment would stay absurdly delicious even if it became expensive.

"No. My book."

"Book?"

"I'm writing the death of the protagonist this very afternoon."

"Your title?"

"*Spooked: The Life and Death of a Black Southern Conservative.*"

"*Spooked.*"

"Or, *Rebel Yell.*"

"I prefer *Spooked.*"

"I prefer *Rebel Yell.*"

"Who did it?"

"I suspect various people will have various opinions. There will be consensus but not conclusion. Perhaps consensus will go only as far as agreeing Abel's dead."

"And you, what do you think?"

"I think he decided to grow up and disappear."

"Why would he do that?"

"The picture."

"The man covering himself?"

"Absolutely."

"A man covered himself. Why was that significant?"

"Just that he was a man."

"The dignity of Adam."

"There is that."

Nicholas offered sarong-wearing Abel a cigarette. Abel accepted. Nicholas lit one for Abel, then another for himself, off Abel's.

"We did not go the wrong way. We went too far."

"You went the wrong way."

"Spoken like a commie."

"I am a commie. But you could have saved me the trip. I'm old."

"While they were chasing you, they didn't chase me."

"Thank you."

"And now they're chasing Hope. The Lord didn't show up with mercy."

"Your lovers did."

"Each in their own way."

Nicholas looked at Abel dressed so strangely. Soon it would be time for Nicholas to wade back to his boat. Now was a time to kiss and know Abel was right. Kiss and know Abel was gone. Kiss and move beyond policing evil toward increasing good. Kiss and know and never tell Abel good-bye. Kiss and play Sheherazade.

"Abel was a cross-dresser?"

"In my dreams."

"You didn't come in a professional capacity."

"I lied."

"Not about anything important."

Hope kissed Nicholas on both cheeks, then again on the first, kissed him formally. They had gotten back to good friends.

TWENTY-NINE

Settling into the leatherette comfort of first class, after boarding, Hope took a Xanax and started drinking sweet drinks. Halfway across the Atlantic, orange juice and champagne gave way to Baileys over ice. Between sips of beigey brown cream, she eased herself into her last journey with Abel. This time they were headed in the same direction.

Twenty minutes later she and the plane were high. Part of what Abel had loved about Rome, and what, eventually, Hope loved best about Rome, was the fact that, in a *Casablanca* kind of way, Rome was all that remained of the long day of their marriage. Rome, a short (not even two-minute) Mississippi John Hurt song, "My Creole Belle," a promise, and Ajay.

She had promised him, that first summer in Rome, that she would bury him in Europe. The conversation had begun after she had showed him her mother's grave and he had asked that Hope bury him "beyond America, out of Dixie." She had promised. And he had prodded to make sure she understood the significance of the promise. He had reminded her of the Road Mangler, the legendary roadie said to have kidnapped Gram Parsons's body and buried it at Joshua Tree. And she had said, "Even if I have to go to jail I promise." Then he had asked her where she wanted to be buried, and she had said, speaking seriously because she finally understood that he was speaking seriously, that she didn't want to think about dying.

Abel had liked the way Canary's freedom, her life beyond stereotypes, expectations, and America, had looked on Hope. He had wanted that one day for his own child. And they had achieved it.

How could she once upon a time have known a man that well, then known him not at all? Maybe she couldn't. Maybe it was just like when a scientist gets a key fact wrong and all the other analysis goes haywire. She had gotten a key fact wrong. Abel had been competent.

And she had gotten key facts right. Abel had been raised in a time and place of terror. It had provoked a permanent wariness. She understood that. She knew what it was to be weary from worry.

Flying literally and figuratively, she understood another thing that had changed on September 11, 2001: Abel had never again enjoyed flying. His safe, optimistic place had been removed. And somehow the way it had been removed, the way the damage had touched all, blindly and equally, had made him finally feel more American than black. But at the last he hadn't been American, or black; he'd been a daddy.

As the plane made preparations for its final descent, Hope started thinking about gold, frankincense, and myrrh. In the little crèche that Hat had whittled for Hope, Caspar, Melchior, and Balthazar had approached Jesus with gifts in their hands.

As a child Hope had loved wondering who had carried what. Later Hope and Abel had debated both what the gifts meant and what had happened to them. Had they been stolen by the men who later hung beside Jesus on the cross, as some folks said, or stolen by Judas, as others insisted? What Hope knew for sure about the gifts was that they were remembered.

Gold. Frankincense. Myrrh. The gifts were remembered and so was the trip. And so was the Wise Men's change of mind. Matthew 2:12. "And being warned of God in a dream that they should not return to Herod, they departed into their own country another way." Staying true to the baby, the Wise Men had betrayed Herod. Hope didn't know how Abel had done it, but she sensed that Abel had passed into his own country another way. Abel had changed masters. She couldn't prove it but, half high and sobering, she knew.

He passed. That's what the aunts would have said. They would have meant he died. And they would have meant he pretended to be white. And they would have meant he lived before he died.

You pass away, and it is a vanishing and an estrangement. You pass on and move into another realm. You pass for white and wear a mask of manners and skin. You march. You parade. You are present. You are seen. You pass. You are not a zombie.

American black people, quiet as it's kept, fear zombies. She remembered the day the aunts let her in on the secret. Her toes had stung where Hot had used the nippers too vigorously before attacking with the nail-polish brush. The old fashion curling iron that had been heated up in the open flame of a gas stove top was perilously near her cheek. It radiated an itchy heat that reminded Hope of Inkwell Beach and the scorch marks that adorned her skin her first summer on U Street. Three faint brown dashes—one near her widow's peak, one at her nape, one near her ear—were all she had left of the moments she had jerked her head in an unexpected direction before Sweet could jerk it back and away from the burn. The little scars itched when she refused to know what she needed to know. She remembered Hot concluding, "That's how you tell if someone's black or not. You figure out if they know 'bout zombies."

For a minute Hope had thought the aunts had been pulling her leg. Then she had realized they hadn't been. They had been pressing curls and painting her toenails, wondering if she wasn't really white. The aunts knew you could be the color of Alabama honey, a most pleasing shade of brown, and be snow white.

Abel lived before he died. Abel passed. Finally it was sad.

She was in a cab driving away from Rome's Da Vinci Airport. The cab was just exiting the grounds of the airport when the phone in her purse began to sing, "Oh my darling, Clementine." Waycross was calling. He and Ajay would be home the day after next. She promised she would be waiting at home when they got there. Another promise she would keep.

She urgently wished to give up her polyandry. Though she was intensely interested in the most intimate of all speculative fiction, what might have been if the love had been better, larger, truer, somehow different, she would let a fondness for presence, presents, and the present win out. She was a practical and passionate woman.

The cab came to a stop outside the walls of Vatican City. She was wearing the same clothes she had worn at Arlington, but now the coat was across her arm, her sunglasses were on her face, and she had thrown out the underpants because they didn't wash and dry as quickly as her body did. The gold locket Abel had bought Antoinette, in which Antoinette had placed the first lock of Abel's hair ever cut from his head, was around her neck.

She was on the Vatican garden tour. People chattered around her in English. She leaned over to smell a yellow rose, she touched the earth. The tiny loop of curl was in her hand. Hope took the lock of hair Antoinette had clipped from Abel's head and she buried it in the Vatican garden.

Sheltered by the Swiss Guard, Hope buried a little bit of Abel in the green gardens that had known and outlived every kind of crime, political and private, in the name of God and in the name of greed, in the name of pleasure and in the hope of pain, confessions spoken and unspoken, in every language of the earth, near the pope's own hotel and helipad.

In a place where she knew prayers would be spoken as long as prayers were on this planet, Hope returned a bit of Abel to earth. This place would best mark the length of his journey.

The place where he had said, so silly, so slyly, so simply, "Popes come and go, talking of Michelangelo."

Long before he read, or met, or denounced Edward Said, Abel had chosen Rome. Rome had fed his southern bred-in-the-bone taste for a kind of numb classicism, for the unbreaking frames that absorb pain.

Having shattered so many promises she had made on her wedding day, Hope kept another: she buried Abel in Rome.

In the end what it meant was that he knew she knew him. Once upon a time, the ends of the universe had met in their kiss. Once upon a time they had redeemed everything, and then it had all fallen back to war. But he knew she would know what he meant by black sand and a Ringling Brothers ticket, the prisoner of Saint-Pierre. The fountain in the park had been sculpted by Emma Stebbins, a friend of Alice Williams. That had pointed Hope back to Rome along a new path, as had *Where the Wild Things Are* and the *Epitaph of a Small Winner.* They all pointed to S———'s friend who had helped found the Lampadia Foundation, who had always wanted Hope to write a novel about a black Confederate. There was a black Confederate in Arlington Cemetery who had been carved by a Jewish Confederate, and that had meant something to the boy from Nashville with German-Jewish ancestors. There was a place, once upon a time, where they had met. Abel had trusted she would remember the place and find her way back to it. Trusted she would seek him by the Spanish Steps drinking coffee, or maybe he would just be laughing. At the end Abel would have imagined Hope chasing it all down, imagined Hope connecting some unconnectable dots for him one last time, and he would have smiled. He would have imagined a scene just like at the end of *The Age of Innocence* except that it would be she, not he, who had to sit out on the bench in the park and not go in, because someone had seen and cared, and that someone had been a wife.

Abel had attained this height: a woman had loved him.

THIRTY

HER MEN WERE on the road home. She prayed she didn't still smell of aging dandy. Abel was buried. When the moment had come to put Abel first, she had put Abel first.

Waycross was at the wheel driving south. He and Ajay were listening to a bootleg CD titled *Idlewild Mix*, a whiplashing playlist of jazz trios and early Motown that they had purchased at a one-pump gas station.

While Ajay had pumped the gas, Waycross had called Ruby. He had told her "it" was over. She had hardly known what he'd been talking about. It had been a good little while since they had last been together, maybe before he had married Hope. But they had left the door open. Now it was closed. Ruby had made it easy for Waycross. "Let's just pretend we had this conversation fifteen years ago, and we're fifteen years into 'just good friends.'"

Waycross would miss the same thing Ruby would miss: holding someone who remembered the world that was segregated, black, and southern—the world before Hope and Abel's world, a more vicious but less bruising world. A vanished world.

Ajay and Waycross had gotten back on the road. They had gotten the music going. Waycross was telling Ajay about Ziggy Johnson and the big-legged beautiful women who had danced at the Paradise Club. He had already told him about Lottie the Body and about how once a year a dancer had been painted to look like a gold statuette.

"Why did he love black Confederate soldiers?" asked Ajay.

"He thought predictable responses were pathetic," said Waycross.

"Daddy told me if anything strange ever happened to him get to Idlewild and I would find him there," said Ajay.

"I guess he meant metaphorically," said Waycross.

"I understood literally," said Ajay.

In preparation for her son's return, Hope changed the linen on Ajay's bed and picked up the clothes that had been lying across his floor since before he'd left. Then she poked through his CD collection to see if he had a copy of Prince's *Purple Rain*. He didn't. She would buy him one. And some Talking Heads. Hope wanted Ajay to know who Abel had been the day they had made him.

Humming softly the melody to her favorite Prince single, "Kiss," the part that hung under the words "act your age, not your shoe size," she put the four books she had found on Abel's bedside table, *Epitaph of a Small Winner*, *Eugénie Grandet*, *Man's Fate*, and *Where the Wild Things Are*, on Ajay's.

Into the Balzac she slipped the photograph from Bohol. On the back she had written, MAMA AND DADDY 1986.

She shuffled the *Epitaph* to the top of the pile. Abel had been proud of Machado and she wanted Ajay to believe what Abel had believed: that the greatest novelist of the West was the grandson of slaves, was brown and brilliant, was Machado.

Hope suspected it would be years, perhaps decades, before Ajay understood that in part Abel had loved *Epitaph* because it suggested that Big Abel had lost simply by playing the male role necessary to conceive a being born to taste and swallow the sorrows of the world. What she wanted Ajay to understand soon was what she had learned so recently: Abel had won by creating Ajay.

She picked up the book on the floor beside the bed, a book Abel had given their son years earlier. A silver bookmark, a circle that slipped onto the top or the side of a page, had been, Hope remembered, the significant present. The book, *Black Southerners in Confederate Armies*, was, Abel had said at the time, just the wrapping the gift came in. Hope opened the book to the page marked and read aloud the words that had been underlined.

Bob, I will never forget you and our trip home in 1862 through the mountains of New Mexico, when you had the smallpox and no one would go near you in the wagon but myself. And afterwards when you had gotten well and I had the measles, you stayed by me as I had you. On our trip alone from San Antonio you stuck to me when I was sick. And this trip, Bob, is heart bound one white man and one negro together. You had lost your master in the battle of Glorietta, I had lost my health, but to each other we stood true, and are today enjoying the blessings that were bestowed on but few of those old boys. Long life Bob. Nora and the boys all send love to the "Old Rebel Negro." Write soon to your old comrade and friend.

Slipped inside the book was a photograph of Hope walking down Circuit Avenue, a photo of Hope that first summer on the Vineyard with her hair hacked off, wearing painter's pants. One day Ajay would have a child. One day Hope would tell that child the history of Hope and Abel at the carousel.

Sixteen-year-old Clementine Hope Morgan, no longer answering to Clementine, walked down Circuit Avenue headed in the vague direction of the beach. When she saw the back side of a delicious-looking beige boy walking toward the Flying Horses, she changed direction.

Almost immediately she was waylaid by two St. Paul's boys pedaling past on bikes who stopped to snatch quick hugs. When they continued on their way, she continued on her path to the amusement shed.

The boy-who-might-be-beautiful was walking away from her again but this time he was walking on a revolving platform as it began to turn, changing one horse for another, taunting and cuffing the younger boys, kissing and flattering the girls and the women before finally making a choice. The first time she saw his face he was laughing and golden surrounded by what appeared to be family.

Antoinette was there; Hope didn't know her name then, or that for sure she was the mother, huge and beautiful, in size-twenty-two L.L. Bean clothes she had bought from a mail-order catalog. She was splayed across a thing that looked like a sleigh, dangling her feet in the air looking as if she could pluck a brass ring from the bar with her toes.

He was on a yellow horse frozen rearing up. Someone had told Hope on her first day on the island, on her first trip to the Flying Horses, trying to explain why this merry-go-round was so wonderful, that when the horses had been new the manes and the tails had been made of real horsehair. That day she hadn't understood. But on this day the silly horses that didn't go up and down, that just went round and round, were magical—because the pretty boy was astride the one with the green saddle blanket and the red saddle.

He noticed her watching him. He had noticed her earlier talking to the white boys on the Gitane Super Corsas. Abel had a Gitane Grand Sport—an excellent but slightly less excellent ride. He had noticed her because the two white boys that had been talking to her had been talking to a black girl just exactly the same way they would have talked to a white girl. And she was exactly like a white girl, almost plump and careless and fresh, soft, in a way he hadn't known people like him and like her could be.

It made him sorry she was dressed strange. Who wore cream-colored painter's pants and espadrilles with a Lacoste shirt? She had her hair all cut off in a strange bush of tiny curls. She looked like a pretty boy with big breasts and a melon butt. He wanted to get inside of her.

This surprised him. He had as yet never been inside of a girl, and only one woman. Most girls looked polluted or boring, or worse, like something you fell into and got gobbled up by, vanishing. This girl was different.

He loved anticipating and talking with his gang of private-school boys about the promised joys of oral copulation. The other act, the alleged main event, the one he had, in fact, experienced, seemed too much the exact opposite of being born.

He had come out of a woman's twat. He didn't know why he would want to go back into one. In his head it was too much like dying.

He knew—hungering for the world, he read much—that the phrase for orgasm in French was *la petite mort*, the little death. And he knew orgasm, from alone with himself and from, once, an older girl at school. Alone with himself there was nothing to vanish into except the hand that was already his own. The almost-woman had been different. He had felt lost inside of her even as he had felt pleasure.

If he could possess this girl first, then plunge into her, maybe then after he vanished into her he would be vanishing into himself. He laughed aloud.

This girl in the strange clothes laughed along with him as if she heard the silent joke and wanted him to know she got it.

Or maybe just to get him to look at her more carefully. He complied. There was a line to ride the horses and she was in it. As she waited, she openly stared. Abel observed that waiting her turn was a novelty for this girl. The way she offered her stare as a gift made Abel jealous. She expected people to enjoy being caught in her gaze. He wanted that for himself.

He stared back at this girl who had no idea in the world what it was to cringe, flinch, or hang your head; who didn't know there once had been a crime called reckless eyeballing, and his father had defended people prosecuted for it.

He wondered where she was from. Island gossip had it

Washington, but he didn't think that could be right. She didn't seem like any bougie black D.C. girl he knew.

He would have wanted to slap the stare out of her eyes if she hadn't been so obvious she envied him back.

She envied him. He saw that clearly. Usually this was not a surprise. He was a prince of the Negroes. With this peculiar girl staring at him, the words "prince" and "Negro" for the very first time didn't rub each other wrong.

He was approaching the gold ring. It was within his reach. He left it for a younger rider. His mother smiled approvingly. He was beyond toys. They had given him education and social status; it only remained for him, according to them, to make a fortune. A million dollars, a single million, was the gold ring his family hoped he would reach out and grab. His own ambitions were different.

He didn't care if he was rich. He only wanted two things: to see the world and to love whoever he wanted to love, not to choose from those assigned to him. He was only seventeen years old but he knew this much about himself.

And he also knew, staring at the insolent girl, who had no clue she was insolent and didn't know that her short hair and her painter's pants made her look like a boy, that she just might be somebody he wanted to do those things with.

Other girls joined her. Girls he knew. Appropriately skinny black girls with biggish butts wearing Lilly. These louder, less confident girls with diamond tennis bracelets had fathers who were doctors and lawyers. They were PLUs who knew their place in the world and on the island of Martha's Vineyard.

He didn't know what this girl's daddy did but he was willing to guess he wasn't a doctor or a lawyer. He had heard someone say they thought her father was a gangster, that she went to some boarding school, and not one of the black ones, like Palmer or Piney Woods, and not one of the regular white ones black people had been going to since the fifties, like Northfield Mount Hermon and that Quaker school, Oakwood Friends.

When an older woman, someone who looked like somebody his mother might hire to cook, or clean, or keep the kids, called out, "Hope, Hope," the girl scooted out of the line and out of the shed. "Hope." He smiled. Her name was more perfect than the rest of her. And she had a nanny.

The platform was still turning, the horses were still flying. He couldn't get to her but he knew her name. He laughed at another instance of his own bad luck. Hope snatched the older and darker woman's hand and continued her ramble to the beach.

She got out her heavy black skillet and prepared to start frying chicken. Ajay and Waycross would for sure know they were home when they saw the bright orange chicken breasts on the pristine squares of white bread. She would make it so hot it would "get their heads straight right off." Hot chicken stones you, and the high is always a first-time high.

According to local urban legend, people had been known to detox from crack on hot chicken and prayer. Hope mixed up her own special paste of cayenne and fine-chopped habaneros. She would get all their heads straight.

That day as she chopped the peppers her hands were stinging and her eyes were tearing and her mind was thinking about Washington and the Lord, about elephants and Jesus and Washington.

Not for fame or reward, not for place or for rank,
Not lured by ambition or goaded by necessity,
But in simple obedience to duty, as they understood it,
These men suffered all sacrificed all dared all . . . and died.

Those were the words inscribed on the Confederate Memorial. Pregnant words, particularly interesting to Hope as she pondered the fact that the plaque on the monument had been placed there by the United Daughters of the Confederacy, magnolia-white southern women, who themselves had faced the privations of war with an obedience that could never rightly be called simple.

Betrayed and betraying, cosseted and corseted, plagued and ignored, these women were peculiarly bound. They had served on an invisible front, gaining intimate knowledge of duty and the double-edged sword of freedom that attends it: the freedom to transcend or transgress, balancing the freedom to commit and serve.

There was a story about Elvis and his manager, Colonel Tom Parker, that Abel and Hope had liked together. The Colonel had started business life as the owner of a circus. He knew elephant handlers. Eventually he learned the big secret of the elephant tent. You get a little bitty baby elephant and a great big rope. You tie the rope around the elephant's neck with a slipknot. You poke the elephant with a sharp stick. The elephant tries to break free of the rope and the rope tightens around his neck and holds. You poke him again and again until he learns not to try to break free, till the elephant knows the rope is stronger than he is.

You can tie that elephant down with that rope for the rest of his life—no matter how big he gets—as long as you never poke him with a sharper stick. As long as you don't give him cause to discover his abilities have increased, as long as you keep him hobbled by memory, tethered by, and to, past realities.

Simple obedience requires complex illusions. "Duty as they understood it." The words were a fitting epitaph for Abel, a man who was ever balancing freedom against duty and duty against freedom and fear against them both.

When the chicken was fried, each breast sitting on its square of Wonder bread with a near-fluorescent disk of green pickle, lightly flecked with cayenne, speared to its top like a medal, Hope walked into the library, found her DVD of *Munich*, the movie about the men who were secretly sent to avenge the Israeli athletes who had been massacred at the Munich Olympics in 1972, and pushed play.

Watching *Munich* it seemed like Abel had always been a spy. Not a lawyer at the Pentagon and an ex–Foreign Service officer and eventually a spy, but a spy always. That was the part of Nicholas's story that conclusively persuaded.

She couldn't trust all of Nicholas's stories, for many reasons; the greatest of these was that Nicholas had a taste for mirrors. He would want to see Abel a spy. Want to see Abel gay. Want to see Abel returned to the Philippines.

Hope loved Abel differently. Negroes who survive to thrive exhibit highly original adaptations to life. As Prince sang, "Animals strike curious poses." Hope wanted to invite the ghost of Abel to touch her stomach and feel how it trembled inside. She wanted Ajay to know her as a satisfied woman. Satisfied by Abel and satisfied by Waycross. That was a part of her duty: to teach her son that women could be satisfied. She would take Ajay someplace Antoinette had not taken Abel.

Finally, her white meal, or at least the moonshine in a Mason jar. The turkey on white bread with mashed potato sandwich looked too sad to eat when she pulled it from the freezer. She watched *Munich*, drank moonshine and Soir de France tea, missed Waycross, worried about Ajay, and just a little bit hated on Ari and Sammie. The movie was over when Ajay and Waycross walked through the door.

They ate their dinner talking about Idlewild instead of Abel. Hope, this once, sat at the head of the table so she could reach out a hand to both of the living men she had been missing without having to stretch too far. Waycross said Idlewild had become a sad place. It had been empty and run-down for a long time, but now it was newly populated with the returning and disappointed.

"Old folks looking for something that's not there anymore," said Ajay.

"Like me?" asked Waycross.

"Yeah," said Ajay.

"You going to school tomorrow?" asked Hope.

"Yeah."

"Sure you shouldn't wait?" asked Hope.

"I'm sure," said Ajay.

"OK," said Hope.

"I love Daddy, but I'm not sure I liked him," said Ajay.

"I'm sure he loved him some you," said Hope.

The son with dark and silver dreads rose from the table, kissed his mother on the top of her black and silver head, then walked out of the room. Waycross dropped his voice down low.

"Did I just hear you lie?" asked Waycross.

"I don't think so," said Hope.

In the same moment Hope and Waycross each leaned in toward the other. Their foreheads touched. Almost to his room, Ajay remembered he had left his phone on the table. Halfway back down the stairs he saw heads touching above the table and toes touching below. Hope and Waycross looked like exhausted boxers hanging on to each other to keep standing. Ajay turned and continued his upward march without disturbing his family.

Later that night Hope went upstairs into her son's room just before he fell asleep. She sat in the chair nearest his bed.

"You didn't know what Daddy did, did you?"

"No."

"Did you know?"

"When I was really little, he used to tell me that he was double oh seven."

The ability to see beauty beyond torture and desecration is the ability to love in ways that cannot be brought to disorder.

Later that night, or some night soon, in her red silk bra and panties Hope would slide beneath the sheets and onto Waycross's side of the bed.

Ajay returned to school. Hope got back to her studio and her little bit of green day-trading. Holiday mode, and survival mode, were over. It was past time for Hope, daughter of a coal man, wife of a do-good doctor, mother of an expensive son, to get back to profitably investing in companies that invested in wind and solar energy—and her sculpting.

Eventually Hope went to talk to her shrink about Philoctete— the mythological creature, not the dog—about his wound, and his stench, and how she dreamed his sore had healed. With Nicholas gone she needed her shrink again.

She wanted to tell him about Bohol. How the Agency had approached her and she had agreed to help them in Bohol. How she had stepped off the ledge just about the time Abel had stepped out onto it. Or maybe she hadn't. Maybe she had stepped out onto it one time in Bohol. Maybe there had been an arms dealer staying at their very hotel. Maybe there had been a diving accident. What was for sure: having her baby had been her way to make sure she never was lured into service again. The baby that had tied her to domesticity had tied Abel to paranoia. She kept her silences. Instead she told her shrink that her friend Moses Henry had turned out to be some sort of spy and Abel had too and so had Nicholas. Her shrink said she was a "spy magnet." They laughed hard. It was the first time she had truly laughed since Thanksgiving.

Just before the end of the hour she told the shrink about a question Abel had asked her just after Ajay was born. It might have been in the middle of the night of his christening when they were in New York at the United Nations. Abel had woken up and asked her, "If God told you to choose between Ajay dying and all of England what would you say?"

"Poor England," Hope had replied. Her shrink said a second thing. "Poor you. Poor Abel. Lucky Ajay."

★ ★ ★

Christmas was coming. She would get her red gown, her mother's gown, out of the cleaners. And she would take out Aunt Hot's old jet-beaded pocketbook. She would take care of her family.

"What's a zombie?" asked Hope.

"A dead person walking the earth," said Sweet.

"And they ain't all folks that died neither," added Hot.

"No sir, most of 'em never lived," said Sweet.

"Born right out of their mother's asses dead," said Hot.

"They be born out of their mama's pocketbooks like everybody else on this earth, but you know what Hot means," said Sweet.

And Hope did know. "Pocketbook" was the aunts' euphemism for vagina. The girls of Milleville would eat that up. Only she wouldn't be telling them. She would be keeping community secrets. If the aunts told her there were zombies walking the earth, she would believe there were zombies. She knew exactly what to say. She had good home training.

"I think my papa was a zombie," said Hope.

"We been wonderin' 'bout that," said Sweet.

She put out the crèche. She planned and cooked the meals. They moved to and through the longest night and shortest day of the year, to and through Ajay's first Christmas without Abel. New Year's they ate black-eyed peas and greens and began again.

THIRTY-ONE

TWELFTH NIGHT. EPIPHANY. Little Christmas. January 6, 2006. Whatever you call it, the day chosen to celebrate the arrival of the Wise Men at the manger was the day Mo chose to check on Hope. He invited her to lunch. First they caught up on the gossip.

"I hear you made a trip to Italy."

"To Rome."

"Sammie took her kids to Alaska for Christmas."

"That's wild."

"The boys went hunting from helicopters."

"Oh, God."

"Now, she's thinking of running for mayor of Decatur."

"No."

"God told her. And some mayor or former mayor she met on the trip said she should go for it."

"Wild."

Hope told Mo about the carousel. The piece was progressing. It now had a name. "Your Flying Horses." She was not a mechanic but she would find a way to make it turn. And there would be music. Dispatch. *The General* and *The Flying Horses*.

She would paint the notes for the melodies to those around the top. She had started some of the figures, his black Confederate soldier, his Lauro, and his Moses Ezekiel. She was sketching ideas for his Fanon and his Balzac. There would be W. E. B. and Booker T. and Adam Clayton Powell and even General Cleburne, who had fought for the inclusion of blacks in the Confederate ranks, and there would be John Henry. She would carve a tiny horse for each. She told Mo she was going to carve a Mo.

Coffee and desserts, two slices of king cake, were ordered. Halfway through her first cup Mo pulled a pouch from his breast pocket and announced it was a present from Abel. Pulling out a double strand of real black South Sea pearls, he said, "He gave them to me five, maybe ten years ago, he said if anything happened to him wait a while and give them to you."

"Wow."

"Did you ever see *Waist Deep*?"

"No."

"You should watch it sometime."

That was the last thing Mo Henry ever said to Hope that wasn't about a drink or a flirtation. When she finally got around to watching *Waist Deep* she was surprised to discover it was an urban melodrama about a father stealing money to ransom back his son who has been taken by drug dealers. At the end he dies and then he shows up on a beach and the man and the boy and the girlfriend live happily ever after. The dad even brings the kid the toy he promised.

Hope loved her some optimistic Mo.

★   ★   ★

Near the end of January Hope downloaded what she thought were photographs Ajay had taken of Abel on Father's Day weekend. She saw pictures of Ajay, pictures of Ajay and Hope, and two pictures of Abel himself.

Abel had commandeered Ajay's camera—shooting over Ajay's pics, leaving his. And so it was that Hope saw herself, saw Ajay, saw Abel, as Abel had seen them.

In the first shot, one of Ajay holding his littlest half sister high above his head, the ripped muscles of his triceps were clearly visible. In the second shot Ajay's eyes were cast down. In Abel's pictures everyone other than Ajay was less.

His portraits of Ajay amazed. Here was the strength wrestled out of the coalfields of West Virginia and tobacco lands of North Carolina married to the strength he had earned running on the lacrosse fields of Middle Tennessee. All the great expectations that had crowded round Abel's crib had bloomed in Abel's son.

Everystuff. Everything he had wished to protect first in himself, then in Tess, everything once precious in himself, then desecrated in himself, was pristine and present in Ajay. He was the only black male Abel had ever found completely beautiful.

There was a picture taken at the Ronald Reagan Airport of Ajay and the new senator from Illinois, a man with a strange name and dark skin who didn't see everything in black and white, through the lens of being formerly enslaved. A man from the other end of Abel's universe.

Finally she realized who Seamus was. The marine mentioned in the big speech of the Democratic National Convention. Between Seamus and the photograph, Hope understood that Abel would have been both shamed and inspired by the existence of a man who had done everything Abel had thought could not be done. Abel, who had spent time wanting to die and be born again as his own son, had captured the full brightness of this man *of his own generation* who made radically different things of this world's realities. Compared with the senator from Illinois, Abel was just too pale. Someone had taken a picture of the three of them together. Abel looked puffy and old-fashioned.

Perhaps confusing himself with Hannibal and the senator from Illinois with Jesus, Abel had prepared to act.

Most likely, something about the way Ajay loved him, wide-eyed yet getting weary, roused Abel from slumber and he started wondering how many boys he would kill tomorrow because he had been afraid yesterday. Wondered if it was enough that he didn't break bodies, he just broke minds.

Somehow it came clear that he did not wish to be present the day his son discovered who he had been, wasn't convinced that Ajay would agree that Abel had parsed correctly the damage of *perpetual detainment* to freedom.

Someday too soon Ajay would associate his name with the Metropolitan Detention Center, with Guantánamo, with Abu Ghraib, with John Ashcroft.

There came a day when he understood that the identity he had adopted to afflict himself and his father was an identity that could defeat Ajay. That was the day he decided to go to the Rebel Yell. There came a day when Abel knew his fate was not to find a way or make a way but to block a way.

Hope got it: earth without Abel was safer for his kid and her kid and all the kids being called to the big bad war.

THIRTY-TWO

A S T H E A M B U L A N C E doors shut, Abel consoled himself with his rule of mud: *They can do no worse to me than I have done to others.* The important preparation for this odd eventuality had occurred years earlier.

"He don't need that, he needs some more CPR." The red-cheeked redneck EMT talked out loud to himself as he changed course, laying aside the full hypodermic of adrenaline he had been holding. Yancey was responding to Abel's smile.

This was good. Abel soon felt the man pressing on his rib cage until another bone snapped. This was very good. Abel had provoked an event. The power to escalate is a control. *When you can't reach the brake, sometimes you can reach the accelerator.*

Abel let himself yelp. A yelp was better than a smile. He was forgetting the rules and he had written the rulebook. The attendant was neither a professional nor severely and recently aggrieved. The man wouldn't have much stomach for pain without humiliation. If Abel could make him see his pain without showing weakness, the man would flinch. Abel might live till he got to the hospital.

The vehicle began to accelerate. Abel had barely started to

wonder what kind of ambulance he was in, *what are the capacities*, before he stopped himself. The difference between possessing lifesaving technology and having a will to use it was well known to him. *Personalities are more significant than technologies.*

Speed intensified Abel's awareness of being cocooned or coffined. *Privacy is dangerous.* He wanted the door to open. He wanted windows, windows so large everything could be seen. *Wrong.* The Popemobile flashed into his mind chased by an image of the navy blue Lincoln Continental car that had driven J. F. K. through Dallas on the last day of his life. Rolling slowly behind that was their old Flying Crow—the Thunderbird, the car in which he had felt so unsafe. Abel edited his thought. *White men are safer in enclosed spaces. Dark men are safer out in the open. I am a white man. I will be safe.* He wanted to smile again but this time he remembered not to.

Not much good ever happened after the prisoner smiled. And nothing good happened after the prisoner cried. Abel kept his face as blank as he had been taught by experience and instruction. Slow the pace.

He wanted to inventory his surroundings but his neck wouldn't cooperate. Thinking about his neck made him think about his wives.

On the blue leatherette cot that Abel, assisted by the hillbilly EMT, intended as Abel's deathbed, he understood himself to be a polygamous man deprived of some of his spicier privileges. The responsibility to write a child-support check should come with the right to do that which surrounds the getting of the baby you are called upon to support. It angered and confounded him to have baby-made responsibilities without baby-making rights. It felt unnatural—like the itchy blue blanket resting atop him.

Wives and necks. He wanted to be the head of the family, and she, both shes, had wanted to be the neck, turning the head whichever way they wanted. Like gravy over army meat, wives and necks were necessary evils, something to make the unsavory palatable.

Wives and necks and gravy. Marines and army and navy. He was glad he had recommended arming American ambulances in the Red Zone even if it was against the laws of war. *Jus in bello;* aggressive protection for the vulnerable; sweet legacy.

He almost wished this man standing above him were part of an extraction team, part of a plan to get him somewhere safe, somewhere in the center of the wild of the war, somewhere his death could be heroic.

Then he didn't. It pained Abel to wish for what could not be. He would not spend the last minutes of his life in pain. He wanted to think about Sammie. He needed to think about Sammie.

Abel wasn't sure if he hoped or feared that something between an assassination and a lynching, something other than the natural course of a freak illness, was occurring in a tin box of a trauma twinkie rolling through the Smoky Mountain night, rolling through the state where Martin Luther King (called by some denizens of East Tennessee Martin Lucifer King) had died.

Political murder is a king's end. And King's end. He had been working on a definition of torture right up to the moment he had left on his Thanksgiving break. That work would stop now. Torture would be defined differently in his absence. Who and what would the difference serve?

★　★　★

This feels too much like a lynching. Training was failing him. He didn't want to pee his pants. But he would rather pee his pants than wear diapers. Lynching was a vertical death. Abel's departure was to be horizontal. He found comfort in the geometry. He held his water.

There was a statue by Moses Ezekiel that haunted Abel. A statue he'd never taken Hope to see. A statue on the grounds of the Virginia Military Institute. *Virginia Mourning Her Dead.*

At the end of the day of a battle he was losing General John C. Breckinridge had hollered, "Put the boys in and may God forgive me for the order." The boys, students some as young as fourteen, none older than twenty-two, had turned the tide of the battle. Moses Ezekiel had been one of those boys, one who had survived the battle, who had earned for VMI, the Institute, the right to fix bayonets during parades. The Confederates had won that day. Abel didn't believe God had forgiven Breckinridge. He wondered if God had forgiven Bevel and King. *Soon I will see.*

He would go lying down. Lying down was a soldier's way to die. *When you die lying on the ground, the earth groans as it accepts the stain.* A *quimboiseur* in Saint-Pierre had told him that way back when Hope loved him. *She may love me again, now. She may love me again.*

Everything was right again. He didn't know what the man in the blue shirt was doing; he couldn't feel what the man in the blue shirt was doing; and if he did, he didn't care.

The air doesn't care. Feet dangle; necks snap. The air is unmarked. The carefully evolving convolutions of Abel's thought were lulling him back to the radical contentment of simple knowledge. He would die horizontal.

Or, he would not die now. There was a possibility he wouldn't die now. Again, he wanted to smile but he did not. "It requires more to torture the dignified than it does to torture the quickly humiliated. It requires more to torture the fearless."

When Abel had made that statement, at a private estate on Catoctin Mountain (not so very far from the Naval Support Facility Thurmont, commonly known as Camp David), some heads had nodded in acknowledgment; others had stared, challenging his attempt to pontificate on the unpontificatable. He didn't let it bother him. He knew what he was talking about. Abel was a prodigy.

Fearless and dignified is usually foreign. He didn't tell them that. *To torture requires familiarity and antipathy.* He didn't tell them that either. He said, quoting an Agency psychologist, "Simple and most satisfying to punish is what we hate in ourselves. The puny and the humiliated catch particular and peculiar hell." Abel would not be puny or humiliated ever again.

Waddell the ambulance man called back to Yancey the EMT with his estimate of the number of minutes before arrival at the hospital: nine.

"We don't want to jostle him," the old EMT hollered back, smirking. The vehicle slowed just a bit. The EMT smiled. By his best guesstimate if the trip took ten more minutes the nigger would expire in the vehicle.

Abel kept his face blank. Abel could use ten minutes. "Good enough for a white prince, good enough for me," mumbled Abel. Assassination was a king's death.

The EMT couldn't make out the words, didn't know what

Abel was talking about, wouldn't have known if he could have made out the words. Abel was talking about Sammie.

Abel was remembering swearing to himself that he wouldn't ruin his second marriage as badly as he had ruined his first. The creature whose hand he had been holding then, Sammie, was far less promising than the woman who first had worn his ring, Hope, but he thought it possible his second bride would make it through to the end.

Abel would give Samantha less to contend with. He wouldn't burden her with his dreams, his desire, or his love.

Abel was remembering all of that. He could not remember what had never left his mind. What had never left his mind he could just keep knowing. Dreams, desire, love, had all been given away, to a woman, Hope, who had discarded it all. Or so Abel had thought on the day of his second wedding.

In the ambulance he thought something different. Even as he remembered consoling himself with the knowledge that however hard the afternoon of the wedding was for him, it was harder for Hope; even as he remembered consoling himself with an imagined truth, as people often console themselves with what they know to be a lie. Abel had seen Hope the morning of his wedding to Samantha.

Hope had been hurrying Ajay along from the opposite side of the door as he dressed to participate in his father's wedding. Finally dressed, he had called her back in. As she had tied the pale blue tie around Ajay's neck, Hope had thought without wishing to think it: One dream we had came true.

Just then it seemed enough. *A sudden sight of himself in his son's eyes killed Big Abel.* That's how Abel saw it just as the ambulance man could sense the life leaking out of his cargo. The ambulance man didn't want anybody to die on his watch. Get tortured a little, maybe; die, no. Humming the *Dukes of Hazzard* theme song, he put the pedal to the metal. The ambulance streaked a little faster through the soft southern night.

You and the father are in your room. It is a Saturday. You have just turned thirteen. The father has come to give you a whipping. When he closes the door to the room you are shivering. He is hissing words you have not heard him speak.

"Fuck them," the father says. "They can't do anything but scare you. Fuck them, child."

You hate the sound of his voice saying "fuck." You hate the fact he has fucked and you haven't. You hate the way he swaggers through a world of grown folks and strands you in a world of children. You don't hate him enough to say any of that. "What's wrong, child?" he asks.

The door is closed and locked and quiet. Your pants are folded neatly on a chair. Your boxers, soon to be around your ankles, are snug about your waist. All is black and red. All is death and blood. There are no other colors and nothing else the colors mean: not apple, not pomegranate, not stop, not alarm, just blood; not night, not coal, not emphatic, not ink, not raven, just death.

Blood is running down your nose. He hasn't touched you. There is blood on your fingertips. Your nose is bleeding. Because you think you are about to die, you tell the truth.

"I wet myself," you say.

"I've seen men in the war wet themselves," the daddy says. His tenderness is a heavy weight. Your thought is narrow, compressed, flattening. The father is the weight pressing your thought down. You say, "You. Ashamed of you, Daddy," you say.

You don't know why you say it and he doesn't either. You start crying. You are looking into the face of the father. Your nose continues to bleed. The daddy is reaching to reassure you but you do not deserve reassurance. You are a smart boy and you know this. You push him away. You must protect him even if he can't protect you. You are a pollution but he doesn't know this. You are smarter than the daddy.

Your eyes are mirrors. You try to imagine what someone opening the door would see. You stand close together, face-to-face, toes touching. You look up into the daddy's face. The daddy looks down at you. You touch your forehead to his. You see him and he sees how you see him: smaller than the policemen, smaller than the firemen, smaller than Ben's father.

This new connection, a shared and profound cocreated humiliation, is immediate and volatile. You are contagious to each other. You taste your own blood and cry harder. He gives you a Kleenex. You come undone and he comes with you.

You are in your bedroom. The father has come to whip you for wetting your pants. Then he closes the door to the room but you are shivering so hard the father takes you in his arms and tries to stop your shakes. His touch constricts. His hands are nowhere near your neck, nowhere near any part of you he shouldn't touch, but it feels like he is strangling you and violating you and you shake harder to shake him off. When he helps you into your pants his hands are shaking. Your shakes are contagious.

"You 'shamed of me?" asks Big Abel.

"Shame," you say like it's his name. And he doesn't slap you hard; he kisses the top of your head and takes you in his arms a baby again.

He drops the belt to the ground. Your fear is more than pain can chase away. You will not be scared into manhood. The father had wanted that, to give you the freedom of having your worst day in your past, but to go one step forward would break you. He will not break you. He kisses your forehead and your ear. The scent of you makes him worried and curious. Then he discovers, by sound, and scent, and taste, by a tingle on his lips, that you are already broken, and you believe him to be more broken still.

The father takes you in his arms and tries to get you not to shake but it feels like he is strangling you and you shake harder.

The father wants to laugh at this colossal and unanticipated, by him, consequence of integration's progress. You are ashamed of him. He kisses you again and pats the top of your curly-kinky crown. You are ashamed of him. The breach is a reciprocal bond.

Ultimately it is not strange and dramatic occurrences that shatter; it is a shivering hug that can not matter enough.

Later you lie and say it was altogether different. Later you fear your own son and the fun-house mirrors his eyes have become. You un-tell the lie but just to yourself. Later, you translate an utter and tender, complete and mutual defeat into the oldest and most powerful male story you know—domination and transferencc. When you tell the rape tale, you elevate, you believe, father and son. *At long last, love.*

A lei. A hula girl. A baby born across the world. The last bed-time story. Once upon a time, with nobody watching, in the early days of August 1961, a skinny brown baby, six pounds and a few ounces, was born, unwitnessed, born with black eyes in the maternity hospital founded by Queen Kapi'olani, a woman who would birth no children from her own body, a grand-daughter of Kaumuali'i, the last king of Kaua'i. *Unwitnessed is free-ey.* Though the delivery was contorted (in ways that were to become customary celebrations of science), just after the birth the mother, a slip of eighteen barely become a woman, high on the hot colors of the Hawaiian sky, held the son to her breast and let him suck, dreaming she was rain and he was earth.

Early days. She sang "Ahe Lau Makani" and "Beautiful Are the Flowers of Ko'olau" thinking this baby is a flower of the world. She sang, "You are a flower of Paradise." There was no "John Henry" sung around this bed or "Hoochie Coochie Man." This boy's world was so different from that boy's world. That boy's mama so different from this mama. And all the choices after, so different from my own. *Good night, sweet prince.*

The earth does not require our wretchedness. Abel got the news via television. He watched the man the Hawaiian baby had grown to become give a speech in Boston. Heard him talk about the marine Seamus. Near to where pilgrims once sought to build a city on a hill, a new Jerusalem, Abel caught a glimpse of a new happily ever after. *My feets is weary but my soul's at rest.*

★ ★ ★

Abel noted the final acceleration. He was near to the place— Waynesboro, North Carolina—where the last shot of the Civil War was fired. He had indulged his memory for eight of the nine minutes he had allotted himself. When he ceased to wish for night, not death, to enclose him; when all he could see was the woman in the green and black corduroy dress tying a blue tie around his son's neck, Abel ordered his conscripted tears to roll down his cheeks, then marshaled his almost-last-breath to beg.

A pillow, soft and clean, swooped down to assist the inhaled horse dander. Abel smiled again. *Absolutely.* He could already see the carousel.

ACKNOWLEDGMENTS

I have known my editor, Anton Mueller, since I was a twenty-two-year-old girl writing love poems, country songs, and magazine articles about the Talented Tenth and he was a fresh-out-of-Hampshire-College kid writing a review of an early Ondaatje book for the *Washington Post*. Good ride, cowboy. I want to thank my agent, Amy Williams of McCormick and Williams, for getting my work from first read. Jay McInerney is a sweethearted man. He has been generous with encouragement and introductions and bold in championing my work from the get-go. He helped me get to this third novel.

My writing process includes talking out the narrative with D. Kirk Barton. I thank him for his most profound understanding of story. Siobhan Kennedy, retired pop star and mama, helps me manage the practical realities of my Nashville life.

I want to thank the readers of my working drafts, Houston Baker, Lizzie Brook, Daniela Croda, Kimiko Fox, Lovalerie King, Carter Little, Jenny Miyasaki, Mimi Oka, Stephanie Pruitt, Tracy Sharpley-Whiting, Hortense Spillers, Breck Walker, and Jane Waterlow, for their thoughtful responses to the evolving manuscript.

Thadious M. Davis, Geraldine R. Segal Professor of American Social Thought and Professor of English at the University of

Pennsylvania; Vanessa D. Dickerson in *Dark Victorians*; Leigh Anne Duck of the University of Memphis; Lori B. Harrison-Kahan with Freshman Seminar 40e, "Rewriting America: Race, Feminism, and Classic Narratives," at Harvard University; Michael Kreyling of Vanderbilt University; Lovalerie King of Pennsylvania State University; Andrea Elizabeth Shaw in *The Embodiment of Disobedience: Fat Black Women's Unruly Political Bodies*; Hortense Spillers, Gertrude Conway Vanderbilt Professor of English at Vanderbilt University; Nell Painter; and Patricia Yeager in "Circum-Atlantic Superabundance: Milk as World-Making in Alice Randall and Kara Walker"—all have honored my work by engaging it in a particularly interesting book, article, chapter, course, or roundtable and I thank them for it.

As writer-in-residence at Vanderbilt University I am heiress to a rich literary tradition. I want to thank Tony Earley for introducing me to the Vanderbilt English Department and for being a friend. I also want to thank Richard McCarty for originally bringing me on board; and our inspired chancellor, Nicholas Zeppos, for encouraging me to stay. Developing courses with Cecelia Tichi is one of the great pleasures of being at Vanderbilt. Developing courses for Jay Clayton, Tracy Sharpley-Whiting, and Charlotte Pierce-Baker (in the English, African-American and Diaspora Studies, and Women's and Gender Studies departments) is another great pleasure. Janis May is the Queen of Institutional Memory and Administrative Insight in Benson Hall. Lucius Outlaw and David Williams were my first champions at the university and remain my dynamic allies.

I would like to thank my godchildren, Kazuma, Charlie, Moses, Takuma, Lucas, Cynara, and Aria, for being their amazing (shockingly athletic, quite beautiful, often particular, always kind, fiercely poetic) selves. They inspire me.

Mimi, Jun, Kimiko, David F., Kirk, John S., and Reggie, you are the siblings of my soul. Godmommy Lea, Flo, Edith, and Joan, thank you for finding a way to treat me like you were treated—as a treasured daughter. David Ewing, you are my husband dear to me like no other.

Black American culture recognizes the exalted tie of "play cousin." I claim many joyfully: Amanda, Ann, Caroline, Debra Gail, Hope, Kate, Martha, Matraca, Perian, and Tracy, as well as Alex, Bob, Brad, Brad, Carter, Howard, Jonathan, Marc, Marq, Matthew, Neil, Ray, Rex, Steve, Steve, and Zick.

One of the pleasures of life in the South is a calendar of parties and celebrations that rarely changes. My year begins with fireworks on the Ezell porch, moving on to black-eyed peas later in the day. The third Monday of every month is Link meeting. Easter means the Foxes will be here; we will be talking about the time Caroline found the golden egg with Steven's help and watching the itty-bitties toddle across the lawn in linen and bows while the steeplechase is about to be run. The Fourth of July finds us on Whitland Avenue with the Stringers and half the world we love. Then school starts and we give out candy on Nichol Lane. Thanksgiving means the Makihara-Oka clan will arrive for my favorite holiday of the year and it's time to start baking herb crisps and sweet potato pie, after bolting down the Boulevard and eating the Hammocks' breakfast casserole. Then it's on to the breakfast we give the Saturday before Christmas, and Sue Atkinson's for December 23, then the Cheeks' for Christmas Eve, and Christmas Day it's breakfast with the Richard Ewings at Flo's, where Maddie dazzles and Richard shines. Then we're on our way to God-mommy Lea's for dinner when we're lucky enough to get her. And on the finest days, and there are many, there are impromptu tea parties with smoked salmon, and Irish Breakfast tea, and vanilla pudding, and flan. I thank everyone who cooks for me and who allows me to cook for them and has eaten my poached pears for keeping life sweet.

Through the years I have cooked for no one more often or lovingly than Caroline Randall Williams, my daughter. I hope she will always be able to find me in the strawberry cakes, and blueberry crepes, and corn bread madeleines; in milky Earl Grey tea, and smoky Lapsang souchong; in little salmon sandwiches; and in peanut butter on a silver spoon. And when she can't find me there I know she can find me in a Steve Earle song or a Guy Clark fable we sang along to when she was a baby and after she became a woman. I hope one day she hands down her Riverside Shakespeare to a son or a daughter. If that child makes half as much of it as Caroline made of mine, she will be a very lucky woman. Being Caroline's mother is my greatest joy and the most significant responsibility of my life. Watching her become a young poet and a young woman has renewed my sense of wonder.

Over and over when I was a girl my father, George S. Randall, charged me with "speaking for those who cannot speak for themselves." I thank him for obliging me to write and for loving me into voice.

Alice Randall is the author of *The Wind Done Gone* and *Pushkin and the Queen of Spades*. Born in Detroit, she grew up in Washington, D.C. As a Harvard undergraduate majoring in English, she studied with Julia Child, Harry Levin, Alan Heimert, and Nathan Huggins. After graduation Randall headed south to Music City where she founded with friends the music publishing company Midsummer Music with the idea that it would fund novel writing and a community of powerful storytellers. On her way to writing *The Wind Done Gone*, she became the first black woman in history to write a number one country song. She also wrote a video of the year, worked on multiple Johnny Cash videos, and wrote and produced a pilot for a primetime drama about ex-wives of country stars that aired on CBS. She has written with or published some of the greatest songwriters of the era, including Steve Earle, Matraca Berg, Bobby Braddock, and Mark Sanders. Two novels later the award-winning songwriter with over twenty recorded songs to her credit and frequent contributor to *Elle* magazine is Writer-in-Residence at Vanderbilt University. She teaches courses on country lyric in

American culture, creative writing, and soul food as text and in text. Randall lives near the university with her husband, a ninth generation Nashvillian, who practices green law. Her daughter is a student at Harvard. After twenty-one years hard at it, Randall has come to the conclusion that motherhood is the most creative calling of all.